JUDGMENT

BOOK FOUR OF THE *LALASSU*

Text copyright © 2018 Jennifer Carole Lewis
Cover copyright © Streetlight Graphics and Jennifer Carole Lewis
All rights reserved
Printed in the United States of America

Published by Past the Mirror Publishing.

ISBN: 978-1-989561-01-0

Judgment:

BOOK FOUR OF THE LALASSU

Jennifer Carole Lewis

Praise for Judgment:

"In a horrible world where Martha is trying to raise her ghost-afflicted daughter while on the run from Nazi-like scientists, it becomes a struggle to survive or do the right thing. But with Lou, her newfound protector and bear skin-walker, Martha may finally have the opportunity to do both. Thrilling, horrifying, and incredibly romantic, *Judgment* will have you rooting for its unlikely heroes and on the edge of your seat, hoping for their success." - Amanda K., Proofreader, Red Adept Editing

"In *Judgment*, the latest installment of the *lalassu* series, Jennifer Carole Lewis takes us on a wild adventure through the Arctic and Pacific Northwest. Martha and Lou seemed doomed from the start, but when they fall in love, they must contend with Martha's daughter's ability to communicate with ghosts, Lou's status as a transformative, and a government plot to confine the *lalassu* to work camps for medical testing. Throughout, we're forced to confront basic questions of good and evil, and readers will undoubtedly find themselves rooting for Martha and Lou. There's a lot to like in *Judgment*, and readers of supernatural romance won't be disappointed." - Kate B., Line Editor, Red Adept Editing

Praise for the *Lalassu* series:

"I've always enjoyed stories of the supernatural living unknown among us and Jennifer Carole Lewis' Lalassu novels are a welcome addition to the list. With kick-ass women and men in over their heads, what's not to love?"
-    Bestselling Author Tanya Huff

Praise for *Revelations*: Book One of the *Lalassu*:

"A fabulous and even dangerous heroine, an intriguing paranormal world, a diabolical plan to harness supernaturals AND a sweet romance combine to make REVELATIONS an engaging debut."
-    USA Today Bestseller Deborah Cooke

To Any and Alix, two of my first fans who were complete strangers
before reading my books.
They reminded me of why I'm doing this.

Lalassu, (Sumerian noun) definition: ghost, hidden or secret

We are all contained within our immediate worlds
Locked into ignorance of the worlds around us.
But if we want to change the injustices of the world,
We need to explore.

There are six stages to gaining greater awareness:

Denial
Knowledge
Self-Awareness
Negotiation
Anger
Action

Prologue

The dirty laundry in the hamper brought Martha down. Numb and in shock, she didn't realize she'd physically fallen at first. The smooth hardwood pressed painfully against her knees while her lungs struggled to expand inside her rigid ribcage. She stared at the dirty clothes as a clear thought slowly seeped through her stunned mind: The life she'd known was done, and she had no idea what would happen next.

Her husband, Derek, had taken his soiled clothes out of the plastic hamper, leaving hers behind. She'd already seen the empty space in the garage, the gaps in the closet, and the bare drawers left hanging from the dresser. Until she saw the laundry, she could lie to herself and pretend he was only taking a break in a fit of temper. She had held tight to the fiction that he would return after he'd calmed. An urge to flee could be perfectly understandable in their circumstances, but she couldn't imagine him actually abandoning his family.

But if he'd picked through the clothes, tossing aside her things and taking his own, it was no mad dash for temporary freedom. He must have planned it for the one hour each week that she wasn't in the home.

Maybe there's still a chance. If we talk, I'm sure we can work it out. She fumbled for the cordless phone with numb fingers. It took her three tries to dial the familiar number.

"We're sorry. The number you have dialed is no longer in service." The simulated sympathy in the computerized voice punctured Martha's shaky reserve, and tears began to flow down her cheeks.

He really did it. We're on our own. The phone dropped as her fingers braced against the floor. The receiver bounced soundlessly, the battery pack breaking free to skid across the hardwood. Martha's voice stayed locked inside her throat. She tried to call out and beg for help, but no sound could escape.

A triple chime yanked Martha out of her deepening depression. *The door. Bernie and Jackie are back.* She couldn't have said how long she'd been sitting there, staring at the empty basket, but it was long enough for her back and legs to be stiff and her throat and cheeks to be raw from her tears. She stood up, wiping her face. There was no more time for self-pity. *Time to go back to work.*

Her body felt robotic as she made her way down the stairs with her face locked into a pleasant mask. Just inside the front door, a young blond woman was helping Bernie out of her coat.

"Hi, Mrs. Anderson," Jackie called, her attention on the little girl beside her. She kept one hand on Bernie at all times, nodding at the little girl's chatter. "Bernie did great with her exercises today."

"Wonderful." Martha forced her smile to spread even wider.

"I want to go watch TV with Chuck." Bernie's brown eyes were bright with excitement.

"Bernie, is Chuck real or imaginary?" Jackie's firm tone demanded the right answer, and Bernie's head hung low.

"Imaginary," she said reluctantly.

Martha wanted to tell her daughter not to worry about it, but Jackie and the other therapists insisted that it was a problem. If she didn't want Bernie's grip on reality to continue to slip, they couldn't allow the girl to indulge in any flights of fantasy, no matter how innocent.

"That's right. You can watch TV while I talk to your mom." For the first time, Jackie looked at Martha. Based on the other woman's shocked expression, Martha wasn't doing a particularly good job of covering up her distress.

Bernie ran down the hall to the family room, barely managing to avoid tripping over the scattered toys. Jackie swallowed, her eyes wide. "Is everything okay, Mrs. Anderson?"

"It's fine, Jackie," she said in a polite but firm tone. If Martha had to explain what happened or deal with questions, she would collapse again. "We'll see you tomorrow."

Somehow, she got the therapist out and locked the door. Taking a deep breath, Martha shoved aside worries about how she would continue to pay for the intensive daily therapy sessions or the house or food—*stop. Bernie needs her mother. There will be plenty of time for despair after Bernie is in bed.* One way or another, Martha would come up with a plan to make sure Bernie got what she needed.

After another deep breath, Martha found the strength to join Bernie in the family room. The TV cast its flickering blue glow over the worn couches, discarded toys, and inexpertly mended furniture. Unlike the rest of the house, the two of them could relax in the casual atmosphere.

The animated characters on the screen were smiling and singing. The talking pig was apparently forgiving a dancing bear for eating a sandwich. But Bernie didn't seem happy about it. She was scowling at the screen and shaking her head. "It's not okay. He should be angry."

There was a long pause, and Martha's heart sank.

Bernie spoke again. "It doesn't matter if they can make another one."

"Who are you talking to, baby?" Martha tried to be gentle, but Bernie still shrank back.

"No one." Her daughter wouldn't meet Martha's gaze and picked at the couch upholstery instead.

"Would you like to talk to me about it?" Martha tried not to be hurt when Bernie shook her head. *Redirect.* That was what the therapists recommended. "What would you like for dinner?"

"I'm not hungry." Bernie bit her lip, staring at her fingers. "Chuck said that Daddy left us."

Caught without a comforting lie ready, Martha could only stand there silently. She wanted to reassure her daughter that her father hadn't abandoned them but also didn't want to build up false hope.

"It's all right, Mommy." Bernie stood up and wrapped her tiny arms around Martha's hips, pressing her head into Martha's belly. "We'll be okay without him."

Martha hugged her daughter, willing those words to be true. *We* will *be okay.* When Bernie's grip loosened, Martha knelt down. "Did Daddy talk to you before he left?"

"No." Bernie's gaze focused on an empty spot on the floor. "Chuck said he took all of his stuff and that he's never coming back. He's in a bar now, drinking and laughing."

It was all too easy to picture the scene exactly as described. Derek hadn't been excited about the idea of children to begin with, but Martha had thought he'd changed his mind after Bernie was born. He'd seemed excited to show off his baby girl to friends and family, at least until the doctors told them that Bernie wasn't just a creative child with a vivid imagination. She couldn't distinguish between reality and her fantasies and constantly talked to people who weren't there. After the diagnosis, Derek kept pulling back while Martha marched forward, determined to get Bernie the help she needed.

But how does Bernie know? It wasn't unusual for her father to work late and miss their evening time together. She hadn't been upstairs to see the gutted master bedroom. Martha sat next to Bernie on the couch, cuddling her daughter and trying to puzzle it out. Eventually, she gave up. Bernie was an intelligent child who noticed more than anyone gave her credit for. She could have picked up on any number of cues. *I have more important things to worry about now.* Martha had quit her job to take care of Bernie, and the therapy bills alone were thousands of dollars each month. Somehow, she doubted that Derek intended to help out financially. She would have to fight him for every penny.

Anger slowly forged her sadness and fear into steel braces that stiffened her spine. No matter what it took, Martha would make sure that Bernie got what she needed. If Derek thought she would roll over and let him quietly opt out of their life, he would quickly discover how wrong he was. *There is no creature fiercer and more dangerous than a mother defending her young.*

Denial

Chapter One

"I hate you!" Bernie's shrill declaration passed easily through the thick log walls of the cabin. Sitting on a low bench outside the door, Martha winced at her daughter's outburst.

"Don't worry. He's heard worse." Lily leaned over, her black hair gleaming in the late spring sunlight. "That patch looks much better than the last one."

Martha's attention wasn't on the ripped jeans lying across her lap, an uneven patch covering the worst holes in the torn knees. A heavy thud shuddered the cabin walls. When they'd first arrived in Bear Claw National Park and the tiny *lalassu* community of Ekurru, Martha had been nervous about Bernie taking lessons from Lily's brother, Andrew. He was a shaman, and while she believed in his skill with spirits, he was also a skin-walker who was able to transform into a giant grizzly bear. The idea had terrified her—she'd wondered what would happen if he lost control during a lesson. The whole family frightened her, along with the other *lalassu* residents. But she'd come to Ekurru anyway, hoping for a miracle.

A wordless, high-pitched shriek echoed from inside.

"She's not any worse than I was at that age." Lily's attempt to reassure weren't helping. Martha appreciated the young woman's efforts. Without Lily's determination to create a friendship, life in the isolated subarctic community would have been a lot more lonely. But if she was alone, then she would have an excuse to go inside and intervene.

Please, Bernie. Just try. Dampness pricked the inside of Martha's eyes, and a swollen lump settled at the top of her throat. From the way the lessons had been going lately, it seemed that coming to Ekurru was going to be another entry on her list of ultimately futile attempts to help her daughter.

"I won't do it! He's my friend!" The door slammed open, and Bernie stormed out. She was transforming from a little girl into a stubborn teenager.

Andrew followed her out, his short dark hair framing the concerned expression on his lean tan face. "Bernie, Chuck is dangerous."

"He is not! He takes care of me!" Bernie's angry gaze fell on her mother. "This is all your fault!"

Martha accepted the blame as Bernie's furious words struck home, slicing deeply into her parental confidence. *I couldn't have made more mistakes if I'd planned them.* Intellectually, she knew it was impossible to expect herself to have realized that Bernie's voices and visions weren't signs of childhood schizophrenia. They were actually ghosts, but it didn't change the reality of eight years of intensive therapy and increasing doses of medication. The overall effects on Bernie had been devastating. The antipsychotic medication sent her into violent emotional swings. The grind of endless therapy had dulled her spirit. In the past two years, Martha felt as though she had gotten her daughter back.

Bernie didn't wait for her mother to respond. Instead she stomped across the narrow clearing, heading for the trees. The sunlight picked up the golden threads in her sandy-blond curls and mercilessly illuminated the strip of pale skin showing between the low boot tops and her worn cuffs. *She shouldn't be living like this.* At twelve years old, Bernie should have friends and pretty clothes, not patched, too-short jeans.

"I'll go after her," Lily volunteered, setting aside the mending. "Maybe some time playing with the cubs at the Colony will cheer her up."

Martha nodded her permission, and the other woman loped away. She caught up with Bernie just inside the forest. At first, Bernie shoved aside Lily's gentle touch, but she quickly calmed as Lily spoke to her. The two of them were nearly the same height—more evidence of Bernie's latest growth spurt. As they walked away, they made a pretty picture together among the fresh greens of spring growth. Lily's tan skin, bright-blue jacket, and dark hair contrasted with Bernie's pale coloring and red jacket.

This is what it might have looked like if she'd had those friends. The intensive therapy and her violent outbursts had made it impossible for Bernie to go to school or have the usual childhood friendships. And since they'd discovered the truth, they'd been hiding from those who wanted to exploit Bernie's gifts as a medium. Someday, when Bernie looked back at her childhood, there would be nothing except black marks on Martha's mothering report card.

"She is very stubborn." Andrew rolled his shoulders as if trying to relieve tension. It wasn't the first time that Bernie had stormed away from her lessons, but something in his expression told Martha it might be the last.

"She still won't banish Chuck." Martha wasn't asking a question. Bernie and Andrew had been fighting about exorcism for at least half of the previous year. He insisted it was necessary. Bernie refused to give up the only friend who had stuck by her since she was a toddler. Martha was torn. She didn't like the idea of forcing a child—even a ghost child—from his home. But he'd been growing more erratic, which made her uneasy. She had to admit that, after over a decade of Chuck-inspired tantrums, the idea of a life without him was tempting.

"No. And I can't help her and fight him at the same time." Andrew's blunt answer didn't leave any room for misinterpretation.

"I see," Martha said softly, keeping her voice level and her face blank in the way that only came after long years of practice. *Of course, Doctor. Yes, I understand. I know you tried your best.*

"Even if…" Andrew's voice trailed off, and he shook his head. "There's nothing I can do."

"I'm sorry." Martha's apology was automatic, a reflex from hundreds of unproductive therapy sessions, some of which had ended much more violently than this one.

His usual stoic expression softened as he faced her. "Maybe if we take a break and allow tempers to cool, we can try again."

She nodded, accepting the polite lie. She'd heard enough professional surrender to recognize yet another death knell.

I'm sorry, Mrs. Anderson, but your daughter has schizophrenia.
The medication isn't working.
The therapy isn't working.

Hit after hit beat her down. Each one inflicted its own set of scars on Martha's psyche and made it harder for her to react to the next one. One therapist had marveled at how calm Martha remained when receiving bad news. Martha had wanted to scream, *I'm not calm. I just don't have the energy to panic any more.*

"Martha." Andrew reached toward her.

She stepped back, holding onto her control. "We'll take a break and see what happens."

"Michael will be here next week with the supplies. Perhaps he will have some new suggestions."

She knew he was attempting to be optimistic, but it sounded forced and flat. It made Martha feel even worse. Andrew's comfort zone was in caustic comments. His awkward sympathy only emphasized the empty ache inside Martha. There were too many disappointments to risk letting herself become fully aware of them. She shoved them deep inside, even though it left her feeling hollow. As much as she would like the luxury of hope, there wasn't any to be had. Michael had been her therapist for years, and he cared about Bernie as if she were his own daughter. If there was a better idea, he would have shared it. "I should go and catch up to Lily and Bernie. Thank you for all of your help."

Her words were cold and robotic, and she kept her eyes down, not wanting to see any hurt in Andrew's face. It wasn't his fault, and it wasn't her fault, but they'd still failed.

She hurried to the forest, her head and heart nearly bursting with anguish. *Don't think about it.* If she let herself fully realize the truth of their situation, she would lose the control she was barely holding on to. *One foot in front of the other.* The woods closed around her, shielding her from watching eyes. The awareness she'd been holding off crashed into her, leaving her no shelter in denial.

I can't do this again. I can't. The pitiful plea shattered her illusion of calm and locked her chest in a crushing vise. Martha dropped to the ground, unable to draw breath through the pain. Her mouth contorted around a silent scream. Fat tears splattered against the hard-packed dirt.

Her chest felt as if she'd been physically hit. Her bruised lungs slammed against ribs that felt on the edge of shattering. A faint, choked whimper escaped, only to be immediately lost among the surrounding trees. Hot tears continued to drip down her face, melting a path down her frozen cheeks. She squeezed her eyes closed and tried to hold it all inside, but there was too much to squash.

The doctors called them panic attacks. *Try to relax and reduce your stress,* they'd said, as if she had any real chance at either. Instead, she'd learned to suppress as much as she could and then ride out the inevitable explosion.

Her rough nails caught on the cool earth, scraping along the surface as her fingers curled. Once again, the promise had become a lie. The adventure of life with her baby girl had become a never-ending swirl of worsening symptoms and horrible events. Intentions didn't count when they caused so much pain.

Slowly, the despair began to lose its hold and settled into the depths of Martha's mind. She stayed on her hands and knees with her eyes closed, each breath burning into her battered lungs. *I can't give up. I have to keep moving. Bernie needs me.* She slowly rose to her feet and the chill breeze bit into the tear tracks on her face. A jumbled nest of sets of parallel, shallow scratches in the packed dirt matched her red and stiffened fingers.

She needed to get herself back under control before she went to the Colony to find Lily and Bernie. Her hazy memory suggested there was a stream nearby where she could at least wash her face. The rest of her wasn't too bad. Pale dust clung to her jeans, but she was otherwise unmarked.

The stream was more or less where her memory placed it. She splashed the cool water on her face and rinsed the clinging dirt from her hands. The small gesture centered her mind once again. *If Andrew can't help*—despair threatened again, but Martha ruthlessly quashed it—*then we'll find something else to try.*

She started moving toward the Colony, finding the trail between Andrew's cabin and the Colony's cliffs. Frequent foot traffic had crushed any green sprouts, leaving a track of gray-brown dirt. She kept her eyes on the immediate path and her feet, not wanting to trip on any unforeseen roots or snags. Which is how she bumped into a flesh wall.

Martha bounced back from the solid impact, and her knitted hat tumbled forward into her eyes. Shoving the mass of pink wool back, she lifted her head to see what exactly she'd run into.

It wasn't a "what" but a "whom," Andrew's twin brother, Lou.

He glared down at her. Martha wasn't short, and Lou still towered over her, easily passing the halfway mark between six and seven feet. His sleek black hair fell unfettered down his neck and across his bare shoulders. Despite the post-winter chill lingering in the air, he only wore a pair of dark leather pants, held together with a drawstring. His naked chest was twice as wide as her entire body, sculpted from the sort of thick muscles that should only appear in celluloid. He might have qualified as a model if it weren't for the scowl twisting his mouth and narrowing his eyes.

"Excuse me." The words were automatic, even as Martha suppressed a powerful surge of irritation. He must have been standing directly in her path and deliberately hadn't moved.

Lou didn't say anything as she steadied herself, but his gaze followed her. Heat burned in her cheeks because of her disheveled appearance. Lou had been the most determined opponent to her and Bernie's move to Ekurru. She'd only seen him twice in the past year, and he'd been scowling both times. His obvious dislike would be much easier to take if Martha didn't end up feeling like a flustered teen girl with a crush every time she saw him.

"Take your daughter home." His deep, gravelly voice surprised her.

Martha straightened and blinked at Lou. *Did he really speak to me?*

If he had, he didn't seem inclined to repeat himself. Instead, he began to shift as if preparing to stalk back into the woods.

"Wait. What?" Martha's question dropped into the silence like a stone into a pond.

Lou stopped and slowly turned, his scowl growing fiercer. He looked as if he was offended that she dared to ask for clarification. "She doesn't belong at the Colony. Take her away."

Take her away. The words made her blood boil. She'd heard variations on them for years as Bernie talked to invisible people. From the librarian at story time: *You need to leave. We can't have her frightening the other children.* From the manager at the movies: *Please don't make a fuss. You're already disrupting the other clients.* Wherever they'd gone, she and Bernie were always unwelcome.

Suddenly, all of her pent-up frustration and fear had a perfectly acceptable outlet. Martha forgot that he could probably pick her up with one hand and break her in half with the other. "Excuse me? She can go where she pleases."

Facing her again, he loomed over her. "This isn't her place."

The weight of his attention might have intimidated her two minutes before, but his words made Martha lose the sketchy grasp she had on her temper. "How dare you!"

His eyes widened briefly, a hint of confusion blooming in their depths.

Martha narrowed in on that tiny weakness, eager to shatter his superior sulkiness. "We didn't ask to come here. You've made your feelings quite clear, and trust me, it's as uncomfortable for us to be here as it is for you to have us here. But this is where we need to be to keep Bernie safe. So you can keep your opinions about our right to be here to yourself."

He seemed uncertain, his eyes darting to the side in search of escape. But when she paused for breath, he growled. "I am the Guardian here."

"Then shout it to the trees or the rocks or whatever you have to do in order to get it off that ridiculously muscled chest. But don't you dare tell me or my daughter that we don't have the right to be here."

He opened his mouth, but Martha stopped him with a single upheld finger. "Unless you are about to apologize to me, I am not interested in any more of your opinions. I suggest you go about whatever business you have and let me go about mine." Martha was rapidly running out of steam and decided it was as good a point as any to make her exit. She walked past Lou with her head held high and her back and neck forming a rigid line of righteousness.

She half expected him to try and grab her as she passed, but he stayed absolutely still, a brooding mountain of man flesh. His disapproval bore down on her like smothering snow, but Martha was used to silent judgment. As long as he kept his opinion to himself, she would do the same, but it felt good to finally lash out instead of meekly turning an embarrassed cheek.

Speaking out felt great after a lifetime of being told to be quiet and not make a fuss. But as she angrily followed the path to the Colony, guilt made her reconsider. He'd been rude, but he hadn't deserved to be the recipient of all her repressed anger.

Sunlight dazzled her as she stepped out of the shady woods and into the clearing below the Colony's pale granite cliffs. Dark cave openings dotted the switchback path that ran along the steep rock face. Most caves had reddish-brown masses of fur resting in front—the grizzly bears who called the Colony home. Martha shaded her eyes and spotted Bernie's bright-red jacket next to Lily's bright-blue one. They were on the second level, and Bernie was playing with a small blob of fur that was likely one of the cubs.

"Ah, good." The man's voice behind her made her jump. "Lou managed to find you."

Martha inhaled a calming breath, not wanting to vent her remaining fury on an unsuspecting target. She made herself smile at Doc, the elderly biologist who helped to protect the Colony. His wire-rimmed glasses glinted in the sun as he smoothed his long gray-and-white beard.

"Malila is a little protective of her cub. It's her first one, and like any new mother, she's nervous." Doc sounded as proud as any grandparent. "Lily is with them, but it would be best if Bernie finished up before Malila gets anxious. Lou promised he'd find you and bring you back here so that you could take her back to the cabin."

Just my luck. I finally vent, and it turns out I had the situation wrong. Still, Lou could have taken the time to explain what he wanted rather than tersely barking orders.

Doc continued. "I probably shouldn't have let her play with the cubs in the first place, but Lily said she'd had a hard day. I wanted her to have something special to cheer her up."

"Thank you," Martha said automatically before calling Bernie's name.

The blob in the red jacket stood up and waved. Bernie and Lily began to pick their way down the narrow path. With her burst of justified anger stolen, Martha didn't have anything to distract her from larger issues. Bernie needed a medium to teach her, but no one could tell them where to find one. They couldn't stay in Ekurru, but they wouldn't be safe outside of it. No matter which way she turned, there were only dead ends.

Chapter Two

Ouch. Skin-walkers might heal quickly, but Lou felt as if he'd been raked by claws. The woman had attacked like a kestrel defending its nest. It wasn't something he'd expected from the woman who'd spent most of the last year hiding. That burst of fire was the first time he'd seen evidence that her soul hadn't been snuffed out long before.

He'd resented their intrusion into his community. The child was gifted, but she wasn't one of the Marked—she was able to hide in ordinary society. Ekurru was for those who needed a sanctuary, not for people who could pass. He'd been annoyed by Martha's presence, especially when her disgust for his family's way of life was clear. If it were up to him, he would have suggested another of the *lalassu* sanctuaries, even if it meant that Andrew had to travel with them for a time.

Of course, no one had asked him for his opinion in advance. Since she had been there, he'd done his best to avoid contact with her. She'd gotten her share of his hunting and trapping efforts, and he did his best not to think about it. Lou continued on the path to the family's cabin. Even though half of his attention was occupied with his thoughts, his bare feet made little to no noise, and he barely disturbed the surrounding plants. Birds called to each other, and insects clicked and buzzed. None of them were alarmed by his passage. He took pride in his ability to blend in with nature, even in the skin.

He touched his chest briefly. "Ridiculously muscled" hadn't sounded like a compliment. He growled at the memory. Outsiders were crazy, and letting any of them into Ekurru had been a mistake. Lily's mate had been the first, and he'd ended up leading a madman's special forces straight to their doorstep. Lou had been relieved when the former soldier left. If his sister hadn't been devastated by the man's absence, Lou would have wished for him to stay in the south. When he came back, Lou wasn't happy, but at least Lily was.

Winter still held Bear Claw in its grip when Andrew had returned from his journey south, dragging the woman and her daughter with him. He had expected Lou to find the pair shelter and food. Lou had spent days fixing up the old cabin in the woods to make it sound enough to hold heat. Then he'd spent two weeks roaming the bitterly cold woods for sufficient game to feed them. Luckily, he'd found a caribou with a broken leg and put it out of its misery. It had taken another day to butcher it and five days to haul the frozen carcass back to Ekurru.

The disgusted expression on her face when he'd arrived with the meat still stung in his memory. She hadn't offered any thanks for his efforts. Lily and Andrew tried to excuse her, telling him that she was used to city living and must still be in shock from having to be on the run. He hadn't bothered to argue or defend himself. His siblings had apparently decided to set up an open-door policy, and neither of them truly understood the woods the way he did. His youngest brother, Mark, would probably bring a whole field team from the university in Alaska next. Martha's outburst was even more evidence of how ill-suited she was to life here. But something about it nagged at him. There had been echoes of something else under the anger, like the echo of a second wolf pack howling along with the first.

Thin scratches on the path caught Lou's attention, and he stopped to examine them. Someone had knelt on the ground long enough to press shallow depressions into the hardened earth. The scratches didn't seem consistent with an effort to dig or an attempt to deliberately mark an area. It was as if someone's nails had scraped away the top layer of dirt wherever a hand happened to fall. He frowned, measuring the marks with his own fingers. Whoever had made them was smaller than he was and had more delicate hands.

He spotted faint discolorations on the ground where the earth was slightly wetter. Most woodsmen would have missed them, but his senses were highly attuned to any change in his territory. *This isn't making any sense. What*—realization dawned on him. Someone had fallen to the ground, crying. Given the freshness of the marks, it could only be Martha. He twisted to look down the path where she had gone, atypical guilt weighing on his heart.

She'd collapsed, alone and overwhelmed. From the markings, she'd cried for a long time then pulled herself together on her own. She must have still been raw when he'd confronted her about her daughter playing with the cubs at the Colony. She'd lashed out, like any wounded animal faced with more pain. He found himself reliving the confrontation. Her eyes had blazed, and the heat had risen in her cheeks. She'd been like an entirely different person, which upset his careful understanding of everyone's role in the community. Perhaps he had misjudged her. Maybe she did have the kind of fire it took to make a life in the north. He noticed he was touching his chest again and dropped his hand irritably.

It didn't change what needed to happen. The girl shouldn't have been interacting with the cubs. The bears in the Colony needed to live as wild animals, regardless of whether they were skin-walkers or only bears. If they got used to interacting with people, they could end up hanging around so-called civilization, where they might find themselves shot as nuisance animals. He drew in a deep and uncertain breath. He didn't want to hurt her further, especially since he'd seen the evidence of her collapse. If Martha was unstable, she could be a risk to Ekurru and the Colony.

A crow cawed a warning and alerted him to an incoming presence before he could decide. Lou stood and scuffed at the dirt. Martha had hidden herself to cry, and Lou didn't want anyone else to see the marks. Besides, he could guess who was coming.

"Ah, there you are." Andrew appeared, his arms crossed over his wiry chest. His short black hair blew into his eyes. "I've been waiting."

Lou shrugged and grunted an acknowledgment. He and his twin didn't often see eye to eye, and he'd learned not to get drawn into debates. Andrew was skilled with human language, where Lou struggled to make the words line up.

"Oh, good. I see that we're practicing our Neanderthal, just in case a time vortex opens under our feet to send us back to the cave days. Very practical." Andrew shoved his hands into his green plastic-coated jacket. "I see that you're dressed for the part as well."

Lou didn't bother answering. He hated flimsy store-bought fabrics, preferring his own sturdy tanned leather. Andrew ordered all of his clothes out of catalogues. Sometimes, Lou wondered if his twin insisted on such things as an escape from his path as a shaman. It seemed like a waste of energy to Lou, but he wasn't the one training with Grandfather.

"Have you seen Martha or Bernadette?" Andrew asked.

"The girl is at the Colony. I passed the woman." Lou hoped his twin would accept the information and move on.

From the sharpening of Andrew's gaze, he could tell it wasn't going to be so easy. "Did she talk to you?"

"We exchanged words." Lou thought of simply changing into the fur and leaving the conversation. Maybe he could stay in bear form for the summer and forget all this human nonsense. He could lose himself in seasonal gorging and not speak to anyone until winter closed in again.

To Lou's surprise, Andrew seemed to lose his confidence. The arrogance melted from his spine, and his shoulders rounded. "Did she tell you?"

Lou stayed quiet. He'd already accidentally hurt someone who was already in pain. He wasn't going to do it twice in one day.

"Of course she told you." Andrew raked his narrow fingers through his hair. "I wish it was different, but I can't help Bernadette. She refuses to banish Chuck."

"I thought you and Grandfather banished him." Lou frowned, studying his twin. From the stiff way Andrew moved, his muscles must have been knotted tightly.

"We sent him away, but she called him right back." Andrew sighed. "We tried convincing him to move on from the earthly plane, but he's too powerful for only two shaman."

His brother lifted his head, and his lost expression reminded Lou of when they were children. Their father had been killed, and their pregnant mother had lost herself to grieving. Instantly, Lou had stepped into the role of protector and provider. He wouldn't let his family suffer if he could prevent it. "Turn around."

"Thank you." Andrew closed his eyes and turned. Lou began to massage his brother's shoulders, easing the knots and stiffness. When Grandfather began to train Andrew as a shaman, Lou had volunteered to train as well after seeing the strain it put on his brother. Grandfather refused, since Lou didn't have any shamanic gifts, but Lou found other ways to help Andrew through the process.

"The child doesn't just speak with ghosts. She actively pulls them in," Andrew continued. "Do you know how many lost hikers have died in Bear Claw over the last hundred years?"

Lou had always been more concerned about the living ones. A still-breathing lost hiker could tell people about Ekurru and the people there if they made it out after finding the community.

"She's pulled in seven so far. Seven! All of them wanted messages sent on to their families." Andrew sighed. "Nothing I've tried has worked, and she's been getting more and more hostile toward me."

Lou hadn't seen his twin so upset since their first encounter with the spirit world. Grandfather had brought them both into the sweat lodge, and while all Lou experienced was a relaxing time in the warm steam, Andrew had emerged tight-lipped and pale faced, terrified by whatever he'd seen. He had never wanted the burden of being a shaman. All he'd wanted was to be able to help and heal people. "You did what you could."

"It doesn't change the fact that it wasn't enough." He scrubbed his palm across his face. "When I told Martha, the look in her eyes… It was like I handed her a death sentence."

A low growl threatened to vibrate out of Lou's throat. He swallowed it, but his inner bear was agitated and demanding action. Except it didn't want to avenge his brother's pain, which was confusing.

"Are you okay?" Andrew twisted and faced Lou.

Lou stepped back, flexing his hands, his arms and legs aching from the impulse to shift. "Not a great day."

"That makes it unanimous. I'm terrified about having them leave. I don't think Martha understands how dangerous Chuck can be. I'm not even sure she quite believes in him." He straightened.

Lou tilted his head. He'd heard Andrew worry about the ghost before, but he couldn't understand how a child ghost from a previous century could be such a threat. "He's been around the girl all her life. He can't be too bad."

"He's isolated her, encouraging her to be violent and act out. He has made himself into her entire world." Andrew lowered his voice. "I can't hear or see him, but I can sense him, and he's overwhelmed with jealousy and anger. I'm afraid that his plan might be to arrange for Bernie to join him in death so that the two of them can be playmates forever."

"He can do that?" If Lou had been in bear form, his fur would have bristled in an impressive display of dominance. His human skin only pebbled in a pathetic imitation.

"You remember a few weeks ago when she went out on the ice?" Andrew asked.

Lou nodded slowly. The child had left their cabin while the mother slept. The temperature had been hovering in dangerously warm territory, weakening the ice covering the river.

"She said that Chuck had told her about someone lost on the other side of the river. But we never found anyone."

He remembered, and it still annoyed him. He had spent days on intensive but fruitless searches when he should have been setting spring traps.

"I don't think anyone was there. And if that's true, Chuck might have been hoping that Bernadette would fall through the ice." Andrew sighed. "There have been a few other incidents that could all have innocent explanations, but taken together, they could be more. Or maybe not. The two of them certainly aren't used to our way of life. After the river incident, Bernie simply refused to follow anything from my lessons."

"The ghost sees you as a threat." Lou didn't need to hear more. His brother had convinced him. Driving off a rival was a universal strategy in nature, which meant the dead boy was a threat to Ekurru as well as to the woman and her daughter.

"She's a good kid. Now that she's off the drugs, she's got a real chance. But not with Chuck."

"What happens now?" Lou asked, hoping his twin wouldn't launch into a tangent of might-have-beens. There was no benefit in wishing for blackberries while the salmon were running. They needed to focus on what was still possible to do, rather than pining for what they might have done in the past.

"I wish I knew." Andrew sank back against a tree as if unable to bear his own weight any longer. "They're going to leave Bear Claw, but I have no idea where they can go to get the help that Bernadette needs. She's too isolated up here, and she won't let us banish her oldest friend."

Lou should have felt relief at his twin's words, but instead his shoulders tensed.

"Wherever they go, it'll be a risk for us. If someone realizes that she's one of the *lalassu* and she tells them about us, it won't matter how isolated we are." Andrew closed his eyes for a moment.

It was exactly the kind of complication that Lou hated about the human world. Things weren't easy in nature, but humans spun out issues faster than any spider building a web.

"I wish there was a way we could keep an eye on them, but there's nothing else I can do. Even if Grandfather was okay with me leaving Ekurru, Bernie doesn't trust me. And even if I find a way to force the ghost away, if it's done without Bernie's consent, she could end up like Mother."

The words sickened Lou. Their mother might not have sacrificed her body when their father was killed by a poacher, but she'd certainly allowed her mind and heart to be sealed in the grave with his corpse. Her light and warmth had vanished, leaving an empty hide draped over a frame.

Andrew's pinched expression suggested that he was having similar thoughts. He offered a faint smile that vanished too quickly to be genuine. "I'm not expecting an answer. I've spent weeks meditating and hoping for some divine inspiration, but the Goddess isn't hinting."

"Wait and watch." It didn't bother Lou nearly as much as it would his twin. He was used to being patient and watching for unpredictable opportunities. The forest wouldn't always give a person what they expected, but there was always something for those willing to be aware. Andrew liked to be in control, and despite the time that he spent in the fur, he had never quite accepted that control was an illusion.

"On to different topics." Andrew stood. "Lily tells me that you cancelled the trip to Russia to meet with the Kamchatka clans. What happened?"

Speaking of control. Lou shrugged. "Too much to do here."

It wasn't a lie. There was always too much to do. Leaving to visit another skin-walker clan should have been a welcome break and an opportunity to see a little more of the world. But it wasn't quite what he wanted. It wouldn't satisfy the restless itch building inside. He wanted more than to just take care of his community. Selfishly, he liked the idea of a partner in his life, someone who would both give and take. Maybe some cubs to teach and raise. He should have been excited at the opportunity, but instead, he'd found an excuse to shut it down.

"If you don't go now, you'll have to wait until next summer."

The idea didn't bother Lou as much as it would have a few years back. He shrugged, hoping his brother would leave it alone.

Andrew frowned. "I don't understand. When you talked with Lily-"

Lou growled. He never should have tried to share his thoughts with his sister. She'd been fighting her own mating impulse, and he'd only wanted to try and help. His family had latched onto his confession and now assumed he was hiding some deep and dark longing instead of a perfectly understandable biological desire.

"Hit a sore spot?" Andrew frowned, and Lou tried to pull himself together. Andrew didn't deserve snarling and snapping right now. Kin stood by one another. For most of his life, Lou had protected his family from potential threats. But as the silence stretched on, broken only by the honking of geese overhead, he wasn't sure if he could stand guard against the danger that the woman, the girl, and the ghost posed to Ekurru.

Chapter Three

"Is Michael coming today?" Bernie asked for at least the twentieth time as they meandered beside the swift-running river, but Martha found the patience to answer without snapping.

"As long as the weather holds, Doc and Michael will be here today." The two were flying up on Doc's little plane, *Angel,* along with a bunch of supplies for the community and, she hoped, some ideas about what to do next.

Without Andrew's lessons to fill the hours, both of them were restless. The last week had been one of the more difficult ones in recent memory. Bernie was bored and starting to show signs of teenage defiance. Avoiding the Colony had eliminated one of the major opportunities for distraction in the immediate area, and Martha hadn't found another option. She was trying not to reveal her own uncertainties and worries about their future, but she knew she'd been more irritable than usual. She'd felt guiltier, too, if she was honest with herself.

She shouldn't have lashed out at Andrew's brother. Heavens knew she was used to odd looks and subtle requests to move along. She'd seen them at the parks and in the grocery store, with their pinched mouths and judgment-laden whispers following them as Bernie talked to herself or burst into unprompted laughter or tears. Martha had years of emotional calluses built up from pretending to ignore them.

The drone of a small-engine plane interrupted her self-recriminations. Bernie began to run upstream to Doc's usual landing area. Martha started to call out, wanting the two of them to stay together, but stopped. Bernie couldn't get lost between the two points. There were no strangers who might be a threat to Bernie or who might get hurt if she lost emotional control. And with all the noise Bernie was making, not to mention the proximity of the Colony, there would be no ordinary bears or other wildlife caught in a surprise encounter. Martha followed along at her own pace, watching the gap between herself and her child grow wider and wider.

The small seaplane puttered up to the makeshift dock as Martha arrived. Most of the community had turned out. Andrew stood beside his sister, Lily, both of them wearing plaid flannel shirts and jeans. The ranger, Bill, stood a few steps back in a worn denim shirt, shading his sun-creased eyes against the reflected light. Lily's husband, Ron, looked ready for action, with his flannel shirtsleeves rolled up to reveal his muscular arms. Georgette was off to one side, her gray-hued fingers contrasting sharply with her cherry-tinted tan skin. A brilliant artist who used her tactile abilities to weave incredible textiles, Georgette had enjoyed a fair amount of success with the southern markets and invested her earnings back into Ekurru.

Behind them all was the person that Martha had been trying to avoid thinking about, Lou. He'd managed to cover up completely, and Martha told herself that she had no business being disappointed about it or imagining what was beneath the dark-brown leather. After years of trying to function on a purely practical level, her erotic awareness was coming back to life with a vengeance. She couldn't have picked a worse target for her fantasies, but her subconscious wasn't ready to listen to common sense. *I should apologize for shouting at him.* Instead, she hid her tongue-tied preoccupation like a coward and focused on Bernie, who was bouncing on her toes in excitement.

Martha wrapped her arms around her daughter, squeezing gently.

The pressure seemed to help, and Bernie slowed, leaning into Martha's embrace. "Chuck says that Michael's there, and there are lots of boxes," Bernie said.

"That's nice. I hope Chuck won't spoil the surprise if there are any presents." Figuring out how to manage her daughter's ghost hadn't been covered in any parenting manuals, so Martha generally treated Chuck like she would have any other child—not one that she could see or hear or touch, but a child nonetheless. Andrew's warnings echoed in her mind, and she pushed them aside. Chuck was a fixture of Bernie's life, and she couldn't just yank him away from her.

Doc stepped out of the plane as it approached and leapt lightly onto the dock, catching *Angel* before it could drift into the rough wooden planks. His gray-streaked beard had been trimmed while he was away, but his wiry hair was still caught in a narrow ponytail. Doc tossed a rope to Ron, who tied off the front of the plane while Doc secured the back. Only then did Doc's passenger emerge.

"Michael!" Bernie burst free of Martha's hold and threw herself at Michael with such enthusiasm that Martha was afraid they would fall into the river.

Tall and slender, with windblown brown hair tangling across his face and shoulders, Michael looked as if he'd be more at home at a poetry reading than standing on a dock in the far north. But if he felt uncomfortable, he didn't show it. He held Bernie tightly, listening attentively to her chatter as she attempted to fit six months into less than sixty seconds. He tucked his long hair behind his ear, and Martha spotted his leather gloves with a purely mental sigh of relief. She knew the truth about his abilities, and they were always the first thing she checked for—without them, Bernie might end up overwhelming him in her enthusiasm. Before she'd known about the *lalassu*, he had explained the gloves as a precaution due to a severe allergy, but he was actually a psychometrist. He could pick up emotions, memories, and impressions from any person or object he touched with his bare skin. Without the protection of the leather, he would be overwhelmed by psychic impressions and possibly thrown into a coma from the overload.

Martha noticed Andrew and Ron holding back, clearly waiting to unload. "Bernie, let Michael come off the dock before you tell him everything."

"Come on, Bernie-pie. Let's help unload, and then we'll have our visit." Michael ruffled Bernie's windblown hair before letting her go. Doc had opened *Angel*'s small cargo doors, revealing tightly packed cardboard and wooden boxes. Michael pulled out the first one and handed it to Ron, who passed it on to Andrew, who placed it safely on dry land.

Bernie helped with a few of the lighter boxes before retreating to her mother's side. Martha smiled her approval until she caught sight of Lou staring at them with his mouth set into a thin line. *Is he upset with us? Does he think Bernie should be doing more to help? Is this a soft Southerner versus self-reliant-and-proud Northerner thing?* An urge to give him another tongue-lashing built up, and Martha hastily stopped her train of thought. She would not use him as an outlet for all of her accumulated frustrations. Not again.

Angel was swiftly unloaded, and the community started to disperse with the supplies. Georgette left with several flats of canned food and a box of concentrated dyes. Bill received a crate of food and a box replenishing his supply of tranquilizer darts. Andrew had several books, and Lily got a box of sewing supplies and another full of paperbacks and magazines. Ron got a packet of letters from his family.

Martha picked up a box of clothes for Bernie and dissuaded her daughter from immediately opening the crate of art supplies. They followed Michael and Doc to Doc's cabin. Andrew came along, helping to carry the food supplies that Doc had brought up for himself. Despite balancing a heavy load, Michael kept up a cheery conversation with Bernie. Martha wished she had the energy to join in. All that week, she had been both dreading and looking forward to Michael's arrival. *He must have some idea of what to do next to help her.*

A low growl behind her sent shivers up Martha's spine. She turned and found a large dark-brown bear standing on the path, its golden-brown eyes staring right at them. She would have been terrified if she hadn't also noticed a pile of crumpled dark-brown leather cached in the branches of a nearby tree. Lou had changed into his bear form. He stared at her, and Martha could see that it wasn't with the attentive watchfulness of a wild animal. There was an intelligent purpose in his eyes, as if at any moment, she would understand the message lingering just out of her reach.

"Mom! Hurry up!" Bernie's impatience broke the connection.

Martha realized she had stopped, letting the others pass her. She glanced down at the path then swung her gaze to Lou, preparing to apologize.

But the bear had disappeared, leaving no trace of its presence except the bundle of discarded clothes. Martha caught her breath and looked around. She couldn't see anything except moss and trees.

"Mom!" Bernie shouted again.

"Coming," Martha called, moving once more and shoving the puzzle of Lou into the back of her mind.

When she caught up with the others, Andrew stared at her. His blank expression would have fit in at any poker table, but Martha sensed he was examining her behind his pose of neutrality. She tightened her grip on the box and lifted her chin, refusing to be intimidated or embarrassed. He nodded before walking on. Martha refused to ask him what he thought he'd seen because it would give him too much satisfaction. The childishness of her reaction bothered her, but she clung to her stubborn pride.

"Mom, Doc says we can stay here tonight so we can visit longer with Michael!" Bernie announced. "Is that okay?"

"Of course." Martha got a brief hug from her daughter before she scampered off to help Andrew warm up the prepared stew for dinner. Doc headed outside to stow the supplies while Martha and Michael cleared his papers off the tiny table to make room for them all. Martha smiled to herself as her daughter managed to keep up a constant chattering monologue explaining the stew's ingredients, how the stove worked, and a dozen other topics. Michael kept his attention on Bernie, seemingly fascinated by the stream of information, but Martha saw shadows of worry behind his attentiveness. Throughout the simple meal, the knowledge of the unpleasant conversation to come kept her from relaxing. Instead, she watched Andrew and Michael, wondering if they would bring it up in front of Bernie or wait until she was asleep.

Bernie took the decision out of their hands. "Chuck says that the government is rounding up *lalassu* and sending them away. Are you coming here to stay with us?"

Michael coughed. "No, I'm going back to Perdition after my visit here."

"But what if Special Investigations gets you?" Bernie asked.

"Is it true?" Martha didn't want to accept Chuck's word blindly. "Are they rounding up people with special powers?"

"It's true." Michael pushed his plate back. "After the presidential announcement that our abilities were real, people started to panic. When André Dalhard used his abilities to break out of prison and take over

Perdition, the government started to panic too. There have been riots and lynchings of people suspected of being *lalassu*."

Bernie didn't need that kind of detail. Martha frowned, and Michael caught her hint.

"The government announced that they wanted to protect their citizens." Michael's mouth twisted bitterly. "Those with special abilities would be taken to an evaluation camp, which would put them out of reach of reprisals and allow the government to understand their gifts. There was a whole advertising campaign. They had pictures of the camp near Fairbanks that made it look like a spa with log cabins and beautiful scenery. It's even called 'Woodpine.' They talked about how we would be able to use our powers openly to help others. What if your doctor could look at you and see what was wrong without an expensive MRI scan? What if someone could walk through rubble to find survivors trapped in the debris?"

Bernie snorted. "That's stupid. X-ray vision and phasing aren't real."

"We should let Michael finish." Martha's stomach clenched painfully around her half-eaten meal. It didn't take a history expert to realize that isolating a targeted population never went well. The thought of Bernie being wrenched from her again brought sour bile to the back of her throat.

"At first, we thought the campaigns might help people to see us positively. There were plenty of us who volunteered to be evaluated, and they were told that the relocation would only be temporary. After the tests were run, the government would help the *lalassu* settle in to new homes. Then the ads started to encourage people to report those they thought might have powers, and those people started to disappear. As far as we can tell, no one is coming back from the camp. It just keeps getting bigger and bigger to accommodate the new arrivals."

"It's worse than we thought," Andrew said quietly.

"We might need the sanctuary of Ekurru more than ever," Michael finished.

"We'll help, but we can't take on entire populations. It would only expose us and leave us all vulnerable." Andrew crushed the frail seed of hope before it could take root.

"We're working on alternatives, but they'll take some time. We're all investigating as best we can. We even sent some undercover people to work at the camp to find out what's going on." Michael turned to Bernie, a bright smile firmly in place. "Why don't we clear the dishes, and then we can play some cards?"

Bernie eagerly accepted the change in topic, bouncing up to help Andrew with clearing the table and washing the dishes. Martha watched Michael carefully. A decade of reading between the lines of optimism told her that their efforts to infiltrate the camp hadn't gone as hoped. She wasn't surprised when Michael asked to speak privately with her. They walked outside, stopping a short distance from the cabin.

Despite the late hour, plenty of light still flooded through the forest. Martha could see Michael fidgeting. "There's more you haven't told us."

He sighed. "I hate to do this, but we're running out of options. Do you remember Hood and Harley?"

Vague memories surfaced. "They worked with your friend Joe, didn't they?"

"With his girlfriend, Cali. Hood ran the organization, and Harley is a hacker."

Martha kept her face smooth as the details returned. Joe was a policeman, but his girlfriend had been a professional thief.

"They've gotten positions in the camp, and what they've found is worrying. The conditions are pretty bad. They're holding families in rough barracks inside a barbed-wire perimeter. There's not enough food or clothes or other supplies. But they've also found evidence that some *lalassu* are being taken from within the camp and disappearing." Michael glanced back at the cabin.

"Are they being sent somewhere else?" Martha doubted they were being given the promised new homes.

"They're not leaving camp or escaping. The exits are too tightly monitored. From what Hood and Harley have found, we think they're being selected for medical experimentation. There's a doctor at the camp, Dr. Coulon, but he doesn't treat the *lalassu* or the camp staff. He's got one of the larger buildings in the camp, and no one is allowed inside except medical staff."

Martha's hopes sank as she realized Michael's intent.

"There's a job opening. With your background as an ER nurse, you would qualify for it," Michael urged.

"But we're on watch lists…" *Surely he can't be suggesting that I go undercover?*

"We can provide false identities for you and Bernie—"

"Absolutely not! I'm not taking her within a hundred miles of one of those camps!" Martha closed her eyes. "I can't believe you would even consider it."

"If you don't want her there, we can find someone else to take care of her, and you can be reunited afterward." Michael made the offer, but they both knew why it couldn't be.

After André Dalhard had used his psychic gifts to manipulate Martha into surrendering custody of Bernie two years before, she'd fought like hell to get her daughter back and keep her safe. But those few days of believing her mother had abandoned her ended up scarring Bernie deeply. Martha couldn't place her in a situation that could open those wounds again.

"Having her there could protect you. They won't expect a spy to have a child in tow." Michael scuffed at the terrain with his foot. "I'm sorry to have to ask, but these are desperate times. The Goddess has warned us that if we don't take action soon, disastrous consequences could follow."

Fury snapped Martha's eyes open again. "The same Goddess who didn't stop the government from finding out about the *lalassu* in the first place?"

"I don't pretend to understand how it all works." Michael's hazel eyes were dark with shadows. "I've been reading the journals of the High Priestesses before Dani. The Goddess only gives us enough to get us into position for a possibility of success—sometimes, just the possibility of survival. Whatever's happening at Woodpine is a key moment in history, and we have to figure out what it is."

The weight of responsibility pinned Martha in place. *It's too much.* All she'd wanted was to be a good mother and to raise a happy, healthy daughter, but instead of playdates and kindergarten graduations, she'd gotten hospital visits and intensive therapy. Bernie was supposed to be thinking about starting high school, not hiding in the middle of nowhere and being asked to help save the world. *This isn't supposed to be how parenting* works!

"Martha?" Michael asked.

She held up her hand. If he said anything else, it would tip her precarious mental and emotional balance. "Tell Doc and Bernie that I've gone back to our cabin for the night."

She knew her words were flat, and she hated it. But it was the only way she could speak without screaming. "She's been looking forward to seeing you and shouldn't be disappointed. I'll be back in the morning."

Michael said nothing as she stumbled away into the fading light.

Chapter Four

"The response to the new campaign has been better than expected." Priya Jeevan handed Karan Samil a slim folder as they rode together in the back seat of a limo. They were scheduled to appear at a political fundraiser. The cause was unimportant to Karan. What mattered to him was the opportunity to influence and manipulate those with power.

He glanced at the numbers in the folder and nodded his approval. His sister had a true talent for propaganda, and her latest series of advertisements had increased reports of potential *lalassu* by twenty percent. "Any problems within the Bureau of Special Investigations?"

She shook her head, setting her heavy gold hoop earrings swinging. "All of my people have been carefully chosen. They understand what is at stake and keep the rest of the agency isolated."

He accepted her statement at face value. The president had appointed someone as the nominal head of Special Investigations, but Priya effectively ran the division. Her government connections and his own position as the head of the international conglomerate of Dalhard Industries put them in a unique position to take advantage of the recent upheavals. After decades of working from the shadows, he felt immensely satisfied to move openly.

The limo slowed to a stop, and he took a moment to check his appearance. His matte-black tux set off his bronze skin perfectly. His unlamented former employer had possessed a particular talent for using clothing for intimidation, and Karan had picked up a few of his tricks.

"Don't worry. You look as handsome as ever." Priya smiled at him as she smoothed her fitted blue gown.

"And you look beautiful." The pleasure of such mundane exchanges still surprised him. Most of his life had been defined by two truths: first, that Priya had been murdered by their father's master's son, and second, that he had been the only one in their family to inherit the gift of unaging immortality. After more than six hundred years, he was still adjusting to the discovery that he had been wrong on both counts.

They stepped out of the limo into an onslaught of flash bulbs. Behind the dazzling lights of the media, chaotic shouts and waving placards announced the presence of protesters. Whether they were for or against *lalassu* was irrelevant. Their presence increased tension and created opportunities. A rare genuine smile parted his lips as he followed his sister up a short flight of marble steps and joined the glittering throng milling in the grand ballroom.

"I see the Humanists are gaining in numbers," he murmured to Priya. She nodded, surveying the waving signs. The Humanists were a newly hatched hate group that were focused on the *lalassu* as dangers to the community. Priya had been tracking them over the past year, keeping a careful eye on them.

"Ah, Mr. Samil, so glad you could join us this evening," Senator Paterson, the representative for Alaska, said as he approached.

"Always a pleasure, Senator." Karan bowed slightly, enjoying the other man's uncertainty as he tried to pull back his outstretched hand without making it obvious.

"Have you seen the view from the upper balcony? It's quite magnificent."

Recognizing a request for a semiprivate meeting, Karan permitted himself to be led upstairs.

The senator did not waste any time admiring the lights of the cityscape. "This camp is proving to be a damned mess. I've got environmental activists complaining about the impact of so much building in such a short time, native lobbyists who are angry at not being consulted, and enough bad press to sink a ship." The senator scowled out the window at the protesters below. "Those idiots down there are getting louder and more violent. You heard about the kid who was hanged in North Carolina? I'm getting hundreds of angry letters about it every day."

"Now, Senator, if no one was angry with you, then you would not be doing your job," Karan interrupted smoothly before the old man could get himself going on a long-winded rant.

"You said this would be temporary. Instead, I've got nearly a thousand people jammed into barracks that were meant to hold half that number, and more are arriving every few weeks." Paterson tugged irritably at his collar. "Who knows what these loocies are capable of? It's like sitting on a damn bomb."

Karan did not react to the slur but was pleased to see it being used more and more frequently. It was a sign of public fear and served to further isolate the *lalassu*, which was exactly what he wanted. "Surely, there are some positives. Increased jobs, for example."

"I want them out of my backyard. There must be somewhere else we can send them."

"I understand your concerns, and I share them." Pretending to sympathize had always been one of Karan's weak points, and Priya had suggested some techniques to help. "You have made a valiant effort, and we can't thank you enough. We needed someplace isolated for the initial site so that no one could be tempted to escape. Your generous offer was exactly what we needed, and I can assure you that we are doing our best to find alternative solutions."

Paterson huffed. "You've been promising alternatives for six months. I need them out now."

Perhaps Karan's social tutoring was not progressing as well as he had hoped. "That will not be possible."

The senator's usual affable mask vanished, replaced by beady-eyed aggression. "You're going to find a way to make it possible, or some very unpleasant details are going to find their way into the public record." Paterson's satisfied smile was designed to provoke insecurity and frustration. The old fool made a show of tolerance but inherently believed in his own cultural superiority. He expected Karan to be intimidated, and that was where the senator made a fatal error.

"A threat, Senator?" Karan inclined his head, and Paterson visibly swallowed. "Does this mean our partnership is at an end?"

"You—"

Karan took a deliberate step forward, and the senator paled, his mouth opening and closing soundlessly. Too bad that laughing would ruin Karan's aura of menace. "That would be unfortunate."

"I know things!" Paterson blurted, backing up.

"I am certain you do." Karan took another slow step. "As do I. For example, your former mistress's suicide caused quite the scandal, but I imagine it would be worse if the press found out your role in her death. You addicted her to drugs in order to keep her quiet and abandoned her when she became pregnant."

"There's no proof."

"I have copies of your emails, even videos." Karan made a mental note to thank Priya for her electronic invasion of the senator's computer. "As you said, very unpleasant details."

"I see." Paterson straightened. "Perhaps we should get back to the party."

From the way he clenched his teeth, Karan guessed that the senator was still planning defiance. Unfortunately, he was too used to being a big fish in the pond to know when he was beaten. Karan would have to educate him before he did something stupid. "Perhaps we should, in a moment."

Paterson hesitated, his arms half-raised as if he expected Karan to physically attack him. As if Karan would need to resort to such undignified methods.

"I have always admired your intelligence, Senator. A foolish man would be planning to eliminate me, but you are far too clever for such trivialities. Right now, we are still allies." Karan slowly raised his hand to brush an imaginary spot from the senator's jacket. The man flinched at the touch but held still, much to Karan's pleasure. "Do not push me into becoming an enemy."

Martha couldn't stop pacing back and forth in the tiny cabin, trying to figure out a way forward that didn't involve having to take Bernie into a prison. *There must be someone else who can teach her what she needs to know.* Michael had brought them Shawna after Bernie was rescued from Dalhard. She'd taught them about life on the run and helped Bernie with her gifts. She had been a medium herself but had struggled to teach Bernie, admitting that Bernie's gifts were far out of her league. *Maybe that's the answer: a stronger medium to guide and teach Bernie.* The only problem was that they only knew one other medium, and Gwen had been driven insane by the dead's constant demands. She tripped over the low bench.

"Dammit!" Her hands scraped over the raw wood of the wall as she caught herself. Tears threatened to spill, but Martha refused to give in for the second time in less than a day. She dropped onto the bench and stared resolutely at a pile of Bernie's notebooks. "I can do this. It's no different than what we've done before."

Except it was. When Bernie was first diagnosed, they'd begun with medication and daily therapy. The medication hadn't worked at all, and the help from the therapy had been patchy at best. Then Derek left, and suddenly she had half the resources she'd had before. She and Bernie moved to a tiny apartment so that Bernie could continue therapy, but her daughter kept getting worse, losing touch with reality more and more. Any attempt to bring her back only triggered violent and destructive tantrums.

That was when André Dalhard and his fake therapy center pretended to come to the rescue. They'd promised free treatment if Bernie went to live at the center. Martha had been in the process of having to order a new bed after Bernie ripped the old one to pieces during a twelve-hour screaming session. The money in her account had dwindled to almost nothing, so she'd ignored the niggling warnings in her gut and agreed. It had only taken a few hours to realize it was a mistake, but by then it was too late.

And then we were on the run. Michael and his girlfriend, Dani, had helped to rescue Bernie and set things up. Apparently, Dani's family had lots of practice in helping people to disappear and evade notice. They'd found Shawna, and when she was arrested, they got Martha and Bernie out before Special Investigations could arrest them as well. With every change, their resources and options had dwindled. Sooner or later, they would run out of options.

A job would give me some money. Real money, not the minimal cash I managed to scrape together doing under-the-table jobs while we were in hiding. Martha shook her head wearily against the temptation. Since she stopped moving, she could feel the ache of her tired bones. *I should go to bed and see if tomorrow looks any better.*

Snuggling under the covers, she closed her eyes and enjoyed the quiet. She hadn't had any real privacy for months. Her mind wandered back over the day's events, but it kept returning to Lou and their moment on the path.

It was so embarrassing to be attracted to a man who clearly disliked her. *My libido should have more self-esteem.* Even when she'd been furious with him, there had been no denying his raw beauty. He always wore fur and leather, nothing store-bought or that he hadn't made himself. In the winter, he wore a thick, irregular poncho of overlapping furs, which gave him an air of wildness and isolation. He seemed like a man imported from another time, where survival depended on his own two hands and mind. A flicker of warmth sparked in Martha's belly.

She clenched her teeth, shifting in bed to ease the building tension between her legs. But the sensual side of her personality refused to be shunted aside any longer. Closing her eyes, her hand slid down past the waistband of her old sweatpants. She was tired of fighting, and for one night, she was going to enjoy both her privacy and the fantasy that an extremely attractive man might be attracted to her.

It didn't take long for her memory to furnish details. His massive arms, full of muscles bunched into tight curves, seemed designed for her daydreams of being held in their shelter. The way his long, silky dark hair seemed to float in the breeze invited her to imagine running her fingers through it. His entire body was so powerful that it should have raised feelings of alarm, but instead it appealed to some deep primal instinct. *My inner warrior groupie. Besides, it's only a fantasy,* she reminded herself as she lightly stroked the soft nub tucked between her moist folds.

She imagined that the weight of the covers was his arms around her and that his fingers were the ones exploring and teasing her clit. In her mind, rather than disdain, his eyes burned with passion for her.

His growl would send shivers down her spine. She would smile and let him lead her into the forest. He would pin her against a tree, his lips pressing hot kisses along her jaw and nuzzling into her neck. She would cling to him, burying her fingers in his thick hair to hold him closer and wrapping her legs around his waist.

Her fingers increased their pace, and habit made her bite her lip to keep from crying out. Silence reigned in the cabin even as the fantasy played out in her mind and she ignored inconvenient real-life details such as clothing, insects, or bark friction burns.

She imagined his fingers stroking just as hers were. In her mind, he was devoted to her pleasure, determined to bring her to release before burying himself in her. She pictured the thick length of him, ready and eager to plunge inside. How good it would feel to be stretched and filled by a man who wanted her as much as she wanted him.

The orgasm burst free and swept down through her. Her whole body tensed, her legs went rigid, and her back arched as heat crashed through her muscles. Her mouth locked in an open circle. She panted soundlessly as exultant sensations seized her body and left it shaking with exquisite pleasure.

Slowly, she relaxed back into reality, into the unbroken dark silence of the cabin rather than the sunlit grove of her imagination. She drew in ragged lungfuls of oxygen, giving her heart time to slow and the flush to fade from her skin. *Very satisfying.*

As always, an inconvenient twinge of reality threatened to spoil the afterglow. The real Lou wasn't interested in her and probably would be offended by the idea that she'd used him as a prop in her fantasy. Sleepiness was making it hard to think, but she found herself wondering again about the moment on the path. He hadn't seemed angry at her. *I should apologize to him tomorrow.* She wanted to make things right between them before she and Bernie had to leave.

Martha rolled onto her side, ignoring the whispering voice that insisted it wouldn't make a difference. It said she'd never get it right and that she would spend her life miserable and alone. It told her that she needed to concentrate on being a mother. The really poisonous one insisted that a woman like her would never have a real chance at a man like him and that she'd never have someone to hold her and make love to her again.

Pushing her dark thoughts away, Martha refused to dwell on disappointments. Reality was reality, and if a quick trip into fantasy helped her to get through the next few days, she wasn't going to get all mopey about the differences between the two.

Chapter Five

"Did you get any sleep last night?" Lily asked as Martha arrived at the family cabin. A basket of wet laundry rested at Lily's feet. The short walls still looked peculiar to Martha. Even though she wasn't particularly tall, she could almost see over the tin roof. Inside, there was plenty of room since the cabin extended down into the earth, but from the outside, it still looked wrong.

Martha shook her head and picked up a soggy pair of jeans to wring out. She didn't quite trust her voice. She'd slept, but her dreams had been a tangled mess of nightmares and desire. *Too much fantasy.*

"Michael told us what he asked you to do. It's unbelievable." Lily snapped out a wet shirt with profane force before pinning it to the clothesline.

'Unbelievable' is the perfect word. No one could possibly believe that the fate of thousands could rest on me, Martha Anderson. I'm not heroine material. I'm not strong and sassy. I don't have any powers or skills that could help with an infiltration.

"He had no right to ask. You and Bernie have been through enough." Lily bent to grab another shirt out of the basket.

"He said they don't have any other options." Martha slowly folded the jeans over the clothesline, smoothing out the wrinkles with more care than was necessary. "They need someone to document what's happening in the camp, or people won't believe it."

"People believe what they want, even when the truth is shoved in their faces."

Martha frowned at the quiver of hurt underlying the harsh buzz of anger in Lily's voice. There was a hint of tears in the other woman's dark eyes. "What's wrong?"

"Nothing's wrong." Lily squared her shoulders and snatched up another piece of laundry, twisting it so tightly that it was impossible to identify.

"I won't ask for details you don't want to give, but I don't think you're this upset on my behalf." Martha reached out and put her hands over Lily's, easing the sodden mass of cloth out of the other woman's grip.

Lily wiped at her cheeks with the back of her hand. "Ron wants a baby."

"Oh. And you don't?" It was a tentative guess.

"I do." Lily's shoulders slumped. "But I don't think we can have one together. We're too different genetically. It's been over a year, and every month we go through the same disappointment."

"I'm sorry." Martha gathered Lily into her arms, holding her the same way that she held Bernie when her daughter was upset.

Lily leaned her head against Martha's shoulder. "I know it's trivial in the face of everything that we're dealing with, but…"

"But it still hurts." Even with more than a decade of life to dull the memory, Martha could easily remember the crushing ache of the cycle of failed fertility. She'd tried for two years before getting pregnant with Bernie, and every month had been a special hell of hope and despair.

Lily wiped at her eyes. "Before Ron, I wasn't even sure if I wanted cubs of my own. I felt like I should, since skin-walkers are practically an endangered species, but it wasn't personal. And then I met him, and suddenly I wanted them more than I could have imagined. I thought it would just be a matter of time. We fought so hard for each other, but things were going so much better."

All part of the happily ever after. Except life doesn't always work that way. Martha closed her eyes against her own tears. Sometimes the universe could be incredibly cruel, twisting dreams into nightmares. Even if Lily and Ron had gotten pregnant, their hopes could still have been destroyed. All sorts of things could go wrong with a child, and it was random chance that decided whether things would go smoothly or abruptly change direction.

"I'm sorry." Lily pulled away, wiping at her eyes. "I wish there was someone I could talk to. Someone who could tell me if we even have a chance. But we've been living in secret for so long that it's like we're living in the Dark Ages. You must have felt the same way when you found out Bernie was a medium."

I would have sacrificed anything for a clear idea of what to do. Raising a child who could speak to the dead hadn't been covered on any of the parenting websites. Instead of a support network of information, they'd been driven underground and forced into hiding. Instead of resuming her career, she stood in the middle of a primal forest, hanging laundry with a were-bear. *Too bad there isn't a medium here. That would solve all our problems.*

The wind shifted, and the coppery smell of blood cut through the clean scent of the freshly washed clothes, causing Martha to gag on her inhaled breath. She spun around and saw Lou standing a few feet away, watching them. Several limp rabbits hung from his hand.

"Oh, good, you were able to find something fresh for dinner." Lily switched from personal distress to business without a hitch, something Martha had never been able to manage.

"I'll prepare them for you." His dark eyes flicked briefly over Martha. The implied dismissal delivered a sharp stab of humiliation. *He'd be horrified if he knew I fantasized about him.*

"Thanks. I'll do up a stew. Andrew promised to bring in fresh plants as well." Lily went back to hanging up laundry. "Bernie raved to Michael about Grandfather's stew. She and Doc took him on a tour of the Colony this morning."

Martha's attention was still on the man moving around the cabin's outer walls. The sled dogs, obviously hoping for a treat, were alert outside their little huts. One of them bounced up as Lou passed, its mouth open to snatch at the dangling rabbits. Without breaking stride, Lou cuffed it on the muzzle with two fingers. Not in a hurtful way, but to remind it who was in charge.

The rest of the laundry went up on automatic pilot as she snuck glances at Lou, trying to decide why her subconscious had settled on him. He was attractive, but so was his twin brother. Ron was, too, for that matter. And it didn't need to be someone there—her imagination could have pulled up anyone. But it kept returning to Lou.

51

He stripped off each rabbit's fur in a single tug, leaving pale-pink, stiff-limbed bodies. Martha swallowed, bothered as she was forced to confront that her next meal had been running around the forest a few hours before, even though she'd never had a problem eating meat in her old life.

Maybe that's the source of his appeal. Lou was intimidatingly self-sufficient. He navigated the forest as Martha could navigate her old neighborhood. He made his own clothing and sent furs south in trade to support his family. He hunted and tracked and could survive the harsh environment with only what he carried with him. *He belongs here. This is his place.* She'd never had a home that fit her as well as his fit him.

"Hey, Mom!" Bernie's shout ended Martha's opportunity for introspection.

Her daughter was leading Michael out of the forest, and Doc followed behind them. Martha smiled when she saw the young woman coming out in her little girl.

"You should have seen it! Malila brought her cub out for Michael to see. They were playing and climbing all over him." Bernie beamed with pride.

"I'm glad it went well." Martha hung a set of mismatched knitted socks, which was the last of the laundry.

"Are you and Michael going to talk more about the camp?" Bernie asked.

Martha stiffened, and she shot an accusatory glance at Michael. He raised his gloved palms and shook his head.

"Chuck says we should go soon so that Leanne can start teaching me." Bernie shrugged. "It sounds a lot better than staying here. There's water and electricity and a real house where I could have my own room again—"

"Bernadette Anderson!" Martha interrupted before Bernie could say something truly offensive. "There's no need to be rude. Lily and her family have been very good to take care of us."

"Oh." Bernie turned anxious eyes on Lily. "I didn't mean to hurt your feelings."

"You didn't." Lily ruffled Bernie's hair. "I know this hasn't been what you're used to. I'd be excited about the idea of my own room, too."

Martha could see Lou watching them out of the corner of her eye, but she couldn't read his expression. She wanted to apologize to him for Bernie's denigration of his home, but he turned away and went inside before she could figure out how to do it. Besides, she had her own crisis to suppress. "We're not going to the camp."

"But we have to." Bernie sounded like any teenage girl being deprived by her elders. "Chuck said that he could help us with the spying, figuring out where the secret places are so that you can find them. And Leanne already said she'll help me."

Martha took a deep breath and resolved to deal with the crisis one step at a time, starting with the unfamiliar name that Bernie had already said twice. "Who is Leanne?"

"She's the one who can hear Chuck." Bernie rolled her eyes in the universal teenage response to parental denseness. "She has her own ghost, Henri."

Martha sucked in a breath. *A medium. Presumably one who wasn't insane. At the one place that I won't dare go.*

"And she's at the camp?" Michael stepped forward with his gloved hands clasped in front of him.

Bernie nodded. Martha noticed a smirk twitching in one corner of Bernie's mouth. She was enjoying being the center of attention. Martha wanted to grab her daughter's shoulders and shake her until she understood how dangerous the situation truly was. It wasn't some grand adventure. If they went into the camp, there was no guarantee they would be able to get out.

"It sounds like you would have an ally already in place, in addition to Hood and Harley. They've been sending us information for the last month." Michael looked hopefully at Martha.

Not helping. "It's too dangerous."

"Actually, it might not be," Michael replied. "I didn't get a chance to tell you last night, but with Dalhard's list destroyed, the government is relying on a simple chemical-reaction test. It's supposed to test for an enzyme unique to *lalassu*. Except we already know that the test doesn't catch about thirty percent of us."

"That's still a seventy-percent chance of being caught. I'm not risking my life and Bernie's on those odds." Martha curled her fingers around her arms to prevent herself from snatching up her daughter and running away.

"I have the chemicals for the test here with me. We can make sure that Bernie doesn't test positive." Michael would win against a hungry dog in a soulful eye-begging contest. "Please, Martha. If the test shows her as a *lalassu*, I won't ask again. But if it doesn't, please consider it."

There's a medium there. And money. And a chance to do some good. Her optimistic side was in full cheerleader mode. Her negative side was already imagining being buried in an unmarked grave.

"Please, Mom?" Bernie wrapped her arms around Martha's waist.

"Fine. We'll try the test." They would need to know no matter what happened. No matter where they went, the risk of discovery would always follow them. She held Bernie tightly. *This time, I'll do better.*

Michael disappeared inside the cabin, emerging a few moments later with a plastic-wrapped tube. He ripped it open, unscrewed the cap, and pulled out a long cotton swab. He rubbed the inside of Bernie's cheek then put the swab into the clear liquid at the bottom of the tube. Gently shaking it, he held it up to the light.

The fluid remained clear.

"What does that mean?" Martha asked.

"She doesn't test as a *lalassu*. If she had, the chemicals inside would have turned black." Michael beamed as if Bernie had won a national competition. "Psychic gifts are the ones most likely to be overlooked."

"But they have to know that their test doesn't catch everyone." Martha's certainty was crumbling under her feet.

"They know it's not perfect, but it's close enough," Michael replied. "I know you can do this, Martha. Please, just listen to what we have."

She listened as he explained, numbly absorbing the details. So many things aligned that it was beginning to feel like predestination, but Martha was tired of being a plaything for fate. Her gut told her that going to the camp would be asking for disaster, but she had no reason that she could give to anyone else. Maybe she could find a critical flaw in Michael's planning.

Several hours later, Martha's hopes were beginning to run thin. She used her spoon to push chunks of rabbit stew around, trying not to look at the end of the table where Lou sat. *Is he disappointed that I'm not leaping at the chance to be a hero? Not that it matters. I have to do what's best for Bernie.*

If only deciding what was best for Bernie was as simple as it had been when she was little. Martha had covered all the basics, providing food, shelter, and love. She hadn't blinked when the doctors recommended therapy.

But she faced a much more difficult decision. If she agreed to Michael's insane plan, she could repay some of her debt to the *lalassu* as a whole. While they were there, Bernie could work with Leanne. If Chuck's word could be trusted, then Leanne was a medium who had managed to avoid going insane from the attention of the dead. Without her help… The memory of Gwen's dark and smelly prison rose up, providing a worst-case scenario. Gwen's parents loved their daughter but had been forced into making the horrible decision to physically isolate her inside a sealed room meant to minimize ghostly access.

But to get Leanne's help, Martha had to put her daughter into a trap and hope that it didn't snap shut around them. Michael and his friends were taking every precaution to make sure that didn't happen, but Martha knew there were no guarantees.

"What are you thinking?" Lily asked quietly.

Martha's fingernails scraped along the wood of the table. "I'm frightened."

The room fell silent. Everyone was looking at her. Andrew and Ron had been arguing about whether or not she should go, but they were eyeing her as if she might burst into a fit at any moment. Michael sat beside Bernie, both of them looking expectant. Behind them, Andrew and Lily's grandfather was in his rocking chair, staring at the fire as if he could read the future in its flames. At the foot of the table sat Lou, with his face cloaked in shadow.

"I'm not strong like Dani or able to transform like Lily or change my face like Cali. I'm an ordinary person." She took a deep breath. "If someone at the camp realizes I'm there to gather information or that Bernie is a *lalassu*, then there's no way I could fight back—"

"I could go with you."

Lou's rumbling statement obviously took them all by surprise. Martha's stomach felt as if it were trying to do a backflip. *He can't possibly mean what it sounds like he's saying.* Andrew and Lily started talking over one another. Grandfather held up his hand, and they quieted.

Lou stood up, dominating the space with shoulders nearly as wide as the table. He turned to Michael. "The camp is in the wilderness, right?"

Michael nodded. "The camp is so isolated that it would be suicide to try and escape into the wilderness."

"Not for me." Lou met Martha's gaze, his dark eyes steady and clear. "If they tried to hold you or your daughter, I could get you both out and take you to safety."

"Why?" Martha asked. Her subconscious kept trying to throw in memories from last night's fantasy, making it hard to keep her face and voice calm.

"This needs to be done." He shrugged as if it were of no more consequence than any other chore.

You were expecting a declaration of undying and passionate love? Apparently, her subconscious hoped that his decision to volunteer had something to do with her personally instead of his sense of responsibility and duty. Martha wrestled down the piece of her that had clearly read too many romance novels. It was time to accept her fate. "All right. We can all go to prison."

CHAPTER SIX

"What exactly are you thinking?" Andrew snarled at his brother.

It wasn't about thinking. It was something more primal. Ever since the day on the path, Lou had become more and more aware of Martha. He would linger near her cabin or shadow her and Bernie as they walked in the woods. At first, he told himself that he was keeping an eye on a potential threat, but surveillance wasn't what kept him going back day after day.

"You can't possibly think this is a good idea!"

Lou ignored Andrew and checked his possessions to decide what to take. A few pairs of leather trousers and his fur poncho were folded into the cedar box under his bed. An assortment of tools hung from pegs on the log walls of the cabin. His trapping gear was in the corner, though he doubted that he would need it. He could make do with thick wire for snares if necessary.

"What happened to your obligations as a Guardian?" Andrew's rant had begun shortly after Martha and the others left, and he'd barely paused for breath since. "Remember the reason you didn't want to go to Russia?"

It hadn't been the only reason, but Andrew wasn't looking for answers. Lou weighed a hatchet in one hand. It was lightweight, designed to chop branches rather than entire trees. *Could be useful.*

"You can't think they'll let you bring that into a prison!"

He might be right. Lou lowered the hatchet. "I'll cache it outside."

"Wonderful idea, except for the part where you're going to have to leave from Juneau. They'll search your luggage before you board the plane." Andrew pointed at the small axe. "The axe will be confiscated and held, marking you as a troublemaker."

Shrugging, Lou laid the hatchet down on the blue-and-gray quilt covering his narrow bed. When he went into the wild, he didn't usually take anything. His bear form was more than adequate for any survival challenges. But if he needed to escort Martha and the girl back to Bear Claw, some basic tools would make things much easier. He placed his fire-starting kit and the first aid kit beside the hatchet.

Andrew grabbed Lou's shoulder, trying to force him to turn around. Lou settled his weight, becoming immovable. Andrew might not match his twin for physical size, but he was still strong. Usually, Lou didn't bother to resist and allowed his brother to be the dominant one. But he couldn't allow Andrew to control him.

Failing to move Lou by force, Andrew circled around to face him. "You have no reason to go."

Maybe not, but I'm still going to go. He needed a reason that his brother would believe. "Ekurru must be protected."

"And how will you protect us if you're in Wood—" Andrew sucked in a sharp breath. "You're worried about them telling someone about us."

No. The denial was instinctive, though he couldn't say why. Martha was fragile and had already broken once. It wouldn't take much to break her again, but if he was there, he could keep her from being trapped in a place where she could break. Lou picked up a pair of dirt-stained leather pants. The hide was still sound. He added it to his pile to pack.

"You can't wear those. You need to fit in." Andrew snatched them back. "And we need to talk about this. Could you kill Martha and Bernie if they betray us?"

His twin's assumptions hurt like porcupine spines latched into his flesh. After forty years together, surely Andrew knew him better than to believe something like that. "No."

"Then what is it?"

"I can get them out if needed. Before someone asks them dangerous questions." Lou couldn't explain it to his twin. He could hardly believe it himself. His decision wasn't about the safety of Ekurru. It wasn't even about wanting to see more of the world. He could claim either reason, but neither was the whole truth. Going with Martha and her daughter was something he needed to do. It was as instinctive as gorging on summer food to prepare for winter hibernation. But he couldn't find the human words to share his certainty.

"Someone needs to go, but that doesn't mean it has to be you." Andrew's fingers bit into Lou's arms. "You have no experience outside of Bear Claw. You could get confused and make a mistake, revealing what you are."

Anger tensed Lou's muscles at the implication of incompetence.

Andrew immediately let go. "I'm sorry. That came out wrong. What I mean is that life below the Arctic circle is a very different world than the one you're used to."

It was exactly the reason why he needed to go. Lou laid out a selection of knives, the blades shining in the steady light from their oil lamp. "You, Lily, and Mark have all managed. I will do the same."

"You—"

Lou shook his head, stopping Andrew's next objection before it could get started. "I am the best hunter and woodsman in Bear Claw, in either form. The territory near the prison is difficult even in this season. I am the best chance she has to escape."

"And thus the best chance to convince her to go," Andrew grumbled. "I still don't think we should be worrying about this so-called evaluation camp. We're safely hidden here, and doing this only risks us being discovered."

Lou didn't believe that his twin meant what he was saying. It belatedly occurred to Lou that Andrew might be worried about him in the way that Martha worried about Bernie.

"Are you even listening to me?" Andrew pleaded.

Lou nodded. "It will be dangerous and uncomfortable and difficult. But I will go."

Andrew sighed, and his shoulders slumped down. "There's no arguing with you. Fine, if you have to go, you have to go. I'll pack you some herbs in case you need them, including the tea that prevents transformations."

Lou hadn't inadvertently transformed for over a decade, but he sometimes shifted to the fur to avoid uncomfortable conversations. Still, it would be a relief to have his brother's medications ready. Skin-walkers didn't always react the same as humans did when it came to drugs. With his brother's concoctions, Lou would be safe.

Andrew picked up the heavy fur poncho. "You are not going out into the world sporting this homemade Neanderthal chic. You need a new wardrobe."

For the first time, Lou felt a stirring of alarm about the plan. "What?"

"You need to wear clothes from a store, not leather and fur. In the south, killing animals for clothing is a big moral trigger." Andrew pulled aside the curtain that separated the bedroom from the cabin's main room, reaching over to snag a thick, glossy catalogue off the nearby bookshelf. Thumbing through, he paused at one page. "Something like that."

Lou looked down at the man in the picture. He was pale skinned and wore blue jeans, a striped shirt, and pale-yellow leather gloves. An axe rested on his shoulder, and there wasn't a scratch or nick to show it had ever been used, despite the prominent stump in the image. "You think I should look like him?"

"It's what the other men will look like. Think of it as protective camouflage."

The material would be thin, flimsy, and easily torn. It would offer little protection against thorns, rocks, or claws. It wouldn't keep out the cold like his fur poncho did. It would itch and chafe at the seams, and it would cost money that their family couldn't afford to spend. But if that was what he needed to do in order to go, he would make it work.

"You awake, Bernie?" Chuck woke her up immediately. He never whispered.

Bernie opened her eyes and shifted on her narrow and lumpy mattress. Chuck stood in front of her, his gray clothes and pale face glowing like a dim night-light. To her, he seemed just like anyone else. He even cast a shadow in the moonlight streaming through the cabin's window on the opposite wall.

"I'm glad we're going to be leaving soon." He poked at the thick quilt, his finger going through the bright-yellow fabric.

"Me too." Bernie yawned then froze as the bunk below hers creaked. She didn't want her mother waking up and catching her talking to Chuck when she should be sleeping.

"Come outside so we can talk," Chuck said.

Bernie waited until her mother's breathing evened out before moving. Her thick woolen socks made it hard to feel the rungs built into the wall as she eased out of the bunk, but she'd had plenty of practice. After the accident on the river, she'd promised her mother that she wouldn't go outside with Chuck again, at least not without telling someone. But the promise didn't slow her steps. Chuck had stood by her and watched over her for as long as she could remember. He'd never let her down, and she trusted him absolutely.

As she crept across the cabin, her socks itched and bunched up on her feet. She hated them, just like she hated the rest of the stupid place.

Not Lily and Doc and the Colony. Her inner voice threatened to disrupt the sullen anger building up in her chest, and Bernie recklessly shoved it aside. She was tired of hiding and of pretending she was just like the other kids without getting to do any of the things that the other kids did. It wasn't fair. Jamming her feet into her stiff boots, she glared at her mother's sleeping back. Her mom was the one who'd decided to bring them to stupid Bear Claw, where it was always too dark or too light.

She wanted to clomp across the floor and slam the door. *I should, but I'm not petty and childish like* some *people.* She could be considerate. She eased the heavy door open and stepped outside, closing it behind her. The cool wind cut through her T-shirt and pajama pants, and she shivered.

"Come around here so you can sit out of the wind." Chuck pointed to the side of the cabin.

Bernie hurried around the corner. "Are you okay? He didn't hurt you, did he?"

"He couldn't hurt me even if he wanted to," Chuck bragged.

She wrapped her arms around herself, shivering. "I wish we could talk in the morning, when its warmer."

"They'd all be listening then." Chuck scowled. "I keep telling you that we can't trust them. They don't understand us."

Stung by his repetition of things she already knew, Bernie rolled her shoulders forward and tucked her hands under her arms.

"I'm sorry, Bernie. I just get so mad at how they keep trying to break us up." Chuck got darker as he got upset, but she could still see him clearly even though it was night. It was kind of like a dark glow. Bernie couldn't have explained it to anyone who couldn't already see ghosts.

"I know." *He has every right to be upset. Mom doesn't really believe in him, Andrew's trying to get rid of him, and I'm the only one he can talk to.* It was understandable that he would be jealous, even though she didn't like it. He'd always been a good listener, back when he was the only person she had to play with besides the therapists. He'd told her stories and sung songs to her and always watched out for her, telling her when people were planning to hurt her so that she could stop them.

"I went to the camp and talked to Henri, Leanne's ghost." Chuck settled beside her, pretending to lean against the wall next to her. Bernie realized she was finally taller than he was. He'd seemed so big when she was little. It was strange to be the bigger one. "Leanne is getting everything ready for when we get there. Henri knows where they keep the guards' weapons—"

"Wait a minute! Weapons? I thought we were going to sneak onto the plane and run away." Bernie started to shake as she remembered the escape from the awful testing place. The quiet man, Karan, had shot Nada, an old woman, right in the head. They'd only been a few feet away from Bernie. It had been horrible and not like the movies at all.

"If Leanne has a gun, she can make the pilots fly the plane to wherever you want." Chuck seemed surprised at Bernie's hesitation.

Threatening to hurt someone was wrong. Michael and her other therapists had told her that again and again. Except Bernie was only hiding because other people were threatening to hurt her, and no one was telling them it was wrong. She hunched, trying to warm her cold hands. If the government was bullying them, then maybe it was okay to threaten the government. It wasn't as if they planned to actually hurt anyone. It still didn't feel right, though.

"It'll be okay, kid. I promise. Once we get away, we'll go someplace where none of the bad people will ever find us again, and we'll be together forever." Chuck smiled. "You know I'll take care of you. Haven't I always?"

Bernie nodded. He'd stayed with her in the awful testing place, helping her as much as he could—not like her mother, who'd sent her there in the first place. Anger tightened the sour knot wrapped around her chest. If her mother hadn't sent her there, they wouldn't have had to run and hide. Mr. Dalhard would have never known about her, she would have never seen Nada get shot, and Michael wouldn't have gotten hurt and nearly died.

"Leanne told me that it's gonna be important for you to find her as soon as you can. I can show you where she lives when you go into the camp." Chuck flickered in and out of her view as he lost the mental control he needed to stay visible. He did that a lot when he was excited. "She's going to need you to borrow some of your mom's clothes."

"Why?"

"So Leanne can wear them to sneak out of camp." Chuck started to laugh. "She's got 'em all fooled. She pretends to be this crazy bag lady so no one will recognize her when she's clean and all gussied up. The two of you will be able to walk right onto the plane."

"Maybe we won't need a gun, then." She would feel much better if that were the case.

"Maybe not. But it's better to have one." Chuck didn't sound optimistic. "And we have to make sure that your mom and Michael don't try to find us."

That was going to be tricky. "I don't know."

"Michael wants you to be happy. If you send him a message saying that you're safe and happy, he'll probably let it stand. And you can keep in touch through Gwen." Chuck's confidence transformed to slyness. "Your mom is going to be the hard one."

No kidding. Bernie wiggled her cold toes and fingers. She knew her mom felt bad about sending Bernie to the testing place. She'd said hundreds of times that she'd made a horrible mistake, and she'd tried to change it as fast as she could. Bernie believed her, but she also knew why her mother had done it in the first place. Chuck told her.

Her mom was tired of taking care of her. Her dad had left because

Bernie was too much work, and after that, her mom had been all about making Bernie better. They didn't read stories or play games or do other things that mothers and daughters did. It was all work, all the time, and Bernie often heard her mother crying in the night. It made Bernie angry, which made her do bad things like rip up the furniture in her bedroom or empty all of the jars and cans in the kitchen.

She couldn't shake the idea that, if she were gone, her mother might be happier. For all those years, her mother had treated Bernie like she was broken, but she wasn't. She was just different in a way that her mother couldn't ever understand. She didn't need to be fixed. She needed to be left alone.

"We might have to do something serious to keep her away," Chuck said.

"No." Bernie might be mad at her mom, but she didn't want to hurt her. "We'll figure something out. Maybe Leanne will have an idea. She's a grown-up."

"Your mom isn't going to want to go into the camp. Look how scared she is of going to see the *lalassu* here in Ekurru."

It was true that her mom didn't leave the cabin very often. She only really talked to Lily and Ron. But Bernie wasn't sure if her mom wanted her to stay at the cabin because she was scared. The whole conversation made her feel uncomfortable. It felt like Chuck was asking her to choose between her mom and him. "I'm cold, and I want to sleep."

She trudged back to the door, her anger at Chuck keeping her warm. *He should trust me the way that I trust him.* She wrestled the door open, got back inside, and stood still for a minute, listening.

Her mother's breathing was still even. Bernie kicked off her boots and climbed back into bed, the warmth from the stove easing the chill in her arms and legs. She wriggled around on the lumpy mattress and tried to pretend it was her own bed back at home. Wherever she and Chuck ended up would have real beds, other kids to talk to, and fresh fruit to eat all year. It would be warm and fun, and she wouldn't have to be afraid. *No matter what, I'm never coming back to Bear Claw.*

Knowledge

Chapter Seven

"Your plan failed." Karan dropped a stack of newspapers onto Priya's desk, which created an exasperated-sounding outflow of air. "The government voted against mass testing."

Not unexpected, Priya thought. Although she'd managed to keep the flaws in the testing process a secret, she'd also been aware of the fluctuations in public sympathies. Relatively harmless *lalassu* were appearing on screen and in newsprint with stories of heartstring-tugging puppetry. She had attempted to counter them with examples of criminal behavior and other socially repugnant life choices. Keeping the momentum of hatred and fear going was difficult without the proper tools.

"The latest patsy accomplished nothing." Karan sank into the visitor's chair and drummed his fingers against the high armrests.

At his indiscreet words, Priya glanced at the hallway. Most of her staff had departed for the day, and she'd carefully chosen her employees, but recklessness offered no benefit. A depressingly large number of investigators truly believed they were doing a necessary civil service. Luckily, none of them appeared to be within earshot. *He needs to be steered back into line...* She folded her hands on her desk. "It's true. The psychic only dug out a few secrets that would have eventually made their way to the tabloids, anyway. It was hardly the sort of display that would inspire torches and pitchforks. This place is too used to scandal."

"We should forget about creating a spectacle and concentrate on harvesting *lalassu* who can be useful to us." Although he was clearly attempting to appear calm, his rapidly tapping fingers undermined his façade.

"Spectacles are only as valuable as the *lalassu* on display." Priya kept her voice low and her hands still to counter her brother's irritation. As tempted as she was to snap back at him, experience had taught her to entice rather than bully her opponents. "If we could find another transformative—"

"Not this again. Last time, we lost an entire team and could not contain the creature. The risk and the cost are too much." Karan slashed the air with his hand.

Priya shrugged. "Then we shall proceed with the current plan and continue to keep the public stirred up while we wait for the doctor to discover an appropriate *lalassu*."

"The press is against us." Karan tapped the newspapers again.

Priya kept her face calm. The physical papers were no longer the authoritative voice of the public. "The government's decision has sparked a new wave of protests. Five are scheduled in the next week. Three of them are being led by the Humanists."

"They are becoming too radical," Karan interrupted. "They could drive away our support."

"They draw the radical element to them, which prevents it from gaining a foothold in the other organizations." She'd worked very hard to ensure a proper balance between hatred and the group's actions. Too much hatred, and the authorities would swoop down and disband the Humanists before she could use them properly. Too little action, and the violence seekers would go elsewhere, making them harder to predict. "The problem is the doctor."

"You cannot expect the man to make an omelet with nothing but rice flour." Karan stared past her with distant eyes. "The truly powerful *lalassu* are escaping our nets, likely due to the interference of their so-called Goddess and her conduit. We need to take down the Harris family."

She couldn't allow her brother to fall down the same rabbit hole of obsession that had swallowed his former employer. She gracefully crossed the office to prepare a cup of jasmine tea. Karan didn't speak. He barely glanced at her as she handed him the cup and knelt beside his chair.

"Karan," she said softly, "you've been dealing with so much over the last year. I can understand how frustrated you must feel. Great men are always frustrated when dealing with their lesser counterparts."

Her brother lifted his eyebrow but didn't comment on her flattery. He set aside the tea, dropping the cup onto her desk with complete disregard for what it might do to the documents she'd carefully laid out. Priya nearly frowned as she realized it was resting on a copy of her latest press release about the evaluation camp, which announced a dramatic increase in construction and medical staff.

"We must be patient. We're only missing one piece: a *lalassu* who can frighten this country into giving over complete power to Special Investigations." The right display would spark panic, which in turn would drive the *lalassu* to follow Karan as a leader. Between the two of them, they would be able to manipulate any situation to their advantage.

"The plan only works if there is a suitable *lalassu* in the camp waiting for the doctor to find them." Karan irritably brushed her aside, his fingers returning to their manic drumming.

"Perhaps we're taking the wrong approach." Priya rose to her feet. "Perhaps we're casting too wide a net."

His fingers slowed. "What do you mean?"

Priya waited until she was seated behind her desk before speaking again. "*Lalassu* powers are part of their genetic code. What we need to do is target specific bloodlines, the ones with useful talents. You must have some idea of the possibilities after your decades of working with them."

If only we still had the list. Karan's list of *lalassu*, their powers, and their families tracked across more than a century. But it had been destroyed by the Harrises and their allies in a brazen display of defiance that still brought an aching clench to her jaw. With the list, she could have chosen precisely the *lalassu* she needed for the display. Instead, Special Investigations and Dalhard Industries were stuck playing catch-up.

"Your point is valid," he finally said. "Perhaps we should bring the doctor in for a consultation."

"An excellent suggestion." She inclined her head and lowered her eyes, signaling submission that she didn't feel.

Karan's spine straightened. "We also need to be prepared for his failure. An army of *lalassu* could take over this country, properly led."

"Of course. It's only prudent to consider other options." *No matter how shortsighted they are.* She kept her smile fixed in place despite the growing ache in her cheeks. If global domination was that easy, any number of sociopathic megalomaniacs would have done it, whether or not they had supernatural abilities. Their best efforts could only establish temporary empires on constant verge of a collapse. Power couldn't be taken without those it was taken from wanting it back.

But it could be coaxed out of distracted hands and emotional minds. Give them bread and circuses, as the old proverb said.

"What is the timeline?" Karan asked.

"We would need the spectacle within a month. Six weeks, maximum." If they waited too long, her carefully orchestrated manipulations would pass each other in the void, rather than clashing in a transforming explosion.

"That does not leave a great deal of potential opportunity. I will make the arrangements to have the doctor flown down." Karan rose to his feet, automatically buttoning and smoothing his suit.

"The lack of communication with the camp has been an ongoing barrier to our success. Perhaps we should remove the electro-dampeners." Putting those things in place had been a mistake from the first day. Their signal-jamming might prevent anyone from taking a digital photograph or using a smuggled cell phone to contact the outside world, but it also meant that the only way to speak directly to the doctor was either to bring him south to do so in person or try to have complicated conversations through a shortwave radio. The jammers also prevented anyone in the camp from using a computer, which meant that reports had to be hand typed and then physically transported via messenger.

"No, there's too great a risk of hackers being able to get into the system." He shook his head.

You mean that you're afraid of Vapor, your old partner. Vapor was another immortal, but he was firmly on the side of the Harrises and their kin. His hacking skills made him invaluable as a forger and information gatherer. Letting him escape was one of her greatest regrets. He was the only one whose skills might have allowed him to penetrate their defenses, requiring their ridiculous reliance on analog methods.

"You showed me how vulnerable electronic information was,"

Karan continued.

Priya nodded, graciously accepting the compliment and the rebuke. After centuries apart, she'd hacked into Karan's systems to smooth their reconnection. Languages came easily to her, even the binary language of the digital world. And once she understood a language, it was only a small step to comprehending what she needed to say in order to get what she wanted.

"Just remember, Hood and Harley will be there to help you, and Gwen will be listening for messages from Chuck." Those had been Michael's last words to Martha as she and Bernie left the hotel. As she surveyed the long stretch of the departure lounge at Juneau's airport, she wasn't reassured by the idea of relying on either strangers or a ghost for backup.

Most of the seats were full, the rows dotted by heads bent over books or tablets. A few children were running around, earning irritated glances from passengers as they took advantage of their last chance to spread their limbs for a while. Bernie was staring out the large windows at the airplanes, looking every inch the sullen teenager with wires trailing from her ears to the player in her pocket. *I should be grateful she hasn't been talking to anyone that others can't see.* Martha checked their tickets again and tried not to wonder where Lou was.

She hadn't seen him since they'd arrived in Juneau three days before. He and Andrew had disappeared as soon as they stepped off Doc's plane. She had the papers for their false identities: they were Martha and Louis McKinnon and were traveling with their daughter, Bernadette. The aliases didn't seem particularly convincing or clever since it only changed their last names, but at least she wouldn't forget which one was hers. At least the documents fooled the company doing the interviews for the camp. Lou had gotten a job on one of the construction teams, and she was going to be the doctor's assistant for the next twelve weeks.

"You folks going out to Woodpine?" A cheerful young man ambled over to them, his smile echoed in his blue eyes. His close-cropped brown hair had hints of blond from the sun, and Martha couldn't help noticing that he filled out his flannel shirt and jeans nicely.

"Yes. I'm Martha." She smiled at him and received a bright flash of teeth from his easygoing return grin.

"Ryan Blake. Is this your first time on rotation?" he asked.

"How did you know?" *Is it obvious that I don't belong here?*

He winked at her. "You can always tell the new folks by their jitters. Like those two over there."

He pointed at two men sitting in the waiting room's plastic seats. One tapped his toe hard enough to set his entire leg moving in a rapid-fire bounce. The other was fidgeting with the straps on his backpack. Martha scanned the lounge again and realized that most of the occupants were young men of various ethnicities. There were only three other women and the two boys who had been running around earlier. Otherwise, it was all men. *What have I gotten myself into?*

"I've been there for the last nine months. Only left because I had to use my vacation hours. Anything you need, just ask me. It's a different world up there." Ryan glanced over his shoulder then leaned in closer. "I know it can be nerve-racking, travelling with a child to a new place, so I wanted to introduce myself and lend a hand."

Martha thanked him, torn between an old instinct to hide and a vague certainty that spies were supposed to cultivate connections.

"I'm a pretty good judge of character, and I think you'll fit in well. We lifers are a solid community up there, all looking out for each other," Ryan continued without any prompting, chatting easily, as if they'd known each other since childhood.

"Do many people stay to work at the camp? I thought it was a strict rotation." It wasn't exactly critical information, but she thought it could help.

"That's how it's supposed to work, but about half of every rotation is regulars. Not everyone can handle being up at the top of the world, only a half mile away from the loocies." Ryan nodded at the two men he'd pointed at earlier. "Those two will probably wet themselves the first time they have to face a loocy."

Martha struggled not to correct him on the term. Michael had warned them about the derogatory slang for the *lalassu*. She hated hearing it but couldn't afford to draw suspicion.

Ryan must have noticed. "Officially, they're called O.H.s or occu-somethings, some Latin stuff that only the execs and the scientists care about. For the most part, they're not too bad. Creepy, but they keep to themselves and mostly don't cause trouble. And for the ones that do, we have the shock collars and detention cells."

It sounded more dreadful the more she learned. Martha noticed Bernie scowling despite her headphones and decided to change the subject before her daughter lost her temper. "Where do you work, Ryan?"

"I'm a guard. We man the exits to the camp and the tower. If there are any problems, I'll take care of you." He pointed his index finger like a gun and clicked his tongue.

"What do you mean, shock collars?" Bernie asked, her nose twisted in disgust.

"Oh, it's not so bad, little girl. It's a little collar around their necks, tiny enough that you would hardly notice it. The guards all carry special controls, and at the press of a button, we can drop 'em to their knees." Ryan clearly wasn't bothered by the barbarity he was describing.

"Can't they just cut it off?" Bernie asked.

"Not if they want to keep breathing." Ryan winked. "Why, one time..."

Martha thought he was pausing for dramatic effect until she noticed that Ryan's attention had shifted to a point behind and above her.

"Martha."

Lou's gravelly voice had never been so welcome. She turned around, ready to pretend to welcome her fake husband. But the words died on her tongue.

He didn't look anything like the half-feral mountain man she was used to seeing. He wore blue jeans that were snug at his hips and stretched over his broad thighs. A gray denim shirt complemented his tan skin and emphasized his powerful chest and arms. His long dark hair was tied back with a leather thong, the only trace of the old Lou. He even wore steel-toed boots.

"I was starting to get worried." She heard a note of breathiness in her voice and made herself clear her throat. Blond hair and a squeaky voice did not leave an impression of intelligence and determination. "This is Ryan Blake. Ryan, this is my husband, Lou."

"Guess we'd better get on the plane." Ryan gave Lou a cool look before shifting his attention back to Martha. "I'll see you around camp."

He walked off, whistling, to join the line of people shuffling into the elevated corridor to the plane.

Lou watched him go with an evaluating look in his dark eyes.

"Can we go now?" Bernie whined.

Martha nodded before it occurred to her to check with Lou. "Are you all right to go?"

He inclined his head once.

And we're back to the strong-and-silent routine. Martha guided Bernie to the line. Lou followed them, looming behind her like her own personal mountain. He didn't say a word to anyone as they showed their tickets and fake IDs to the company agent at the gate. His footsteps boomed on the carpeted walkway, causing it to shift with each step. Martha wondered whether it was old or if it hadn't been built with skin-walkers in mind.

Inside the narrow plane were twin rows of double seats. Everything was worn and outdated. There were no overhead bins or seat-back screens. Martha let Bernie claim the window seat and settled herself in the aisle. Lou took the seat across the aisle from them. No one tried to move past him to claim the empty window seat.

The final few passengers filed in. Then the airplane's doors sealed with a solid thud, like the doors of a prison.

Chapter Eight

"They are coming, *mon coeur*." Henri's voice always sounded as if it was coming from another room. Leanne couldn't see him, but she could sense his presence, a sort of fullness to what should be only empty air. Smiling in triumph, she wrapped her frayed woolen blanket tighter around herself. Once the little girl arrived, the countdown began for Leanne's ticket to freedom.

"Come on, Looney." One of the guards was trying to coax her to join a work detail.

Leanne cackled at him, enjoying watching the young man swallow hard. He was probably fifteen years younger than she was and woefully softhearted. If it hadn't been for his jutting ears and nonexistent chin, she might have considered seducing him. "Wants me to crack my fingers to the bone, he does."

Henri chuckled. "Bet you that he calls for backup."

She tapped her left index finger twice, accepting the bet. The boy would run out of the barracks in terror before calling for help. He just didn't know it yet. She crawled out of her bed, using swift, jerky movements that she'd seen in a horror film. The guard stepped back, his hand hovering over a small device clipped to his belt.

The reminder ruined Leanne's fun. If he was close enough when he pressed the button, the shock collar fitted around her neck would send electricity jolting through her body. No matter how much she manipulated the guards, she was still a prisoner. She didn't dare get any closer to him or she'd be in range. Instead, she grabbed handfuls of her ratty layers of skirts and curtseyed. "A good day to you, my lord."

"Come on, Looney, you don't want me to drag you down to detention." He beckoned to her with both hands, speaking slowly and calmly. "Come on with me down to the laundry. It'll be nice and warm."

Warmth was a temptation. Even in the start of summer, chill winds still blew through the rough walls of the barracks. She'd already had one stint in detention, where she'd been under the thumb of the doctor. Those marked as troublemakers were "volunteered" for further experimentation, and no one walked out of that unscarred. But she couldn't afford to set a bad precedent by cooperating. Leanne made her eyes go wide. "Mother told me to beware of young officers. They'll seduce a girl and leave her ruined forever."

"I resent such implications," Henri grumbled. "I was always a gentleman."

You also weren't a soldier. A smile would ruin her performance.

The guard stepped closer. "That's not why I'm here."

"No, you're here to cut me open and find out how I tick." She made a clicking noise with her tongue.

"Hey, you still trying to get Looney to the laundry?" Another guard poked his head inside the door and glared at her.

"Yes, sir." The boy's shoulders slumped in defeat.

"Forget it. They need you over by the chow line. Let her stay in the barracks, out of everyone's way. Then no one has to deal with the stink."

Leanne blinked innocently as if unaware of what they were saying. Instead, she stared at a spider crawling up the wall as if it was the most fascinating thing she'd ever seen. From the moment she'd been snatched from her tarot booth in New Orleans, she'd been playing the part of a crazy bag lady, including wearing layers of smelly old clothes snatched from the other internees.

"All right. You stay here today." The first guard backed away, keeping a wary eye on her.

Leanne saluted him. "Aye, aye, captain."

The two men left, closing the door behind them. Leanne began to laugh, knowing it would only add to her reputation of insanity. While other internees toiled away at what amounted to slave labor, she had the whole barracks to herself.

"Neither of us won the bet. It's too bad because I was looking forward to watching the boy soil himself." Henri's voice drifted closer. "Should I make contact with the girl once the plane lands?"

"Get her here as soon as possible. The faster I can shake this dirt off my feet, the better." Leanne moved back to her cubicle and settled onto the bed. "Has her ghost finally decided to share any more details?"

"No," Henri replied. "We get the girl out of here, and then he says that he and she have a place they can go."

She didn't particularly like being kept in the dark, but if ignorance was the price of leaving, she would accept it for the time being. Once they were away from Woodpine, she could press the girl for more details and make certain they really did have somewhere to go. A sheltered suburban child wouldn't do well on the streets.

"What about the mother? She could cause trouble," Henri said.

"She'll be too preoccupied with her so-called secret mission." Leanne snorted. It was the most ridiculous idea she'd ever heard. As if a soccer mom could possibly uncover a secret that didn't involve a recipe.

"They're trying to do the right thing. We could help," Henri offered again.

"We've done enough." Leanne considered the merits of taking a nap versus doing some strategic scavenging in the other empty barracks. "None of them tried to help us. We have to look out for ourselves."

Henri didn't answer, which relieved her. She hated the rare occasions when they argued. *Besides, what does he think we can do?* Everyone knew what was going on in this place. The old doctor and his creepy experiments. He ran intensive tests on every *lalassu* who came here, keeping them in isolation for days and sometimes weeks. There were rumors that some never made it out of isolation, at least not with a pulse. Others disappeared, never to be mentioned again.

It's not going to happen to me. Ever since her arrival, she'd been talking to herself about any topic under the sun to disguise her conversations with Henri. Not even the other *lalassu* suspected that she was one of them. There were plenty of so-called normal people who'd been caught up by the government's ridiculous test, and they were stuck on the latest low rung of the discrimination ladder. Leanne wasn't going to lose any sleep about it. The important thing was that everyone had become used to seeing her around camp, and no one thought anything about it. It made her effectively invisible.

Leanne curled up on the thin mattress and went over the plans for her escape. She and the girl could hide in plain sight aboard the biweekly supply-and-personnel plane. Her ghost and Henri would provide distractions and lookouts as needed. By the time anyone would think to search for them, they'd be long gone. The only tricky part would be the shock collar. After what happened the last time, she didn't dare try to cut it off. *Once I'm back in New Orleans, I can find someone to take care of it.* The fellow from the tea-and-spice shop near her booth occasionally "fixed" ankle monitors, and he would probably be able to get rid of it. Until then, she could keep it covered. Without the guards' triggers, it was just an ugly choker.

If the ghost and the girl didn't have a place to go, she thought she might use the girl as an apprentice. She could run two-man cons again. "It would be nice to have a partner again."

"What am I? Last week's leftovers?" Henri sounded amused, not offended.

"A physical partner," Leanne corrected herself.

"That could work. But you should be careful. They wouldn't be hiding like this if someone didn't already want the girl."

True. And people who want something are usually willing to pay for it. If the child proved difficult, there were always other options available.

Bears are not meant to fly. The plastic armrest creaked under Lou's tense fingers. He had flown before with Doc, but it had been a different experience. *Angel* was a small cargo floater plane, and Doc flew it with the winds, moving as a part of the environment. Inside the jet, Lou couldn't feel any part of the outside world. Artificial air circulated, artificial materials were under his feet and hands, and artificial people were crushed together. The walls were too thick to get any sense of the air currents, and the plastic window only showed the tops of clouds. He had no idea who the pilots or any of the passengers crammed in around him were. To add to his frustration, his store-bought clothes were chafing his neck, wrists, and waist.

He glanced across the aisle at Martha. She held a book but wasn't reading. She kept looking at Bernie, who was slumped in the window seat with tiny headphones shoved in her ears, scribbling in a new notebook. She had it angled away from her mother. Martha tried to speak to her a few times, but Bernie gave one-word answers.

Maybe I should try to talk with Martha? She liked talking. She and Michael hadn't been quiet once during the trip down to Juneau. Their constant chattering had made Lou's head ache. Add in the drone of hundreds of people talking at once, tinny music blaring inside buildings, and the purring growl of dozens of motors, and he'd decided that the outside world was crazy because it couldn't hear itself think.

Movement behind him caught his attention. The man who'd been talking to Martha in the airport was watching her again. He held a magazine loosely, but his gaze hadn't left her for more than a few minutes at a time. Lou's hackles rose, every animal instinct warning him that the man was trouble. Andrew had cautioned him to wait for human proof before acting to defend Martha, Bernie, or himself, so Lou wouldn't rip into the interloper yet. But he also didn't intend to give the man much leeway. His human shape might not be different from the others on the plane, but Lou had already marked him as a scavenger who would steal what he had not earned.

He may not be a problem. He's already submitted. Indeed, the man had nearly piddled himself when Lou arrived to protect Martha, and it was an immensely satisfying memory. *No scavenger will go far while the scent of blood is in the air.* If he tried anything, Lou would ensure he regretted it. As a Guardian, it had always been his job to stand between those he protected and the rest of the world. He was the one who went out in subzero weather to make sure no poachers or trespassers were in Bear Claw. When his father died and when Andrew went away for school, Lou was the one who'd stayed and kept everyone safe and fed.

The task carried much more prestige back home than it did

anywhere else. Lou shook himself. He'd listened to his siblings talk about the outside world, but he hadn't understood how easy everything was.

At home, if he wanted new clothes, he needed to find and kill a suitable animal. He would store and preserve the meat then spend over a week tanning, stretching, and smoking the hide to make it into usable leather. Next, he had to cut, shape, and stitch the leather into the clothing he wanted. On their first day in Juneau, he and Andrew had walked into a massive store full of ready-made clothing in different sizes, colors, and fabrics. Within an hour, he'd bought a wardrobe that Andrew considered suitable for blending in. There had been other stores lining the street. Meat was pre-butchered and ready for cooking. Metal tools shined without a dent or mark. All was available at everyone's fingertips.

If that was the kind of world that Martha was used to, then it was no wonder that she and Bernie had trouble adjusting to life in Bear Claw. It was hard for anyone to learn to value what they had when so little effort went into acquiring an item. There was no need to hone the skills to make and mend when it was far easier to simply purchase something new.

Martha twisted a strand of honey-blond hair around her finger, creating a tight curl. He knew she wasn't happy about having accepted this work but was going to do it anyway because it was necessary. His respect for her increased. She'd been faced with a difficult decision in choosing whether to protect her cub or the community. Once she realized it was possible to do both, she'd agreed.

She noticed him looking at her and smiled briefly at him. "We'll be landing soon."

He nodded, acknowledging her words.

"I hope it doesn't take too long to get settled." She pressed her lips together as if sealing words inside before they could spill out.

She and Bernie would likely not return to Bear Claw. The thought ached like a half-rotted tooth. Without any conscious intention on anyone's part, she had become one of his charges. He put the thought aside. Worrying about the future got humans into trouble in the present.

"Thank you for coming with us," she said softly, resting her fingertips on his arm.

"You are welcome," he replied, surprised when his skin warmed under her touch as if in summer sunshine. The heat stayed even when she pulled away and returned to pretending to read her book.

He resisted the urge to touch his forearm to see if it truly felt warmer or if it was all in his imagination. He shook his shoulders in the way he would shake the ruff of fur around his neck when in bear form, but the sensation didn't dislodge as easily as biting flies or clinging ice.

The jet bounced much harder on landing than Doc's usual easing into the water. Lou clenched his teeth to suppress a building growl. *How does anyone live this way? Trusting strangers only leads to disappointment.*

He shouldered his bag along with Martha's and Bernie's in spite of Martha's objections. It was the point where they were most likely to be discovered. If they needed to run, the females needed to be unencumbered. Keeping close to the two of them, he saw Bernie scanning the horizon of the small airfield, her eyes stopping on sights invisible to others.

"My music isn't working anymore." Bernie yanked her earbuds out of her ears, keeping distance between her and her mother.

"It's not going to work while you're here, kid." The man from the plane, Ryan, approached them again, all smiles and friendliness. "Nothing digital does. Phones and tablets are all just bricks. It's one of those dead zones."

Lou stared impassively at him, but Ryan seemed much more confident now that they were in his territory. He grinned at Bernie, who crept closer to her mother. Martha put her arm around her daughter, her worried eyes seeking Lou's. "They didn't mention anything about that in the interview."

"It's not one of the selling points of this place. There's a shortwave radio in the Hub if you need to get in touch with the outside." Ryan's smile went wider when he met Martha's eyes.

Lou stepped between the two of them, breaking the other man's line of sight.

Ryan backed up a step but then shook it off and puffed out his chest. He indicated the school bus waiting on the airfield. Its surface was more rust than yellow. "Better get moving so you can all get a seat together on the bus."

Martha and Bernie started walking. Ryan tried to slip in between Lou and the girls but fell back when Lou's long legs threatened to trample him.

The bus rapidly filled with people, but Lou secured two seats for them. Martha and Bernie sat behind him, and he piled the bags beside the window. No one asked him to move.

Their pest managed to get a seat near Martha and talked throughout the drive to Woodpine. He pointed out the massive two-story administration building, calling it the Hub. Beside it was a reinforced gate. "There's a kind of no-man's-land between the Hub and the loocies. We've got the warehouse, the medical building, and even a school in there."

Lou tuned him out, studying the camp itself. Long stretches of barbed wire cut it nearly in half. Inside the fence were squat metal and plastic box structures lying in long rows against the grayish-brown mud. Outside the fence were more prefabricated trailers set in grids. There were only a few feet between each one, which would make it very easy to overhear the neighbors.

Ryan was still talking. "The trailers are pretty good. They're hooked up to a generator, so they've got some power. Enough for lights and stuff."

"They seem very small," Martha commented.

"No kitchen and only one bathroom. You'll be lucky. They'll probably give you a family unit. Most of the rest of these guys are going to be dealing with at least two roommates." Ryan leaned closer. "I get my own place. Part of the privileges of rank."

"If there's no kitchen, where do we eat?" Bernie asked.

"All the meals are served at the Hub's cafeteria. Don't worry, kid, I'll save you a spot." Ryan winked at Bernie.

It lets them keep an eye on everyone. Lou could see the sense in forcing everyone to go to one place to eat. Communal meals would be more efficient but would deny potential escapees the supplies needed to survive. Lou gazed at the thick forest surrounding the camp's cleared earth. Even in summer, it would be too easy for the unprepared to get lost and wander until they collapsed. In winter, it would be suicide.

The administrative building wasn't a prefabricated structure like the others in camp. Built out of bricks and cinderblocks, it towered over the camp. The name "Woodpine" was spelled out in big block letters over the double front doors. Barbed wire topped the fence sealing in the prisoners. As they filed off the bus, Lou felt dwarfed by the structure and oddly small. His animal instincts insisted that it was a time to creep quietly, lest he attract the attention of a larger or more dangerous predator.

The new arrivals were hurried through the doors, bags still in hand. To the right, the air smelled of stale food. Rows of tables disappeared into the gloomy light. On the left was what might as well have been another world. Windows on the second floor spilled their light onto his fellow passengers as they shuffled into seats. None of them seemed to recognize how foolish the design was. It would be nearly impossible to keep warm in winter with such a high ceiling.

At the end of the room, a woman stood up from a desk, scowling at them all. She was a person of authority. Her thin dark hair barely covered her scalp, and her pale skin glowed like mushrooms deep in a cave. The hairs on the back of Lou's neck rose. She reminded him of an ermine, a small weasel that challenged much larger predators for their kills.

"Everyone, take a seat," she called out. "I have your housing assignments here, and I'll pass them out as soon as we complete the final genetic test."

CHAPTER NINE

Another test. Martha's fingers started to cramp from her tight grip on her bag. They'd already done the standard test in Juneau, and Michael hadn't said anything about a second test at the camp itself. *What if it's a different, more accurate one?* Bernie had resumed her aloof stance, but her hand was clamped tightly around Martha's. She kept raising her eyes and quickly looking down. *Are there ghosts here? Or is it something else?*

She snuck a glance at Lou. He sat on his creaking plastic chair, slowly scanning the room. He didn't seem to be the least bit concerned about any of it. If she hadn't noticed his fingers digging into the armrest on the flight, she would have thought him incapable of nerves.

"Don't worry about it." Ryan's friendly smile took on a malicious tint as he surveyed the room. He'd taken the seat directly in front of her.

Please go find someone else to talk to. She wished she could close her eyes and pretend none of it was happening. *I shouldn't be here. We shouldn't be here.*

"Can you believe that some loocies have tried to get into this place on faked tests?" Ryan clucked his tongue and shook his head. "Now we have to have the test done by the doctor himself."

It was valuable information, but Martha would have traded it all to be safely back in her comfortable home, never having heard of the *lalassu*. *Except then I wouldn't know how to help Bernie.* She reached over and squeezed Bernie's hand.

"It's a prison," Bernie whispered.

Ryan guffawed loudly as if she'd made a joke. "You should see a real prison, darling. This is nothing."

Martha couldn't agree. The waiting room resembled a typical government office, with rows of plastic molded chairs and bland posters and calendars on the wall. But the walls were painted cinderblock, not plaster. The receptionist had gone back to making notes in a ledger. Her desk was piled with notebooks and folders. Next to it was a heavy door of clear glass or plastic, framed by shining steel. A small room with a second door was in the back, creating something similar to an airlock.

She snuck another look at Lou. He seemed bored but watchful. His head and neck never moved, but his eyes flickered briefly. *What will he do if the test reveals us?*

A loud bang cracked through the room like a gunshot. Martha jumped in her seat, her fingers tightening around Bernie's wrist in a crushing grip before she realized it was the door opening.

"Nothing to be nervous about, Martha." Ryan grinned at her. "This is my third time through. It's a piece of cake."

Well, it's my first. She kept her retort to herself.

A tall skinny man in a white lab coat was standing beside the receptionist's desk, the corners of his narrow mouth twisting down in irritation. He held a tray of plastic tubes in his green-gloved hands. She couldn't make out his eyes behind the glare on his glasses. The round lenses of reflected light made Martha think of a menacing insect. Behind him were two large men in body armor, each carrying a rifle.

"Exciting, huh?" Ryan winked at her.

It wasn't the adjective that she would have chosen. She wasn't sure which frightened her more, the doctor or the guns.

"Line up against the wall. Spit out any gum or breath mints." The man in the lab coat ordered, not bothering to introduce himself or explain the procedure.

Martha followed the others, lining up against the wall and feeling as though she was preparing for an execution by firing squad. Lou's massive presence beside her was reassuring. If things went badly, she and Bernie could take shelter behind him.

The doctor moved slowly down the line, flanked by the armed men. Each person had the inside of their cheek scraped with a thin plastic tool. The scrapings went into a plastic tube, which the doctor sealed before applying a preprinted sticker with each person's name.

When they got to Martha and Bernie, her daughter's hand tightened on hers. She met the doctor's eyes as he stripped the plastic film from a fresh tool. "Is this really necessary? She's only a child."

She could see his eyes behind the glare, and there was no compassion in their cold dark depths. "If she wants to stay here, it's necessary."

Martha coaxed Bernie into cooperating. Once the sample was collected, she opened her mouth for her own turn. The plastic rasped harshly against the inside of her cheek, and the scraped spot burned as she and Bernie moved back to their seats.

The doctor's fist was tight as he reached up to scrape Lou's cheek. The guards' weapons were higher than they'd been with her and Bernie. Seeing the evidence of their fear made Martha feel perversely better, as if her team had scored a point.

"You know, it's hard to picture a gal like you with someone like him." Ryan's low comment quickly swept away Martha's brief rally. "Does he ever talk?"

"Only when he has something to say." Bernie glared at the blond man.

She again caught the predatory glint in his eyes as his grin widened. *Is it Bernie he's after?* She was all too aware that children living with a single parent were at greater risk of abuse. After Derek left them, she promised herself that she would do whatever was necessary to protect Bernie. She'd only failed once.

Lou moved between them as he returned to his seat. Ryan eyed him. "Your girl here just told me you're not much of a conversationalist."

"I did not!" Bernie's voice carried across the room. Now the people around them were all watching the minor drama unfold.

So much for a low profile and flying under the radar. Everyone would know who they were and keep an eye on them, hoping for more excitement.

Lou didn't respond to Ryan's verbal jab, continuing to stare straight ahead as if the other man simply didn't exist. His indifference was annoying Ryan, based on the tension creeping into his friendly grin.

"If that's right, then it's too bad. There's not much to do up here except talk to one another." Ryan's tone was pleasant, and his words were reasonable, but there was an edge of mockery underneath.

Maybe she could divert him. "I hope they'll finish up soon. It's been a long day, and I, for one, could use some rest before starting tomorrow."

A few murmurs of agreement came from the others waiting.

"It doesn't take long to run the tests, unless they find something," an older man offered as he pushed up his glasses. He only had three fingers on his right hand. The pinky was a stump.

"I don't care if I work or have to sit on my ass, as long as I get paid what they promised," a younger man said, leaning back in his chair. He didn't seem old enough to be out of school.

"Oh, it's definitely good money. And most of it goes right to the bank if you don't get stupid." Ryan captured the attention of the room. He went on to talk about how expensive it was to order things during the regular mail runs. Martha allowed herself a soft exhale in relief, hoping that he would keep on basking in the others' attention and stop trying to provoke Lou.

The doctor and his guards had disappeared while Martha was distracted.

"I'm tired," Bernie whispered.

Martha kissed the top of her daughter's head. "I know. It should all be over soon."

Bernie shook her head. "No, it won't."

Had Chuck warned her? If the new test identified any of them, they would all be in trouble. Martha's heart pumped faster, the blood spinning so quickly through her system that it left her dizzy.

A warm weight settled on her shoulder. Lou was still staring straight ahead, but he'd reached out to her and rested his hand on hers.

I'm not alone. If this goes wrong, he'll get us out. Martha took several deep breaths to calm herself down. After a few seconds, Lou removed his hand and put it back on his knee. She wanted to thank him but worried about drawing more notice. Knowing he was paying attention to her and that he was ready to protect her gave her comfort that she hadn't known since Bernie was first diagnosed.

The door opened again, and four armed guards emerged with a cart loaded with dull-gray binders. One guard carried a black metal clipboard and handed it to the receptionist.

"Blake, Ryan," the receptionist called out.

"That's me." Ryan stood up and winked at Martha. "See you around."

The receptionist didn't seem impressed. "Unit H-11. Training begins at eight a.m. tomorrow."

Practically whistling a jaunty tune, Ryan accepted a binder and a key attached to a red plastic circle before leaving.

"Burke, Cameron and George."

Two men rose from their seats. Their features were so similar that Martha guessed they were brothers. As they got their key and binder, she felt a tap on her shoulder. She looked back to see an older man with a scruffy beard hiding his wrinkled face.

"Don't pay too much attention to that blowhard, miss." His voice was scratchy, and it was hard to understand even in the relative quiet. "He's not typical of the people who work here."

"I'm relieved to hear it," she replied, keeping her voice equally low.

"For most of us, this is a job. We don't go out of our way to be cruel."

But do you go out of your way to be kind? Martha didn't see how they could, but maybe she would be surprised.

"Just keep your head down and do your work. You'll get through it okay." He patted her on the shoulder again.

She glanced at Lou, uncertain if he'd been listening.

"Knight, Tyrone," the receptionist droned.

The man who Martha had thought was too young to be out of school stood. His cheeks were too smooth to need to be shaved more than once a week. He held out his hand for his key and binder.

"Test failed."

For a moment, Martha didn't understand what had happened. The receptionist's voice was the same dull monotone it had been since they'd begun. She certainly didn't sound like someone handing down a sentence on someone's freedom.

Tyrone clearly didn't understand, either. The top of his nose wrinkled, and his mouth was open as if he was trying to figure out what question to ask.

The only ones who acted were the guards. The first two immediately pointed their weapons at the boy while the second pair moved around and grabbed him before he could react. They slammed him into the floor, and he cried out in pain.

His captors didn't seem to care. They yanked his arms back and tied his wrists with a plastic zip tie. Tears built in Martha's eyes, and she held tight to Bernie. *This is not cruel?* If the goons tried to take her little girl, she would have to fight them.

"This is a mistake!" Tyrone didn't struggle as they lifted him.

"Take him to detention for evaluation." The receptionist ignored his shouts as the door behind her opened, and the guards carried him through. "Lochlan, Timothy."

Another young man swallowed nervously as he cautiously stepped forward. He froze as the door reopened and a second pair of armed guards came in to replace those escorting the unlucky Tyrone to his fate.

"Unit B-3. Training begins at eight a.m. tomorrow."

Timothy accepted the binder and key and hurried down the stairs.

"McKinnon, Martha, Louis, and Bernadette."

Lou stood up first, and Martha and Bernie followed. Martha's mouth was dry as they crossed the suddenly vast expanse to learn their fate. *Surely we can't have failed. There aren't enough of them to take us all. Or maybe only one did. Or maybe there are more guards waiting out of sight.*

"Unit F-12. Training begins at eight a.m. tomorrow."

Martha blindly took the three binders and the tiny key. F-12 was marked in small white letters on the red circle. *At least we can't get lost.* She kept her head down as they walked down the stairs, afraid she might burst into hysterical giggles since the moment of truth was over.

She moved automatically down the hallway, the key digging into her fingers. Bernie kept pace, her eyes fixed on the floor. When they reached the main doors, Martha consciously ordered her plodding feet to stop. *I'm the adult. I can't fall apart now. Time to get back to being the responsible one.* Looking around, she frowned. No one waited for them.

The man with a missing finger passed them and headed out the doors, walking toward the rows of trailers with his bag on his shoulder.

Channeling her confident-parent persona, Martha made a decision. "I suppose we walk. It isn't that far."

Bernie rolled her eyes—presumably at her mother's efforts—but didn't protest as they left the building. The ground was slick and muddy. There had been some attempt to gravel the road, but most of the stones had been scattered or had sunk into the mud. Lou managed easily, taking long strides despite carrying their bags. Martha and Bernie picked their way through the muck more carefully.

Trailer F-12 proved to be a double-wide unit at the back of the rows, one of the farthest away from the compound and only twenty feet from the trees. Its beige plastic exterior walls were speckled with dirt and unidentifiable dark smudges. Martha pulled open the narrow screen door and unlocked the inner one.

Inside wasn't as bad as she'd feared. The main room was long and contained a shallow sofa, a pressboard coffee table, and a small round table with four plastic chairs. A small set of empty shelves was fastened to one wall. Three cardboard boxes were waiting in front of the sofa, proving that the belongings they'd shipped had made it. Grimly, Martha wondered what would happen to Tyrone's belongings.

She opened each of three doors to reveal a full bathroom and two nearly identical bedrooms. The only difference was that one had a double bed while the other had two singles. Martha swallowed. They hadn't discussed sleeping arrangements. *Will he expect me to stay with him in the double bed?*

Bernie flopped on the sofa and began flipping through the binder. "It says we have to eat at that nasty cafeteria place."

"It will be an adjustment." Martha walked over and ran her hands over the dusty cardboard box on top. "We should probably unpack."

Lou set down the bags carefully. "I will scout the area."

"Be careful." After she'd spoken, Martha wondered if he would be offended. He was there to take care of them, not the other way around.

His expression didn't change. He nodded to both of them and left the trailer. Watching from the windows, Martha saw him walk straight into the woods. *Not exactly a surprise. I wonder if he'll shift shape. Is he stripping down and transforming into a bear right now?*

Thinking about him taking off his clothes was a mistake. Her cheeks flushed, and she turned away from the window as if she'd been caught peeping.

"Chuck says no one is watching us," Bernie announced. "There's a spot in the woods out back where the guys go to drink beer and have a fire, but no one is there now."

"Please thank Chuck for me." Martha rubbed her fingers with her thumb as she looked around.

"Am I still going to get my own room?" Bernie asked. "Or are you going to make me share with you again?"

Martha ignored the sullen tone of the request. It was natural for Bernie to want her own space and privacy. "Why don't you take the room with the big bed, and Lou and I will take the one with two beds."

Bernie's eyes lit up. "Really?"

"Really." Martha smiled softly, enjoying the proof that her daughter hadn't been submerged into adolescence yet.

Bernie grabbed her bag and hauled it into the bedroom with the double bed. A few minutes later, she came out and retrieved the box with her name on it. Martha picked up her own box and bag and carried them into the other bedroom.

It reminded her of a cottage with its minimal furniture and veneered-wood paneling. She wondered how warm it was during the winter. *We should be long gone before then.* Flicking the light switch turned on two overhead bare bulbs, one over each bed.

She had just opened her suitcase when the first knock banged on the door.

Chapter Ten

Martha reminded her racing heart that it didn't need to compete with whoever was banging on the front door. *There is absolutely nothing to panic about.* Too bad she didn't believe herself. They were spies in enemy territory, and she'd never heard a version of that story where things didn't go badly.

As she crossed the room, visions of being hauled away by the guards with their guns kept her adrenaline flowing. *If they do, I'll shout at Bernie to run. She can get out through the window and go into the woods. Lou will find her and get her somewhere safe.* Ready to sound the alarm, Martha opened the flimsy front door.

Two black men stood outside. The first was tall and muscular enough to give Lou a run for his money. The second was leaner and had sad eyes. Both were wearing jeans with T-shirts, not guard uniforms.

"Martha?" The first one asked. "Martha McKinnon?"

She nodded, still tense and ready to warn Bernie if necessary. She doubted the two men were part of an official welcome wagon.

"I'm Hood, and this is Harley. We need to get inside before someone notices us."

"Oh." Embarrassment replaced adrenaline. Martha stepped aside to let them in. She hoped they wouldn't assume she had hesitated because of their skin color or gender. Then she wondered guiltily if she would have reacted differently if it had been two women, but she forced her brain to stop wallowing. These were the contacts that Michael had told her about, and she wasn't giving them the impression of competence. "It's nice to meet you."

"Likewise." The second one, Harley, smiled at her, but the flash of white teeth did nothing to lift the sorrow in his eyes. "Our daughter, Eva, works in the kitchens. If you need supplies, let us or her know."

"Things are far more precarious here than we initially thought. I'm sorry we brought you in like this, since I'm sure it's the last thing you wanted to do, but we really had no choice." Hood stood beside the window, checking to see if anyone was in view. Martha's skin chilled as she realized he was standing so he couldn't be seen from outside.

"Lou is out doing a patrol." Her fingers crept up to her neck and began twisting a strand of her hair.

"I hope he doesn't go too far. There are rumors that the camp planted mines around the perimeter." Hood frowned.

Mines? Martha twisted her strand of hair so tightly it yanked painfully on her scalp.

"I'm sure he'll be fine." Harley shot an irritated glance at Hood.

"We need to start with some history. The government initially promoted this camp as a temporary measure to evaluate *lalassu* and their abilities." Hood sat down at the small table, and the light shone off his bald head. "Except once people were here, no one was in a rush to let them go home."

"We decided to come up here to investigate," Harley continued as he and Martha sat down as well. "We needed to get out of Perdition for a while, and since we're not *lalassu*, we weren't worried about getting caught. I'm pretty good with computers, so I thought I'd be able to hack into their records and get everything we needed. Except there are no computers."

"What?" Martha searched her memory, trying to recall whether she'd seen a monitor on the receptionist's desk. It wasn't something she would consciously look for since computers were so omnipresent that they were effectively invisible.

"No computers. Not a single one anywhere in the camp," Harley said grimly. "Officially, it's because the generators can't deliver enough power."

"Except there's plenty of power. It's all going somewhere, but we can't figure out where." Hood grimaced. "It's not the shock collars, though they're not shy about using them."

"Internees disappear during work shifts and sometimes out of their beds in the barracks." Harley's hand slipped into his husband's. "We've been trying to find them, but it's like they vanish into thin air."

Or shallow graves. Martha couldn't stop thinking that isolated wilderness was the perfect place to make people vanish.

"We've checked the detention cells, the warehouse, and even the storage sheds out by the landing strip. There's no sign of where they could be." The tiny muscle at the corner of Hood's jaw flexed. "We're completely on our own up here. The only way to communicate with anyone outside is to smuggle a physical message or break into the radio room."

"It's not just the lack of signal. The phone doesn't work at all." Harley pulled a slim mobile out of his pocket and showed Martha the absence of bars. He lifted it to take a photo before showing her the screen.

The image was badly distorted and full of black-and-white dots.

"Any digital camera is affected. We brought these little button cameras, and all we have is static and blurs." Hood leaned back in his chair, frustration pinching his mouth and eyes. "We needed to get cameras with actual film up here."

Harley slid the phone back to his partner. "It's all old-school spy stuff, but we're using it to document what's happening here. I've gotten some pictures of the results of experiments in the detention areas, and it's bad. Sleep deprivation, submersion in ice, or deliberate burns, all in the name of testing *lalassu* powers. But we think there's something worse happening with the doctor. One of the internees told us that he saw bodies in pieces."

Martha shuddered.

"The internee was killed in an escape attempt later that day," Harley continued. "I think he was deliberately killed to keep him from talking. Luckily, they didn't connect him with us, but it's put an end to us wandering around. That's why we brought you in."

"To be the camp nurse." Martha waited for the two men to explain further.

Harley leaned forward and lowered his voice. "We need copies of the doctor's records. He's the type who would document his atrocities."

She knew it was going to be one of those moments where she would later wish that she could un-hear what she was about to learn. She could feel the tension thickening the air.

"Don't go near the detention area. We've already covered it, and if you get caught there, it could raise suspicion." Hood stood up to check the windows again.

After what she'd heard, Martha was more than happy not to go anywhere near it.

"We might not be able to find where he's holding the internees, but if we can find the records of what he's doing to them, we can still use the information." Harley's dark eyes held hers again. "He's supposed to be evaluating the *lalassu* gifts and sending reports to the government about how to deal with the different abilities, not torturing them in the name of science."

She was right. It wasn't something she wanted to know. Her hands rose to slowly cover her face. *I want to go home.*

"I wish there were another way, but there's too much information. You understand the medical jargon, which means that you can pick out the files we need," Harley pleaded.

The light from the overhead lamp filtered through her fingers, creating stripes of light and dark, bordered by thin strips of red. Martha drew in a slow breath, refusing to let her brain get too far ahead in its panic. *It's too late to give up. I'm already here. So I need to stop hiding and start getting the job done.* She drew on the coping skills she'd learned in Bernie's early childhood and shoved her emotions aside to focus on what was needed. *One task at a time.* Her fingertips slid down her face, skating along the surface as if shaping a mask. "It's just the records you need?"

"That's all we're asking for. Get us proof that the experiments are happening and that Dr. Coulon isn't being honest." Harley's knee bounced under the table. "We don't want to put you or your daughter at risk."

Hood stared at her coolly from the corner with his arms crossed over his broad chest. Martha didn't need him to speak to understand his disapproval. He and his husband had put their family at risk to help the *lalassu.* Martha and Bernie had been helped by the *lalassu,* and yet Martha wasn't volunteering to help them in return. She felt the guilt trying to break out from her mental box, but she kept it all tightly buried. *I'm not a horrible person.* She cared about the people being forced to stay in the awful camp and hated the idea of medical experimentation. But she also had responsibilities and no one to pick up the slack if she faltered. She was doing what she could, and no one had the right to judge her for it.

"We've sent out proof of the inadequate housing and the shock collars." Harley was still speaking. "It's turning public opinion but too slowly. People are scared of the *lalassu.*"

"So you need proof that Dr. Coulon is another Mengele." Martha's shoulders curved under the lead-like weight of more responsibility.

"Get the film to us, and we'll take care of sending it south." Hood's indifferent voice struck a harsh blow to Martha's emotional balance. "No one needs to know you were involved." *Coward.* His unspoken word echoed in her head.

Martha nodded. "I'll get you what I can." *Sure, I can go into an evil scientist's lair and bring out proof that he's evil.* It sounded too ridiculous to be real.

Harley caught her gaze again. "Thank you." The sympathy and understanding in his eyes offset his husband's cold contempt.

Martha reminded herself that it wasn't about making friends and being popular. It was about finding the truth and preventing cruelty.

Harley pulled a travel makeup kit, a black metal box that fit comfortably in his palm, out of his pocket. He opened it to show the mirror in the lid, along with a space for lipstick and an eyeliner pencil. Pale powder, sealed with a clear plastic lid, filled another compartment.

Martha took the kit from him and turned it over in her hands, trying to guess how she was supposed to use it. *Maybe the powder is to reveal lasers?*

"It's a camera." Harley grinned. He took it back and showed her how the hinges parted to reveal a long, narrow lens. "It's a Cold War photographic document scanner. Roll it along a document, and it will take a copy of everything it sees. The film roll holds up to fifty pages." He gave it back to her.

A photocopier that fits in my pocket. And all mechanical. Maybe this task won't be impossible after all.

"We also have some wide-angle cameras disguised as pens." Harley handed over two slim, blue-plastic pens that were indistinguishable from any of the dozen varieties of bulk office supplies. "When the nib is retracted, the first click takes a photo of whatever the opening is pointed at. The second click extends the nib. Each holds twenty pictures. I've got replacement rolls of film for both the scanner and the pens."

It all sounded very James Bond. Martha supposed she should be grateful she wasn't being presented with a catsuit and a martini. "What happens if I get caught?"

The two men looked at each other. Their expressions mirrored the one on her face when Bernie asked an awkward question and Martha had to decide whether to tell her the truth or a comforting lie.

"We would do our best to get you out," Harley began.

"Don't get caught," Hood finished, his dark eyes boring into her.

Martha's shoulders lowered as she relaxed. They'd told her the truth. She met Hood's penetrating gaze with her own. "I need a promise from you."

They waited silently. They were fathers, which meant they would understand what she was about to ask.

She kept her voice low to keep Bernie from overhearing. "If I disappear into that camp, then I want the two of you to get Bernie out. Take her back to Michael and the Harrises. Don't wait for me. Don't try to rescue me. Just get her out."

Just get her out. Martha's words replayed in Lou's head as he crouched beside the trailer. He'd finished a preliminary search of the woods and was about to search the perimeter of the camp, but he'd wanted to check back with Martha first to make sure she was all right.

He straightened and began to walk back into the woods. The ground was too soft to risk leaving footprints where anyone else could see. He'd have to make a wide circle to avoid leaving traces.

Maybe I should switch to the fur. A bear wouldn't excite the same attention as a man, but if he was spotted, the woods could fill with trigger-happy guards playing hunter. *Better to stay in the skin for now.* The chilly air clung to his hands and face as the sunlight finally began to fade.

Don't wait for me. Don't try to rescue me. Just get her out. The words sparked pride and frustration in equal measure. Her cub was everything to Martha. Like any good mother bear, she would sacrifice herself in a heartbeat to save her offspring. At the same time, he wanted to rush into the flimsy trailer and shake her until she understood that she had to fight for herself as well.

He moved through the trees, the barely-visible fence a constant marker to his right. There was a wide clearing surrounding the camp, but he couldn't see or smell any sign of guards posted around the perimeter— only the cold bite of barbed wire strung around wooden posts. They'd woven it tightly enough that anything larger than a fox or a rabbit would have trouble getting through, so perhaps they assumed that escape was impossible.

More likely, it was the fear of what lay beyond the fence that kept the *lalassu* prisoner. Even the more nature-based talents, such as the ability to find edible plants or water, wouldn't be enough to keep someone alive during the long trek to civilization if they didn't also know how to survive on the harsh land, especially when the temperatures crashed low enough to freeze exposed skin in the night.

Still, he would expect someone to be watching out to make certain that the prisoners weren't caching supplies or weakening the fence. Just because he hadn't spotted a guard didn't mean there wasn't one there.

"The man is walking through the woods around the camp. He must like having his nuts frozen into icicles," Henri reported.

Leanne huddled deeper inside her woolen blankets. The rough walls of the barracks didn't stop the wind from whistling inside, even though they'd stuffed the chinks with mud. She curled her fingers around the orange-sized stone in her bed. She'd left a pair of them on the stove in the center of the barracks, wrapped them in old T-shirts, and brought them back to keep her warm through the night. The stove was supposed to warm the entire building, but the heat never quite seemed to reach the farthest bunks.

I hate this place. It was much worse than any of the prisons she'd spent most of her adulthood moving in and out of. Ironically, she hadn't even been doing anything illegal when they found her.

"Do you want me to keep watching him?" Henri's voice soothed her, bringing up memories of the long nights he'd watched over her when she was a child, singing her songs and telling her stories, making her forget that she was hungry or hurt. Sometimes he felt so real that she forgot he was dead.

"Keep an eye on them all." Leanne pulled her thick hat lower on her head.

"I'll bring the girl to you tomorrow," he said quietly. "The others are agitating to get to her, but I'm keeping them contained."

The other ghosts in the camp were real nuisances. There were a few who were self-aware, but most were locked into endlessly repeating moments. With her help, Henri had pushed them out of range. Leanne's breath froze in the air, a soft wisp of cloud. "Let them come."

Henri shared his opinion of her plan with a muttered explosion of French cursing.

Leanne smiled. "It will distract the girl and give her incentive to come to me."

"Chuck already agreed to your plan," Henri said.

"It wasn't my plan. It was his." She quieted as a cough, and a grunt from her neighbors reminded her that some things are best not spoken aloud. She rolled over and faced the wall. "I don't trust him."

Henri stayed silent for a long time. "You may be right. Now that I've seen them, I have a bad feeling about this. He's a lot older than I thought." The older the ghost, the more powerful it became. Henri liked to pretend he was from the French Revolution, but he had only died about twenty years ago.

"How old?" she asked.

"Almost a century. But it's like he's never learned anything. He was shouting at the ghosts in the Hub today, trying to get them to go away. He doesn't seem to know how to join to the girl to push the others away."

Leanne curled tighter, disturbed by the warning. She'd never heard of a ghost that old who wasn't trapped in a particular place.

"He's erratic, too. His color comes and goes." Henri's voice was tense, even more afraid than when he'd tried to warn her that Special Investigations was coming.

"Shit!" Leanne cursed.

"Shut up, Looney! People are trying to sleep!"

Her neighbor's shout put an end to the conversation. Leanne felt Henri leave, but she kept muttering bits of poems, television shows, or whatever else came to mind. *Let the others shun the crazy woman. I have a ticket out of here with the little girl.* If her ghost was unstable but also ignorant, Leanne should be able to show the girl how to control or even exorcise him. The most important thing was that Leanne's days of being trapped were numbered.

Chapter Eleven

"Excuse me? Hello?" Martha half-raised her hand, hoping to catch the receptionist's attention without also drawing her irritation.

The dumpy woman scowled as she shut the ledger with a determined thump.

"I'm Martha Mc—"

"I know who you are. I suppose you want a tour." The receptionist stood up, eyeing Martha up and down. "It's not complicated."

Martha did her best to smile through the implied scorn. "Thank you, Mrs....?"

"Fitz. I run this place, no matter what the doctor thinks. He tells you to change anything, you run it by me first. Got it?" Mrs. Fitz glared.

Martha had hoped the other woman would be a potential ally if she could get on her good side—assuming she had a good side, which seemed less likely with each passing minute.

"You'll be holding office hours between eight thirty and five every day. Staff take precedence over the internees." Mrs. Fitz picked up a keychain attached to a thick piece of wood. "If you need keys, you come to me, and bring them back when you're done. Lose them, and you'll be facing a prison sentence."

Martha reached out, and Mrs. Fitz pulled the keys back.

"You won't be needing those. Dr. Coulon will come for you."

The woman seemed to be hoping for a confrontation, a chance to put Martha in her place. She reminded Martha of one of the hospital administrators she'd worked for, a man who continually manipulated his employees. He encouraged suspicion and backbiting, preventing the staff from working together. Martha's long-buried professional instincts were slowly waking up, warning her away from doing anything that might seem like a challenge to Mrs. Fitz. She nodded, keeping her hands clasped in front of her and her eyes wide for an illusion of confused innocence. *Might as well let the dumb-blonde stereotype work for me.*

"Wait there, and don't get in my way."

Martha sat in the indicated chair, keeping a careful eye on Mrs. Fitz as she opened the ledger again. There had been a hint of breathiness when the administrator said the doctor's name. *Professional admiration? Maybe an office crush?* Either way, she crossed the woman off her mental list of possible allies.

A clock on the wall clacked out the seconds, each one echoing slightly in the relative silence. Mrs. Fitz's pencil scratched along the paper as she wrote. Martha's fingers tightened around her bag as the seconds ticked into minutes, marking time in an endless symphony of ordinary sounds made sinister. When Mrs. Fitz turned a page, the loud rustle startled Martha. She shifted, and her chair scraped against the floor. Mrs. Fitz glared at her as if she'd done it deliberately to interrupt.

"Mrs. McKinnon."

Martha barely heard the thready whisper, and it took her a moment to recognize her alias. Looking up, there was no one by Mrs. Fitz's desk to her left, but when she turned her head to the right, there was an older man in a white lab coat standing less than three feet from her.

A rib-contracting twitch almost pushed a startled squeak out of her mouth, but Martha swallowed it. *More proof I wasn't meant for this kind of work.* The man beside her already looked annoyed, with his narrow lips pursed. His sunken cheeks gave him the air of constantly sucking on something sour, while the light reflecting off his glasses masked his gaze. Martha recognized him as the man who had collected the blood tests the day before. *How did he sneak up on me?*

"Follow me." He walked swiftly to the door beside the receptionist's desk. His hard-soled dress shoes announced each step with an authoritative tap.

Martha hurried behind him, struggling to catch up. He unlocked the heavy door and pushed through, not looking back to see if she'd made it before the steel frame clanged shut, like the bars slamming closed on a jail cell.

She tested the door and discovered that it had locked automatically. Her new boss opened the second door and stalked through, again without waiting or checking on her.

Apparently, Dr. Coulon isn't much for small talk. Or introducing himself. Keeping her real work in mind, Martha tried to pay attention to everything she saw.

The administrative building stretched up and out to either side, forming a solid wall between those who were kept in the camp and those who kept them. Chain-link fencing sprang up on either side, stretching ten feet into the air as it outlined the so-called "neutral area." To Martha's left was a long, low building with dull-blue siding. Ryan had identified it as the medical building they'd driven past the day before. To her right were two other structures: a smaller rectangle painted an ugly and uneven green and a large, horizontal, metal half-cylinder. She identified them as the school and the warehouse, based on the notes in the orientation binder.

Martha would have liked to escort her daughter for her first-ever day of school, but class didn't begin for another hour, and Eva had volunteered to take Bernie to the school. As Martha hurried to match Dr. Coulon's brisk pace, she noticed a crowd of people gathering behind the second line of fencing. Unlike the crisp uniforms and business-casual clothing worn in the neutral area, those behind the camp fence wore mismatched clothing that was clearly too large, too small, or out of season. The fabric showed patches, ground-in dirt, rips, and wear. The sight made Martha ashamed of her own dress pants and fitted blouse.

She hadn't wanted to help the internees because it would have put her and Bernie at risk. The danger of the situation hadn't changed, but it was much harder to focus on it when she saw the faces of men, women, and children being held like unwanted animals. *I'm doing what I can. I'll get the information they need, and then we can get everyone out of this awful place.*

"Mrs. McKinnon," the doctor snapped as he stalked through the open door to the medical building.

"Coming, sir." Martha lowered her head and moved faster.

Inside was a narrow room set up like a typical school-nurse's office. A long plastic-covered bed and molded-plastic chair stood against one wall. The other held cabinets and a counter with a tiny sink and jars of gauze, tongue depressors, and cotton swabs. The cabinets all had large padlocks on them. Dr. Coulon unlocked a second door at the back.

Four locked doors so far. There had been two in this building and two in the administrative center between her and the relative freedom of the staff trailers. If Dr. Coulon got suspicious, it would be too easy to trap her. The thought should have choked her mind with fear, but Martha's brain was falling back into old habits, firing faster than it had in a long time. She was aware of more going on around her and could analyze the pieces to put together the larger picture. For years, everything had been focused on Bernie, but now other parts of herself were waking up.

The inner room was Dr. Coulon's personal office. A bookshelf filled with medical texts loomed behind the steel-and-glass desk. A few folders were scattered across the sterile top, but there were no knickknacks or mementos. *His work is everything.* Martha cautiously took the chair in front of the desk.

Dr. Coulon picked up a folder and opened it, his skinny fingers skittering along the edges like spiders. "Your application was unexpected, Mrs. McKinnon. I don't care for surprises."

"Yes, sir." Martha kept her chin tilted down and her gaze lowered. *He wants to feel in charge and wants me off-balance.*

"Your résumé says that you spent several years as an ER nurse and then moved on to be the head administrator of a private clinic." He paused, obviously expecting a response.

Vapor had put together a fictitious work history for her based on her real experiences. He'd assured her it was similar to what he'd done for other *lalassu*. Martha spent days reviewing the details until she knew them all by heart. "Yes, sir."

"I have copies of glowing reviews and letters of recommendation. With your experience, I would expect you to be running a private hospital instead of applying for a temporary job here." He closed the folder and put it back down on the glass desk. "We generally receive two types of applicants. Those in it for the money and those seeking adventure. You could make more money elsewhere, and you don't strike me as an adventurous sort. Which leaves me to ask why you applied to come here for what is effectively a scut job."

Martha's lips stretched into the bright, willing-to-get-my-hands-dirty smile that she'd used at the start of so many interviews to get Bernie into treatment programs. "I wanted a change from traditional—"

"Stop."

The single syllable squeezed around her, blocking any escape. Her clasped hands tightened to the point of cramping.

"It was an impressive work of fiction." Dr. Coulon tapped his bony fingers on the folder. "Yet, when I contacted your previous employers, none of them could remember working with a Martha McKinnon."

The one time an employer decides to be thorough. The moment was everything she'd feared. The walls of the prefabricated building suddenly seemed thicker, forming an impenetrable trap.

"It seemed rather strange to me, since their written words were so full of praise. But I never turn away from facts, no matter how strange or unexpected. And the facts are clear. You are not who you claim to be."

Her dry mouth threatened to choke her as she tried to swallow. There must be something she could say to ease his suspicions. *How long will it be before someone misses me? Will one of the men realize something went wrong in time to get Bernie out?* Logic reasserted itself. If the doctor suspected her, he could simply take her into custody. The camp didn't need to justify its actions. *Keep calm. There's something more going on here.*

"There is a third type of person who applies to work here. Those looking to expose." His chin lifted, and his upper lip twitched in disdain.

"Expose?" Martha needed to buy herself some time. *Think!* It was clear that the doctor liked to be in control and have a feeling of power over those around him. He'd waited until she was in his presence to confront her. He suspected her, but he wasn't certain.

"This camp serves a vital function. It is imperative that we understand what these *occulata hominem* can and cannot do." Dr. Coulon folded his hands, his cold gaze studying her. "There are those who come here with an agenda, either to show us as villains or to take out their frustrations at life on our charges. Neither is acceptable. The purpose of this camp is scientific study."

It was a lecture, not a conversation. Martha nodded attentively.

"To protect our work, I've learned to become quite adept at spotting those who do not belong here. And you, Mrs. McKinnon, do not belong."

A hint of a satisfied smile curled the edges of his pale lips. "I ask again, why are you here?"

Taking a deep breath, Martha threw aside her memorized history. She needed to stay as close to the truth as possible while still protecting Bernie and the others. If she could make herself appear vulnerable, he might be satisfied. She stared at her clenched hands and whispered. "It's because of my ex-husband."

He tilted his head like an insect deciding where to bite. "Go on."

"He didn't want the responsibility of having a child." Her voice wavered as she opened up the box of emotions that she usually kept shoved deep inside. "One day, he walked away from us without any warning. I'd already given up my job to stay home with her, and then everything I'd relied on was suddenly gone."

As she watched the reflection in the glass desk, the doctor's expression and eyes stayed blank, leaving Martha with no idea if she was making any kind of impression, much less the right one.

"It wasn't a smooth divorce." She'd fought hard, demanding unilateral ownership of the shared family home so that she'd have a nest egg to support Bernie and her. Derek had fought, but he'd been eager to move on to marry his new pregnant girlfriend. "He blamed me."

"She belongs in an institution, and if you were a real mother, you'd know that! But you'd rather waste time and money pretending to fix her." Even in memory, Derek's words burned like a red-hot stove.

Dr. Coulon showed a hint of interest, tilting his head forward.

"Two years ago, he kidnapped our daughter." Not Derek, who had happily forgotten them to focus on his so-called "normal" family. But she couldn't mention the name André Dalhard without explaining why he'd been interested in Bernie, which could reveal her as *lalassu*. She would have to pretend that Derek had done it all. "His lawyers attacked me, claiming I was unfit. I got her back, and we went on the run."

"I see." Dr. Coulon's cold eyes bored down like a drill, piercing her protective layers to expose the truth. "You're not worried about him finding you here?"

She couldn't allow him to contact Derek and unravel her new lie. She lifted her head and met his gaze, allowing herself a small moment of defiance. "I was able to convince him that leaving us alone was the best choice for him."

"A moving story. But it does not explain why you're here."

He thought he'd trapped her. She could almost feel the touch of cold steel bars. Martha lowered her eyes again. "I need to rebuild my life. I have no home, no savings, just a few things in suitcases. I might have qualifications, but I've been a ghost for two years. No hospital or clinic would hire me. But I heard you were having trouble finding someone to come out here and work near the loocies." *I'm sorry, Bernie.* "I used my fake ID to create a résumé and took a chance."

"Do you have any of the skills you've so blithely claimed?" He wasn't persuaded yet, but he wasn't seeing her as a threat any longer. *No one ever suspects the overweight, middle-aged woman of anything but being pathetic.*

"I do. I've done everything on my résumé, just not with that name and at those places." She put her hands on the glass, not quite begging but in the same spirit. "You said you needed someone to deal with day-to-day injuries and help with your research notes. I know I can do that."

"And will you tell me your true name so that I can verify your story?"

"I-I-I can't." She slumped in place. "While we were on the run, I… did things to survive. Illegal things. If the government finds out where I am, they'll arrest me." The excuse sounded contrived to Martha, and she winced as Dr. Coulon stood up, his chair scraping against the cold concrete floor. She braced for him to call in the guards. *Please, just let them get Bernie away.*

"You were right that we've had difficulty finding someone for this position." A metallic shriek announced the opening of a file cabinet. "Particularly someone familiar with using a typewriter instead of a computer."

Martha straightened in surprise. "You mean you're still offering me the job?"

The doctor was holding a sheaf of handwritten notes, flipping through them with his free hand. "You may be more valuable than I first thought. Many of our subjects have existed in the criminal fringes of society. Your experiences could give insight into how they interact. If you perform well, then we may be able to make this a more permanent position. You would not need to worry about your secret being exposed, and you could certainly earn enough for a certain level of comfortable obscurity."

Martha knew there was a *but* coming. Men like the doctor didn't exert themselves to help others. She didn't have to wait for long.

Dr. Coulon held the papers out to her. "However, should you cause problems or fail to fulfill your tasks, I will find your ex-husband and make certain that both he and the government are aware of your fraud and crimes. Are we clear?"

"Yes, Doctor." Martha did her best to seem defeated instead of relieved. She put the papers in her lap so they wouldn't rattle in her shaking hands.

"I expect those to be neatly typed by the end of the day. You'll find what you need in the front office. This camp is in an unusual location. Electromagnetic interference causes problems with any kind of computer or digital work." He peered over his glasses at her. "I prefer it that way. Computers are too vulnerable to alteration. An error or false entry could greatly undermine my work here."

His preference wouldn't explain the digital distortion, but Martha wasn't about to poke holes in Dr. Coulon's explanation.

He stared at the wall behind Martha's head. "*Occulata hominem* are the greatest discovery of this generation. My work with them will be my legacy."

There. That was what mattered to him: he wanted the respect of future generations and his professional peers. She also knew that, for as long as he believed she would help him toward that goal, she would be safe.

"The guards will be bringing you internees from detention. I expect you to treat their injuries and any other day-to-day incidents and keep them from disturbing me." The doctor opened up a leather-bound notebook and began to write rapidly in it.

After a few seconds, Martha got up as quietly as she could and returned to the front office. She opened the door and found an older woman and a little boy waiting outside. Both of them had narrow gray collars circling their throats.

"They said you would treat us." The older woman was holding on to the boy's hand hard enough to dent his skin. He kept looking off toward a line of people stretched out across the neutral territory. "He has an infection."

Martha blinked at the woman's hostile tone, but she made herself smile. "Of course. Come on in."

"Nana, I don't want to miss breakfast." The boy tugged on her arm.

Breakfast? A sickening realization burned in her stomach. She stared at the line again, noting the children sprinkled along it, leaning against their parents' protective legs. Their silence shredded any comforting lies she might have told herself. *Any hungry child would be throwing a tantrum or whining, but they aren't. They know there is no hope of change.*

Chapter Twelve

Bernie kept her head down and her attention on answering the questions that the teacher had given her, trying to behave like the other kids. Twenty-two other students, ranging from a foot-swinging four-year-old to a clutch of teenagers gossiping in the back, sat at the folding plastic tables arranged in neat rows.

"Forget all this stuff, Bernie. Let's go find Leanne." Chuck poked an insubstantial hand at her test paper.

Bernie shook her head, moving it as little as she could. It had taken a lot of arguing to convince her mom to let her go to school instead of working on her exercises at home. She wasn't going to waste the chance, even if it wasn't exactly what she'd expected. She stole a glance at the three girls her own age, who sat together at a table two rows back and to the right. They kept looking at her then huddling back together to whisper. *Maybe I'm making mistakes.* Bernie's heart sank.

"I could tell you what those brats are talking about."

She shook her head again, refusing Chuck's offer.

"Is everything all right, Bernadette?" Mrs. Chin asked brightly.

Bernie's tongue was scratchy and dry, and it took her two tries before she managed an audible "Yes, ma'am."

"All right. Let me know when you've finished." Mrs. Chin walked back to four little kids and continued to explain their spelling lesson. Three of the children had a gray strip around their necks with a small box on one side. Shock collars.

"All of you, stop chattering and listen to me!" Mr. Marshall thundered from the front of the class. Bernie didn't like him much. He looked like he'd smelled something awful, and he had a nasty thick mustache that reminded her of a dead caterpillar. He kept bending down and peering at the kids' necks. She'd much rather talk with Mrs. Chin, who had a nice smile and wore a pretty blue dress.

The screaming lady ran past the school window again, shouting for someone to help her. She'd done it four times so far that morning, but none of the other kids reacted to her shouts. Bernie kept her eyes on the papers in front of her, filling in the answers with her pencil.

"This is such a waste. Like you're ever going to need to know when Columbus came to America." Chuck grew darker.

Bernie hoped he wasn't going to get angry enough to cause an incident. During therapy, he'd often shorted out light bulbs when she'd tried to ignore him. *Doesn't he remember that I'm not supposed to talk to him?* It was harder than she'd thought it would be. She hated when Chuck was unhappy. He'd been her friend for a long time, and friends were supposed to help one another. She finished the last question and raised her hand.

Mrs. Chin came over and collected the test, checking her watch. "All right, children. I think it's time for a short break."

Mr. Marshall started shouting again, drowning out Mrs. Chin's words. Bernie bit her lip, trying to watch the other kids without being obvious. They weren't reacting to Mr. Marshall, so she figured he was probably a ghost like the screaming lady.

The kids all got up from their chairs, surprising her. The younger ones ran outside, shouting, while the teenagers sauntered along and acted as if they were too cool to care. Still, Bernie noticed they weren't wasting any time. Mr. Marshall shouted at them to slow down, following them outside.

"Bernadette, is everything all right?" Mrs. Chin asked.

Only one other kid was still in the classroom, a little girl, about eight years old, with dark hair in long braids. She smiled sadly as she walked through the wall to the playground.

"I'm fine, Mrs. Chin," Bernie whispered.

"Are you having any trouble with your work?" Mrs. Chin was using the slow, patient voice that adults used when they thought a kid was stupid.

"You should knock these Bug-Eyed Betties into next week." Chuck's fists clenched, and darkness swirled around him.

I promised Michael I wouldn't let Chuck talk me into hurting anyone. Bernie closed her eyes for a moment, trying to remember what Mrs. Chin had asked her.

"I'm sure it's a big change. Your records say you were homeschooled?" Mrs. Chin prompted.

"Yes." Bernie kept her gaze on Mrs. Chin, ignoring the screaming lady's shouts again.

The teacher's pleasant smile began to look pasted on. "We'll have plenty of time to talk later. Why don't you go and play with the other children outside?"

Bernie dragged her feet outside. She'd failed some kind of test, which marked her as a freak. The other kids could see it. Mrs. Chin could see it. They could tell she'd never been at a school before.

It wasn't anything like what she'd expected from a one-room schoolhouse. It didn't look anything like the *Little House on the Prairie* books. The tables and chairs were plastic with folding metal legs. There wasn't even a blackboard, just a big pad of paper clipped to an easel. A couple of cheap bookshelves held lots of paperbacks of varying thicknesses, but otherwise, the room was more like a storage room than a school.

Outside, the kids had divided themselves into two groups, and those with the gray shock collars and those without kept as far away from each other as possible. Bernie stood in the middle, not sure which way she should turn. The girls her age were clustered together, fingering the gray bands encircling their necks. On the staff kids' side, some of the little ones were playing a game, throwing a rock back and forth. Bernie wanted to join them. *I'm probably too old for that kind of thing.* Tears stung her eyes, and she wished she could go home.

"Don't cry, *petite,*" a man's voice interrupted. "The other children will jump on you if you start to cry. Just start walking toward the fence."

Bernie obeyed, keeping her head high. When she reached the fence, a man waited on the other side of the chain-link barrier. He looked funny, with thick black hair and a long nose. He wore a long blue velvet coat with a white puffy thing at the front.

"Much better. Pleased to make your acquaintance, *mademoiselle*. I am Henri." He stepped through the metal lattice as if it didn't exist.

"I don't like you." Chuck materialized beside the two of them.

"After all of our conversations? I am wounded, Monsieur Charles." Henri's hand fluttered to his chest, a gold ring glinting on his third finger. He winked at Bernie, inviting her to share the joke. She smiled, liking his playful sense of humor.

Chuck grew darker, the gray of his pants and cap deepening from overcast to storm. "Go away."

Worry cut Bernie's good mood short. When Chuck got dark, he could hurt people. And since no one would believe he existed, they would blame her.

Henri bowed, using his arms to sweep the long tails of his coat back. "Please accept my apology, monsieur. It was only a joke, but I see you are not in a joking mood. I only wished to introduce myself to the *petite mademoiselle*."

"Don't be mad, Chuck," Bernie whispered, checking to make sure no one would hear her.

Chuck lowered his head, but Bernie still caught the hurt in his eyes. "I don't like this."

"I can understand," Henri said gently. "We would rather meet under different circumstances. I hope you have not changed your mind about the lessons?"

"No." Bernie suppressed a shudder. She didn't want to end up like Gwen, trapped and insane. "I want to learn."

Chuck stared at the ground, his arms and legs rigid.

"Chuck?" she whispered. Henri waited silently with his hands folded together.

Slowly, Chuck raised his head. "I know we have to do this, Bernie. I'm just worried."

She smiled in relief. "It'll be okay. Right, Henri?"

"*Absolument.*" Henri bowed again. "After school, I will take you to Madame. Then your real lessons can begin."

"Hold your end steady, Chief," the foreman shouted.

Lou grunted under the weight of the massive steel beam. *Why do humans always feel the need to chatter at one another?* He'd rebuffed several attempts at chitchat already, and it was only his first day. For some reason, the humans seemed to find his silence hilarious. He'd nodded to acknowledge his name when the foreman called it, and the others all laughed.

"Not much of a talker, huh? Guess we got ourselves a regular 'Chief' here, like *One Flew Over the Cuckoo's Nest!*" The foreman elbowed the others, eying Lou as if he expected the other man to attack.

Lou didn't particularly care what they called him. He knew it was offensive and intended to hurt, but the term had no personal negative associations, and he did not think it was wise to fight them on it. Let them attempt to ruffle his fur with their blunted weapons. He would stay focused on his work. The weight of the beam lessened as the others banged the support posts into place beneath it. Lou studied the concrete bases and mentally shook his head. The posts would sink and rise with the thawing and freezing of the ground. The building would probably collapse within a year or two.

Of course, it would still be better constructed than the flimsy shacks on the other side of the fence. Made of thin boards, they would be impossible to keep warm in winter. They should be reinforcing and insulating the barracks instead of building something new in the neutral area.

From where he stood, he could watch the children in the small schoolyard. Martha's daughter stood alone by the camp fence. He instinctively weighed the distance and the obstacles. It would take less than a minute to cross to her and only a few seconds more to either jump or break down the chain-link fence. Another three minutes, and they would be in the forest. He'd tested the outer fence the night before, and it would be easy to breach in either of his forms.

Having the child within reach was reassuring, but being unable to see Martha made his bear side edgy. It wanted to go searching, find her, and make certain she was safe.

A pair of guards strolled by, rifles in hand. A low growl resonated in Lou's chest. It was the third time Ryan and his partner had sought out the construction crew. Each time, the man made a point of joking with the others, excluding Lou in an attempt to dominate the situation by building up connections, like a beta wolf gaining the support of the pack before challenging the alpha.

Too bad for him that Lou didn't play by wolf rules. Bears might acknowledge physical superiority, but they didn't indulge in pack-animal politics.

"All right. The beam's good to go."

Lou stepped away as the foreman ordered, rolling his shoulder to ease the ache. From the corner of his eye, he saw Ryan stop talking and his hands tighten around his rifle's grip. When Lou bent to pick up the level to check the support, Ryan relaxed, and the chatter started up again.

"Let's get the walls up, boys." The foreman kept them moving with no time to rest. Lou's stomach grumbled, reminding him that he'd missed the communal breakfast. Hunger made it hard to concentrate on human things. He could smell the bounty of the forest, full of rich, satisfying food that would see him through the winter, but it was just out of reach.

"Aw, shit! Look out!" someone shouted in alarm.

A young man was staring at his hand, eyes wide as blood spurted from a deep cut in his palm. The other men were shaking their heads and backing away, the sour tang of fear rising from their bodies.

Lou dropped the piece of lumber he'd picked up and quickly walked to the injured man. "Hold still." Grabbing the bloody hand, Lou pressed his fingers and thumbs into the flesh beside the slash and lifted the hand into the air. The pumping blood slowed to an ooze.

The foreman pushed through the crowd. "What's going on? Dammit, Tom! Chief, get him over to medical."

Lou tucked one hand under the injured man's armpit in case he collapsed. Based on the paleness of the boy's skin, there was a good chance of him fainting. Tom was babbling, but Lou ignored his words, moving quickly to the medical building.

As soon as he opened the door, he caught the scent of blood and burned flesh. Martha was applying dressings to a young woman with a red, raw burn down her arm. Two guards stood nearby, watching her with guns in hand.

Seeing Martha unharmed relieved his inner bear, but his human mind couldn't share in the sentiment. She lifted her head as they came in, and he saw the fear in her eyes.

"I need help," Tom gasped.

"He needs immediate attention." Martha turned toward the woman still on the office's lone examination bed. "Can you—"

The nearest guard didn't wait for Martha to finish. He yanked the internee off the bed, grabbing her burned arm. She cried out, falling to her knees.

"You didn't have to do that." Martha started to bend to help the girl.

"Treat him first," the guard ordered.

Lou held back a growl, tensing in preparation for a fight.

Martha bit her lip but didn't disobey. She began searching the cupboards, fumbling with the keys to unlock each set.

Lou helped Tom up onto the bed. The young man clutched at him, clearly afraid.

"It's bad, isn't it?" Tom wouldn't look at his hand. Lou still held it high to slow the bleeding.

Martha tugged on a pair of green gloves that smelled of baby powder and rubber, scents Lou remembered from Andrew's kit. She reached up and gently lowered Tom's hand. "I've seen worse. We'll get you patched up soon. What made the cut?"

Tom's eyes were squeezed shut as Martha examined the injury. "I was cutting a board, and it splintered. Some of it got jammed in the electric saw, and I reached in to get it out. Then the saw started up again."

"Next time, it's a good idea to unplug the saw before clearing a jam. You're lucky it's not fingers," Martha told him matter-of-factly as she inserted a small needle into the skin near the gash. "That should feel better in a minute."

She kept talking to the young man as her fingers danced around the wound. Lou was still holding tight to keep pressure on it, and her touch was like a bird's, barely enough to register before it disappeared. Tom seemed to take comfort from her words, relaxing against Lou as Martha cleaned and stitched the wound together before wrapping it with gauze.

"There." She stepped back and looked at the young woman, who was still kneeling on the floor in pain. "I can finish your dressing now then get you both medicine."

Her efficiency impressed Lou—she had obviously invested long years of practice in her skills. But it only brought the gap between them into relief. Animals healed on their own, or they died. She was a human, with skills for the human world, not his.

Tom was quiet, still leaning against Lou for support as Martha finished sealing the burn behind a layer of gauze. She searched the cupboard again and measured out pills into two envelopes.

She handed Tom the first one. "Take these now and then every eight hours. Come back tomorrow, and we'll check for infection."

Tom accepted the small envelope. Martha held out the second to the girl, but the guard snatched it away.

"Medication here only. We don't need a drug problem in camp." He seemed bored and restless.

"But those burns are going to be excruciating. She'll need a regular dosage." Martha shook her head in confusion.

"I'll come back. It's okay." The young woman seemed eager to go, despite the clear pain on her face.

"I hope you've learned your lesson. No more gambling in camp." The second guard seemed a little more sympathetic.

"Yes, sir." She left, followed by her escort. Once Lou, Tom, and Martha were alone, it was harder for Lou to ignore the scent of fresh summer flowers in the room.

"I don't understand this place," Martha said sadly. Her eyes met Lou's for the first time since he arrived. "Will you take him to his trailer? The medication will make him sleepy."

He nodded, accepting the task. Tom seemed much happier since the bloody gash was no longer visible. Lou opened the door to leave.

"Wait," Martha called out.

Lou turned to look at her.

She twisted the green gloves in her hands. "Will you be home later?"

she asked.

He nodded again, balancing the injured man with one hand.

"Thank you." She smiled at him. The sight of her grin was like the first rush of warmth in the spring. He wished he could think of the right words to say to keep that smile in place.

Tom groaned before Lou could assemble his thoughts into words.

The smile vanished from Martha's face. "You should go. I'll see you after work."

Lou hefted the wounded man upright and helped him to the gate out of camp. As they trod the muddy path between the camp and the trailers, Tom began to walk more easily. It gave Lou time to go over Martha's reactions and relive their exchange. She seemed different than she had back in Bear Claw, commanding circumstances and her environment rather than being buffeted by them.

"She's a nice lady," Tom shared into the silence. "Much better than the doctor. I hope she stays."

Lou could neither agree nor disagree. If they were successful, the camp would be dismantled. He refused to think of what would happen if they failed.

"You really don't talk much, do you?" Tom pointed at the next trailer. "This one is mine."

Lou unlocked the trailer and helped Tom inside. It was much narrower than the one he shared with Martha and her daughter, with a set of bunk beds across the back. The air was stale and stank of acrid tobacco smoke. His neck itched as his hackles tried to rise in human form.

Tom sat down at the small table and began taking off his boots. "It's kind of a nice change, you know? The not-talking thing. All the other guys were talking when I got hurt, but you stepped up and did something. Thanks."

"You're welcome," Lou replied.

Tom blinked at him, his foot propped up on the chair to make it easier to undo the laces.

"Do you need any more help?" The stale air burned in his lungs, but he held his ground. He wouldn't leave before making certain Tom was okay. It was what he had promised Martha.

"You're a decent guy. I don't know why Mr. Blake is talking trash about you." Tom yawned as he lowered his foot back to the floor, still in its boot. "I thought he was supposed to be nicer after they made him take some time off. Hey, can you tell them that I got ordered to rest? I don't want to get my pay docked."

Lou nodded. He knelt to strip Tom's boots off his feet. From the way Tom was rambling, his brain was already asleep. *His body hasn't caught up yet.* He caught Tom before the man could overbalance in his attempt to crawl into bed.

"Be careful about Mr. Blake. He scares me. He's got his own gang with the guards, and he works a lot with the doctor." Tom's head hit the pillow.

The same doctor who makes people disappear into tortuous medical experiments. Martha's direct boss. *And they expect her to spy on him.* Anger brought his bear close to the surface. The scents of the forest called to him as he left the trailer, but Lou's attention stayed on the camp, searching for any trace of Ryan. *He hunts for the doctor.* He could be hunting for Martha and Bernie while Lou took care of Tom.

If he was, he would soon discover that even a wolf pack was no match for an angry bear.

Chapter Thirteen

"Ms. Jeevan, how do you respond to accusations that your evaluation center is no different from Nazi concentration camps or the internment camps for the Japanese in World War II?"

Smiling sweetly at the reporter's question, Priya kept her temper. *This is an opportunity.* No matter that she would have preferred to remain behind the scenes. But Director Fangato had come under criticism lately about the optics of a white man persecuting a newfound minority. Priya didn't trust any of the other staff at Special Investigations to remain calm and on message, so she reluctantly agreed to step up.

As she expected, the reporter was beginning to show signs of discomfort with the hard line of questioning. Priya remained pleasant and calm, causing the reporter to visibly doubt her own certainty. "I can understand why people are concerned, and indeed they should be. History is full of bad precedents."

The reporter shifted in her seat, and Priya continued smoothly, preventing the other woman from regaining control.

"I hope everyone understands that Special Investigations isn't motivated by fear, nor do we have any intent to harm the O.H.s under our care." Priya let the smile drop and allowed concern to furrow her features. "We only want to dispel the cloud of uncertainty and learn the truth about these new abilities."

The hot lights of the television studio shredded the illusion of comfort created by the casual couches and fake living room set. Two massive cameras stood sentinel at the abrupt edge of the plush carpeting, each poised to seize on any sign of weakness or vulnerability.

"Then you deny the allegations of inadequate shelter and food?" The reporter leaned forward, obviously hoping to catch some sign of discomfort, but Priya had been playing the game for too long to be caught off guard by a woman in a pink Prada knockoff.

She leaned back in the gray armchair, allowing her smile to slip into an expression of disappointment. She kept her voice soft and low to reinforce the impression of innocence and trustworthiness. "We had some problems initially, since we weren't expecting so many O.H.s to comply with our requests. Northstar Construction has hired additional construction crews at their own expense to meet the demand. And Lantern Security, who runs the day-to-day operations, has begun hiring O.H.s to see to the necessary work in the camp, allowing them to earn a decent wage while they are being evaluated. The staff and O.H.s work side by side to make certain that everyone's needs are met."

The reporter checked her notes again. Priya tried to remember the woman's name, but it was her fourth interview that day, and the names of unimportant, fleeting contacts were rarely necessary. Instead, Priya decided to appeal to the woman's professional pride. "I want to thank you for being so diligent in your research and making sure the public stays informed. This has not been an easy process, but we have everyone's safety as our first priority."

No sign of a flattered flush or unconscious pride. Only the intent gaze of a woman preparing to pounce on a prize. "Aren't Northstar and Lantern both subsidiaries of Dalhard Industries?"

Priya kept her face smooth. "I believe you are correct on that point."

"And the head of Dalhard Industries, André Dalhard, died last year as part of his attempt to take over one of the outskirt communities of New York City by using O.H.s and their abilities. In fact, my sources indicate that he was obsessed with those abilities and used his multinational corporation to search out and kidnap O.H.s and coerce them into working with him." The reporter's eyes gleamed in anticipation.

Poor girl. Priya was already prepared for such questions. "André Dalhard was one man with an unfortunate mental health issue. The company he created employs hundreds of thousands of people across the globe. Surely you are not suggesting that each and every one of them is equally complicit in his actions?"

The reporter's eagerness vanished. Priya smiled sweetly and continued in her ruthless, soft-spoken assault. "In fact, is it truly such a surprise that those who have worked within Dalhard Industries would be familiar with the O.H. community and abilities, making them invaluable resources to the Bureau of Special Investigations? Or that some of the brave men and women who have done such work might feel guilty at some level for their employer's sins? That they might then volunteer to serve in very difficult and isolated conditions because they feel passionately about doing the right thing for the nation as a whole?" It was all complete garbage, of course. Those at the camp were there for money or power, not for any kind of altruistic martyrdom. But the statement was plausible enough to be believed by the uncritical and contained enough truths to spin strength out of its potential weaknesses.

"So you still maintain that separating and isolating those identified as O.H. is the best course of action for the nation?" The reporter appeared to be regrouping. "Is that why you've continued to push for mass testing?"

"First, Woodpine is only a temporary measure. The isolation is to protect both those in our care and the general public. After decades of suppressing their abilities, the O.H.s need space and freedom to learn how to control what they can do." Priya considered getting the woman's name after the interview was done. Ambition could be useful if directed properly. "And yes, the Bureau of Special Investigations is disappointed in the government's recent decision to forego mass testing. We believe it is important for all O.H.s to be identified as such, both so they can receive proper legal protection and so that the public can be kept safe. It would be awful if, for example, an O.H. had the strength to shatter bones with their bare hands and the police were unaware of it when they came with an arrest warrant."

"Yet several independent laboratories have claimed that your tests are hugely ineffective with a high rate of false positives."

It was information that should not have been available outside of Special Investigations. Priya raised her hand to her cheek as if shocked. "Our own lab has done extensive testing—"

"But your lab isn't exactly impartial, is it?" The reporter shifted to face the camera. "I have a list here of over a hundred American citizens who were falsely identified as O.H.s due to your test. They were taken to your evaluation camp and haven't been allowed to leave. Their families are considering filing a class action lawsuit. Do you have a response?"

"I would hope that the families would contact the Bureau of Special Investigations instead of lawyers. We insisted on rigorous evaluation before releasing the test for use. The test only identifies *occulata hominem.* However… Oh dear, perhaps I shouldn't say anything before knowing all the facts…" Priya lightly touched her lips as if shushing herself.

The reporter's righteousness played right on cue. "What could you possibly say that would justify imprisoning innocent Americans?"

"Well—and please understand this is only my personal speculation at this time—it could be possible that some people could be O.H. and not realize it. They could have these strange gifts and only find out during some kind of crisis situation, perhaps harming someone without ever meaning to." *Seed planted. Now the public won't know who to trust—not even themselves.* "However, please, I would ask that these families contact us for more information and further testing. I will give you a special contact number to pass on to them, if you would be so kind. And again, thank you for your diligence."

Priya stood up and detached the microphone, unthreading it from her clothes before the reporter managed to gather her thoughts enough to ask another question. She smiled graciously, shaking hands with the entire crew as she made her way to the door. Storming out of an interview only made a person look guilty. But pretending that an agreed-upon conclusion had been reached would make others hesitate to contradict it.

Her phone rang as soon as she settled into the limousine. Priya exhaled softly, slipping her aching feet out of her high heels before answering. "Director Fangato."

"Who the hell leaked that information about the test?" her putative boss demanded.

"I'd like to know that myself." She had a few ideas. Not everyone at Special Investigations shared her agenda.

"This is turning into a public relations nightmare." Fangato continued to rant, and Priya listened with only half of her attention as she mentally reviewed her schedule for the rest of the day. *No more interviews, thank goodness. I should touch base with my brother and see if the telekinetic can be made useful. If only I could convince him to go after the transformatives near the Alaskan border…*

"…that's why I need you to attend this charity fund-raiser this evening."

The director's words snagged her focus. As much as she wanted to refuse, it wouldn't align with the carefully crafted persona that she used with him. "Of course, if it will help. I'm afraid I'm not familiar with the group."

"They call themselves The Other Acts of God. They're raising money for those attacked by O.H.s," Fangato explained.

"A religious group?" Priya picked up her tablet to scan through the group's website. She needed to thread a fine needle, encouraging fear of the *lalassu* without publicly stepping into obvious bigotry.

"Not exactly." The director coughed. "You know how the insurance companies refused to pay out for damages during the incidents last year? They claimed that people with powers qualified as an act of God and thus wasn't covered. This group has taken it as a rallying cry, using the slogan: one act of God deserves another."

"With the other being charity. How clever. I'm sure I have something suitable at home for a black-tie event." *Perhaps the blue silk gown.* It flattered her complexion, and the cool color created a sense of authority.

"I knew I could count on you, Priya." Fangato sounded exhausted and beleaguered. She smiled in pleasure as they exchanged goodbyes. She'd planned to leak the information about the faulty test after the spectacle to trigger the director's resignation, but she could work with the current circumstances. Her explanation about unknowing *lalassu* would work for the false positives, but when the public also discovered that some *lalassu* tested as false negatives, they would be outraged. With the right spectacle, she could ensure panic in the streets.

Her phone buzzed again.

"Well done maintaining control in the interview," Karan said as soon as she answered.

"I'll be grateful once Fangato can resume his role as the public face of Special Investigations. It's far too time-consuming." Priya glanced at the privacy screen separating her from the driver and decided to be prudent rather than explicit. "Did the package arrive today?"

"It did. But the merchandise is not quite what we hoped for."

Karan's answer was disappointing. So the telekinetic wasn't as promised. "Very well. We'll have to continue to search."

Martha's eyes and hands were aching. She'd treated two bad infections, a sliced hand, and an old man who she suspected had parasites. And when she wasn't doling out medical help, she was reading through the patient files in the flickering light from her single desk lamp. Dr. Coulon's writing was cramped and irregular, and she'd gotten out of practice at deciphering doctors' notes, but she wasn't seeing anything that looked out of place or didn't make medical sense. His notes contained references to age distributions, previous medical histories, and some basic test results, such as guessing cards from another room or disrupting electromagnetic flows. It might be weirder than a typical physical, but it wasn't worse.

Of course she didn't actually expect him to give her access to secret information on her first day. No matter how afraid people were of the *lalassu*, any sort of intrusive medical work would be illegal. So if there were records, they were more likely to be in his office than in hers. *Probably in those notebooks.*

But that was a challenge for another day. It was after six, and she wanted to get home and make sure Bernie was all right. She slowly opened the inner-office door, hoping he wouldn't assign more work when he saw her.

Dr. Coulon wasn't in his office.

Martha frowned and rubbed at her eyes. *Maybe I'm more tired than I thought.* A second, more thorough look confirmed the first glance had been right. Dr. Coulon wasn't there.

He couldn't have left. The only exit was through the front office, and she would have seen him.

Martha's puzzling was cut short as the bookshelf at the back of the doctor's office began to swing forward. She hastily pulled the door closed, leaving only a tiny sliver to peek through.

Dr. Coulon emerged from behind the bookshelf and pushed it back. A metallic clunk sounded like a deadbolt sliding home. He took out a pad of paper and began to write furiously.

Martha held her breath, stepping backward as quietly as possible. She might not have experience as a spy, but she could guess what would happen if Dr. Coulon realized she'd seen his secret exit. *It's not going to be a promotion.*

She opened and closed several cabinets in the front office, not overtly loudly, but not making any attempt to be quiet. After a minute or two of making noise, she tapped on the doctor's door. "Good evening, Dr. Coulon. It's after six, and I should collect my daughter to get something to eat. Would you like me to bring you anything?"

The pad of paper had disappeared from the glass-topped desk. Instead, the doctor had a thick medical text open in front of him, as if he'd been doing research. He shook his head, his glasses flashing in the dim light. "I will expect you at eight thirty tomorrow."

"Of course, sir. Good night." She closed the door and exhaled silently. *First day done.* After gathering her things, she hurried outside.

A large shadow loomed from the dark side of the medical building.

Martha sucked in a breath that sounded suspiciously like a squeak. She wrapped the straps of her bag around her hand, getting ready to swing it in the face of her attacker. But as he stepped into the light, she realized that it was Lou.

"You frightened me," she snapped. After a long day of tension, the last thing she needed was him jumping out of the shadows at her.

He swallowed, his eyes dipping down. "I was watching Bernadette."

She felt like a complete jerk. Lou always seemed to catch her in breakdown moments. Parental worry soon superseded apologies. "Is she okay?"

"She is unhurt. But after school, she went into the camp with the other children." Lou's low, gravelly voice sent a distracting shiver sliding under Martha's skin. She'd always loved deep voices. "She went into one of the barracks and stayed there. I checked, and she seems to be speaking to one of the women. The other *lalassu* call her Looney."

The long, low building had nothing to distinguish it from the others except for a weatherworn three painted on the narrow side. Most of the *lalassu* were leaving the barracks and lining up for their dinner. Martha's stomach growled. "Let's go get her then get something to eat. We can talk back at the trailer."

Lou fell into step behind her as she walked toward the gate between the neutral area and the actual camp. Having him there was comforting, like having a personal army. *Don't get silly about this and make an idiot out of yourself.*

The guards at the gate put their hands on their guns as she and Lou got closer but relaxed when they saw they were staff instead of internees. They let the two of them pass without comment.

There was no lock on the barracks door. Martha hesitated, unsure if she should knock or go in. Before she could decide, a young Asian woman opened the door and froze.

"Hello," Martha began awkwardly. "I'm Martha. I'm just here to pick up my daughter."

The girl visibly relaxed, making Martha wonder what kind of surprise visits happened around here. "You mean Bernie? She's in the back with Looney."

"Thank you." Martha waited, but the girl didn't offer her own name.

Instead she stepped back and held the door for Martha. "Listen, you don't have to worry about Looney. She's noisy but harmless. I think she's been happy having someone to jabber at, which might mean that we can get some sleep tonight."

Martha thanked her again and stepped inside. The light was dim and came only from a few kerosene lanterns placed on hooks running down the center of the long room. Half-height wooden partitions separated the interior into eight sections, with a broad aisle between. It looked rather like a barn but without doors for the stalls. Inside the first section were two narrow cots with metal sides and legs, a set of shelves, and two wooden boxes. Not exactly luxurious living.

An older woman with short dark hair and a wide, round body

scowled at Martha from the second stall but didn't move from her cot. Martha hurried past, even more grateful that Lou was still with her. She didn't think the internees would attack, but she could sense their resentment.

"So what do you do when there's no one inside a ghost?" Bernie's voice echoed through the barracks.

"Those ones are difficult, *petite*. You can't argue with a recording," a woman's voice replied, the thick French accent lilting like a song as it drifted below the range of Martha's ability to overhear. But she didn't have long to wait to discover its owner.

"Hi, Mom." Bernie's greeting rang out as soon as she came into view. "This is Leanne."

"A pleasure to meet you." Martha held out her hand to the woman sitting on the bed. She wore two knit caps on her head, both worn and full of holes. A long sweater similarly revealed the cotton shirt underneath, and she wore so many layers of skirts that she seemed like a kind of homeless Southern belle. But her face and hands were clean, and while the clothes were shabby, they were clean as well.

"Likewise. Henri has told me a great deal about all three of you." Leanne gestured with bony fingers that she arched as if to clasp an invisible cigarette. "Come back tomorrow, and I'll tell you more ghost stories to chill your blood."

Bernie laughed, sounding much lighter than she had in at least a year. The sound warmed Martha's heart, even as it made her sad that someone else had lifted her little girl's burden. "Thank you, Leanne."

"See you tomorrow!" Bernie hopped off the stool. Martha bit her lip rather than remind Bernie that she should ask permission before making plans. *They have to spend time together if Leanne is going to teach her.*

To Martha's surprise, Leanne followed them to the door, tugging her tattered sleeves down over her bare hands. Outside, the Arctic twilight cast long shadows across the barren stretch of no-man's land. Leanne reached out and grabbed Martha's arm.

"There isn't much time," the medium hissed.

Lou's powerful hand clamped down on Leanne's, prying it off Martha.

Leanne glared at them both, cradling her wrist. "You need to find what you came for quickly."

"You could help me with that." Martha held her arms rigidly to stop herself from snatching Bernie back from the hate-filled eyes of the madwoman. *Ghosts could help to search the camp and wouldn't have to worry about being caught.*

"And just like that, you decide to use our gifts for your own advantage?" Leanne cackled at Martha's embarrassment. Bernie looked horrified at her mother's suggestion. Even Lou seemed disappointed.

"That's not what I meant—"

"I know what you meant." Leanne cut off the hasty apology. "And it's so noble of you to ride in and try to rescue us poor people who are only here because we dare to be different. You could never understand what it is to be one of us."

A low growl from Lou cut off the taunting, and Martha walked away with Bernie in tow, feeling guilty, unsure, and very much alone.

<h1 style="text-align:center">CHAPTER FOURTEEN</h1>

"Chuck said you found the secret door today." Bernie yawned as she climbed into her double bed. "That's good."

Martha wished Chuck had kept that particular tidbit to himself. "Why is it good?"

"The door is where the bad stuff happens. The things that Michael wanted us to find out. So once you get inside, you can leave." Bernie bunched the thin pillow into shape and lay down on her side.

"You mean we can go back to Bear Claw?" Martha pulled the prickly wool blanket up, though she knew Bernie would shove it aside.

When her daughter didn't answer, Martha leaned in to press a kiss on Bernie's forehead. If she kept asking questions, Bernie wouldn't answer, but if Martha stayed silent, there was a chance her daughter would open up to her. She smoothed locks of hair away from Bernie's face. The wispy curls were changing into thicker, wavier strands. *She's going to be stunning, with those rich sandy browns and bright golds.* Of course, she'd probably want to dye her hair black, just to defy any expectations.

"Mom?" Bernie said softly.

"Yes, darling?" Martha kept stroking Bernie's hair, but all of her attention was on what her daughter would say.

"Do you think Lily and Doc would be mad if I didn't go back to Bear Claw?"

"They would miss us," Martha said quickly. "But they wouldn't be mad."

Bernie sat up. "If the tests don't show that I'm different, couldn't I

130

find somewhere else to live? Vapor could get us fake IDs, and I could go to school like any other kid."

The hope in Bernie's eyes broke Martha's heart. She couldn't destroy the dream of a life without lies and secrets. "We'll have to see."

"Do you want to go back to Bear Claw?"

It was a tough question, particularly with Lou waiting in the other room. *Here goes another attempt at diplomacy.* "I want us to be safe."

The smile disappeared from Bernie's face, and she flopped down, facing away from Martha. "Fine."

"Sweetheart, I want us to have that kind of life too—"

"But we can't because I'm a freak." Bernie's sob-roughened voice echoed off the wall. "It's why Dad left and why you can't have a job and why we always have to be alone."

"No, Bernie!" Martha grabbed her daughter's shoulders, wrapping herself around Bernie in a protective cocoon. "You are not a freak."

"Yes, I am!" she shouted. "I belong with all the other freaks!"

Martha's breath caught in her throat. *No one belongs here. You're not a freak. I love you just the way you are.* Struggling to find the right words, she missed her opportunity to find what to say. "You're not—"

"You don't understand." Bernie shrugged off her mother's embrace. "Leave me alone."

Martha retreated, standing on shaky legs. "I love you, Bernie. We can talk more tomorrow."

Bernie didn't say anything, her bony spine bristling under her nightshirt like a porcupine's back. *Approach at your own risk.*

Martha closed Bernie's door, her eyes and throat burning. *What can I say to fix this?* Bernie's comment about her father had caught her by surprise. She'd always made it clear why Derek had left: because he didn't want the responsibility, not because of anything related to her or Bernie. *It's not our fault, it was a lack in him.* She thought Bernie had understood that.

A warm hand touched her shoulder, and without thinking, she turned and buried her face in Lou's shirt. Tears flowed fast, ripping their way out of her swollen, scratchy eyes. She bit down on her fist, trying not to make any noise. She couldn't add her own problems on to Bernie.

Lou cradled her gently with his big arms. She shook under the force of her escaping emotions, but he remained rock steady, supporting her easily when she thought she might fall to the ground. His shirt grew soggy and cool as it absorbed her tears, but he never wavered or retreated. She gave up all pretense of control and surrendered to the overwhelming misery and guilt. She could let it all out, confident that he would watch over her. She'd fought her feelings for as long as she could, and it was better to let them out with Lou instead of having a panic attack at some random moment. For once, she didn't have to be the lone guard at the gate. There was someone else ready to share her task.

Slowly, the intensity waned. Her eyes were burning. All of the liquid was gone, leaving them red, dry, and irritated. Her throat felt as if it had been scraped raw and then sealed shut, gluing itself together. Her chest ached, the ribs bruised inside from rapid, panting breaths. Her legs were wobbly, her fingers were numb from being clenched into fists, and her mind was starting to realize that she'd had a breakdown in front of the man of her fantasies. *I might be the first recorded case to die of embarrassment.*

She pulled back slowly, not sure what to say. *Should I offer to buy him a new shirt? Wash this one? Apologize? Thank him?* Somehow, Emily Post had never quite covered the appropriate response in that situation. She kept her gaze focused on the checkered fabric, wrinkled from her death grip.

Isn't he going to say anything? Martha would have been grateful even if he started in on a speech about why women were too emotional and how she needed to toughen up. Anything to break the awkward silence wedging between them.

She couldn't put it off any longer. She would have to look at his face. Mentally preparing herself for the worst, she took a deep breath. *He probably hates me. He wants to leave but is too polite to.* She raised her eyes and stared.

There was no judgment on his face and no hint of disgust curling his mouth, only concern as he watched her. It wasn't the wary type of concern, the sort one would have when facing an unpredictable wild animal. It was just awareness with compassion. If she still needed to cry, it was okay. If she was ready to move on, that was okay, too. Either way, Lou would accept it, if she was reading him correctly.

The idea of complete acceptance left Martha paradoxically shaken and off balance. She didn't know how she should react or what she should do next. *Thank him? Apologize? Ask him to let go? Climb him like a tree?* The last thought came directly from her libido. It was perfectly happy to overlook her raw throat and swollen eyes, but Martha stepped back quickly before that newly reawakened side of her could prompt her into trouble.

Lou's arms fell away as she moved. His dark eyes stayed on her as she fumbled for the door to the second bedroom. His hands were outstretched as if he expected her to fall and was ready to catch her.

I'm being ridiculous. Martha took another deep breath and made herself face him. "Thank you. I don't break down often." At least he didn't know about her meltdown in Bear Claw's forest.

He nodded slowly before bending to continue the task that she'd interrupted. He was making a bed on the narrow sofa. He spread a gray woolen blanket over the worn tan upholstery, tucking it carefully around the cushions.

"You're planning to sleep out here?" Martha wrapped her arms around her stomach. "Why?"

He straightened. "I will not impose."

Impose? The sofa was less than five feet long. His head and feet would both dangle over the end. And Martha doubted that his shoulders would fit across. The twin beds in the other room might be cramped, but he could at least stretch out on them. "Don't be silly. We can both sleep in here."

He tilted his head as if questioning whether or not she meant the offer.

"We're both adults, and there's no reason for you to sleep on a couch that will give you back problems or worse. I'm sure I can restrain myself from jumping you in the middle of the night." *Oh my God, did I really just say that?* Her cheeks were burning, and she had no idea what to do with her hands.

One corner of his lips pulled back in a lopsided smile.

If he laughs at me, I'm going to have to hit him. She tried to shove her hands into her pockets before remembering that her dress pants didn't have pockets. She settled for hooking her fingers into the belt loops.

"Thank you." He bent down and picked up his duffel bag.

As he carried it into the room, the realization hit her. He was really going to be there all night, only a few feet away. He would see her when she first woke up with smushed hair and drying drool on her lips. *Well, if there was any chance that he wanted an out-of-shape single mom, that should cut right through my glamorous allure.* Her shoulders slumped. She shouldn't waste time on impossible fantasies. It hurt too much to return to reality. Drawing in a breath, she gathered her thoughts and repeated the mantra that had gotten her through her loneliness since Derek left. *It doesn't matter if anyone wants me. I have a responsibility to Bernie, and I don't have time for romantic relationships. All of the statistics say that, if I did, I would be increasing her risk of abuse. I would never forgive myself if she got hurt, and I can't trust myself to see it coming.* She hadn't seen Derek's abandonment coming, after all.

Reality duly reestablished, Martha went into the bedroom to pick up her pajamas, dull-gray loose pants and a matching baggy shirt. Both were worn, soft, and comfortable. *Real fantasy material,* her sarcastic inner voice jabbed. Grabbing her clothes from the drawer, she hurried to the tiny bathroom to change, avoiding her reflection in the mirror. She didn't need that big a dose of reality, thank you very much. When she returned to the bedroom, she stopped dead in the doorway.

Oh. My. God. Lou had stripped off his clothes and stood with his back to her. His body was every bit as amazing as Martha's fantasies. His muscular shoulders made two perfect v's, pointing at a pair of firm, round butt cheeks that begged to be cupped. The long line of his spine was like the trail in an ice cream after the first satisfying cone-to-crown lick. His hair was loose, falling in a silky sheet that made her want to bury her hands in it, parting it to tongue the sensitive flesh at the base of his skull before tasting his tan skin—

Stop. She shut her eyes, but there was no halting the buzzing thrill of interest from her long-deprived body. Her breasts were full and heavy under the loose shirt, with nipples hard enough to etch glass. *Maybe he'll think it's the cold?* And maybe he'd believe the wetness between her thighs was because she'd been swimming.

"Martha?" Lou sounded worried.

She refused to open her eyes in case he'd turned around, no matter how much she wanted to peek. "Mm-hm?"

"Are you all right?"

"Fine. Just fine." She patted the wall to her right until she found the light switch and flipped it off. Under cover of the safe shroud of darkness, she opened her eyes and fixed them firmly on the carpet as she made a beeline to her bed and safely tucked herself under the covers. Then she turned and faced the wall to avoid temptation. *Just stay focused on what you have to do.*

Karan arrived empty-handed at Priya's modest apartment. Already irritated by an evening spent in meaningless conversation at the fundraiser, Priya didn't bother to hide her frustration, turning abruptly on her heel and walking away from the open door.

"Good evening to you, too, sister." Karan stepped inside and closed the door. "I ordered a light meal. It should be arriving shortly."

The gesture soothed her temper. A little.

"You remind me of Mother. She was always quiet when she was angry." Karan chuckled.

"What happened with the telekinetic?" Priya was not in the mood for reminiscence.

"A few floating papers exhausted her. She would not be able to sustain the sort of demonstration that we need." Karan stood just outside her small kitchenette, hands folded behind his back.

Too bad. A few cars flying through the air could have been very effective on the six o'clock news. "What was your idea?"

"I should introduce you to the bakery near my apartment. They make the most delicious almond cookies."

He was toying with her. She hadn't welcomed him into her home, so he was keeping his information in reserve. The blatantly transparent manipulation attempt threatened to snap Priya's temper, so she assumed a pleasant smile in order to recover the social high ground. "Forgive me, brother. It's been a trying day."

"I saw the Channel 3 interview." Karan inclined his head. "It was unpleasant but no reason to blindly panic."

Does he truly think I'm panicking? It was unbelievable that he'd survived so long and accomplished so much without acquiring a basic understanding of the tangled web between those who made the decisions and the general public.

The phone rang, announcing a delivery. Reluctantly, Priya permitted them to bring up their stacked plastic containers. Karan remained standing in place, unruffled by her continuing lack of hospitality. His poise aroused her suspicion. *Does he have something that would give him an advantage in pursuing his own goals?* She waited until the delivery people left, giving herself time to regain her composure. "All right. Sit down, and we can discuss this like adults instead of undisciplined children."

Karan opened the first container, releasing the scent of warm milk, saffron, and raisins. "I remember how much you loved Mother's kheer. This is the closest I've found to her recipe."

Priya preferred Italian or Thai food, but the smell of the sweet rice pudding tugged at memories of more sheltered times. She accepted the bowl from Karan. Tradition meant that she was also putting aside their argument by eating with him.

She watched him carefully, noting the subtle signs of subconscious relaxation as he poured himself a cup of badam, warm milk flavored with almonds and spices. His hands were loose on his wrists, and he briefly turned his back to her as he put the extra food on the counter before joining her at the island. *He still trusts me.* Or rather, he trusted her as much as he trusted anyone.

"Thank you, Ekie." She used the old pet name deliberately, curious to see his reaction.

He smiled at her. "We are partners, are we not?"

"Of course." Her suspicions sharpened. In her experience, people rarely stated such things unless they were attempting to lull her into a false sense of security.

"I've decided that, as your partner, I should be taking your advice."

She stirred the kheer with her spoon, waiting for Karan to continue.

"I have resisted harvesting the skin-walkers from Alaska because of the potential cost. I was certain that we could find an appropriate *lalassu* who would be easier to control. But the ones we have are not sufficiently frightening. Accusing clairvoyants of spying or having a telekinetic pinch a blood vessel to cause a heart attack is not visually dramatic enough." Karan paused.

It was a point that she'd made months earlier but he was now repeating as if new. *Very well. I'll play along for now.* "Any *lalassu* that we can control is unlikely to be powerful enough to ignite the public terror that we need. Those who are suitable would be too dangerous to try and bring under our control. It's a difficult line to walk."

"It is. But I had not realized what a valuable resource you could be." Karan lifted his mug in a salute. "Watching you deal with the reporter was an enlightening lesson."

Intriguing. His lips were pursed slightly. He'd done the same thing as a boy when they'd planned mischief together. It suggested he truly did see her as a partner. The thought warmed her, reminding her of the times he'd argued with their parents on her behalf rather than joining in the "accept your fate" chorus. It amused her to realize how far she and he had surpassed their family's limited dreams.

"If we could find a way to collect the creatures, do you believe you could use your talent for manipulation to ensure it could not turn against us?" he asked.

Yes. Instead of answering directly, she pretended to consider the question. "Your notes said that the transformatives displayed considerable loyalty, even at high cost to themselves?"

He tapped his fingers against the thick-sided mug. "That is correct."

"Then I should be able to use their family ties to create a suitable leash." The creatures might make ideal personal guards for herself and Karan once they were co-rulers. The older creatures would have to be eliminated, but children were always easy to manipulate. Even if they were a different species, the cubs should be malleable. "How many communities did you discover?"

"Three so far. The original one in Bear Claw and two more. One in Kamchatka, Russia, and one in northern British Columbia."

"Did they have cubs? Or were there only adults?" she asked.

"They all appear to be breeding populations. I had the same thought to harvest the cubs for future use." Karan pursed his lips again. "I believe that we could move in on the Bear Claw location with sufficient forces to capture a few adults and cull the rest.”

“I’ll begin immediate preparations for a suitable holding place within the city. It would be best to scatter the creatures to prevent a mass escape.” Excitement rushed through her veins at the prospect of finally enacting the next stage of her grand plan.

“I’m sure the doctor would appreciate having some samples for his experiments.” Karan picked up his own bowl of kheer and began to eat. Through the meal, the siblings spoke of other minor annoyances and challenges that had cropped up. Priya found herself preoccupied with mentally designing and redesigning the propaganda material that she intended to create. The images and sequences were so clear in her mind that getting actual film seemed superfluous. Rather like the message she’d sent to her former masters when she’d finally tired of being their kept slave, there would be no room for interpretation. She paused to admire the bangles on her wrist. Even after centuries, they still gleamed. It had been well worth the effort to remove all of her former owner’s blood.

CHAPTER FIFTEEN

"Don't worry, Martha. I'll take good care of her." Eva's bright smile didn't seem to lift Martha's spirits, at least not from Lou's point of view as he lurked to the side. Martha kept reaching toward Bernie then dropping her hands back to her sides. The little girl sat with her back to her mother and her nose buried in a book.

"Thank you, Eva. You can call… oh, I suppose not." Martha flushed, the rush of pink briefly hiding the dark circles under her eyes.

"Don't worry." Eva didn't seem bothered by the mistake. "It took us a while to remember the no-phones thing, too."

Martha didn't meet the teen's gaze, and her hands were constantly tugging at her sleeves or sweater hem. Lou wondered if he should say something. She hadn't slept well, constantly shifting from one side to the other or adjusting the covers and pillow. When she'd first woken, the marks of a wakeful night had been starkly visible on her pale skin, like the shadows of fish moving under the river ice. His own sleeplessness wasn't so obvious.

Harley stepped in. "If there's a problem, Eva can send a messenger to the medical building for you." He hugged his daughter, tugging at her long ponytail.

"You two should get going." Hood took Harley's hand and pulled him close for a tender kiss. "Be safe today."

Harley leaned his forehead against his husband's. "You too."

Martha's expression caught Lou's attention. She had turned aside as the two men embraced, but her gaze kept flickering back to them. Her soft lower lip disappeared between her teeth, and her eyes were sad, as if watching something she could never have but desperately wanted. His instincts pushed him to embrace her again, but his human awareness held him back. Perhaps he'd made a mistake the night before and triggered her restlessness by offering her comfort.

"I'll see you after school, Bernie." Martha slowly gathered her things.

"Sure." Bernie didn't look up as her mother left, accompanied by Harley. Lou frowned. In nature, the parents pushed away their offspring when the caretaking period was over. Bernie's withdrawal seemed premature.

"Our turn to go, big guy." Hood opened the trailer door.

"See you tonight, Dad." Eva shared a brilliant smile, sparking one from Hood in return.

Lou and Hood left the trailer to walk down the wide, muddy road to the camp. Hood did not suffer from the human need to continually chatter, earning Lou's gratitude. Silence gave him a chance to try and sort through the confusing tangle in his mind.

Something had shifted between him and Martha. Or maybe just in him. *Or was it there all along, and I missed it?* Ever since that day in the woods, she'd crept into a permanent place in his awareness. But the night before, thoughts of her had crowded out everything else in his mind. As he ignored the shouts from a passing truck, Lou wondered if he'd been fooled by his own instincts.

Back at Ekurru, he'd thought it must be the skin affecting his mind. Bears mated once per year. Humans mated constantly and frequently. His human body could have been reacting to the presence of an attractive and compassionate woman. He'd told Andrew that he'd come to protect Martha and Bernie, and that was still true. But as he'd stared at the web of brown water stains on the trailer's ceiling through the night, he'd been forced to recognize that it had never been the only reason.

Would I have realized it earlier if we'd spent more time together while she lived in Bear Claw? Or was this always the time and place that fate had chosen for me to realize that my spirit chose Martha as my mate? He hadn't believed the mystical alignment would ever happen to him, but he couldn't deny it.

Somewhere, the gods were laughing at him. He understood why Lily had been so resistant to his anger when she defended her mate. The order of the universe had shifted, placing Martha directly under his protection, above his duties and his family. But he wanted to be more than only a protector to her.

The memory of their embrace sent blood rushing below his belt. Lou shifted uncomfortably, wondering who had designed jeans to chafe so badly. His leather pants allowed plenty of support and room and didn't have anything resembling a seam in the worst possible position. His senses recreated the moment, torturing him. Her honey-blond hair had been so much softer than he'd expected, catching on the rough calluses of his fingers and palms. Her scent had filled the room they shared, all spring flowers and fresh greenery.

What should I do? She wasn't game he could track and hunt. He had no clue how to read the spoor or even which direction to go. He could pursue a full partnership and complete the mating, but was that what Martha would want? She wasn't one of the *lalassu*. She had hated Bear Claw—not overtly, but he'd seen the signs. He couldn't abandon his family and the Colony. He wished he could speak to Andrew. His twin would help him understand what to do next.

Except Lou couldn't wait until he got back to Bear Claw. He needed to find resources at the camp. Lou considered the man walking beside him. Hood was human and a parent, and he'd been mated for a significant time. He might be able to untangle the thorns of human custom for Lou.

"Go through these files and find examples of physical anomalies in the O.H. subjects." Dr. Coulon gestured at the dozen legal-sized boxes sitting in his office. He didn't bother to even raise his head. "I need the information by Friday so that I can prepare a report for my trip."

Sixty files per box. Twelve boxes. Seven hundred and twenty files. All to be processed in only a few days. *Sure, Doc. Want me to organize them all by blood and tissue type, too?* Keeping her lips sealed over her inner sarcasm, Martha picked up the first box. "How long will you be gone?"

"Three to five days. I close the office when I'm not here. You will assist Mrs. Fitz if there are any medical emergencies." He glanced at the box in her hand. "I will not be tolerant of failure due to lack of effort."

It was hard not to stare at the shelves and wonder how to get at the door behind them. Martha nodded and carried the box into the front office. *Maybe I'll be lucky and find something useful in one of these.*

It was easier to think about the files in the boxes than the secret door, and she kept wondering how she could sneak in. Dr. Coulon was in his office before she arrived and still there when she left. If he hadn't changed his clothes, she would assume he hadn't left. His trip should be a good opportunity but not if the office was going to be locked.

She began going through the files, skimming them for physical anomalies, but she only got through a few before the first knock on the door.

It was the old woman and her grandson from the day before. Eyeing her suspiciously, they still wouldn't give her their names, but the cut across the boy's leg was less swollen and red. She gave them another packet of antibiotics along with a surprise. She'd grabbed an extra granola bar from the kitchen this morning. "Here. I thought you might like this since you missed breakfast yesterday."

The boy reached for it but faltered, checking with his grandmother.

Martha held out the granola bar, waiting for the woman to make up her mind. After a long, evaluating look, she nodded. The boy snatched the bar, and the two of them left without a single word.

Unsure whether or not to count the encounter as a win or a loss, Martha sat back down to continue going through the files. Maybe she should go to the construction crew and check up on Tom. *And see Lou,* her libido whispered.

Stop thinking about him. He'd hugged her. That was all. Just because she'd seen him naked didn't mean that her lady bits should be all fired up. For years, she'd focused on her roles as a mother and a provider, shoving the other sides of herself into a deep dark box. *Maybe I shouldn't be surprised that my passionate side is demanding to make up for lost time.*

She shifted on her stool, trying to ease the ache between her thighs. *I have a newfound understanding of how teenage boys feel when they're trying to hide surprise erections.* Which led her to wonder what Lou had done as a teenager and if he—

"Crap." She couldn't remember anything that she'd read in the last two files. She picked them back up and stared at the first one. *I am a grown woman, and this is getting ridiculous. I am way past having crushes.* She buried her face in her hands.

"Hey there, gorgeous. What's up?"

Martha jumped and spun around to see Ryan standing in the doorway with a rifle held loosely in his hands and a sly smile on his face. He clearly enjoyed her reaction and keeping her off-balance. She forced herself into a semblance of calm. "Ryan. Is anything wrong?"

"Oh, I'm as healthy as a fiddle, sweetheart." He winked. "I thought I'd come and check on you."

"On me." Martha realized her fingers were twisting around each other and clasped both of her hands tightly together.

"This can be a scary place. But you don't need to worry. Me and my boys will keep you safe with this." He patted his rifle affectionately before putting it on the counter.

Having the gun so close repulsed her, and she said the first thing that came to mind. "I didn't realize you were in charge of the guards."

"I don't like to brag. So how are you settling in?" He leaned in closer, and Martha tried to breathe shallowly through her mouth to avoid inhaling the miasma of sour sweat and cheap cologne.

Eww. Time to put an end to this farce of flirtation. "I'm quite busy. Is there something you needed?"

"Just stopping by." He briefly ran the edge of his thumb along her upper arm. "And then I saw some of the loocies leaving, and it made me worried."

His touch locked Martha into a rigid pose. *Say something or don't say something.* No matter which option she chose, he would turn it around on her. If she complained, he'd act disappointed and claim it was an accident. If she said nothing, he would continue to push the boundaries. *I'm really not cut out for this.* Dani or Cali would have him spilling whatever he knew with a wink and a flirty hair flip. Lily would be able to knock him into next week, even without transforming into a bear. All Martha could do was sit politely and hope he didn't hear her teeth grinding.

"You know, if you're having problems at home, I'd be happy to lend a sympathetic ear. There's a great place near where we have fires. We could sit outside and look at the stars, and you could tell me anything you wanted. I'd never share it with a soul, darling." Ryan's finger ran from her shoulder down to her elbow.

That's it. She stood up, moving out of his reach. "No, thank you."

"Oh, come on, baby. I can grab a bottle of wine from the warehouse." He leaned against the counter.

She suspected the string of endearments was supposed to be charming, but she also suspected that it was because he'd forgotten her name. *Should I remind him of my pretend marriage? Or is this a test?* Maybe a real spy would encourage him to get information, but the thought of more contact with him made her want to reach for the gun. She straightened and made herself meet his eyes. "No."

"Your loss, sweetheart." He shrugged as if indifferent. "We'll try again another night."

"Mrs. McKinnon," Dr. Coulon called out. "Have you completed your review?"

The doctor's querulous voice had never been so welcome. Martha kept her eyes locked on Ryan. "I have work to do here."

"Me too." His hand darted out and grabbed her elbow, pulling her close. His breath crawled on her cheek like an insect's hairy legs as he whispered, "Don't push me away. You could use a friend like me."

She froze, her mind blanking on what to do next. She couldn't fight him off, and she doubted the doctor would be sympathetic.

He let her go and picked up the rifle from the counter. "I'll see you around, Mrs. McKinnon."

Air rushed out of her lungs as the door finally closed behind him. She twisted the lock closed and leaned against the frame, trying to find her calm. The way he'd said her alias sounded as if he was emphasizing it. *Was he warning me that he knows I'm here under false pretenses?* She doubted he was trying to lure her into an isolated area to dispose of her. As head of the guards, he could kill her without any need for pretense.

She stared at the lock, realizing the uselessness of her actions. Ryan undoubtedly had keys. She sucked in lungfuls of air, reminding her body that breathing was a time-honored tradition while she tried to guess

Ryan's actual goals.

If it was easy sex, surely he could find it from one of the other women in the camp. There weren't many, but Martha wasn't the only one to sport a double-X chromosome. If it was about her task for the *lalassu*, he could have killed her on the spot. *He liked seeing me jump.* She exhaled and closed her eyes. It was her fear that was drawing him to her. That was why he'd targeted her.

In some ways, he reminded her of her ex-husband. Derek had been everyone's friend, charming and pleasant. But as their relationship moved past the first blush of romance, he'd begun to distance himself from her. She'd become more like a member of his staff and a prop for stories at social gatherings, not a cherished and beloved partner. It had taken her years to understand that his abrupt departure was only the inevitable end to their continuing emotional separation. He'd chosen to sneak away because it was the easiest option for him. *And he didn't care about what happened to me or Bernie once we weren't useful to him any longer.*

Her chest ached, and a lump of tears crept up her throat. Even after ten years, it still hurt. She held it at bay, swallowing the tears before they could choke her. *It doesn't matter what he thought. Bernie deserves love and attention, and I've done everything I can to help her.* Her guilty conscience tried to chime in, but Martha quashed it. *I'm a good mother, even when I make mistakes.*

"Mrs. McKinnon," Dr. Coulon called again.

Shit. Martha hurried to his office. "Yes, sir?"

The doctor sat behind his desk, his hands pressed together like the hanging blade of a guillotine. "I am not accustomed to having to wait for a response."

"I'm sorry." Martha kept her gaze on the front of the desk. She could see Dr. Coulon in the reflection but hoped that she seemed sufficiently submissive. "One of the guards had a medical question."

"Hmmm." His irritated rumble did not sound promising. "Are the guards your employer?"

"No, sir." The only thing that gave Martha strength to keep up the pretense was the realization that he seemed unaware that she'd seen him use the secret door. There was no reason for him to play games with her, and she had no doubt that he would have her killed in a moment if he'd known of her discovery.

"Do we need to have a discussion about your conduct in the future?" His tone was clipped, but Martha heard the note of relish underneath.

Let him see you're afraid. "No, sir. I-I'll do better."

"Good." The satisfaction of superiority rang clear. "Now let's see if your medical skills are sharper than your social ones. What do you think of this X-ray?"

Martha took the black-plastic film and looked for a light box. *No electronics. Right.* Instead she lifted it high enough that the light from the narrow windows under the roof would illuminate it. It wasn't easy to read the X-ray in such circumstances, but the film showed a woman's torso— she was probably someone in her early twenties. Her ribs and collarbone seemed normal, but the bones were darker than she would have expected.

"Well?" Dr. Coulon snapped.

"The bones seem to be denser than typical." Martha lowered the film and gave it back to him.

He nodded, excitement softening his voice. "They are both denser and stronger than a human's. This girl could be struck with a baseball bat and not suffer a fracture. Perhaps even a car."

Martha channeled her inner Mr. Spock. "Fascinating."

"Include her information in the packet for my trip." Dr. Coulon waved his hand to dismiss her.

Martha backed away, returning to her stack of files. She still needed to figure out a way to try the secret door while the doctor was away. Hood and Harley had worked with thieves. One of them must be able to pick a lock. They could sneak in overnight... *because I'm sure the guards will be completely understanding if we get caught.* She shook her head at her own inner sarcasm.

"Break down the problem," she whispered to herself. One of Bernie's early therapists had told her that. *Don't get overwhelmed by everything. Find one small part to accomplish and start with it.* She needed to get into Dr. Coulon's office without being discovered and with enough time to find the secret mechanism to release the door. She needed to find out what he was hiding in a place that he already ruled absolutely.

SELF-AWARENESS

CHAPTER SIXTEEN

"All right, break for lunch," the foreman called out, his reddened skin bright with sweat. Lou could smell the sour stench easily, despite being at least a hundred feet away. The other men set down their tools and began to walk to the administrative building, but Lou hung back, staring at the medical building.

Ryan had gone in there during the morning. When he'd come out, he'd looked straight at Lou and saluted before walking away. Since then, Lou had been keeping careful watch on the building, but there had been no sign of Martha. His inner bear was restless, which made it hard to resist the urge to go and check on her.

A large hand clamped on his shoulder. Immediately, Lou shrugged it off and turned to face his attacker. The muscles in his neck, back, and arms began to ripple as he prepared to shift.

"Come on, Lou." Hood spoke each word clearly, his hands lifted with his palms facing out. "We should go get our food before it's gone."

There was no one else nearby. Lou took a deep breath, testing the air for foreign scents. Nothing. His body and spirit calmed as he realized he'd mistaken Hood's touch for aggression. Still, he couldn't help staring at the walls that hid Martha from him.

"She's okay," Hood warned in a low voice. "But if you keep drawing attention to her, she might not be."

She was supposed to be his wife. That was the lie they'd told. *Human husbands check on their mates, don't they?* Reluctantly, Lou followed Hood. If the other man said it would be a mistake, Lou needed to trust him. With

149

the mating instinct so new, restraining himself would be difficult, but no more than wading through thigh-deep snow to check traplines. It was unpleasant but necessary.

The meal waiting for them in the cafeteria did nothing to distract him from his mental obsession. It was a glue-like mixture of processed cheese and pasty noodles along with a hard brown roll. Lou watched it glop off his fork and wished he could go hunting for some deer—even rabbit. The only thing appealing about the mixture was the number of calories he would gain. Thick with fat and sugar, it would build his reserves for winter.

Hood ate quietly beside him. None of the other construction workers tried to join their table. Their chatter quickly filled the room with meaningless noise. Lou reminded himself again that humans made noise like crows. He and Hood sat together, the only silent ones in the flock.

"Hey, bro. You slackin' off again?" Harley clunked a plastic tray on the table as he sat down. Lou's fingers tightened over his fork. He hadn't heard the other man approach over the general noise.

"Be quiet, or I'll tell Momma that you've been disrespectful." Hood grinned. "Sit down and fill that ugly maw of yours."

Lou watched the two men trade friendly insults. Their bodies were telling a different tale from the one that morning in the trailer. Then, they'd been birds building a nest together. In the cafeteria, they were more like two rocks tumbling down the same slope. There was no real connection other than a shared direction.

"So, you're into Martha, huh?" Harley's words burst out of the background noise like a flower on a barren field.

Lou straightened his neck, scanning the room. None of the other men were paying attention.

"Keep it quiet, big man. We're just a couple of guys talking about women. Nothing unusual." Hood followed his own quiet advice, poking at his meal with his fork.

Lou did the same, but his arms and legs were tense and ready to move at a moment's notice.

"You're wondering how I knew." Harley's smile only grew wider. "Trust me, I can recognize the look on a man's face when he finally realizes that he wants someone."

"Careful." Hood laid his fork flat on the table.

"You worry too much, brother." Harley emphasized the last word. "So what are you going to do, Lou?"

"About what?" Lou asked cautiously.

"About next year's presidential candidates." Harley snorted. "About Martha, duh. Are you going to ask her out?"

"This isn't our concern." Hood glared at his husband.

"Oh, please, like you aren't as curious as I am." Harley waved off Hood's complaints. "If you want a romantic meal from the kitchen, I can oblige. Speaking of which, here." Harley slid each of them a sealed yogurt. "Compliments of Eva."

Lou tore off the plastic top, enjoying the mixed scent of cream and blueberries. He ate the contents quickly.

"So, enough stalling. What are you going to do?" Harley asked eagerly.

"I don't know." Lou sniffed the emptied yogurt container and reluctantly put it aside.

"Oh, I get it. You like her, but you haven't gotten the courage to act on it yet." Harley shrugged. "That can take more time."

More time wouldn't make their differences any easier. And it would only make the mating urge harder to fight.

"Maybe he doesn't want to talk about it." Hood's glare had no impact on Harley's enthusiasm.

"You strong, silent types are all the same. Trust me, Lou, this is one of the many times when using your words is better than the alternative."

Lou regretted sharing his feelings with them. There were enough conflicting thoughts in his head without adding more opposing voices.

"What are you boys talking about?" An unwelcome interruption broke the conversation. Ryan walked toward their table with his rifle slung prominently over his shoulder.

Lou stared at him, unblinking, letting his feral nature rise to just below his human surface.

Ryan's steps faltered and slowed as he came to a stop several feet away from the table. He seemed confused. He wanted to dominate Lou, but from the way he moved, deeply buried physical instincts were warning him away, screaming at him to run. Lou leaned back, wondering if the man would realize his mistake.

"Having trouble, Chief?" Ryan's words cracked aggressively.

The room had fallen silent, with everyone's face turned to Ryan and Lou.

Lou continued to stare at him with a bear's eyes, weighing the effort required for a kill against the gorging possibilities after. He would not start the fight, but if Ryan insisted on pursuing violence, Lou would finish it. Meanwhile, he would not engage. Bullies like Ryan were comfortable with conflict. By refusing to participate, Lou could continue to make him more and more unsettled.

When it became clear that Lou was not going to respond, Ryan began to look foolish. A few quiet chuckles throughout the room brought a red flush to his ears. Ryan shot all three of them an irritated and suspicious frown before backing down and retreating. Lou kept his eyes fixed on him until Ryan started talking loudly to the kitchen staff.

"That man will be trouble," Hood said. "I haven't seen him like this before."

"He can tell that Lou isn't impressed by him, and it's driving him nuts." Harley stirred his yogurt.

The airport. Ryan had been frightened by Lou's initial appearance, and his attempts to frighten or attack Lou could be an effort to balance the scales. It was eventually going to build up to a physical challenge. Ryan couldn't win, but the fight would likely reveal Lou's true nature.

"Is he why you don't want to talk about Martha?" Harley asked. "Trust me, she doesn't like him. But I think she likes you."

"There's too much going on to add a relationship into the mix." Hood's fork banged against the tray in emphasis.

"Oh, please. That's what you said when we were taking down the Black-Swan trafficking ring." Harley reached out and squeezed his husband's hand.

Hood jerked his hand away, checking quickly over both shoulders. His action surprised Lou, especially when he saw the hurt expression on Harley's face.

"Come on, Lou. Lunch break is over." Hood stood up, his neck and shoulders tense with anger. Lou rose with him, watching both men carefully for cues.

"I'll get your trays. See you later." Harley didn't make eye contact with Hood, concentrating instead on gathering utensils and dishes onto one tray. Hood walked away without another word. Lou followed, chased by Ryan's triumphant and obnoxious laughter.

Lou and Hood walked in silence through the empty grounds and abandoned construction site. The imprisoned *lalassu* were gathered by the gate, waiting for their chance to feed.

"I hate having to do that." Hood exhaled, staring at the ground. "He just…"

Lou waited for the other man to finish, but no more words came. Hood stood there, his hands on his hips and his head bent, alternating between what looked like anger and shame.

He quickly raised his head. "He knows what's at stake, how careful we have to be. But he doesn't get it down here." Hood's fist circled his stomach.

Lou wasn't sure he got it at all. He knew the two men were hiding their mating but had ignored the reasoning behind it as an incomprehensible human custom. "Does pretending to be mated put Martha in danger?"

"What?"

"You are pretending not to be mated. Is mating dangerous for humans?" Lou didn't think that was the case, but he needed to be certain.

"No." Hood checked the immediate area. "Being married isn't dangerous for you and Martha. But it is for me and Harley."

Lou frowned, not understanding the difference. Hood took him by the arm and began to walk toward the camp fence.

"Can you smell anyone around?" Hood asked.

"We are alone." He wasn't a bloodhound, but years of practice looking for the telltale grass shivers that signaled a rabbit below worked just as well.

"Okay, so here's how it is." Hood began to talk quickly. "There are lots of people who don't like the idea of two men being married. Some people will get angry if they see two men together. Some would try to hurt us or even kill us."

Humans were even more bizarre than Lou had imagined. It was a wonder the species had survived at all.

"A place like this, with a lot of young men all stuck together… it's dangerous for Harley and me. They're all trying to out-macho each other, which means attacking any sign of being gay." Hood sighed. "We knew we would have to hide. I thought we were both ready for it. But it's harder than I thought it would be."

Humans spend so much time in pretense. More than any other animal. Lou had watched other herd and pack animals try rudimentary deception, usually around food. Only humans lied about anything and everything. Hood's confession was the first time Lou heard one admit that it was difficult.

"When we first met, Harley was out, but I wasn't." Hood paused.

"Out?" Lou didn't think he'd heard the word correctly.

Hood started again. "Harley didn't hide that he liked men. He was one of the elite Dark Net hackers, so he could afford to be more obvious. People needed his skills too much. I was in a gang, and he hired us to take down a human-trafficking ring that sold people, usually children."

A growl boiled up, vibrating Lou's teeth as his shoulders bunched.

"Yeah, I hear you, big guy." Hood's anger softened. "Harley and I spent a lot of time working together, and it was torture. My gang didn't know I was gay and would have killed me if they'd found out. And here was this funny, wonderful, gorgeous man with a heart of gold, and I had to pretend I wasn't interested."

Perhaps Hood would be able to help Lou pretend he wasn't interested in Martha.

"We would have walked away from each other and always regretted it if he hadn't made the first move," Hood finished, smiling. Then the smile vanished. "Now I have to do it all again. Pretending I don't feel anything for him, no touching, constantly looking over our shoulders. I hate it!"

The noisy exchanges of other men returning to the construction site warned them that time was nearly up. Lou wanted to do something to help Hood's obvious sadness and anger. He'd seemed happy talking about Harley's first move. Lou asked. "What was the first move?"

Hood straightened. "Excuse me?"

"Harley's first move. What was it?"

"I came home to my bed, and he was waiting for me, naked." Hood's shoulders eased. "After that night, I knew I couldn't go through life without him. Being with him made me happier than I ever could have imagined. I faked my death so my gang wouldn't follow us, and he wrote us new identities. We started our lives together the next day, and we've never looked back."

Lou wasn't sure he understood. "Being naked is part of human mating?"

"Yeah. A big part." Hood's lips curled in a quick smile.

"You boys, back to work!" the foreman shouted. Hood and Lou separated, but Lou found himself dwelling on Hood's words, rolling in them to catch all the flavor.

He'd been so eager to escape from the flimsy, constrictive clothing the night before that he had been solely focused on the relief. He'd noticed her discomfort but thought his error was in not being modest. He hadn't considered she might have believed he was signaling a desire to mate. Her discomfort could have been a rejection. The idea sat heavily in his heart and mind even as he tried to tell himself that it was good if she wasn't interested. He reminded himself of the barriers between them.

"Chief!" the foreman shouted, grabbing Lou's arm. "Think you can pay attention and…"

He trailed off as Lou straightened and looked down at the pale hand gripping his forearm. He reached over and grasped the foreman's knuckles, using a fraction of his strength to slowly and carefully lift the other man's hand away, dropping it as soon as possible.

The foreman squawked and clutched his hand. Lou realized he might have damaged something.

"You son of a bitch!" The foreman began to spew obscenities and insults at Lou.

The wise move would have been for Lou to submit, especially after the encounter with Ryan in the cafeteria. There were too many secrets at risk. But his animal instinct kept his spine straight and his hands loose. The top of the foreman's head only came to Lou's shoulder, and while the man was muscular, he was no match for Lou's bearish build. There was something primal at work, a subconscious hierarchy that had nothing to do with the humans' titles and charts, and Lou could feel it deep in his bones. He could not afford to lose the challenge.

The other men had gathered around, watching to see how Lou

would react to the threat.

"Come on. I'll take you over to medical." Hood inserted himself between Lou and the foreman. "The rest of you, back to work."

A grumble of disappointment rose from the crowd. Lou joined a crew digging a new foundation. Behind him, the foreman shouted orders as he left, washing away the sting of his injury by dominating men who had already submitted.

"Be careful, Chief."

Lou couldn't tell which of the men had whispered the warning. All of them had their heads bent, attention focused on their work. He did the same, wondering if there might be more.

"If you cause trouble, you won't last long out here." It was the man next to him, an older man with only three fingers on his right hand.

Lou glanced at the *lalassu* waiting behind the camp fence, passive, broken, and outnumbering the guards twenty to one. Troublemakers would have been too much of a threat. The guards would have to deal with any defiance quickly and definitively. He'd walked the full perimeter, and there were no signs of carrion pits or graves. *Could they be keeping them all in detention?*

"He works with the doc." The next whisper was even quieter. "Stay away from him."

That was the second warning he'd gotten about the doctor, and Martha spent her days alone with him. Once again, Lou's gaze fixed on the blue medical building with the ease of a compass finding north. The wooden shovel handle creaked in his grip, the thick shaft ready to snap.

CHAPTER SEVENTEEN

Martha's palms were sweating enough to leave damp spots on her trousers as she stood in front of Mrs. Fitz's desk. Dr. Coulon had flown out the night before, and Martha had spent a sleepless night trying to think about how to get into the medical building—or at least not to think about the fact that Lou was sleeping naked only a few feet away.

The office despot ignored her and scratched her pencil across the ledger. The urge to walk away was so strong that Martha's legs trembled, but she held tightly to her courage. Sooner or later, Mrs. Fitz would get tired of her manipulative power plays.

"What is it you want?"

"I'm so sorry to trouble you, Mrs. Fitz, but I need the keys to the medical building."

Mrs. Fitz put down the pencil and folded her hands neatly on top of the desk. "I wasn't informed of a medical emergency."

Martha had spent most of the night crafting her excuse before abandoning it for what was effectively the truth. "I know, but I've been treating one of the internees for a bad infection, a little boy. He needs his dose of antibiotics. I was planning to give it to him when I do the rounds of the camp today."

Eyes narrowing, Mrs. Fitz didn't seem convinced. "The doctor didn't tell me about you doing rounds."

Martha swallowed a hysterical impulse to compliment the other woman on her stern librarian impression. *Keep a straight face.* "He doesn't want the internees bothering him when he returns."

"Why did you not obtain the medication before leaving yesterday?" Mrs. Fitz asked.

Martha made her eyes go wide and kept her mouth from smiling. The rush of a successful lie was more thrilling than she would have guessed. "I'm so ashamed. I forgot about them completely."

"Hmmph." Mrs. Fitz scowled but, as Martha expected, opened a drawer and fished out two sets of keys. Martha recognized one as the set for the internal cabinets, but the other was the much larger bunch attached to the wooden block—they had to be the master keys to the entire camp. "I expect these back promptly."

"Thank you so much." Martha backed away, keeping a firm lid on her impulse to bolt and escape. With Mrs. Fitz expecting her to be in the camp for the morning, she'd have time to search for Dr. Coulon's secret files. The document-scanner-makeup kit and the camera pen were ready in her purse, along with a small flashlight. Once she'd copied what the *lalassu* needed, she could concentrate on keeping her head down for the rest of her contract and keeping a closer eye on Bernie. Her daughter had gotten used to a lot of freedom while they were in Bear Claw. However, Martha wasn't as comfortable with Bernie going in and out of the *lalassu* camp. An undercurrent of resentment and anger could explode with the right spark.

I can't blame them. They'd been taken from their homes, held in a horrific place, and had their families split up, so the people behind the fence had every reason to be angry. But angry people weren't good at picking targets for their rage. They tended to settle for whoever was convenient, and Martha was determined it would not be her or Bernie. But as she glanced over at the kids playing behind the fence, the decision to hold back didn't sit well. *I used to be a good person who helped other people.*

There were nearly thirty different keys on the ring, and Martha tried twelve of them before she found the one that unlocked the front door of the medical building. Hurrying inside, she locked the door behind her. There wouldn't be a lot of time before Mrs. Fitz would expect her back with the master keys.

Taking a deep breath, she made her way to Dr. Coulon's office, taking the time to carefully close the door behind her. Then she stared at the bookshelf, trying to decipher its secrets.

It was about six feet wide and loaded with various medical texts in glossy leather bindings with gold lettering. Faint dents in the industrial carpeting arced to the left, tracing its movement. Martha tugged on the right-hand side, hoping for the obvious and easy solution, but without luck.

Okay, let's look at less obvious ideas. She pulled the flashlight out of her bag, flicked it on, and leaned to the left to shine the light behind the bookcase. A reflection glinted off tiny brass hinges joining the bookcase to the wall at regular intervals. Then she moved to the right, where there was nothing as obvious as polished brass, but she could see two long, slender shadows at the top and bottom, close to the right-hand edge. The gap was too narrow to wiggle her fingers inside, but there was something odd on the side of the bookshelf, about two feet off the ground.

If she hadn't been shining the light, she probably wouldn't have noticed the odd shadow cast by a narrow, flat piece of metal, like a brace but painted to match the pressboard whorls of the bookcase exactly. It was at knee height, placed to run parallel to the floor, and had a small dent in the end furthest from the wall like the divot at the top of the blade of a Swiss Army knife.

Martha dug her finger into the mark, and the metal tab swung out easily. Cautiously, she tried pushing it down. No movement. The fear that someone would notice what she was doing sent chilly tendrils of sweat sliding down her hair. She tried lifting it and discovered that it raised like the latch at the base of a French door.

Inspired by the mental comparison, she reached up to the top of the bookcase and patted with blind fingers, quickly discovering a similar tab. She pushed it up and the entire bookcase swung gently away from the wall.

Her heart thudded as she prepared to run, but there were no alarms or crashing boots. She pushed the bookcase open farther, surprised at how effortlessly and soundlessly it moved. Unlike the rest of the camp's ad hoc construction, it had been made with extreme care and skill. On the back of the bookcase, there were narrow rings and sliding bolts that matched with more rings on the revealed door.

Martha studied the hidden door. It looked like a typical front door, one that wouldn't be out of place in an apartment. She turned the brass tab to unlock the deadbolt, and it clicked back. Taking a deep breath, she opened the door.

On the other side was a dark narrow landing and a set of stairs to the left, leading down. She could see dim light at the bottom. Feeling like the idiot girl in a horror movie, Martha slowly made her way down the steps. At the base was a short hall and a curtain of thick plastic strips that could be used in a walk-in freezer.

Just a few more steps. Then she could snap pictures and hurry back upstairs, leaving no one the wiser about her explorations. She pushed through the plastic strips.

"Well, you certainly aren't what I expected," a wry but soft male voice exclaimed.

Martha gasped, inhaling a lungful of stinging disinfectant and an underlying sour mustiness. The room and its contents blurred as her shocked brain tried to process it, but one thing remained crystal clear. The row of cells along the far wall had people in them.

"You're not like the others." The voice came from a heavy man with dark skin who stood at the metal bars of the cell farthest to the right. "Welcome."

"She can't let us out," the teenager in the middle cell said. His jaw was covered with blond fuzz and acne. He rocked back and forth on a narrow cot.

The cell on the left held a young woman, her short black hair sticking up in spikes. She was curled up in the corner, as far as possible from the cell door and with her face turned to the back wall. All three of them were wearing plain blue hospital scrubs that were far too thin for the damp, chilly air.

"Wasting time," the teenager said, not looking up. He began to mutter to himself. It sounded like mathematical equations.

"Who are you?" Martha asked as her mind tried to scramble for a logical and not-horrible reason why people would be in hidden cells.

"My name is Kaleonahe, but everyone calls me Kal. I taught elementary school in Waipahu, in Hawai'i." The heavy man smiled broadly.

"I'm Martha," she replied automatically, her mind still trying to find a reasonable explanation for why people would be held prisoner down here. Meanwhile, her adrenal glands went into overdrive, prepping her to flee at a moment's notice.

"That's Patrick next door. He lived in a group home for special-needs teenagers. Somewhere in Wisconsin, I believe. And Annika is beside him. She used to work for a company in Los Angeles." Kal settled himself on the cot, reaching underneath it to pull out a tattered book. "It's a pleasure to meet you, Martha. I don't suppose you happened to bring any books with you? I've read this one a dozen times already."

"Sorry, I didn't," Martha said. Kal didn't sound like he was dangerous. Patrick's odd-but-harmless constant calculating reminded Martha of Bernie. Annika seemed more depressed than aggressive. Why—

"We're here because we are the most powerful *lalassu* that Dr. Coulon found here in camp. He has been experimenting on us, trying to understand the limits of our abilities. And yes, I am a mind reader," Kal explained with another smile. "It's such a pleasure to see a friendly aura for a change."

Secret experiments sounded too horrible to believe, but Martha couldn't hide behind denial any longer. The room was a laboratory fit for a mad scientist. A gurney fitted with restraints stood in the center, the pale vinyl surface stained with faded patches of darker and lighter browns, the irregular edges darker than the center. Scalpels gleamed on a metal tray nearby. A wide drain in the concrete floor steamed in the chill air. The walls were all dark cinderblock, except for a second plastic-strip curtain.

Kal pointed to the second curtain. "It leads to tunnels to the other secret areas in the complex. I wouldn't recommend exploring."

Martha only recognized half of the equipment in the lab and didn't want to guess at the other half. "I don't know what to say."

"Take your pictures and make sure that the doctor's actions do not disappear into forgotten history," Kal gently prompted. "And try not to feel badly about us. If you tried to help us escape, you and your family would end up in a shallow grave in the tundra. You need to protect your daughter. I understand that."

He understood, but Martha wasn't sure that she did anymore. Her fingers closed on the camera pen but couldn't quite pull it out. It seemed heartless to simply take pictures and leave. Except Kal was right. If she let them out, there was nowhere to take them but into the camp itself. They'd be recaptured too quickly. *Maybe Lou could help us, get us all out through the woods.* Or maybe not. She might not be an experienced frontierswoman, but she knew enough to know that taking care of three people was a lot different than taking care of six.

Even if she wanted to, she couldn't go ask him. Mrs. Fitz would be expecting her keys back, and once they were in the drawer, Martha would be locked out of the medical building until Dr. Coulon's return. And then she wouldn't be able to sneak past him.

"It's all right, Martha. We understand." Kal leaned back against the wall and closed his eyes. Patrick was still rocking back and forth and chattering his formulas. Annika hunched tighter into a ball, both arms wrapped around her legs.

"I'm sorry," Martha whispered, pulling out the pen camera. She took as many pictures as she could, feeling like a complete failure of a human being.

"Don't be too hard on yourself." Kal pointed through the bars. "He keeps his secret records in there. You should document those as well."

Martha opened the unlocked cupboard and used the document scanner to capture the files inside, each documenting incredible cruelty in neat notes and color photos. Halfway through the first, the reel jammed, refusing to advance. She realized she must have reached the end of the roll. "I have to go."

Kal opened his eyes again. "It was a pleasure to meet you, Martha. I wish you well. And don't worry about the book. We'll be fine."

She went back upstairs, clutching the precious evidence. With everything locked up and replaced, there was no evidence she had been in the secret lab. She could walk away.

The people down there couldn't walk away. Neither could the people trapped behind the fence. Martha stood in the middle of the front office, her feet frozen by conflicting impulses. She wanted to run and hide and pretend none of it had ever happened. She wanted to find her daughter and hold her close, promising to keep her safe. She wanted to scream her knowledge to the world. She wanted to take all of the people here, especially those downstairs, and make sure they were all safe and secure in their own homes. She wanted the world to be a better one than it was.

But it wasn't. It was a horrible, cruel world where doing the right thing would only be punished. The people controlling the camp were powerful, with long reaches and deep resources. Martha couldn't hope to take them on single-handedly. They would squash her and never even break stride.

What can I do? The evidence was in her bag. She could bring it to others and let them fight the Goliaths. That was all she'd been asked to do.

Did they hold Bernie in a place like that? From her descriptions, the lab she'd been held in sounded more like a cheap hostel than a terrifying dungeon. Even so, it was just as bad. Her little girl had been a captive used for experimentation, like the people downstairs. There had been nurses and other staff who had seen Bernie and done nothing to help. They were doing their jobs and nothing more.

Like I'm doing now.

She closed her eyes, guilt pulling her down like lead weights attached to every limb. Her hands landed on the examination bed, fingers digging into the rough wool blanket folded over one end. *How did I get here?* Fifteen years ago, she had been happily married, preparing to become a mother. Life seemed to promise so much back then. *And now I live in a trailer under an assumed name, on the run from the government and trapped in the middle of a camp that would fit right in with Nazi Germany.*

Not exactly how I predicted my life would go. A weak laugh escaped Martha's lips as she rubbed at her face, breaking the immobilizing tension. *Break down the problem.* The first thing she needed to do was to not get caught. Otherwise, all of it would be for nothing, and no one would ever know about it. That meant she needed to take the keys back to Mrs. Fitz and make sure there were no traces that Martha had been inside the building during Dr. Coulon's absence.

The blanket on the examining table was bunched up, and Martha automatically smoothed it. It was there for cases of exposure or shock. *Too bad I can't take it down to Kal and the others. It's so cold down there.*

Martha's hand froze on the gray wool. She couldn't take that blanket down to them. Aside from the fact that it was only one blanket and there were three of them, it would be missed if they did have an emergency. But the warehouse was only across the yard, and she held the master keys. Blankets wouldn't solve everything, but they would help to keep Annika,

Kal, and Patrick warm. Maybe it was only a small act of compassion, but it felt like the first step back to becoming the person she used to be. *And it's not a bigger risk than walking around with recordings of secret documents.*

She cracked open the door and took a cautious look around. There were a few guards visible, but they were focused on the internees, not on the area between the medical building and the warehouse. She eased the door closed again. *Think it through.* She still had to return the keys to Mrs. Fitz, and it had already been too long. There wasn't time to run across to the warehouse then take the blankets down to the cells.

But do I have to return the whole ring? There must have been a hundred keys. *Would Mrs. Fitz notice if one or two were missing?* Martha couldn't guess at how observant Mrs. Fitz was, but as she stared at the silver keys, an idea came to her.

She dug in her purse and found an old set of house keys from two years before. They had belonged to an older woman who had rented her garage apartment to Martha, Shawna, and Bernie. After two months, they'd left in the middle of the night because of an incident with Bernie and Chuck. Martha had always meant to mail the keys back to their landlady, but it never seemed safe to do so.

The door key was a similar color and shape to the ones on Mrs. Fitz's ring. Martha found the key to the medical building again and slowly eased it off the ring, replacing it with the old door key. She locked the door, left the actual key loose in her pocket, and walked briskly to the warehouse.

Finding the warehouse key was easier than finding the one for medical building. One key was larger than the others, with a big square end, like one she'd had to the front door of an apartment. It proved to be one that unlocked the warehouse door. But the lock relocked itself as soon as she pulled the key out. Glancing around to make sure no one was watching, she unlocked it again and eased it open slightly. Kneeling down, she snatched a small rock and jammed it into the gap between the door and the frame.

Then, with her heart pounding, she hurried across the yard and returned the keys to Mrs. Fitz. The other woman barely acknowledged the return, sniffed at Martha's supposed stupidity, and ordered her to return after lunch to organize the file room.

Instead of going to the cafeteria, Martha walked past the door to the file room and straight to the warehouse. The door was still propped open, and she slipped inside, checking nervously over her shoulder.

The blankets were on a shelf near the front. Martha pulled down three, all identical to the gray wool already in the medical building. Walking out, she felt as if everyone would know that she was taking something that didn't belong to her, but no one seemed to notice or care. Fear had dictated her actions for too long.

She walked back to the medical building and let herself in, her heart galloping with exhilaration and purpose. There was no turning back.

CHAPTER EIGHTEEN

"Dr. Coulon, thank you so much for making the trip to speak with us." Karan smiled pleasantly despite the other man's scowl. Priya presented the doctor with a glass cup of steaming coffee on a delicate china saucer. The overhead lights in the office caught the heavy gold bangles on her wrists.

Coulon took the drink with barely a glance at Priya. "Are you going to tell me why I need to be wasting my time here instead of doing my research?"

"We are rapidly approaching the deadline." Karan adjusted his stance carefully, sharpening the regal tilt of his chin but keeping his arms close to his body. The doctor was proud and sensitive, as were most men who dominated through intellect. Too much confrontation, and Coulon would throw a temperamental-artist's tantrum. But with an opportunity to lecture a superior, there would be no shutting the man up.

"All the more reason for me to be in my lab." After taking a hefty swallow of coffee, he lifted his thin eyebrows above the wire rims of his glasses. The surprise quickly changed back into irritation, and Coulon stalked over to the trio of chairs and presided over a selection of pastries and cheeses.

Priya's smooth face betrayed no glee as the doctor willingly walked onto the stage they had set. She offered Karan a white china cup full of jasmine tea, taking her own cup with her to the chairs. He reminded himself to apologize to her after the meeting. Providing Coulon with his favorite brand of coffee had seemed too simplistic to be effective, but the

166

momentary pleasant surprise had derailed the doctor's rant, which allowed them to move on to more productive conversation.

"Do you believe that any of your current subjects might be suitable to inspire public fear?" Priya asked, cradling her teacup with her fingertips.

"No." Dr. Coulon's flat reply didn't offer any room for interpretation. "The telepath is effective at short ranges. Sixty feet appears to be the outer limit. He can pick up any conscious thought but is unable to probe past the surface. The boy's ability to predict future trends through pattern recognition has been lucrative for stock market investments, but he's more likely to inspire greed than fear. The girl is the most disappointing. Her skin is invulnerable, resisting penetration by both scalpel and projectile, but the flesh beneath is not resistant to damage. She does not have above average strength or stamina, making her practically useless. There are a few other candidates within the camp, but they frankly show even less promise. The telekinetic was my most promising subject."

"Then it would seem your experiments are not worth further pursuit." Karan shrugged, aware that the dismissal would further prickle the doctor's ego.

"Or perhaps we've been asking the wrong questions," Priya interjected smoothly before Coulon could react. "The doctor's work could be incredibly valuable after this initial phase is complete."

She had surprised the doctor again. Karan noted a slight loosening of the jaw, barely noticeable unless one was looking for it.

"The boy's ability to examine a wide range of data and provide accurate predictions could be used for more than the stock market. He could be given security data and possibly pinpoint the truly dangerous from the braggart's chatter." Priya turned wide eyes to the doctor. "Isn't that right, Dr. Coulon?"

"Of course." Flattery might have preened Coulon's ego, but it didn't soften his tone. "The telepath could prove useful for interrogations. If we could find or breed others with similar abilities, they would make excellent spies. The girl has no real practical use, but perhaps dissection could lead to improvements in protective armor."

"Excellent points. But we still require a suitable event to catalyze public reaction." Karan leaned forward. "We have a proposal, but we will need your help, Doctor."

Coulon set down his coffee. "What is it you have in mind?"

"In the final year of my employ with Mr. Dalhard, we discovered an enclave of individuals who could physically shift shape between human and animal—grizzly bears, to be precise." Karan noticed the other man's mouth twitching downward in disbelief. "You must have seen the video. I can assure you it was entirely accurate."

"But the conversion of mass—"

"Will be the subject of scientific investigation." Priya leaned forward. "It could revolutionize our understanding of biology and physics."

"I need access to test subjects." Academic greed ignited in the doctor's expression. Karan had seen it before in men whose pursuit of knowledge was unfettered by morality.

"Exactly what we were hoping for." Karan pulled out a tablet from its hiding place, tucked beside the chair. He tapped the screen to begin a video playback.

A pale man in his thirties appeared, his round face and bald scalp marked with cuts and purple bruises. One of his eyes was swollen almost completely shut. Karan allowed his lips to curl in satisfaction. Bob Villeneuve might have thought he was in control, posting the shifting video on multiple media platforms to get back at his ex-wife, but he had quickly learned otherwise.

"My name is Bob, and I used to be a pilot, flying in the Yukon." His words were halting, probably because Bob was still getting used to the gaps in his mouth where broken teeth had been removed. "During that time, I lived in a small settlement in Bear Claw National Park, known as Ekurru. There were many *lal*—O.H.s who were able to transform themselves between human and animal."

The video continued for several minutes as Bob described the Colony and those who lived in it. His bitter eagerness caused him to spit out details faster than his battered mouth could manage as he talked about the Charging Bull family and explained their connection to the giant, intelligent bears who lived nearby. "They can't all transform, but the ones who can have put themselves in charge of it all. Lily Charging Bull is the worst, putting on airs and deciding who can stay and who can go. Her brothers, Lou and Andrew, are the same, no better than animals themselves."

Reluctantly, Karan stopped the video. From there, the man dissolved into ranting, blaming the Charging Bulls for breaking up his marriage, forcing him out of Ekurru, and destroying the social order. Interestingly enough, he never mentioned his ex-wife by name or ability, showing that he still wanted to protect her. It was a useless effort, given that Karan and Priya were already perfectly aware of Evonne Villeneuve and her enhanced tactile abilities, but they had not needed to use it as an encouragement tactic.

"He's telling the truth?" Dr. Coulon lifted his gaze to Priya and Karan.

"His information is accurate, though his interpretation is regrettably biased." Priya sipped her tea. "The data remained consistent throughout rigorous interrogation."

"These creatures could be what we need. But we require someone with your skills and understanding to quickly evaluate the candidates once they have been harvested. Then we can use the largest and most aggressive to launch a public attack." Karan tasted his own drink. He must remember to compliment Priya's people. The flavor was satisfyingly rich, lingering on his tongue.

"You want to attack humans?" Coulon's gaze darted between the two of them.

"A controlled attack with minimal casualties, quickly stopped. We will then show the predators in their human form and reveal the attack was a coordinated effort to free the detainees," Karan said. "Faced with video of a vicious assault by an organized and ruthless enemy, the lagging public support will be revitalized."

"I could have nearly unlimited funding for my research," Dr. Coulon mused.

"Along with a superior quality of test subjects." Priya laid her fingertips on Coulon's arm. "Do we have your support?"

"Of course, my dear." Coulon put his hand over Priya's and squeezed.

Karan caught his sister's nearly invisible flinch at the man's touch. *Do not spoil the deal now*, he reminded himself, reining in his anger at Coulon's presumption. *The man is still useful.* Karan rose, forcing the doctor to do the same. "Dalhard Industries' private jet is waiting and at your disposal. It will take you to the harvesting team waiting in Juneau."

James Bond never has to deal with his heart pounding so fast that it feels like he's going to throw up. Martha swallowed, clasping the blankets tightly despite the rough wool scratching the bare skin above her collar and past her cuffs. Although she'd locked the main door behind her and pulled the bookcase closed over the secret entrance, her feet wouldn't move as the rational side of her brain reminded her of the consequences of being caught. *Just remember, this isn't about being an action hero. It's about being a decent person.*

She made herself take the first step then the next and the next until she reached the bottom.

"Martha, you didn't have to do this." Kal stood by the bars, his round arms folded over his broad chest.

"Yes, I did." She separated the first blanket and pushed it through the bars of his cage. "Is there room to hide it along with the book?"

"There is." He held it as if it were something precious and delicate instead of a mass-produced mash-up of close-woven fibers. "Thank you. And you don't need to be ashamed of yourself. I'm sure even Mr. Bond was nervous in the beginning."

She smiled at Kal's encouragement, pushing the next blanket through the bars of Patrick's cell. It plopped onto the end of the cot, and he didn't seem to notice. Martha weighed the benefits of pointing it out to him. The way he rocked and muttered, he might be caught in a manic state. She remembered Bernie's manic fits too clearly to risk interrupting him. Maybe Kal could remind Patrick about it later.

"Change in variables… Increased probability of detection." Patrick's voice rose, a hint of panic lifting the pitch closer to a child's than an adult's as he began to rattle off numbers and formulas.

"It will be all right," Kal called out. "I'll know when someone is coming, and we can hide the blankets."

"Possibility of successful concealment, seventy-three-point-oh-two-five-seven percent." Patrick's frantic movements slowed. Martha breathed a sigh of relief.

"Practically a guarantee." Kal winked at Martha. He'd wrapped the blanket around his shoulders like a shawl.

Patrick's skinny fingers grabbed the wool and draped it over his legs, leaving his torso free to keep moving.

Annika hadn't changed position or said anything. Martha wondered if she was even aware of what was happening around her. She seemed so small and young, curled up on the cot with her back to the horrors of the lab.

"Hello? Annika?" Martha called out softly, not wanting to wake the girl if she was sleeping. "I brought you something."

The dark-haired girl didn't move, but her breathing sped up. She wasn't asleep, just ignoring Martha and the others.

I can't blame her for that. Whatever they had done to her must have been horrible enough to break her spirit. Martha eased the blanket between the bars. "It's inside if you want it."

She wanted to linger, to do more, but there was nothing left that she could do. But when she turned to say goodbye to Kal, she found him staring at her with an intense expression on his face. He motioned for her to stay where she was.

Martha froze, wondering if someone was coming. Her heart renewed its nauseating frantic pulsing. But there were no footsteps approaching, no echoes of voices.

"Why?" The harsh croak from inside the cell didn't sound like it belonged to the slender waif lying on the cot.

There were so many ways to interpret the question. Martha answered as a mother. "Because it's cold down here."

An ugly laugh brayed, and the girl lifted her head, revealing a swollen and battered face. A purple-black bruise covered her from forehead to chin on the right side, and her eyes were puffy slits. Anger radiated out from her like heat from a stove.

Martha sucked in a hissing breath. "Oh my God."

"He doesn't care." The girl's lips were stiff, barely able to move.

The pain and hatred in her voice broke Martha's heart and firmed her resolve. "Maybe not. But I do. Can you move enough to get the blanket?"

Annika shifted slowly, each movement obviously costing her in pain. Her determination and anger made Martha reconsider her estimate of the girl's age. She wasn't a betrayed teenager. Despite her slight form, Annika must be older.

Her next words confirmed it. "Now that you've salved your conscience, you can disappear, too."

"I'm not going anywhere," Martha said quietly.

"Sure you are." Annika's eyes roamed over Martha in the quick, confidence-shattering evaluation that women performed so easily on one another. "Tonight, you'll go back to your heated trailer, having eaten a filling meal. When your contract is done, you'll go back to whatever white-picket-fence life they pulled you out of. That's if it all goes well. If it doesn't, there's no telling where they'll take you."

Martha took a deep breath, giving herself time to consider her reaction. "You're right. I can't stay in this exact spot forever, but I'm not going to walk away and forget I found you. I'm doing what I can to make sure people know what's going on here. I want to stop all this."

"All about the justice, hmm? I used to think the same way, but now I know that's not how the world works." Annika turned her back to Martha again. "Thanks for the blanket."

Martha left with the other woman's cynical accusations ringing in her ears. The sheer depth and scope of the wrongness in the place seemed to defy any one person's ability to even begin to make it right. In the past years, such awareness had led Martha to withdraw, focusing solely on herself and Bernie. But she took comfort in knowing that she'd taken one small step in the right direction. It might be the equivalent of a tiny candle trying to banish a starless night, but the fact that a few blankets didn't solve the problem didn't smother the spark.

Having erased all signs of her intrusion, Martha left the medical building. The *lalassu* families were lined up, collecting their boxed lunches from the cafeteria under the watchful trigger fingers of the guards. Martha watched them trudge forward a step at a time, and the sight killed what little of her appetite had survived the morning.

Kal, Patrick, and Annika don't even have that much. Kal hadn't mentioned whether or not they were fed when Dr. Coulon was away. As much as Martha wanted to believe that the doctor was methodical enough to ensure his subjects had sufficient nutrition, she couldn't shake the fear that he was cruel enough to include food deprivation in his evaluation techniques. But food wasn't as simple as the blankets. There weren't cans of pork and beans stacked up on the shelves of the warehouse. All of the food was kept near the kitchen. Eva had talked about having to organize it as part of her duties.

Martha hurried into the Hub, heading to the kitchens. She couldn't take long. Mrs. Fitz would be expecting her soon in the file room. Luckily, when she poked her head inside, she and Eva made eye contact almost immediately. Eva stripped off her latex gloves and ran over, her dark ponytail bouncing in alarm.

"You missed lunch," she whispered. "Is something wrong? Is it my dads?"

Martha shook her head, leading the girl into the relative privacy of the staff dining room. Most people had already eaten, and the tables were deserted. Quickly, Martha explained what she had discovered underneath the medical building. She also handed over the fake makeup kit and pen. If someone had spotted her, she wanted the information to be safe in another's hands.

Eva covered her mouth, but to her credit, she didn't waste any time denying Martha's words or insisting on proof.

"Do you think you can get your hands on something portable? Something I can sneak in to them?" Martha asked. She couldn't go back right away, but she'd be looking for another opportunity while the doctor was gone.

Eva nodded. "They keep a close eye on the food for the *lalassu* but not on the stuff for the staff. I can definitely make sure some gets set aside."

"Good." There was still the issue of how she would get the food inside the secret lab without tipping off Dr. Coulon, but Martha had a few ideas. She would have to ask Lou for help, though. "You should get back to work. We don't want your boss getting suspicious."

Eva slipped through the kitchen door. But she immediately reappeared with a small cardboard box that she thrust into Martha's hands. Her confusion must have been obvious, and Eva immediately explained. "It's cookies. For Mrs. Fitz. Everyone knows that she's not happy about you needing the keys this morning. This way, if my boss asks, I can say that you were asking for them to give to her."

"And that will be okay?" Martha didn't want Eva risking herself.

"Trust me. Everyone is equally terrified of Dr. Coulon and Mrs. Fitz, and you work for them both. No one will think twice about it." Eva paused. "Thanks for asking for my help. My dads still think I'm, like, five. They don't want me anywhere near this stuff, and if they'd had anywhere else to leave me, I think they would have ditched me there."

"Parents are like that with their kids." It was a lame defense, but Martha couldn't risk any stones getting thrown in that particular glass house.

"Yeah, I get it." Eva's determined earnestness could only come from someone under the age of twenty. "But I also want to help. Cali's been my honorary aunt forever, and even without that, what they're doing here isn't right. I don't want to sit on the sidelines and not do anything to fix it."

Martha could remember believing not only that it was possible to fix the world, but that she was going to do it. The conviction of her early twenties had slowly eroded under life's pressures, but having reclaimed a small piece of it, she wasn't going to let it go again.

Chapter Nineteen

"So, you've come back to me, *petite*." Leanne smiled widely as Bernie stepped inside the barracks.

Her mom had asked her to stay with Eva after school that day. The two of them had been acting weird for the last few days. Eva kept sneaking her mom food, but none of it ended up in their trailer. Bernie didn't mention it to Leanne. The meals were getting scanty, and the *lalassu* in camp were getting restless. Bernie wasn't afraid of them, though, even if her mother was.

"How was school?" Leanne asked.

"A waste of time," Chuck muttered.

Bernie glared at him. He'd been impossible all day, constantly talking and distracting her. Because of him, Mrs. Chin thought Bernie was too stupid to figure out which part of the chair to sit in, and none of the other kids would talk to her. Then he'd begun flickering the lights, making Mrs. Chin stop and check the generator. It had been less than a week, and Bernie was ready to give up and never go back.

"Charles, I asked Bernadette, not you," Leanne said firmly. Then her dark eyes focused on Bernie again. "How was school?"

It was so strange to hear someone else acknowledge what Chuck had said. Bernie had gotten used to being the only one who heard him. She told Leanne about the day: the gossiping girls who mocked her, how angry Mrs. Chin had gotten about the lights, how hard it was to ignore Chuck.

"Chuck should be careful with the lights. Ghost energy is close to electricity, but it isn't the same. If he blows the circuit, it could affect him," Leanne said.

"Really?" Bernie looked over at Chuck.

He shrugged. "I've always been able to make the lights go off and on. Almost all ghosts can."

"Oh." Bernie sat down carefully on the narrow stool with wobbly legs, careful not to move too quickly and tip it over. "Maybe he should. Then I wouldn't have to go back to stupid school."

Leanne rubbed her bony hands together. "I felt the same when I was a girl. School was for those who were trapped in the mundane world. Not for the likes of us."

It would be easy to agree, but Bernie spoke the truth in a small voice. "I thought it was going to be different. I thought I would make friends." *Real friends that everyone can see and hear.*

Bernie didn't look at Chuck, not wanting him to guess her thoughts. Dry, cool fingers wrapped around her wrist, squeezing gently. Bernie's throat tightened as she tried not to cry.

"Ah, *petite*. I wish it could be different. But the truth is that mediums are often isolated because those who do not see as you do can never understand. But I do."

A weight dissolved from Bernie's chest, letting her breathe easier. *Mom tries to understand, but she doesn't get how hard it is to figure out what other people can see.* Over the past year, Bernie had seen the tired, frustrated look creeping back into her mother's eyes—the same look she'd worn before signing the papers to give Bernie away.

"What is it?" Leanne asked.

"Do you really think that other people can't understand us?" Bernie looked up, not sure what answer she wanted to hear.

"Not even other *lalassu*." Leanne squeezed Bernie's arm again. "You've seen them here, how they call me Looney. Henri told me that you've seen Gwen and how they treat her, locking her away."

"But my mom—" Bernie bit her lip.

"You can't trust your mom. Not after what she did." Chuck flickered, growing darker.

"What did she do?" Leanne asked, and Bernie began spilling the whole story. The years of therapy and medication, being told that she was crazy, all finishing with the terrible day of being hauled away.

"Bernie, you gotta run!" Chuck shouted.

She stared at him, trying to ignore him. Michael and the others kept telling her that Chuck wasn't real, that he was a part of her imagination. Her head and stomach hurt from the clozapine, making it hard to remember what she was supposed to do. She got to her feet and slowly stumbled to the kitchen.

Her mom was talking to two other men in suits. "I'm not comfortable with not being able to see her during treatment."

"We understand, Mrs. Anderson," a man's voice said. "But it's an important part of our treatment model. We need to make a complete break with her ordinary routine."

"I don't know…" Her mom's voice trailed off as one of the men took her hand in both of his. Mr. Dalhard.

"It's been very difficult for you, Martha," he said soothingly. "You've tried so hard for so many years, but you've failed."

Tears flowed down her mother's cheeks. "I tried."

"Of course you did." He patted her arm, still keeping a firm grip with his other hand. "But if you want Bernadette to get better, you need to sign the papers."

The other man slid a neatly stapled pile across the table, along with a pen.

"I want her to get better." Her mother looked at Bernie, her face drawn and pinched. She looked beaten down, not like the mother who used to bake cookies and read stories. That mom had disappeared along with Daddy.

"Then sign, and you'll never have to see her again. You can go back to having a life of your own." Mr. Dalhard's hypnotic voice seemed to fill the room. "It's what you've secretly wanted all these years, isn't it? For the burden to end."

"Yes, I want it to end." Her mother signed the papers quickly, the pen scratching loudly in the silence.

Bernie couldn't understand what was going on. It must be another hallucination, like Chuck shouting from the other room, causing flashes of light and shadow to burst across the apartment. Her mom couldn't be giving up on her.

"Thank you, Martha. Why don't you go to sleep now? Everything will be better tomorrow." Mr. Dalhard guided her mother toward her bedroom in the back of the apartment.

"Mom?" Bernie pleaded, but her mother didn't turn around.

Mr. Dalhard let go and turned to face her, a big grin on his face. "Bernadette, so lovely to meet you. We're going to go for a little ride."

"I don't want to go with you." Bernie stumbled forward. "Mom!"

Her mother paused, her hand on the bedroom door. "Goodbye, Bernie-pie. I'm sorry I couldn't help you."

"No! Mom!" Bernie screamed. Heavy hands grabbed her from behind, and something sharp pinched her neck.

"She's been sedated," the man reported to Mr. Dalhard.

"Good. Don't worry, Bernadette. Everything will be better when you wake up. You're a very important young lady."

"I kept screaming for her." Bernie sobbed into Leanne's arms. "But she never came."

Leanne murmured to her in French, kissing Bernie's hair and forehead. "I am so sorry, *petite*."

It was like a dam burst inside of her. All of the things that she'd never said to Michael or her mother came pouring out. "She never believed me. She told me I was making it all up, and she took me to so many doctors, and I had to take pills, and they dragged me down and made everything foggy and scary. Why couldn't she believe me?"

Leanne held Bernie, rocking her back and forth. "Because she was afraid."

Bernie stilled. Michael had told her that it wasn't her mother's fault, that her mom couldn't have known that Chuck was real, and that Mr. Dalhard had used his powers to control her mom's mind.

"You are special, Bernie. You're so much more powerful than I am. And that power frightens people, which is why they'll try to break you down." Leanne stroked Bernie's hair. "Tell me what she did to you."

Bernie gulped, her throat and eyes raw. "She gave me to Mr. Dalhard, and he sent me to a horrible place. They made me do tests, over and over, when all I wanted was to go to sleep. I was all by myself, except for Chuck. Michael came for me, but then Mr. Dalhard got me again. He said Michael was dead, but Chuck told me that he wasn't. They were going to take us on a plane, somewhere no one could find us, but Nada stopped it with her electrical powers. She was one of the people with Michael who came to rescue me. Then the other man shot her. It was horrible." She shivered, remembering the loud blast and spray of blood and tissue.

"How awful." Leanne hugged her again, giving Bernie the strength to finish.

"Michael and his friends got me back, and I thought we would stay with them and they would help me. And then I would get to be, you know, a real superhero, like Michael and Dani." Bernie leaned her head against Leanne's bony shoulder. It felt good to finally say the words that had been crowding into her head, but she was exhausted.

"Is that what you want? To be a hero?" Leanne asked.

Bernie nodded.

"Such a brave girl. No wonder you're so unhappy here. You need to be somewhere where you can live your dreams." Leanne used her sleeve to wipe the tears from Bernie's face. "Maybe you and Chuck can stay with Henri and me until you get on your feet."

"Really?" Bernie blinked, not sure she'd heard the words correctly. "You would want me to stay with you?"

"I don't think that's a good idea," Chuck said.

"Of course I mean it." Leanne smiled.

"It's a great idea, Chuck." Bernie bounced in excitement. She'd been worried about what she and Chuck would do after they escaped.

"We can disappear into one of the big cities and become real heroes. First, though, we need to get onto the plane. Can I count on your help?"

"Sure." Bernie slowed down. "But my mom might try to stop me. She says she feels bad about before and watches me all the time."

"I know," Leanne said sadly as she stroked Bernie's cheek. "I wish she understood what needed to be done. It's terrible the way that she's made you hide instead of helping you to understand your gift, and all for the most ridiculous of reasons. I'm afraid that she can't be trusted."

Bernie's throat was getting hot and tight as she got too angry to think. It wasn't fair. And it wasn't right. Her mom should have believed in her, not tried to fix her.

"It's because the others are afraid of us. Well, not of us in particular, but of death. We understand death more than anyone else because we are the only ones who speak to the dead. They should embrace us as emissaries, but instead they shun us." Leanne smiled again. "But now we have each other. And together, we can do so much, *petite*."

If Lou were in the fur, the atmosphere of the camp would have sent him moving to higher, more defendable ground. The *lalassu* were sullen, lingering in large numbers near the gate. The guards were tense and kept their weapons ready. The construction crew kept jumping at unexpected sounds, and the foreman seemed to blame Lou for all of it.

"Chief, we're not paying you to stop and stare!"

Human teeth didn't grind well. They were painful, causing the whole jaw to ache as if broken. Lou ignored the foreman, continuing with his work. The idiot kept barking at him as if trying to provoke him. The other men on the crew were getting more and more nervous, dropping tools and fumbling tasks.

"Careful," Hood warned as Lou secured a stud into the framework by driving the nail in with a single hammer blow. The foreman was still chattering away like an irritated squirrel, but that wasn't what Hood was focused on.

The internees were crowding the gate, making big gestures as they argued with the guards. Lou could catch pieces of what they were saying.

"...supposed to be an hour ago!"

"...children are hungry!"

It was later than usual for the meal, mainly because the foreman was insisting on completing this framework before allowing the crew to pack away their tools. As long as there were hammers, saws, and other potential weapons in the neutral area, the guards wouldn't let the *lalassu* out of the inner camp. Lou spotted Ryan stalking back and forth near the gate, his rifle raised.

Movement on the other side of the yard diverted Lou's attention. Martha emerged from the Hub and immediately headed toward the construction crew. Keeping his distance from her had been the most difficult test of his self-control he'd ever faced. She'd invaded his thoughts and dreams, taking over his waking and sleeping life.

As she drew closer, he realized she was upset, based on the way she bit her lower lip and pressed her arms into her stomach. Alarmed, Lou laid down his tools.

"School let out three hours ago, but Bernie isn't with Eva. Do you know where she is?" The worry in Martha's eyes drove away his thoughts of jealousy.

She wasn't going to be pleased with his answer. He gestured with his chin to the inner camp.

Her breath hissed between her teeth. "She's with Leanne? Again?"

As Lou nodded, the foreman shoved in between them. "This isn't personal time, Chief."

The other workers stopped their work to watch the confrontation. Hood had explained that they saw it as entertainment. Lou straightened so that he towered over the foreman, making the other man squint up at him and, more importantly, moving him away from Martha. Lou held still, not confronting the other man but using his size to make it clear that escalating the conflict would not be a smart choice.

The foreman puffed up his chest and thrust out his jaw, playing to their audience. "We're staying until we finish this, even if I have to keep you here until dark."

Shouts from the inner camp answered the foreman's statement. Lou flexed his arms, shaking out any knots, preparing to fight if necessary. *Throat first. Then the back of the head.* He could take the foreman out quickly.

The foreman smirked. "Don't fuck with me. I'll make your life a living hell, you dumb In—"

"Excuse me, is there a problem here?" Martha's quiet words cut through the tension with the precision of a scalpel.

From the sudden sick expression and beads of sweat bursting on the foreman's face, he'd forgotten she was there. Lou took a quick look at the other crew members, many of whom seemed angry or irritated by the foreman's words.

"Well, ma'am, you see, we still have some work to do—"

Lou shifted position, moving to where he could get between Martha and the foreman in a hurry.

"It's after six," she said quietly but firmly. Her chin was held high, a posture that made Lou nervous, since it put her vulnerable throat on display, but it seemed to intimidate the foreman. "Surely you don't intend to work these men all night?"

There were nods and murmurs of agreement from the men. The foreman looked around and realized he had lost the sympathy of the crowd.

"Everyone is ready for their supper." Martha kept her gaze fixed on the foreman with the intensity of a hawk who wasn't quite hungry enough to snatch a mouse but who still might explode into a lethal flurry at any moment.

The crew members' heads were bobbing in agreement. Even Lou could tell that there was no recovering. As long as no one challenged the foreman, he could push them. But since it was out in the open, he had to yield or prepare to fight.

"Fine. Start packing it all up," the foreman ordered.

"Thank you." Martha inclined her head, every inch of her posture shouting control and authority.

The foreman wiped the sweat on his head. "Chief, get—"

"His name is Lou McKinnon. I am certain an experienced leader such as yourself recognizes that it is always best to address others with respect and avoid shallow-minded slurs." The snap of steel in Martha's voice brought a pleased smile to Lou's lips.

"I—"

"I assume there won't be a repetition of this." Martha might have been shorter and smaller than the foreman, but when she stepped forward, the man cringed. She lowered her voice and delivered the final warning. "If it does, it will not be my husband whose life becomes a— quote—'living hell.'"

The foreman moved away, pretending that the eager workers needed supervision as they loaded the construction tools onto the golf cart to take them outside the camp walls. Lou held still, enjoying the rush from Martha's words. Hearing her call him "husband" was far more satisfying than a simple word should have been. "Thank you."

Her eyebrows lifted in surprise and what he hoped was pleasure at his words.

"You got him running scared." Hood didn't look entirely pleased about it.

"Has he been doing that the whole time? Calling you that awful name?" she asked. "Well, it ends now. There's no excuse for it." Her attention drifted back to the fence and the increasingly angry *lalassu*.

"It might not have been a good idea to threaten him." Hood was still watching the foreman. The crew was hiding smirks as they put away their tools. "The risk—"

"Our jobs here don't mean that we have to abandon all of our morals," Martha said absently, her focus on the inner camp. "Besides, I apparently work for the two biggest bullies here. Might as well take advantage of that fact."

"It's still not a good idea," Hood muttered. Lou disagreed. He was proud to see Martha's fire reemerging. He would get her safely through the *lalassu*, who were getting angrier by the second.

Suddenly, she grabbed his arm, her nails digging painfully into the skin. Sharp fear flooded the air between them. Lou immediately tensed, preparing to attack whatever threat she'd noticed.

"Bernie," Martha whispered through pale lips.

It took Lou a moment to spot her. His human vision might be better than a bear's, but it still wasn't great over distance. But he saw the shorter shape near a heavily bundled one. The smaller one's golden-brown hair gleamed in the sunlight, and more importantly, no gray shock collar glinted at her throat.

However, even in the scant minutes since the confrontation with the foreman, the mood of the crowd had worsened. Children were crying. Women were shouting and jabbing through the chain-link fence with accusing fingers. Men were glowering and rolling their shoulders, ready to fight.

Lou took Martha by the hand and hurried to where Bernie stood. The child was less than ten feet from the gate, surrounded by shoving, angry adults. His heart beat faster, all too aware of how easily her fragile human body could be broken. She could be shoved against the fence and crushed, or a random blow could shatter her bones.

"You can't go in there." There had never been a more unwelcome voice or statement.

Lou would have ignored Ryan if not for the rifle barrel aimed squarely at his chest. He stopped, reconsidering his options.

"Please, Ryan, my daughter is in there," Martha pleaded.

Grab the rifle and hit him between the cheek and eye. It would break his rival's orbital bone, giving Lou time to get past him.

"What?" Ryan demanded. The crowd was roaring now, a mixture of shouts and chanted threats. The people were moving closer together, interlinking in an impenetrable wall of flesh. It would take too long for Lou to make his way through them. *Rip through the fence.* He would be outed as a *lalassu,* but it would let him pull Bernie out.

Lou's hand closed around the rifle barrel at the same time that Ryan dropped it. The unexpected lack of resistance sent the weapon tumbling to the ground.

Ryan grabbed at his belt, and suddenly all of the *lalassu* were screaming, dropping to the muddy ground. They were writhing and shaking with stiff limbs. *The collars.* Lou's comprehension didn't slow him down. He ran past the uncertain guards and over the flailing internees. Bernie stared at those around her, mouth open and eyes crinkled in surprised horror. She didn't resist as he picked her up and carried her back through the gate to Martha.

She gathered Bernie to her, but her stunned eyes were on Ryan. "How…?"

"Mass shock switch," he explained proudly. "Head of the guard shift carries it. Drops every loocy within two hundred feet."

"That's horrible," Martha whispered.

Ryan's face darkened. "You'd rather I let them kill your daughter?"

Lou stepped forward, furious at both Ryan's actions and words.

Ryan stepped back, his eyes darting toward the rifle lying on the ground. Instinct must have told him that there was no way that he could get to it before Lou got to him, because Ryan focused on Martha. "As a mother, you should know better than to let your daughter play in the inner camp with the freaks."

<h1 style="text-align:center">CHAPTER TWENTY</h1>

"Things are getting too tense out there." Hood twitched the curtains closed and returned to the table. They had retreated to Hood and Harley's trailer after the riot, where they waited for Harley and Eva to join them. He turned, pinning Martha with his hard gaze. "Confronting the foreman was a mistake."

Martha was still shaking from what could have happened to Bernie and the confrontation with Lou's foreman. Her body couldn't decide whether to be terrified or furious, and she kept flipping between the two. But Hood's comment frayed the last restraints on her temper. She might be more of a housewife than a secret agent, but she also wasn't an idiot. "Excuse me?"

"We can't afford for anyone to pay extra attention to us." Hood glared at Martha. "You're sneaking into the secret lab every day to deliver food, and your daughter is getting training as a *lalassu*. There's too much to lose to risk it all over a bigoted moron."

Lou stood up, his arms and shoulders flexing. Martha stepped in between them. She refused to start a fight, but she also wasn't going to back down.

"It was wrong, he deserved to be called on it, and letting him keep on doing it wasn't going to stop the riot." *Or what happened afterwards.* She still couldn't think about all of those people dropping to the ground without feeling sick to her stomach.

A knock on the door stopped the confrontation from escalating. Martha opened the door, and Harley and Eva trooped in, laden with foil packets from the kitchen.

"Thank you, Eva," Martha said wearily. "Bernie is in your room. Do you think you could take her dinner and maybe sit with her for a while?"

Luckily, Eva didn't ask why Bernie was in her room. Maybe Martha should have claimed parental credit for it as a punishment, but the truth was that Bernie hadn't spoken to her at all on the way to the trailer. As soon as they'd stepped inside, she'd gone right to the bedroom and slammed the door. Martha was too unsteady and raw to face her daughter until she'd had a chance to calm down, so she hadn't pushed.

Eva's quiet knock was followed by a terse invitation to enter. Martha swallowed her disappointment and focused on peeling back the foil to uncover lukewarm meatloaf and potatoes.

She took a fork from the selection of borrowed cutlery and poked at a greasy brown spud, but her stomach refused to consider allowing any food to remain in residence. Instead, she studied the trailer, which was nearly identical to their own, with the same blue-gray carpet, pale fake-wood paneling, and cheap pressboard-and-plastic furniture. It emphasized how the people running this camp saw them all as disposable.

She pushed aside her meal to offer it to Lou. He always had an enormous appetite, no matter how good or bad the food was. A high metabolism must be part of being a skin-walker, because his body certainly didn't show any signs of that much intake.

But Lou wasn't sitting at the small table with the rest of them. Instead, he'd positioned himself by the trailer's door, periodically lifting the blinds to peer out the windows. Protecting them from anyone who might overhear their conversation.

"We have to decide what to do next." Hood used his fork to cut a potato in two. "There are three and a half more weeks until Harley, Eva, and I rotate out. We can take the photos to Dani and Michael, and they will release them to the media. We need to keep a low profile to make sure none of us get hurt between now and then."

"Other people are getting hurt." Martha couldn't get the choked screams from the riot out of her head, not to mention the images of the fresh bruises on Annika, Kal, and Patrick from the asshole guards who were supposed to be feeding them. Each night, it was getting more difficult to walk away.

"There has to be something we can do. Get the pictures out early and raise public pressure," Harley suggested.

"Public awareness takes too long," Hood said flatly in the voice of experienced cynicism. "By the time it leads to action, Dr. Coulon will have destroyed the lab and anyone who's seen it."

Including Kal, Annika, and Patrick. Martha swallowed and noticed Lou looking at her. When their eyes met, he nodded once, a hint of a smile hovering in his otherwise calm expression. *He agrees with me, and he thinks I can come up with a solution.* The realization warmed her, as did the reminder that he would make sure she and Bernie were safe if everything went badly. She could afford to take risks because of his promise of safety. Her memory supplied a flashback to the first night and his spectacular body when it wasn't hidden underneath the denim and flannel.

"What if we could send out a message to get Cali and the others here to help us?" Harley suggested, his words cutting through Martha's recollection before it could do more than spark a zing along her nerves. She mentally dragged her disappointed libido back under control.

"The more we do, the more likely we are to be caught." Hood's cool evaluation earned him indignant looks from both Martha and Harley. Hood raised his hands again. "I'm not saying that I don't want to help, but I also don't want any of us to be the ones in those cages."

"I could get a message to Gwen." Bernie's quiet declaration silenced all of the adults.

Martha hadn't even heard the bedroom door open, but Bernie stood there with Eva beside her. "Thank you, sweetie, but it's too dangerous for you."

Bernie's eyes narrowed. "Because then they might realize that I'm a freak who belongs with the others?"

Parenting autopilot took over. "You're not a freak. You have a gift. And none of the people here deserve to be locked up."

"You don't believe that. You're scared of us." Bernie glared. "Because of you, all of those people got tased today."

"It wasn't your mother's fault," Harley began.

"Yes, it was." Bernie interrupted. "You don't like it when I'm with Leanne. If you'd let me have dinner with her instead of trying to drag me out here, then they wouldn't have used the shock collars."

"They used the shock collars because there was nearly a riot. You have no idea how dangerous those can be." Hood grabbed one of the foil packets and split it open, clearly considering the discussion over.

"I've talked to people who have died in riots," Bernie said calmly. "They got crushed to death, trampled, shot, beaten up, all sorts of things. So I do know how dangerous they are. But it's even worse to be held as a prisoner or killed just because you happen to be different."

Part of Martha wanted to applaud her daughter's words. The other part was appalled. No child should have to know those kinds of things.

"I know a little something about that." Hood laid down his fork.

"Then you should stop being a coward and do something. All of you." Bernie swept them all with an equally indicting glare.

Martha regained her motherly footing. "All right, young lady. That's enough."

Bernie opened her mouth, but Martha held up her hand before she could say anything.

"We're all tired, and it's been an emotional day. As much as I would like to rescue everyone tonight, it's not going to happen. We should get some rest and try to come up with a plan tomorrow."

Hood and Harley didn't argue with her. Eva looked as if she might like to, but she kept her mouth closed. Carrying the leftover food, Martha, Bernie, and Lou left for their own trailer. But once Martha and Bernie were inside, Lou closed the door and disappeared into the night. Guiltily, Martha wondered if he needed to get away from an unpleasant scene so badly that he was willing to forego a meal.

"He's checking the trailers. Chuck's watching him." Bernie folded her arms. "Chuck's been watching the whole time."

"Then I'll thank him for that." Martha took a deep breath. "We need to have a talk about what you've offered to do. I'm very proud of you for wanting to help, but you have to understand—"

"Why?" Bernie interrupted, walking away and yanking the blind open to stare out the window. "You don't understand anything about me."

"Every teenager feels that way about their parents. But I do know you, and I understand more of what you're going through than you'd think."

Bernie whirled in place, her arms tightly crossed. "You think this is about the whole becoming-a-woman thing? As long as I can remember, you've shoved drugs down my throat and told me that what I saw wasn't real. You never knew who I really was."

The accusations bit deeply, striking to the heart of Martha's biggest fears and regrets.

"Even now, you don't get it." Bernie sighed dramatically to underscore her mother's denseness. "You forget about Chuck. He sees everything, and you treat him like an imaginary friend. You're afraid of him."

"Yes, I am." The three words spilled out of Martha's mouth before she could decide whether or not they were wise. Bernie's mouth dropped open, but Martha pushed on, no longer trying to be diplomatic. "I'm afraid of what he's asked you to do. I'm afraid of how angry you've said he gets with you. I'm afraid that he cares more about what he wants than what is best for you."

Bernie's gaze darted to an empty spot nearby. "He understands me. He's my friend."

"Someone can be your friend, and you can care about them a great deal, but it doesn't mean that they feel the same way about you." Martha hoped her daughter would listen and believe her. "They might say they do. They might even believe that they do, but if they are pushing you to put yourself at risk or do something you're not comfortable with, then your feelings for each other don't make that okay."

Her daughter didn't answer, and Martha hoped that the message was getting through.

"People's actions will tell you who they really are. No matter what they say, it's what they do that matters. So, no, I don't trust Chuck. He's asked you to do some truly horrible things, and he kept asking you over and over even when you didn't want to do it. He gets angry with you when you don't do what he wants. He scares you."

Bernie's head snapped up. "At least he's never handed me over to a crazy psychopath."

Martha could only stand there as Bernie stormed back into her room and slammed the door. *Mr. Dalhard used his powers on me. He attacked my mind so that I would give you up.* She'd said it before, told Bernie over and over as she apologized, but she wondered whether it could ever be enough. Martha slowly sank down onto the couch, the thin cushions releasing a burst of ancient cigarette smoke. Her attempts at redirection didn't sweep aside her secret fears that she'd already passed a point of no return, damning herself and Bernie with her ignorance.

Mr. Dalhard's psychic gifts had been irresistible once he was there in person, but it didn't change the fact that Martha had made the initial call before even meeting him. She might not have known that it was part of an attempt to harvest *lalassu* with usable gifts, but she'd known it was a residential treatment program. That had been part of the seductive appeal. After years of being attacked when Bernie went into manic tantrums and of feeling trapped in her own home, the idea of being able to gain some small respite had been too tempting to dismiss. When she'd added in their offer of free treatment and Martha's dwindling savings, she'd succumbed, only to be proven unforgivably wrong.

If Bernie judged her by her actions, Martha was even worse than Chuck. She wanted to tell herself that the circumstances were different, but rational thought crumbled under the emotional weight of too many mistakes and too many failed certainties. Her body felt hollow, as if all of her substance had been scraped away, leaving a thin shell of brittle, empty skin.

The door opened and closed. Martha struggled to get up and present a brave face, despite the lump of unshed tears clawing at the inside of her throat. *I will not break down. There are too many people counting on me.* But her muscles were listening to the soundless howl of despair ripping through her heart and the whispering inner voice reminding her of every incident where good intentions had struck deep wounds that still bled.

Lou knelt in front of her, compassion softening his sharply chiseled features. He reached up and smoothed away the stray wisps of sweat-soaked hair from her cheeks and forehead. The caring gesture threatened to upset Martha's delicate emotional balance and unleash the outburst still waiting to explode. *It doesn't mean anything. He's being kind.*

"You sh-sh-should have something to eat. I'll be f-f-fine." She pushed the lie out, not wanting him to see her lose control yet again. He'd been proud of her when she stood up to the foreman. He believed she would find a way to free Annika, Kal, and Patrick. She didn't want to see him lose that faith in her.

Instead of going to where the congealing meatloaf waited on the table, Lou shook his head. He put his hand on her feet, glancing up at her for permission.

Martha wasn't sure what he planned but was too numb to rouse herself to ask. "It's okay."

He bent and eased her shoes and socks off of her rigid feet. *It's only kindness*, she repeated. Just then, she could use some kindness. Even if it wasn't all that she might have wished for, in that moment, she allowed herself the luxury of accepting it, knowing that he wouldn't do anything to hurt her.

He cradled her left foot in his hands and began to rub his strong fingers along the arch, kneading away the tension. Slowly, her toes unstiffened and relaxed, moving with his steady strokes. He gently lowered her foot back onto the floor, and Martha sighed in equal parts resignation and satisfaction. *It's over. It was nice, but it's over.*

Then he picked up her right foot and repeated the process, easing the knotted tendons into relaxation. Then his fingers began a steady progression up her calf, sliding underneath her dress pants.

Oh. My. God. Martha hung tightly to her expectations. She'd forgotten what it felt like to have a man's hands on her and how they could feel large and powerful but also incredibly gentle and precise. Lou's hands were nearly large enough to wrap around her entire calf, one palm cradling the outstretched leg while the other massaged away the cramps. He kept moving higher and higher, his fingertips brushing along the sensitive flesh on the back of her knees.

A quick peek through her nearly closed lashes let her see his forearms buried under her bunched pant fabric. His head was bent forward so that she only got a glimpse of the intent focus on his features—he looked as if the massage were the only thing on his mind. There were no worries about the past and no hopes for the future—only the moment. She wished she could say the same as he kneaded her muscles into relaxation.

I should stop him. Aside from the impropriety, there simply wasn't enough room, even in her loose trousers, for her leg and his hands. But it was hard to take action as a wave of sensual pleasure briefly lifted her. As she floated back to awareness, it was hard to remember how much of the day had been devoted to heartache and despair.

His fingers went still on her skin, and she bit her lip, wondering if she'd made some noise to make him self-conscious. He lifted his head, studying her face.

"It's fine," she whispered, her traitorous mouth teaming up with her heart to override her brain.

When his hands began to slide back down her leg, she'd accomplished the Herculean task of both keeping a straight face and finding the words to thank him for his effort. By the time he tugged her pant cuff into place at her ankle, she was reasonably certain she could even deliver the thanks without sounding like a desperate hausfrau.

And then he began to work on the left leg. Martha quickly abandoned her efforts at dignified maturity and let herself savor every kneading caress. As he glided his hands down the newly relaxed muscles, she only half-heartedly tried to retrieve her carefully worded message of appreciation. He took her right hand and repeated the process, beginning with the fingers and palms before moving up her left arm to her shoulder. By the time he finished, Martha was ready to start purring. Her body hadn't been this limp and relaxed in years.

But he wasn't finished. "Move." His voice was quiet—it was a request rather than an order.

She slid to the edge of the couch, and he moved into place behind her, his long legs stretched out on either side. His hands cupped her shoulders, and he began to massage inward. She leaned forward to make it easier, resting her lightened arms on one upraised knee and letting her head drop. He ran his hands up and down her spine, and the knots practically untied themselves.

Then his hands were buried in her hair, caressing her neck and scalp. A low moan escaped her lips before she could catch it, and she regretted it when he paused. Maybe he was waiting for her to move away or for her to accept that he'd done more than his share. When she held still, he continued, his strong thumbs alternating strokes on her neck while his fingertips massaged her jaw and hairline.

He'd touched her from head to toe, though with some disappointing and expected exceptions. She shouldn't have been waiting for more, but as he rose from the couch, she couldn't quite find the strength of will to break the blissful lassitude flowing through her. Later, she knew she would be embarrassed at her lack of control, both for the outburst and during his care, but as her eyes rolled closed, she could put all of that aside. She was so tired after everything that had happened that she could hardly keep her eyes open.

His thick arms slid underneath her shoulders and knees, and he lifted her as if she were one of those delicate and slender heroines from the movies. If she moved her hand a fraction of an inch, she could have touched his broad chest. *He hasn't asked you to touch him. Don't take advantage. Don't be that woman who shows her desperation by groping anyone at the slightest opportunity.* There would be plenty of time to remember the massage and fantasize about it going further. *For now, enjoy being carried to bed like a princess.*

He laid her on the covers before smoothing her hair away from her face again. She couldn't read his face at all. *Wistful? Pleased? Or am I reading my own desires into his expression?*

Despite her admonition to behave herself, she reached to cup his smooth cheek, running her thumb along his high cheekbone. Her eyes were too heavy to keep open any longer. As she slipped into sleep, she felt him cradle her hand with his own before tucking it back into place beside her.

Chapter Twenty-One

The first rays of sunlight were pushing back the darkness, but they didn't bring any illumination to Lou. He'd spent the short night pacing back and forth in the small trailer, trying to make sense of his raging human emotions. There were still hours to go before he had to report for work, but he couldn't make himself lie down. His feelings were driving him crazy like the itch of shedding fur, but there was no tree to scratch away the maddening strands.

This is more than the mating instinct. The mating drive pushed a skin-walker to protect, to claim, and to cherish. It merged two spirits into one. He felt the drive with Martha, in the form of a radical shifting of his priorities and a desire to make her happy. He understood it, along with his desire to physically mate.

He did not understand the fantasies being constantly generated in his mind. They went beyond the biological connection but were also obsessively tied up in it. They made it hard to think, as if he'd eaten fermented fruit. But the most frightening part was how they locked him into his human form, denying him the simplicity of the fur.

The night before had tested him past his limits. When he'd seen Martha blinded by despair, there had been no room to remember his self-imposed limitations. He'd gone to her immediately, without any thought of being considerate to her and avoiding further confusing the situation. When he'd touched her, he'd immediately noticed the rigid muscles under her skin and begun the massage.

It had been honest enough at first, but something had selfishly twisted inside him. As he caressed her skin and unknotted her muscles, his cock had swollen to press painfully against his jeans. His mind had begun to obsessively whisper, fantasizing about tearing aside her pants. The material was so thin that it would require hardly any effort to remove them. He'd imagined running his hands along her bare skin, the details forming almost instantaneously. Tasting her skin, cupping her breasts, burying himself inside her as she gasped and sighed—none of it would go away.

He'd only managed to keep from acting it out by freezing in place like a terrified deer. More fantasies bloomed in his mind, like pushing Martha up against a wall and thrusting himself inside while he feasted on her neck or having her rise above him while she rode him. Every thought of her made him want to touch and taste her more, to mark himself on and under her skin. He'd barely gotten himself under control enough to continue the massage. If she'd given him any encouragement, he wasn't sure if he'd have been able to remember why it was not a good idea.

The memory of her soft moan left his cock achingly hard and his whole body rigid with desire, just as it had been through most of the night, despite two trips outside, where he'd used his fist to get some relief.

I have to talk to Hood again. He couldn't trust himself, and he would never forgive himself if he lost control with Martha.

"Lou?"

At first, he thought he was imagining her voice. It was far too early for her to be awake. But when he turned, there she stood, ready for work in a thin blue sweater and another set of flimsy black pants. Her dark-honey hair spilled evenly over her shoulders and around her face as she stared at her fidgeting hands. He had thought he was fully aroused before, but with each second he looked at her, the intensity of his desire painfully increased.

"I… I wanted to thank you"—the blueness of her eyes flashed briefly as her gaze flickered up through her lashes—"for taking care of me last night."

"You're welcome." His voice was lower and hoarser than he'd expected. From the way her shoulders twitched, it surprised her as well.

"You're really good, you know." Her blunt teeth captured a fold of her soft-pink lip.

His heartbeat thudded faster. His tongue darted forward to touch his own teeth, as he imagined kissing the shallow dent. *Focus!*

"You could be a professional masseur," she continued, her gaze fixed somewhere to the left of his hip. "I used to go for regular massages, back when I was still married. It will probably sound silly to you, but I like being touched. I was always cuddling up to my friends or boyfriends. I just like physical contact. Derek didn't like it, though. He said it was smothering him. So he didn't touch me unless he wanted sex."

Anger distracted him from his lust, though he couldn't be sure if it was from the idea of another man touching her or the idea of a man refusing to touch her when she wanted it.

"I'm sorry. I'm babbling." She still wouldn't look up. He sensed that there was something underneath the flood of words that she needed to say.

Lou didn't want her to stop. "It's okay. Go on."

Her eyes briefly met his in surprise before she went back to staring at the floor. "Then, after Bernie was diagnosed and I quit my job to manage her therapy, I would go once a week. Sometimes it was the only time I left the house each week. But once a week, I would have that time to myself. Time when someone was taking care of me instead of me always having to be the one who takes care." She began to fidget with the hem of her sweater. "So it meant a lot to me that you took care of me last night. Thank you."

The sensory memory her soft skin threatened to overwhelm his control. To distract himself, he blurted out the first thing that came to his mind. "It was Andrew."

"What?" Her hands dropped, much to his relief.

"Shaman training is hard. He hated it." Lou threw the human words out, building a barrier between his desires and his actions.

"Why?"

"Hours of sitting in a trance and listening to Grandfather's lectures. He wanted to leave Bear Claw and go to the city." Remembering how miserable his twin had been helped Lou with his own discomfort. "I failed the test."

"What test? To be a shaman?" Martha asked.

He nodded, grateful she'd understood what he meant.

"That must have been disappointing."

Ordinarily, in that kind of conversation, he would be desperate to leave. Instead, he found himself wanting to share this piece of his life with Martha. "I wanted to help him, so I gave him massages."

"No wonder you're so good. You've had lots of practice." She smiled at him.

He shrugged. "It helped sometimes. With the headaches."

"How old were you?" Martha asked, stepping forward and closing the gap between them.

Her eyes were like river-polished agate, speckled shades of blue. Lou forgot to breathe. "I'm not sure. Ten or eleven. Maybe twelve. Our father had just been killed by the poacher."

"Lily told me a little about it. That must have been hard on you. You were only Bernie's age."

His stomach twisted. He never talked about those days. Not with his grandfather, and not even with his twin. But he still wanted to tell her. "I had to take care of Andrew. Grandfather pulled back. Our mother was trapped in her pain. I couldn't let him be alone."

"What about Lily and Mark?" Martha was only inches away, close enough to fill the air with her scent. She was looking up at him without fear and without pity. Only compassion and caring was on her face.

"Our mother couldn't take care of them." He took a deep breath then told her the secret that had weighed on him since his youth. "There was a third cub that didn't survive its first year."

Martha's hand flew to her mouth. "Lily never mentioned that."

"She doesn't remember. I didn't tell her." Memories of the tiny cub filled his mind. He'd struggled to feed all of his siblings and still wondered how he could have done more. *If I knew then what I know now about hunting—*

A warm touch on his chest pulled him from his guilt. Martha's fingertips were resting lightly over his heart.

"I called him *Kots'éen*," he said, covering her hand with his.

"I'm so sorry, Lou. What does the name mean?" she asked.

"Mouse." he smiled, remembering. "In Tlingit. If he'd lived, Grandfather would have given him a Miwok name."

"You must have loved him very much."

"I did." It had hurt for a long time when Kots'éen died. He'd buried the cub near the Colony and built a cairn over the site.

"Is it okay to talk about him?" she asked.

"There isn't much to say. He didn't make it past the spring or find his name." There was only a memory.

"I'm afraid I don't understand about the names." Her apologetic smile warmed him more than the summer sun.

"Skin-walkers aren't part of the tribes. We have our own rituals and traditions. But we are connected." He wished they were back in Bear Claw. Andrew and Grandfather could tell her the rich history and old stories. "We all have Miwok names. Mine is Notaku."

"Like Lily is Litonya when she's in her bear form. Right?" She seemed excited at her comprehension but then frowned. "But everyone calls you Lou when you're in bear form."

He shrugged. "I don't stay in the skin much."

"You must hate it here, being locked into the form you don't like and having to take care of me and Bernie." She started to drop her hand and only then seemed to realize that he was holding it against him.

"I don't," he said quietly.

They stood there, staring at each other. Her hand was cradled inside his. If he bent his head a little, he could kiss her. But he held himself still, refusing to trespass where he had not been invited.

"I'm glad you're here." Her captive hand flattened against his chest. "I don't think I could do this without you."

She doubted herself too much, but Lou was glad he could support her.

"So why did you give him a Tlingit name instead of a Miwok name?" she asked.

"I learned Tlingit to trade. It seemed to fit." He dared to reach out and smooth a tendril of hair away from her forehead.

Her breath caught, and he released her hand. It left a cool, empty spot on his chest.

Martha stepped away, as if she'd suddenly realized how close they were to each other. She exhaled sharply, wrapping her arms around her stomach.

"I saw you the first night," he said quietly, not wanting the conversation to end.

Her head raised in surprise. "You did?"

He'd watched from the forest as Lily and Ron brought them to their new home. There had been a flurry of chatter and excitement, but once Lily and Ron left, the only movement from the cabin had been the slow coil of smoke unfurling from the chimney. He'd stayed as the light faded and Arctic night reigned, staring at the freshly chinked log walls. "You came out to chop wood for the stove. You wore a blue scarf."

Her hair had kept peeking out in threads of gold from the folds of blue wool while she struggled with the axe. He remembered staring at it, as if hypnotized by those sparks of color. Every moment of that night was imprinted on his memory. *I should have known then that she was my mate.* They could have spent the year together. His arms went rigid, trembling with the effort of keeping them at his sides.

"I couldn't leave until you went inside." His fingers and toes would have frozen if he hadn't been a skin-walker. He'd been so uncomfortable, unable to change into the fur.

"You must have hated us then. I remember when you dropped off that frozen caribou. I had no idea what to do, and you just stood there, silent," Martha said. "I didn't understand then."

He waited, wondering what she would say. He'd learned to keep his feelings hidden early on. Whether to protect his family from having to worry or to avoid giving bigots like the foreman the satisfaction of reacting, it was easier to keep it all tucked behind a scowl.

"Now I know how much work it was to keep us all fed. You took care of all of us." Martha kept her voice low. "And you're still doing it. You've done an incredible job, both then and now. I haven't had someone I could rely on in a long time, and I'm out of practice. Your help means more to me than I can say. So thank you."

The words warmed him. "You're welcome."

"You know, when you smile, it changes your whole face. It's much nicer than the angry scowl." She laughed lightly. "Who knew you had this charming, open side? I certainly wouldn't have guessed it when I yelled at you in the woods."

Her beautiful smile made him feel like he'd hunted a whole winter's supply of meat and single-handedly built a cabin for it. He wanted to tell her about the mating bond but held back. Putting that burden of expectation and obligation on her would be wrong. "Before that day, I didn't know you had such fire inside you."

"I guess we fooled each other, then." The dancing joy faded from her eyes. "I used to be a fighter. When I was working, I would go up against the union, the administration, anyone who was taking advantage. I dug into records and found cases of fraud. I helped with recordings when one of the doctors was trying to coerce a nurse into sleeping with him. They started sending me into hospitals to clean them up. I was proud of doing all that. It was the right thing to do, and I was in a position to do it."

He could easily imagine it.

"I know Hood thinks I've made a mistake and that it's too big a risk to help Kal, Patrick, and Annika or to confront the foreman. But I can't ignore it, not anymore." Martha took at deep breath. "I hope I didn't cause you more trouble."

"Don't worry." He moved closer to her. "I can take care of myself."

"I know." Her voice caught.

"You are a fierce kestrel." He cupped her cheek, stroking the cheekbone with his thumb. "She is the smallest hawk but takes on opponents many times her size and defeats them." His self-control faltered, and he bent his head, touching his mouth to hers.

In the back of his mind, he was still planning to do the right thing and walk away. Even the front of his mind was still confident that he could allow a lapse of control and still step away. And he might have had a chance if she hadn't started to kiss him back.

Her lips moved under his, and all brain function shut down to enjoy the sensual pleasure. She tasted sweet and rich, like summer berries and fresh flowers. He could feast on her all day and keep coming back hungry for more. Her hands slid around his neck, pulling him closer as her fingers twined deep into his hair.

His entire body shook with conflicting needs. He wanted to pick her up and carry her to the bedroom. He wanted to tear away the ridiculous thin clothes that separated them. He wanted to lay her down and let his mouth roam over her skin. He gritted his teeth as his swollen cock pushed hard against its denim prison.

She pulled away. Her cheeks turned bright red, and his palms absorbed the sudden inrush of heat. "I'm sorry."

"Do you want to stop?" he growled, aware he was looming over her but unwilling to lose physical contact.

Her head shook once. Twice. And that was all the encouragement that he needed.

He did what he'd been longing to do since she'd walked into the room. He pulled her into his arms, and the feel of her body pressed against his drove him into wild territory. Any doubts he might have held about her eager participation vanished as she opened her mouth under his. Her tongue darted forward and teased his, shattering his lingering concentration and awareness.

He deepened the kiss, swallowing her moans of pleasure. He ran his hands along her back, pressing their bodies tighter together. Her hip rubbed against his heavy erection, and he growled, grinding his hips against hers.

Releasing her lips, he began to kiss along her neck. She tilted her head back, baring her throat to him and letting her soft hair spill over his hands. Tiny, throaty gasps escaped from her with each soft-lipped nibble. He gripped her hips to hold her still as he began to lower his mouth, pushing at the neckline of her sweater to bare the sweet skin underneath.

"Mom?"

Bernie's plaintive cry broke the moment, leaving them breathless and clutching at one another.

"Yes, sweetie?" Martha called out, her fingers still buried in his hair and red marks from his lips visible on her pale flesh.

"Is it time for breakfast?"

"No, sweetheart. You can go back to sleep." She sighed as he pressed his forehead against hers. "I'm sorry," she whispered.

She kissed him again, a soft tender touch of the lips, equal parts apology and promise.

He ran his thumb gently down her face, drawing a line from the corner of her eye down to her chin. She let her hands slide down from his hair only to clutch the fabric of his shirt as if she wanted to rip it aside.

"I want to." She stole another soft kiss. "I want to so much. But I can't, not right now."

He nodded reluctantly. Better than anyone, he understood how responsibility could override personal desire.

Slowly, she disentangled from him, breathing heavily as she retreated to their shared room. Lou watched her go and wondered how humans ever got anything done. The rush had been far more intense than the annual heat of his bear form. *If they can feel like this at any time, why don't they?* Because he knew he would not forget that kiss anytime soon. Exhaling sharply, he did the only thing he could think of and headed back out to the woods.

NEGOTIATION

Chapter Twenty-Two

For Martha, putting aside fantasies of Lou had been hard enough before, but the memory of their kiss that morning made it nearly impossible. And it wasn't only lust and physical passion. She was discovering how kind and considerate he was. He took care of them without expectations or demands, protecting them in spite of the fact that it meant leaving his family. *I have to remember that this is all temporary.* Otherwise, it would be all too easy to find herself deep into an emotional connection that could rip her apart when they had to leave.

Still, that man can kiss. She didn't know where he'd gotten the practice, but his skills were incredible. A heated sensory flashback forced her to pause on the dark narrow stairs to the secret lab, sending a tingling throb through her loins and a rush of heat to her cheeks.

I hope that was out of range for Kal. She took a breath, tightened her grip on the bag of wrapped sandwiches and muffins, and stepped into the lab. Dr. Coulon was still away, but Martha had convinced Mrs. Fitz to let her open the medical building to help calm down the *lalassu*. Tensions were high after the mass tasing. She hoped that treating their bruises and other injuries would help. And maybe it would distract her from thinking about kissing Lou.

Kal beamed at her as she pushed aside the plastic strips. Martha doubted his delighted, knowing grin was about the food. Chickening out, she went to Patrick's cell first. As usual, he was rocking back and forth and reciting his formulas, but he slowed down as she pulled out a sandwich.

"Thank you." He took a large bite. "This is turkey on whole wheat with mayonnaise and mustard."

Martha nodded. "Do you like it?"

"It's good." Patrick took another bite. "My favorite is peanut butter and jelly."

"I'll see what I can do for next time," Martha promised. "Here's a blueberry muffin, too."

He was muttering to himself again by the time she moved to Annika's cage. The girl sat on the cot, facing the bars. "You keep coming back."

Martha decided to treat the sarcasm at face value. "Yes. Are you okay with turkey?"

Annika shrugged and winced, her hand coming up to touch the fading bruise on her jaw. "Food's food. You got any painkillers?"

"I'm sorry. I'm not sure what he's already given you, and I don't want to cause a drug interaction." Martha passed the sandwich and muffin through the bars.

"Yeah, 'cause it would be such a tragedy if I died in here." Annika rolled her eyes but still picked up the food.

"It would matter to me. And not all drug interactions are fatal. They could cause all sorts of problems." Martha curled her hand around the bar, wishing she could go in and give Annika a hug. "None of you should be in here, and I'm doing what I can to make sure that you all get out."

"Right." Annika laughed bitterly. "I know Mr. Teacher down at the end has checked, and you actually believe that. But it doesn't make it true. No one is riding to our rescue."

Martha had tried being nice to break through Annika's thick protective shell. Maybe she should try a dose of unexpected realism. "You're right."

That got Annika's attention. Her head snapped up, and she blinked a few times.

"I wish someone was. I'm not one of the *lalassu*. I'm a nurse. In here, all I can do is bring you food and a blanket to keep your warm. Out there, all I can do is stitch up wounds and give out antibiotics. So that's what I'm going to do." Martha held Annika's gaze. "I wish I had the power to bust through the walls and set you all free."

As Martha walked back to Kal's cell, Annika called out, "They feed us twice a day."

Martha paused and looked back.

"They were here about an hour before you came. You should be more careful or else you'll get caught." Annika bit into her blueberry muffin.

"Thank you." Martha had wondered, especially given the doctor's long absence. It was the first time one of them had shared information with her. Kal kept telling her not to worry about it. "Wait—are they coming through the medical building?"

Annika shook her head. "They come through the tunnels."

Martha had forgotten about what lay beyond the plastic-strip curtain on the far wall. Or maybe she hadn't wanted to remember. *Someone could have come out of there at any time.* Chilly sweat pooled down her spine as she realized how close she'd been to being discovered.

"I would have warned you, Martha," Kal called out.

I guess he would have. It wasn't completely reassuring, but it let her calm down enough to hand over the last of the food to him.

"I'll always let you know if it's safe," he promised.

"So don't come in if it's quiet, huh?" Martha rubbed her arms. *How did he get captured if he can read minds that well?*

"The minds in front of me didn't know anything, and the ones I needed to read were too far away."

"I'm sorry. That was rude," Martha said.

"Not at all." Kal glanced at the ceiling. "I think it would be best if you went upstairs now. Be careful."

Taking his warning seriously, Martha ran up the stairs. Any second, she expected shouts from someone looking for her, but her heart was pounding so loudly that she couldn't hear anything else. She pushed open the bookcase, only to discover no one else there.

Real funny, Kal. She sealed the bookcase door, trying to calm her breathing. Someone could come in at any moment, and she sounded as if she'd been running. As she had the thought, the front door opened, and Ryan walked in. "Hey there, Martha. What's wrong?"

"You… ah, startled me." Martha made herself lower her hand from her chest. "Is something wrong in the camp?"

Ryan's eyes lingered on where her fist had been as he came toward her, placing each foot with deliberate menace as he circled to her left. "I wondered that myself. Especially after the riot. It seems strange to me that you've been pushing to let the loocies out when they nearly killed your daughter."

She had no idea what to say in response, so she kept quiet. He seemed agitated, which would make it very easy for her to misstep.

"I've been pretty busy." He picked up a box of bandages. "Someone has been riling up the loocies. And there have been some thefts. Food from the kitchen, blankets from the warehouse. Do you know anything about that?"

They must have taken a more thorough inventory than Martha would have guessed. She met his eyes and kept her voice calm. "I'm afraid I don't."

"You're different from the others." Ryan's words sent a chill down her spine. She'd heard that tone before, in violent psychiatric patients before they attacked.

"Thank you. I really should get back to work. I'm sure people will be coming any minute." She kept an eye on the half-open door, hoping someone might appear to rescue her.

"We take traitors seriously here." Ryan stopped circling and leaned in. Martha tried to step away, but he had maneuvered her against the long counter, and her escape was cut off.

"I don't know what you're talking about." The words were weak, her mouth too dry to deliver much sound. *Does he know about the film? That Bernie is one of the* lalassu?

His eyes lit up in pleasure. Martha's stomach dropped as she realized that she'd given him what he wanted: her fear. He liked being in power.

She needed to stay calm and keep thinking. If he knew about the photos, he had no reason to keep quiet about it. She should try to keep him talking. Eventually, he would get tired and find someone else to bully. She opened her mouth, but it was too late.

Ryan's hand jammed into her throat, his fingers wrapping around her neck.

She grabbed at his hand, trying to pry at his grip.

"Don't lie to me." He batted away her clawing fingers as if they were nothing.

"Stop," she croaked.

He released her neck. She reached up automatically to check for injuries, but he grabbed her wrist and twisted hard.

A hoarse whisper of a scream escaped her lips. He pinned her against the counter with his body, trapping her free hand between the two of them.

"Where's the uppity bitch who stood up to the foreman now? Hmm?" He wrenched her wrist as if he were trying to unscrew it.

"I'll scream," she gasped.

"Try it, and I can kill you before anyone comes. I'll tell them you were helping the loocies."

His attempt to threaten only brought relief. *He doesn't know.*

"You know, I can't stop thinking about that day." He dropped her wrist and wrapped his hand around her throat again. "Until then, I had you pegged as a real mouse. Now, I know there's some spirit to make things even more interesting."

His closeness made her skin crawl as if it were trying to get away from him. She tried to lean back over the counter, but he only pressed closer. His hand tightened painfully around her neck.

"One word from me, and you, your husband, and your daughter all disappear into the inner camp. Trust me, former staff don't do well in there. You would never make it out," he whispered into her ear.

Nothing was getting through her windpipe. Black flecks started to fill the edges of her vision as she struggled to break free. The doorway remained empty. She'd underestimated him. He wasn't a petty bully. He was a full-on psychopath. There was a real chance that she might not survive. *I'm sorry, Bernie. I'm sorry, Lou.*

Ryan glanced over his shoulder to see what Martha was looking at. His creepy smile grew wider, as if being pulled with hooks at the corners. "So what are you going to do to keep me from tossing you on the other side of the fence with a collar around your throat?"

"Fascinating." Dr. Coulon polished his glasses and leaned close for a better look in the dim early-morning light. After a week away from his lab, his brain felt soft from lack of scientific exercise, but it had been worth it. The young woman kneeling in front of him showed no signs of physical abnormality. Outwardly, she appeared to be Native American, with a genetic background in the Pacific Southwest. Five foot six, maybe seven, with a petite build. Even though she was wrapped in heavy chains looped around her neck, arms, waist, and legs, her captors lifted her easily, which proved that her muscles and bones weren't unusually dense.

But this woman could transform into a massive grizzly bear, one that could stand nearly twelve feet tall and weighed almost two thousand pounds. It was no illusion. A third of the collection team was dead, but Dr. Coulon had what he needed. Five cubs squalled in kennel cubes, and seven adult corpses were being prepared for shipment and dissection. Adding to the din was the yapping and howling of the dozens of dogs, all chained on the far side of the little collection of cabins.

The woman glared at him but held still in the hands of the two men holding her. The chain wrapped around her throat prevented her from changing to a larger shape. It would strangle her before she could break free. *An elegant solution.* He admired whomever had devised it. He would find a more permanent version before bringing her to camp.

Irregular bursts of gunfire nearby interrupted his concentration. The collection team was still securing the other specimens. He was impatient to get back to his lab and begin work but reminded himself not to be hasty. Proper examination took time, and it would be scientifically mortifying to miss a key detail because he allowed himself to become too excited.

"Secure her in a transport cage," he told the two armored men holding her.

They nodded and carried her to a waiting unit. Using the same basic design as medevac cocoons, the transport cages would keep the occupants immobile and lying prone. The cages could then be attached to the exterior of the helicopter or another vehicle, minimizing the risks if a test subject did manage to escape. He was reminded of an important detail. "Tell the others that I need at least two more confirmed transformatives. I want to determine if the subjects remain in animal form when killed or if they revert to a human one."

"Yes, Doctor." They finished securing the specimen inside a cage before rejoining the rest of the team.

Dr. Coulon turned his attention to one of the cubs. It sat in the middle of the kennel, staring at him instead of calling like the others. A long cattle prod lay nearby, and he picked it up, tempted to shock the creature to see if electricity would produce a transformation. It would be a quick field test, something to replicate later in his lab.

The current subjects will have to be moved. The predictive could be sent to Dalhard Industries. Dr. Coulon had learned nearly all he could from him. Special Investigations could have the telepath. The invulnerable was a more difficult decision, but there was plenty of cold storage, so he could keep her corpse until he had time for a detailed postmortem.

"Lily!" A man's voice roared nearby.

Irritated, Dr. Coulon saw a Caucasian man running toward the transport cages. He was over six feet and muscular but moving much faster than one would expect. *Perhaps another potential test subject.* He glanced around, but none of the collection team were nearby. *How disappointing.*

The woman in the cage shouted at the man, telling him to run. That wasn't an acceptable option. These transformative bears might be an exciting new variation, but Dr. Coulon had no intention of abandoning his research into other *occulata hominem.*

The man grabbed the transport cage and began to twist the steel containment bars with his bare hands. *Utterly amazing.* Dr. Coulon moved closer. It should be physically impossible for human flesh to withstand the pressure of the one-inch rods, no matter how much strength the individual possessed.

"Ron! Look out!" the woman screamed.

Regretting the necessity, Dr. Coulon jabbed the cattle prod into the man's back before he could turn around. The man immediately shook in a full-body spasm and dropped to the ground. Dr. Coulon waited then used the prod again, sending even more voltage into the subject's body. He watched carefully, keeping an eye on the man's respiration and reactions. Triggering a heart attack would be frustrating and inconvenient for his research.

Three members of the collection team arrived, weapons drawn and ready to fire. From their bruises and grim expressions, Dr. Coulon guessed they'd already encountered the latest subject.

"Get me the sedatives." He didn't trust the soldiers to monitor the prod's effects properly, and the man's strength removed the possibility of using purely physical restraints. They would need to develop some sort of foam containment to prevent him from gaining the leverage to escape. *Ah well, improvisation can yield unexpected benefits on occasion.*

The clinking of glass vials announced the arrival of the sedatives. Dr. Coulon gave the man another preventative jolt before filling a syringe with ketamine. He would prefer something more precise, but there were too many unknowns that could affect the anesthetic.

Metal rattled as the woman shouted at him, throwing herself around in the transport cage. Dr. Coulon frowned, weighing the risks of sedating her as well. She could damage herself, but if he injected her, he would have to keep her inside the helicopter so that he could monitor her. *Better to transfer her to another transport cage.*

Once the man was unconscious, he directed the collection team to place him in restraints and prepare for immediate takeoff. "I want two men armed with cattle prods inside the helicopter as well as live ammunition."

"Yes, sir. We've acquired one more transformative, but the others have scattered into the forest. Do you want us to track them down?"

Of course I do. But the realities of the clock held him back. It would take another two hours to regroup, another four and a half to fly to Woodpine, and an additional two hours to unload and secure the subjects in his lab. It was not worth the additional delay to waste more time for one or two possible additional subjects. "Prepare for extraction."

"Yes, sir."

"And re-secure that one." He pointed at the woman. She was still struggling to break free.

With his instructions complete, Dr. Coulon left the din of dogs, woman, and cubs so that he could use the satellite phone to contact Dalhard Industries. He would have preferred to speak with Priya. She respected his talent and never argued with him about resources, but her brother would have to do.

"Dr. Coulon, it is a pleasure to hear from you," Karan answered. "Was the collection worth the extended wait?"

It felt like a snide reminder of his objections to the delay. "You were correct. Fewer soldiers might have compromised the collection."

"How many transformatives did you collect?" Karan asked.

"I have one female and one male subject. Your soldiers are tracking a third," the doctor reported. "However, I've also acquired an unexpected subject. He is not one of the transformatives but appears to be a different variety of *occulata hominem*."

"How so?" Karan sounded bored. Coulon could hear computer keys clicking over the connection.

"He appears to be a white male in his mid-thirties but is exceptionally strong. The bars weren't melted or otherwise structurally changed. His hands crushed the steel like clay."

The clicking stopped. "A Caucasian? You are certain?"

An idiotic and insulting question. But Coulon remained calm. *I still need his company's support.* "That's correct."

"You may have discovered a very significant individual, the target of a prolonged manhunt. Corporal Ron McBride," Karan said excitedly.

"He is an O.H.?" Coulon asked carefully. If he was reading the other man correctly, it could be a promising development. The doctor was loath to lose either of his acquired transformatives to public demonstration.

"He is a test subject of my former employer, Mr. Dalhard. His DNA was blended with that of an *occulata hominem*. I want him sent to New York immediately."

Coulon couldn't allow the man to steal all of his potential test subjects. "If I may, he was captured while attempting to free one of the transformatives. A woman. He was entirely preoccupied and didn't react as I approached."

There was silence on the other end of the call.

"If I were to hold on to the transformatives, they could be a useful tool in securing the experiment's cooperation." It would be so much simpler if Coulon could have spoken with Priya instead. But the siblings had insisted.

"I see. You may have a valid point. What is it that you want, Doctor?"

Coulon didn't hesitate. "I want to run tests on the two transformatives. I want a chance to understand them and discover the secrets of their abilities."

"Your devotion to your research is admirable."

Unsure if Karan was mocking him, Coulon continued. "If the experiment is not a true *occulata hominem*, his inclusion in my data will skew the results. Take him and use him as your demonstration."

"I could take all three." Karan sounded bored.

"All three together present a much greater risk of escape. Separate them, and they will be less likely to take the chance. Choose which one you want the most and leave me the others." Coulon hesitated. "I would be… grateful."

"In what sense?"

"You wanted a way to exploit O.H. abilities. Give me this research, and I will find the secrets of their powers." Coulon waited for Karan to reach the only possible conclusion.

"Very well. Keep the transformatives. But send me McBride." Karan ended the call.

Visions of academic papers and speaking tours made the doctor smile. His old university would regret dismissing him to placate the politically correct activists. Those students had known what they were signing up for. The fact that a few didn't survive the testing was unfortunate, but it was no reason to attack his research.

Occulata Hominem *and Their Abilities*. It would be the definitive textbook by Dr. Christoph Coulon.

Chapter Twenty-Three

"I don't want to be a messenger ghost. I hate talking to Gwen." Chuck grimaced as one of the teenage girls walked right through him, pushing past Bernie to join her friends watching the construction crews. Bernie still didn't know all their names, but they'd made it very clear that they weren't interested in being friends. None of the internee kids would talk to her since the riot the day before. They stared at her, fingering their narrow gray collars but not saying a word. Mrs. Chin didn't say anything. She probably thought Bernie was too stupid to notice.

"C'mon," Bernie muttered under her breath. It didn't matter if the kids noticed her talking to herself. It couldn't make her any more of a freak.

"She's a real whacky. Besides, we should be worrying about the plane in three days and how you and me can be on it." Chuck followed Bernie to the far end of the school playground. Henri was already waiting there in his resplendent brocade coat and hose.

"How are you on this fine day, *ma petite*?"

"Fine. Is Leanne okay?" The guards wouldn't let Bernie into the inner camp at all, thanks to Lou hauling her out like a bag of potatoes last time.

"Doing much better. I helped her find a stash of painkillers, since she won't see your mother."

Her mom had convinced them to open the medical building so she could treat the contact burns and sprains from the mass tasing. Some of the *lalassu* would let her help, but others, including Leanne, wouldn't. "I don't blame Leanne. It was all Mom's fault."

"The guards and the shock collars must take some responsibility, *non*?" Henri's smile ignited Bernie's temper.

"Don't make fun of me." From the startled looks around her, Bernie had spoken louder than she meant. She hunched away from the stupid kids with their stupid faces and lowered her voice. "I'm not some baby."

"I know that, Bernie." Chuck said, glaring at Henri.

"And you are right." Henri nodded gravely, adjusting his cravat. "Adults do have a habit of forgetting how much children have grown."

"This whole thing is dumb, and everyone keeps pushing me aside. Like I'm not the one with the most to lose if this doesn't work out." Bernie rubbed at her neck, reassuring herself of the absence of a collar.

"It's much quieter here today." Henri changed the topic. "You were finally able to drive the other ghosts away?"

During their talk the day before, Leanne explained how Bernie could hook her mind together with Chuck's, creating a kind of bridge between them. Since then, they'd been practicing, and that morning, they finally got it to work, creating their own "territory" that they defended with Bernie's living energy and Chuck's ghostly energy. "Mr. Marshall and the screaming lady are gone."

Henri leaned over and winked. "And good riddance to them."

"We decided to let the other girl stay." Bernie pointed her nose at the girl with braids, standing and watching the other kids play tag. "She seemed lonely."

She expected Henri to approve, but instead his colors flickered into dull gray for a moment. Losing colors usually meant a ghost felt sad or guilty, according to Leanne. "That is a very kind thing to do, *petite*. Did Leanne show you this?"

"Not really. But Chuck and I figured it out." It was like issuing a day pass for a visitor.

"Very well done, Mademoiselle Bernadette." Another flicker of gray. "And now I shall treat you like an adult, and we can discuss the plans to escape this place."

Bernie took a deep breath. She hadn't shared any of it with Chuck yet. "I don't think we should leave."

"What?" Chuck's shout echoed across the camp. It seemed

impossible that no one else heard it, though Bernie noticed a few people slowing and rubbing their arms, probably reacting to the increase of tension and heaviness in the air. Henri was pushed back, his feet disappearing into the mud, and the girl with braids had vanished.

Henri made his way back to them, wincing and moving stiffly. There was no sign of the girl. Bernie hoped that she hadn't been hurt. "This place is awful."

"You will get no argument about that from me." Henri tugged at his coat cuffs.

"All the more reason to get out of here." Chuck got darker and angrier.

"Please don't get mad, Chuck." Bernie licked her suddenly dry lips. "I'm not saying I don't want to go, just that I don't think we should right now."

She braced herself for an explosion of temper that could include lights flickering, booming noises, even relentlessly whispered demands in her ear—Chuck had done them all in the past, and he looked perfectly willing to do them again.

"Why?" Henri asked softly.

Bernie had spent most of the day thinking of how to explain it. "We have an obligation to use our gifts to help. Michael used to talk a lot about superheroes and how the good heroes help other people who don't have special powers. Even when it's hard, even when it costs them everything, they keep on helping."

"Those are stories. Real people aren't like that!" Chuck glared.

"Michael is. He and Dani risked their lives to come and rescue me. Dani could have gotten her mind all eaten up by Mr. Dalhard, but she kept on helping. Mr. Dalhard tried to blow Michael up, but he didn't stop trying to rescue me." Bernie took a deep breath. "I thought about what my mom said. How actions count more than what people say. I don't want to be the kind of person who runs away. I want to be one of the heroes."

"*Un coeur plein de courage,*" Henri whispered like a proud dad, and even though Bernie didn't know what his words meant, she like the sound of them.

"Your mom doesn't want you to help. She didn't even want to use you to send a message to Gwen," Chuck pointed out nastily.

His words made Bernie angry. Her mom saw her as broken and useless. But she had a chance to change that.

"She and Eva have been sneaking food to the people in the secret lab. That's helping, too." Chuck wasn't finished. "You promised Leanne she could leave. You want to break your promise?"

"I'm not breaking it, just postponing it." Bernie turned to Henri. "Do you think she'll be mad at me because I don't want to leave yet?"

"She'll be furious!" The air chilled as Chuck shouted. "You're leaving her in a prison!"

"Exactly. This is a prison." Bernie rubbed her arms. "What happened with the collars, I knew they could do it, but when I saw it happen, it was scary. No one should ever be able to do that to someone else, and no one should ever be stuck in a place where they have to be afraid of it happening. The experiments in the doctor's lab, they're awful. Heroes stop stuff like that from happening. We can do that."

Henri knelt on one knee in front of Bernie so that his face was on the same level as hers. "Perhaps we can, *petite*. I will talk with Leanne and help her to understand. But no matter how she or Monsieur Charles feel, I am very proud of you for what you want to do."

Chuck vanished, the ghost equivalent of stomping off in a huff. It didn't bother Bernie the way it usually did. "Really? You're proud of me?"

"*Non.*" He winked at her again. "I am very proud of you."

Mrs. Chin shouted at the children to let them know recess was over. The kids began trudging back to the schoolhouse, but Bernie had one more thing to do.

"Will you check on the little girl with the braids? Make sure that she's okay after Chuck's outburst?"

Henri flickered to gray again but smiled. "*Certainement.* You can trust me."

218

Martha staggered through the front door of the trailer, tripping over the recessed step. Fumbling, she yanked the door closed behind her and slid the lock home. The metallic click snapped through her like a padlock on a chain, making it impossible for her to move. Every step of the way, she'd been focused on what would happen as soon as she had privacy. She'd expected to cry and shake as her mind replayed her encounter with Ryan over and over again. She'd planned to begin packing so they could flee this horrible place that night. But she found herself sitting on the floor like a bump on a log, her mind too numb to think, feel, or plan.

"He's coming soon." She'd gasped out the words.

Ryan had dropped her, looking over his shoulder. She'd scurried away out of his reach.

"Fine. We'll finish another time." He grabbed his rifle. "And I don't think I have to explain that, if you say a word, your family will pay the price."

She leaned back against the wall, cradling her abused wrist to her chest. The cool plastic vinyl paneling popped shallowly beneath her head's weight. Her throat ached in a way worse than any virus or infection could cause. She touched it gently with her uninjured hand, trying to evaluate if the heat and tension were the result of her emotional response or a sign of physical damage. If her throat was swelling, it could cut off her breathing when she fell asleep. And she didn't want to think about having to explain the bruises to her daughter. Or to Lou.

"I'm going into shock," she rasped, her voice sounding as if she were two days into a three-day whiskey bender. The thought made her laugh, jarring her wrist. A sharp spike of agony brought tears to her eyes. She started to cough and wheeze as her body tried simultaneously to not move and breathe. Bracing herself against the cheap carpet, she focused on calming herself down.

Shock. The light-headed hysterical laughter was another symptom. She could run down an entire clinical list, but none of her medical training could tell her how to make herself get up and start doing what needed to be done.

Ryan had only let her go so that he could toy with her. He wanted her fear, and he knew there was nothing she could do to stop him.

People talked about the fight-or-flight impulse, but Martha didn't get either of those in a crisis. Instead, she froze. It was the worst possible option, since it allowed all of her problems to stack together, threatening to bury her in an avalanche of results that she could have avoided.

I'm not going to be stuck staring at dirty socks again. I have to figure out what to do next. She wanted to run. Then, she'd never have to find out if Ryan's threats were theatrical or real. *So what are you going to do to keep me from tossing you on the other side of the fence with a collar around your throat?* Right after he'd said it, he'd taken her aching hand and rubbed it against his crotch as she struggled to breathe. She'd come close to panicking, wondering if he'd keep choking her and all too aware of how the combination excited him. Too scared and surprised to fight back, she'd gone limp, hoping he wouldn't demand gratification right there and then.

The door had been open. Anyone could have walked in and seen them, which meant that Ryan wasn't worried about facing any consequences for his actions. The sour taste of bile in the back of her throat came with the certainty that it hadn't been the first time it had happened. And it wouldn't be the last.

This isn't supposed to be happening to me anymore! She'd been careful in her teens and twenties, never appearing too flirty or going by herself to a bar or some man's apartment. But since then, her life's mileage and motherhood had rendered her effectively invisible. She was the one who made the chocolate chip cookies, not the one who got sniggered at or fantasized about.

Of course, it wasn't really about sex. It wasn't her body or her personality that had Ryan excited. It was the power he held over her. He enjoyed threatening her, Bernie, and Lou.

Ryan had laughed at her before he walked away. Even in her memory, the sound sank deep under her skin like acid. He'd liked her confusion because it only added to his sense of power. And he would come back for more.

I can't afford to indulge myself now. I have to figure out what to do next.

They could run. *But Ryan would go after Hood and Harley. Oh God—what if he goes after Eva?* She was bright, pretty, and young, which meant there was no chance that Ryan wouldn't want to overpower her. Martha gagged on a fresh wave of bile at the thought of him groping and pawing at the girl. Hood and Harley would go ballistic. She wiped at her mouth, working on convincing her stomach not to throw up in a desperate bid to purge the greasy contamination of Ryan's attentions. Closing her eyes, she tried to imagine what one of the other *lalassu* women might have done in her place.

Dani had fought Dalhard's mind-control powers, breaking his hold over her. Lily had taken on an entire squad of soldiers to protect Bear Claw. Cali had not only stopped Dalhard but also managed to pry open Vincent's shell to begin the healing process. Despite being blind, Virginia ran the *lalassu* underground, using her visions and blunt-force personality. Evonne had left Bear Claw to follow her dreams and start a new life. Any of them could have kicked Ryan's ass without breaking a sweat. Martha had let herself believe that she might be like them. She thought that she could make a difference, maybe even find some happiness and love.

Except it just wasn't her. She wasn't a Rosa Parks or a Joan of Arc or a Harriet Beecher Stowe. She was a mom trying to do the right thing for her daughter, not save the world. *Then I need to do the right thing. For now, I need to tend to my injuries. That's the first step.*

She hauled herself to her feet and walked carefully to the small bathroom. She drenched a thin towel with cool water and held the dripping mass to her throat while holding her wrist under the running tap. As she stared at herself in the mirror, it was hard for her to remember that she'd felt hopeful and proud only a few hours before. Lou had kissed her and called her a fierce kestrel. *What would he think now?*

The door to the trailer banged open, and Martha spun around, dropping the towel to grope for a weapon.

Harley stood in her living room. "Mrs. Fitz is on a rampage looking for you."

Oh. It wasn't surprising. She should have been back at the administrative building after lunch.

He came closer, his hands upraised and compassion creasing his thin face. "What happened?"

From the horrified expression on his face, her prayers to avoid bruising had gone unanswered. "Ryan," Martha said in her new smoke-and-whiskey voice, "he…"

"He did this to you?" Harley's mouth narrowed as he knelt down beside her. "We have to tell Hood and Lou."

She grabbed his arm and shook her head. "We can't."

Harley was quick to figure out the reason. "He threatened you. Does he know about the lab? The food?"

"Not about the lab." Her throat hurt more than she could have imagined as she forced the words out. "They found the missing blankets and food."

"Shit."

"I'll be okay." She would make it be okay. The thought of the others playing white knights and getting captured or killed was terrifying.

"Honey, from those marks around your neck, he tried to kill you." Harley spoke gently, as if she might break down any minute.

Abruptly, Martha was sick of being treated like spun glass. She might not be a badass, but she wasn't a complete victim. "I know." Each syllable scraped against her raw esophagus. "I need you to help me get to the medical building. I need a brace for my wrist and anti-inflammatories to prevent my throat from swelling."

He blinked in surprise. "I think—"

"I'm the closest thing to a doctor here. I know what I need." Martha turned around and examined herself in the mirror again, checking her eyes for any sign of burst blood vessels. Her eyes were red and swollen from crying, but there weren't any brilliant spots of red. *I wish I could do a laryngoscopy, but I'll have to settle for treating the symptoms.*

"I'll take care of it." Harley stood behind her, visible to her in the mirror. "Tell me what I need to get."

She opened her mouth to answer, but he shook his head.

"Don't strain your voice. Write it down. I'd rather not face Lou knowing that I caused you more pain than you needed." Harley grinned, handing her the pad and pencil from the table. "His feelings for you are way more powerful than either of you realize."

"He can't go grizzly on Ryan." Martha's heart ached at the thought of him risking himself. "You need to convince him."

"I don't think it'll be as hard as you imagine. Not that he's not willing to rip this place and everyone in it apart for you. But he's going to listen if you say that's not what you want." He motioned at the pad for her to start writing. "He's a rare commodity, Martha. He's spent his entire life in isolation, which doesn't just mean he's got that whole Nanook-of-the-North hotness thing going. It also means that he's never learned to say one thing and mean something else. He's got no idea of the games that civilized people play when they get groiny with each other."

Martha tore the top sheet off the pad and gave it to Harley, trying to keep her face impassive.

"You're skeptical, but I've been amusing myself over the last week and a half, watching Lou get up the courage to admit how he feels about you. He might not be a game player, but he still has some serious alpha-male silence issues to overcome. Or at least he did until this morning." Harley seemed to accept Martha's blush as confirmation. "You're worried he's going to see you differently because of what Ryan did. But that's never going to happen. All he sees is you."

Chapter Twenty-Four

"What?" The human word spilled out of Lou's mouth, despite the fact that the last thing he needed to hear was Hood repeat what he'd already said. The two of them were deep in the forest, past the bottle-strewn fire pit. Hood had made some excuse to the foreman and took Lou there. At first, Lou had assumed it was some sort of human ritual, but Hood's news drove all of that from his mind.

"She's all right. Harley got her what she needs from the medical building." Hood held out his hands with his palms up as if surrendering. The gesture did nothing to calm Lou's anger as the other man kept talking. "He's also got Bernie with Eva, so everyone's safe. But you need to calm down and let me finish before you sprout fur."

Lou's muscles rolled and bunched as he hovered on the edge of transformation. He wanted to find Ryan and rip both hands from his arms for daring to touch Martha. Then Lou would crush the scavenger's ribs and crack his skull.

"You can't go after him. She doesn't want you to."

Lou paused, panting noisily as he struggled to inhale and exhale rather than launch into an attack.

"She can't deal with an avenging rampage right now. She's hurt and afraid and needs you to be with her, not on a vengeance tear in camp that could mean we all get caught and she loses her little girl forever. It's not fair, but it's what needs to happen." The anger in Hood's eyes matched the rage boiling in Lou's chest.

"He hurt her." The growled words came out low and thick, not entirely from a human throat.

"I know. And we will make sure he pays for it later. For now, it has to be about Martha. She needs you." Hood swallowed. "I can't let you go to her until you calm down."

From his sickened expression, Lou could tell that Hood recognized he was placing himself in a dangerous position. But he cared about Martha and understood human customs, so Lou restricted himself to a single growled question. "Why?"

Hood's shoulders relaxed slightly, but he still stood his ground. "Because if you snap while you're listening to her, it's going to hurt her way more than Ryan did. He's an asshole, and she knows it. You, she cares a whole lot about, and she's going to be terrified about how you'll react with her. So you're going to need to be gentle."

"How?" His voice became more human again, pleading rather than demanding.

"Let it out here. Yell at the sky, punch a wall, whatever you need to do." Hood straightened. "Then once you walk through the door, it's all about her and what she needs."

Lou nodded. His body shook from repressing the shift into the fur, so he surrendered— better in the woods than when he was faced with the scavenger. His shoulders and neck thickened while his nose and mouth thrust forward into a muzzle. There were brief sensations of pressure along his neck, waist, arms, and legs, but they quickly disappeared. He dropped to all fours. His claws cut through the hard-packed earth, and he roared, bellowing his fury across the forest. *Let the scavenger hear it and know fear.* He needed to release the rage building inside of him. A tall pine provided a satisfactory target. He reared up onto his sturdy hind legs and smashed his front paws into the tree, snapping the trunk.

Needles rained down, and a cloud of splinters filled the air as the tree fell between its companions. Lou landed hard, his paws crushing the ground under his weight. The tree crashed to the earth a moment later, rattling the ground and sending clouds of birds winging skyward. The cool air stung Lou's lungs as he snapped at the breeze, and his entire coat bristled, the prickly fur standing on end and making his already-impressive size seem even larger.

Beside him, Hood was holding very, very still, barely willing to breathe. A selfish part of Lou was glad. The other man liked to think he walked the path of the alpha predator, but like all so-called "civilized" humans, he'd distanced himself from nature's power. And if Lou couldn't induce pants-soiling terror in Ryan, there was a very human satisfaction in making someone else feel as uncertain and vulnerable as he did.

Short, sharp breaths helped to smother his rage, leaving it banked until it could blast its intended target. The emotion cleared, and Lou's muscles contracted and shrank as he pulled back into the skin. The breeze raised rows of goose bumps along his bare skin as his human body protested being naked in the cold.

Unfortunately, his clothing had not survived the shift. Bits of plaid flannel and dark denim littered the ground along with the wooden chunks and splinters from the tree.

"Okay. Not what I expected." Hood's low voice held more than a hint of bravado covering fear.

"Clothes," Lou growled.

"Yeah. We're definitely gonna need those." Hood nodded to himself, more as if to test his ability to move rather than out of a need to acknowledge. "I thought you'd take them off first or they'd absorb into your body or something."

Snorting, Lou bent down to pick up dark-brown leather tatters still attached to a rubber sole capped with steel. His work boots. Andrew would be frustrated with him if he knew about the destruction. Or maybe not. His twin had insisted on buying two pairs, so perhaps he'd expected Lou's behavior.

"All right. I can get you a spare set of my clothes. They'll be tight, but better that than wandering around naked. We need to get out of here in case someone works up the courage to come looking." Hood grabbed Lou's arm and tried to pull him forward.

"I need to go to Martha." Lou wrenched his arm free.

"Pants first. Martha second." Hood hissed then pursed his lips. "Actually, correction. First, no getting caught, then pants, then Martha."

Lou reluctantly accepted Hood's list of priorities. They began walking toward the camp.

"That was… more than I thought it would be." Hood seemed shaken. He kept glancing back at Lou. "I saw the video, but the live version is way different."

"How?" The shift was natural to Lou, something that all of his family did.

"Your body kind of twists, and then there's a bear standing where you were. A damn scary bear. I'll be honest. I just thought you were going to shout and maybe punch a tree or something. I didn't expect you to go full-on lumberjack." Hood took a deep breath. "This could cause us more problems."

Let it. Lou didn't say the words aloud, and he was aware that there were larger concerns. But he was also angry enough to be eager for a confrontation. Particularly if it meant he could get his claws into Ryan.

They reached the fire pit, and Hood directed Lou to hide while he went to retrieve clothing. Lou chose a tree and hauled himself into the concealment of the branches. He could see the camp, and there were definitely signs of agitation—people shouted and guards ran around. His outburst certainly had not gone unnoticed, and there was nothing he could do to change the outcome.

Regret tainted the fury still simmering inside. The *lalassu* in the camp would suffer because of his lost temper, and while he recognized that the alpha's share of blame rested on those who ran the camp, there was still plenty left to stick to his hide.

Hood returned quickly with a pair of gray sweatpants and a flannel shirt that buttoned down the front. His boots proved to be too small for Lou, so they would have to hope that no one noticed his bare feet. As they drew closer to the camp, it was harder for Lou not to be bent down by guilt. The *lalassu* were already in bad shape after being tased, and now they were slinking around and huddling nearby, looking even more frightened.

He might have begun the mission purely as a protector for Martha, Bernie, and Bear Claw, but Guardianship ran too deeply in his blood to walk away from such callous indifference to the suffering of others. Martha was right. They needed to expose the camp and get everyone out. But first, he needed to make certain they were okay.

As he got closer to the trailer, his heart started to pound hard enough to threaten to escape his ribs. He wasn't sure what to expect as he unlocked the narrow door.

Martha stood by the window in an oversized sweatshirt and jeans, her sunshine hair confined in a thick braid. She spun around when the door opened, and her face lit up in relief. "Thank God you're safe."

He couldn't make the proper reply with his attention focused on the dark nylon brace wrapped around her wrist and the huskiness of her voice. Red scratches and blotches stood out like a snare looped around her pale neck. *Ryan had put those there. Marked my woman as if she were a tree in empty territory.* Lou's nails stretched and hardened into claws, ready to rip a match for each bruise onto the scavenger's flesh. *No. Be what she needs.*

"I'm sorry," he whispered.

She flushed but didn't look away. "It's not your fault."

But it was. He was a Guardian, which meant it was his job to prevent such things from happening. And she was his mate, which made him doubly responsible for her safety.

"It's not my fault, either," she said quietly. "I have to keep telling myself that. I've already decided that I'm not going to let him win. He wanted to scare me, and he did, but in a few days, I'll be healed up. And then I'm going to bring him down." She raised her head, defiant instead of beaten.

Lou exhaled sharply. Whatever happened, Ryan hadn't destroyed her. His strong Martha might be marked, but she hadn't been broken—he hoped.

"Are you okay?" She stepped closer. "I heard the roar…"

"I should have been here." He bit his lip, not wanting to make things worse. Hood's claims about Martha's fragility didn't seem accurate, but maybe he'd seen something that Lou was missing. "Hood told me to take it out on the trees instead of shredding Ryan into fish-bait-sized pieces."

Her beautiful lips quirked in a smile. "Can we keep that option on the table?"

"Say the word," he promised.

She fidgeted with her braid. "You called me a fierce kestrel."

He nodded, holding himself still.

"I used to be someone to be reckoned with. People used to say I was more stubborn than any mule." She wandered to the sofa, not quite meeting his gaze. "But no one ever called me fierce until you. I liked that."

Then, those around her had been blind. The tiny hawk was the perfect symbol for her. Kestrels were devoted mothers who routinely took on both prey and enemies many times larger than themselves.

"I like the fact that I'm becoming that person again. This whole situation might be awful, but I'm not just surviving it. I'm actively doing something to make a difference." Martha sat down, releasing her braid to start digging her fingernail into the seam of her jeans and picking at the stitches.

He knelt in front of the sofa and rested his hand over hers, stilling the plucking.

She lifted her eyes, her long golden-brown lashes glinting in the light. "And then there's you. I told myself that I was comfortable focusing on getting Bernie what she needed and keeping her safe and that it didn't matter if I was alone."

Lou stroked her hand, driving himself wild with the tiny taste of what he craved. Her pupils were wider than normal, pools of blackness in the blue. She seemed restless, but he wasn't sure if it was an aftereffect of the attack or whatever drug she might have taken to help. *Andrew might know.* But her next words drove all thought of his twin out of his head.

"I don't want to go back to being alone. When we kissed, it was like the whole world shifted into color after years of gray." She stared at him as if searching for the answers in his face. "I don't want to lose that."

Her hand broke free from his and reached up to touch his cheek with trembling fingers. He held on to both his breathing and his control with only the tips of his blunt human fingernails.

"I don't want Ryan to take this part of me. What he tried to do, it was about showing me that he had power over me. I don't want it to get mixed up in what is between us." The pink tip of her tongue swiftly moistened her lips. "When we kissed, I liked it. A lot."

His mouth was dry, and his cock stood painfully at attention. *Be what she needs.* He would keep himself under control and run to the woods later if necessary.

"The thing is, I think I need that again." Her fingertips slowly moved down his face, brushing past his mouth and jaw. "But I don't want you to kiss me out of pity or because there's no one else available here. I need to know that it's because you want to and I want to. No other reason."

If he allowed himself to move, he would lose control, so he gave her an opportunity to halt it before it started. "Is this what you want? Are you sure?"

A faint laugh escaped as her hand dropped to his collar. "No, I'm not sure. I'm not sure of anything right now except that I don't want him in my head anymore, and I want you to help me chase him out. Please?" She stopped, pinching her lower lip between her teeth. "If you don't want to—"

"I do. I've never wanted to be with a woman the way I want to be with you." *There.* There would be no way to take it back or pretend it didn't exist.

She stared at him, her forehead wrinkled in confusion as if he'd spoken in Inukititut instead of English. "You do?"

"I dream of you. I think of you. I always want to be where you are." His hands rested on her thighs, ready to strip away the concealing denim. *Control!*

She slid forward a fraction of an inch, and her fingers twisted open the button on his collar. "I think about you, too."

The next button followed. Lou struggled to keep a sober mind through the rapidly rising heat pulsing through his body. She was injured. She'd been attacked. *I should not—*

The rest of the thought was lost as Martha planted her lips on his.

Chapter Twenty-Five

If their first kiss had ignited a fire, the current one threatened to burn down the entire forest. Martha was perfectly happy for it to scorch away the memories of the hours between the two, scalding them out of her mind as if they'd never existed.

The aches in her throat and her wrist faded away under Lou's gentle touch and soft kiss. His care of her healed the deeper wounds in her self-esteem. It was only for the moment—she knew she would eventually have to deal with the memory of Ryan's attack, but for the time being, she would accept Lou's easing of her pain and re-sparking of her expectations. It felt the way a kiss was supposed to feel, something wonderful and exciting to anticipate.

Lou gently pulled her closer, careful not to jar her wrist or neck as his hands drifted from her waist to skim up and down her spine. Undoing the buttons of his shirt was difficult to do one-handed, but she wanted to feel the warmth of his skin under her fingers. Sitting on the sofa with him kneeling in front of her put the two of them in the perfect position. His erection bulged against the sweatpants, and she was delighted to realize it excited her rather than bringing up memories of fear.

She opened her mouth under his, inviting him to deepen the kiss. He accepted, his tongue thrusting into her and sparking delight. He supported her neck and head with one hand while the other parted the gap between her shirt and pants, caressing the flesh at the base of her spine.

A soft noise, something between a gasp and a moan, vibrated through her throat. Growling quietly, he broke to meet her gaze, checking to see if she was all right. She traced the outline of his proud, concerned face with her fingertips. She could see the struggle to hold back in his eyes, and it was reassuring and powerful to know that her comfort and desire were so important to him.

As her breathing calmed, she relaxed in his arms. A smile slowly stretched her lips, and her eyes were wide and bright. Her thumb caressed his earlobe as she whispered, "Thank you."

She leaned forward to steal another kiss, but as their lips touched, the door to the trailer echoed with an urgent pounding.

They broke apart, but Martha's fingers were still twined in Lou's hair. Her body started to shake as she wondered who was out there, a sign that the afternoon's damage would need more than a kiss to make it all better.

"Martha, Lou. It's me."

She recognized Harley's voice, and the tension flowed away in a burst. She started to laugh in relief. "It's like high school, and we've been caught by Mom and Dad."

Lou frowned in concern but didn't ask her to explain. He rose, but Martha caught him by his waistband. His shirt hung open to his waist, and while she wasn't ashamed of what they'd done, she also didn't particularly want to advertise it. "Wait."

As she struggled to close the first button, he began to help. A low growl of equal parts determination and appreciation buzzed past his lips, bringing a smile to her face as she tugged his collar straight and smoothed his hair.

The door banged again, but Lou took the time for a swift, toe-curling kiss before answering. The expression on his face suggested he was ready to scare whoever it was into the middle of next week.

Harley shouldered his way into the trailer and shut the door behind him. "Sorry, I didn't want to interrupt, but…"

Martha slowly got to her feet and went to stand beside Lou. Whatever Harley had come to tell them wasn't good. He opened and closed his mouth several times as if trying to decide what to say.

"Are the *lalassu* upset that I didn't open the medical building? Or has someone found out what happened in the woods?" The urgent questions squeezed painfully through her throat, and her hand flew up to cover her bruises.

"Shh." Lou gathered her close before turning a baleful eye on Harley. "You. Talk."

"Did you hear the helicopters?" Harley asked.

Martha shook her head, and Lou did the same.

"There were three. They landed about fifteen minutes ago. After everything else, I thought I should have a look, and that's when I saw—" Harley stopped, rubbing at the back of his neck.

Any lingering good feelings quickly vanished to be replaced by fear. Beside her, Lou straightened and demanded. "What?"

"Bears. Big ones."

No. Martha's brain refused to leave denial. *It might not be Bear Claw. It could be a coincidence.*

"I'm sorry, man," Harley said.

Lou's muscles tightened under her hands, and his aura of menace returned. He growled a single word: "Where?"

"It makes sense if you think about it, Leanne," Henri insisted.

At least her supposed insanity gave her the perfect opportunity to indulge her temper. "Stuff it."

Two men ahead of her abruptly veered off to the side. Leanne hid a grin, enjoying the feeling of power. She'd joined one of the two groups capable of acting without consequences. She was at the bottom of the social pecking order. She had no family, resources, or friends, which meant there was nothing further that they could do to her. Any attempt at punishment would actually result in an improvement in her circumstances since she would be moved into a warm cell with regular meals. She cackled to herself, not bothering to muffle the volume.

Still, she'd much rather be part of the other group, those so rich and privileged that the world bent backward to prevent them from suffering the results of their bad decisions.

A pair of women talked quietly beside the barracks.

"I thought they were going to treat our injuries. I think Eric's wrist might be broken from falling," a woman complained.

"What else is new? The doctor's purpose was never to keep us healthy." The second woman glared bitterly at the guards walking past, rifles held prominently in front.

"The new one isn't as bad. Felicia said she fixed up her grandson's infection."

Leanne ground her teeth as the first woman defended Martha. *If the stupid woman hadn't panicked about Bernie, none of us would have been tased in the first place.*

"She's just like the rest," the second woman said. "I'm not giving her extra credit for doing her job."

"I've been speaking with Bernie, and there's a real chance that they might be able to get everyone out." For the past few hours, Henri had tried to convince her that the brat's decision to stay was something other than delusional suicide.

Leanne ignored him, her fingers aching in the cold. *Time to head back inside and come up with a new plan to get out. One that doesn't need Bernie's cooperation.* She passed a group of men talking in low voices.

"The helicopters came too quickly. It couldn't have been because of whatever happened out in the woods." The man speaking held himself as if he had military experience.

"Do you think they found a new *lalassu*?" another asked. "Maybe they were testing something."

"Then what are the helicopters here for?"

Leanne touched the pads of her index and middle fingers with her thumb before flicking toward the landing pad, signaling Henri to investigate. Maybe there would be a chance for an early escape.

"I'll check it out," Henri said, "but we're not done talking."

"Well, zip-a-dee-doo-dah." Inspired, she belted out the controversial Disney song, enjoying the irritated and surprised looks from those around her. She sang all the way back to her deserted barracks. At least her cellmates had remembered to keep the stove stoked.

Leanne shoved her hands into the column of radiating heat and sighed as the knotted tendons in her fingers began to unwind. Going out to get the pulse of the camp had been necessary, but she hated the cold, and it prompted a fresh wave of irritation with Bernie. *I'm supposed to be on my way back to civilization, not playing hero.*

"*Chérie*, I know you're disappointed." Henri's voice floated out of the silence.

Leanne flexed her fingers. "Oh, I'm just peachy. The girl decides to hang around and save the world, leaving me trapped in a prison. And you've decided she's the best thing since sliced bread."

"We've known each other too long for that kind of talk. I'm yours, and I always will be," Henri replied.

Leanne ignored him.

"Why are you so angry? I thought you would want to help her and make them all pay for what they've done to you."

"Did you miss the part where I got tased?" Her knees and hips were bruised from the fall to the ground.

"I think that's why she wants to help," Henri said.

"No, it ain't." A new voice joined the conversation. Leanne frowned, trying to figure out if it was male or female.

"What Bernie is doing is very brave, Monsieur Chuck." Henri sounded angry, but he gave Leanne the clue that she needed.

"So why does she want to stay if it's not for the noble purpose of helping others?" Leanne took her blanket from her bunk and put it on top of the stove. In a few minutes, it would be toasty warm.

"She wants her mom to be proud of her," Chuck answered. "After everything that twist has done to her, Bernie still thinks they gotta stick together."

"And you know better, don't you, my friend?" Leanne would have liked to see Chuck's face instead of only being able to judge his reaction by his voice alone. If her gift was as strong as Bernie's, allowing her to see ghosts as well as hear them, her life would have been much easier.

"She'd be better off on her own. With me. I've never given up on her." Chuck's voice deepened, cracking around the edges.

"You know what's going on in this camp," Henri said. "If there is a chance it can be stopped, shouldn't we try?"

Leanne snorted. "I've gotten caught up in the let's-make-a-difference dream before. Let me refresh your memory about how it will go. Public indignation and demands for change will quickly change to a chorus of 'not in my backyard.' There will be a flurry of impassioned sound bites posted on social media and then it will all be forgotten—except by the bigots looking to take out their frustration on acceptable targets."

"Exactly." Chuck sounded relieved. "People keep thinkin' that some big speech is gonna change the world. But I've watched it. The world just finds sneakier ways to be mean and new people to be mean to."

Leanne knew Henri wouldn't let that stand. And she was right. "There have been real changes—"

"Shut up!" Chuck's shout sent a shiver through Leanne, as though an invisible wave of cold water had doused her.

She waited for Henri to reply, but the only sound was the background chatter of the living.

"Stupid frog eater. Thinks he knows everything," Chuck muttered. "That'll show him."

"What did you do, Chuck?" Leanne asked, the hair on the back of her neck beginning to prickle. The older a ghost got, the more powerful and erratic it became, and Henri's silence suggested that she was alone with a ghost who was a hundred years old, the oldest one she'd ever heard of.

"I sent him packing." Chuck confirmed her fears.

Closing her eyes, Leanne tested the connection between her and Henri. It was intact but stretched, the same way it felt when she sent him on long-distance assignments. She pulled the blanket from the stove and wrapped it around herself. "Why?"

"You can make Bernie leave. Take her away from this awful place before they stick her in a hole in the ground and poke needles in her."

Leanne chose her next words carefully. She couldn't make false promises, but she had no wish to trigger further outbursts. "I wish I could, Chuck. But I am not a physically strong woman. I can't pick her up and carry her away, not without getting caught."

The silence reminded her of the pause a child will take when told they won't be getting a cookie before supper. But there was no shaking of the unearthly atmosphere, so Leanne was cautiously optimistic.

"I want to help you. I know that you care about Bernie." She kept her voice soft, as if speaking to a frightened child who was trying hard to pretend to be grown-up.

"I been watchin' over her since she was a baby. Even then, she was special, different from the other kids. They start to talk, and they stop seeing me, but I knew Bernie wouldn't be like that. She would never turn away from me."

"She cares about you a great deal," Leanne said in a soothing voice. "But she's going through a lot of changes as she becomes a woman. It's only normal for her to be confused for a while. It doesn't mean that she'll grow away from you."

"Yes, it does." The three words were no plaintive child's cry but a determined statement from someone who had seen too much to be swayed by pretty sentiments. "All those people talking to her, trying to take her away from me. I tried to protect her from them, but they won't leave her alone. As long as she's alive, they'll keep on her."

As long as she's alive. Leanne's fingers tightened around the blanket as she realized it wasn't a turn of phrase.

"If she was like me, we could go wherever we wanted. See all the places in the world and never have to worry about being caught." He sounded wistful and excited, his voice bouncing like a puppy after a ball. "We would be together forever."

Leanne was out of her depth and had no idea which way would take her to shore. "Not every death creates a ghost."

"I could keep her here as long as it was a surprise and didn't hurt too bad. People don't go right to the light unless they're hurt or they're ready to die." Chuck tossed off this earthshaking tidbit as if it were common knowledge. "You and I could help each other."

"How?" As a survivor, Leanne had made some soul-scarring decisions in the past, but she suspected this one was going to cut deeper than she was prepared for.

"You want out of here before they get you. There's not much time. I've seen where things are going in the world, and it's about to get real bad." The child Chuck was gone, replaced by the eerie persona who wasn't quite an adult but certainly wasn't innocent and naïve. "If you and Bernie get out on the plane tomorrow, you can get ahead of it. Trust me, a few days from now, no one in this camp will be in any shape to go looking for you. You can disappear, free and clear."

Leanne swallowed her response. The air around her prickled and cooled as if he was coming closer.

"Before you do, you'll give Bernie something to make her sleep and never wake up. I'll take care of the rest from there."

Murder. It wouldn't be the first death on her hands, but it would be the first where she knew in advance that it was going to happen.

"If you don't, I'll make sure they hunt you down, no matter how you try to hide. I've been paying attention, and I can send a computer message," Chuck's voice whispered from behind her. "I'll find you no matter where you go. You won't last a week."

She needed time to think without an insane ghost actually breathing down her neck. *There has to be a way out of this.*

"I won't ask for your promise." His voice was farther away, as if he were leaving. "I know that it doesn't mean anything if you see a way to break it. But my promises will come true, and there's nothing you can do to stop me. Catch you later, dollface."

His presence dissipated, leaving her alone in the stark barracks. Leanne quickly weighed her options. If Chuck were older and more mature, she might have a chance at convincing him to change his mind, but he was eternally stuck as a twelve-year-old boy—old enough to cause trouble but too young to understand the nuances of real life. Everything would be black and white to him, and after nearly a hundred years of death, those shades would be locked in.

A practiced medium could exorcise an unattached ghost, forcing them into the light. But the older the ghost, the more difficult it was. And Chuck was both old and attached to Bernie, which meant that Bernie would likely be the only one who could do it.

I could teach her how. But will Bernie believe me about Chuck wanting her dead? And if Leanne told her, then Chuck would have no reason to hold back. He didn't need living intervention to send Bernie to the other side. A well-timed accident was within his abilities.

"Leanne?" Henri's shout started as distant but quickly came closer. "Are you all right?"

"I'm fine. What happened?"

"The little bastard blasted me out of camp and halfway across the Pacific Ocean." Henri began to curse in French.

Leanne nodded. If she'd had any doubts, it proved that Chuck was more powerful than Henri. He couldn't protect her from the older ghost. "What was happening at the landing field?"

"You want to talk about that now?" He sounded surprised. "Three helicopters full of soldiers, with two prisoners and a bunch of dead bears."

"Dead bears?" Leanne couldn't even guess what they were for.

"Dr. Coulon is with them."

She closed her eyes and leaned back against the rough planks. Chuck was right. Things were changing. And if she wasn't on the plane three days later, she would be caught in the middle, and it wouldn't matter what she decided to do.

Chapter Twenty-Six

The door banged again as Martha was applying a fresh compress to her throat. Rising stiffly, she wondered if there was more bad news. Lou and the others were still at the landing field, presumably trying to find out more information. *Hopefully it wasn't Bear Claw.* Lou would be devastated if his home had been attacked while he was gone. She opened the door, half expecting Eva to be bringing Bernie back.

Instead, Mrs. Fitz stood there, with folded arms and her mouth twisted into sour irritation. "I do not tolerate unprofessional—"

From the abrupt break, Martha guessed the other woman had noticed the bruises around her throat. "I'm sorry, Mrs. Fitz."

"Hmm." There was no hint of warmth or sympathy in the other woman's evaluating gaze. "I told you that the loocies would not be grateful for your efforts."

"It wasn't an internee," Martha said angrily before she thought about her words. She had hated the derogative word to begin with, and she'd begun to loathe it with a passion.

"Your husband found out that you've been playing footsie with Ryan Blake? I can't say I'm surprised that he acted violently." Mrs. Fitz's smug pleasure hit Martha like a blow to a sunburn.

"Lou would never hurt me." But she would be the one responsible for hurting him if it turned out he couldn't protect his family because he was busy protecting Bernie and her. Martha's anger abruptly froze as she realized what else had been said. "What do you mean by playing footsie?"

"Everyone knows that you've been sleeping with him in exchange for favors. It's probably how you got the job in the first place." Mrs. Fitz sniffed in disapproval. "He's been reprimanded for allowing thefts of extra food and blankets. We all know that you have a soft spot for the loocies, so it wasn't hard to guess where it all went."

Martha's fingers brushed her neck. *So that's why he attacked earlier.* Being censured by Mrs. Fitz would have hit a man like Ryan hard in the ego.

"At least you won't be doing it anymore. No one could be tempted to feed those nasty creatures that the doctor has dragged in. Dalhard Industries will be collecting the test subjects." Mrs. Fitz straightened. "You'll be docked two days' pay for leaving without notifying anyone. Dr. Coulon will be expecting you tomorrow morning at eight thirty. I suggest you make yourself presentable."

The door closed, leaving Martha confused and upset. *Do they know that I discovered the secret lab, or were they talking about the experiments in detention?* Either way, she couldn't allow Kal, Patrick, or Annika to be taken to Dalhard Industries and be subjected to the same horrible treatment as Ron or Bernie.

She grabbed her coat, mixing up the sleeves in her nervous state and losing precious seconds to get it straightened out. She hoped she would find Lou, Hood, or Harley and that they would be able to help. She figured Hood or Harley would have had experience with breaking people out of prison. She wrapped her scarf around her neck to hide the bruises.

A little voice in the back of her head kept shouting that her plan was stupid. Whisking three prisoners out of their cells without anyone discovering her actions seemed impossible. *Don't panic. The first step is getting them out before they can be taken to Dalhard Industries.*

She hurried along the road, moving past people returning to the trailers after supper. No one seemed particularly interested or alarmed by her presence. As she passed the gates, she saw Dr. Coulon walking into the Hub with Mrs. Fitz.

If he's there with her, he can't be in the secret lab. She froze in place, her fingers wrapped around the chilly metal links of the fence. *It might be the best chance to get Kal and the others out. We could make it look as if they'd escaped after the guards fed them. But it means there's no time to get Lou or anyone else.* It was up to her.

She unlocked the medical building, her mind whirling but her intentions clear. She would get Patrick, Annika, and Kal out of their cells and out of the medical building. Then she'd have to find somewhere to hide them. *Maybe in the warehouse? Or maybe there was an empty trailer? Or the woods?* It didn't matter. *Get them out first and then figure it out.* Dr. Coulon would have the keys to the cells in the lab. She was certain of that. He wouldn't want to waste time fetching them when he wanted to do experiments, and he wouldn't want to carry them around and risk losing them, either. Besides, the guards would need the keys to open the cells when they brought food.

Opening the secret bookshelf, Martha wondered if she was making a mistake. The old self-doubt whispered deep inside her mind. *No, I have to be fierce, not scared.* She closed the shelf carefully behind her and hurried down the steps.

"Martha, you shouldn't be here," Kal hissed as soon as she stepped into the lab.

"Just tell me where the keys are." She yanked open the drawers in the tool chest, scanning the metal surgical tools.

"Low probability of success," Patrick muttered under his breath, rocking rapidly back and forth while tightly hugging his torso.

"Listen to me." Kal's big dark eyes held hers. "I know what happened upstairs today and back at the trailer, and while I'm delighted that your outlook on life has improved, you need to leave now if you want a chance to enjoy this wonderful new romance."

"I am not leaving you down here. Tell me where they are, and we'll all have less chance of being caught." Martha slammed the drawer shut and pulled open the next one.

"They're behind the file cabinet. That's where he takes them from," Annika said.

Martha hurried to the file cabinet. The keys were on a hook, but the angle wasn't good. Dr. Coulon's insect-thin arms might have fit, but hers wouldn't.

Kal tilted his head, closing his eyes. "It's too late. Over there, behind the oxygen tanks. You have to hide. Stay there, no matter what you see. If you're captured, none of us has a chance."

"I need something to reach them." *There must be a stick or something I can use.*

"Shit," Annika said.

"Too late. Hide! Now!" Kal hissed again.

She could hear voices on the stairs. Ryan and Dr. Coulon. Tall dull-blue oxygen tanks stood beside the metal tool chest. There was a small gap behind them, an oddity of construction or sloppy storage. Either way, it was barely large enough for Martha, even if she crouched, and if someone looked directly at the tanks, she would be easy to spot. But there weren't any better options. She crammed herself down into the spot, sitting despite the cold, damp concrete. If she had a cramp and moved, the tanks would rattle and give her away.

"...not how I like to do things," Dr. Coulon complained as he entered the lab with Ryan a step behind.

"You should see the damage. A tree bigger than my waist, snapped like a toothpick. Whoever did it is powerful. We can't let them stay out there without tracking them down," Ryan argued.

"Finding whoever did it is your concern. I have my new work." Dr. Coulon passed out of Martha's field of view. "When can the subjects be moved out?"

"The helicopters will leave in the morning." Ryan moved closer to Annika's cell. "More than enough time for a proper goodbye."

His words sickened Martha and sent a trickle of cold sweat down her spine. Annika didn't seem to be paralyzed by fear. "Come any closer, and I'll rip your freaking face off."

"Not soon enough. I want 347 and 639 out now. I need the space," Dr. Coulon ordered coolly. "Take them to detention."

"That's not a good idea. They could tell others about the lab." Ryan sounded uncertain.

"They do say patience is a virtue, Doctor," Kal announced cheerfully. "Are we travelling by helicopter, then? I've always wanted to do that."

They were distracting Ryan and the doctor from seeing her, Martha realized.

"Enough." Dr. Coulon's voice was closer than she'd expected. "Drug them to keep them from talking."

Maybe we can get them out of detention. Martha still hadn't set foot inside, but Hood and Harley had. It might be easier than getting them out of the cells. She closed her eyes and concentrated on breathing as silently as possible.

"What are you planning to do with me, you pretentious quack?" Annika demanded.

"Nothing at all for the moment." Dr. Coulon didn't seem disturbed by her outburst. "Once I have the time, I hope your autopsy will prove more useful than your previous tests."

Martha crammed her fist into her mouth to keep from shouting. The doctor's calm was chilling as he handed down an indifferent death sentence.

"How nice to know that Patrick and myself can continue to enjoy job security." Kal sounded as if he actually was pleased.

She heard rattling metal, and her eyes popped open to see Ryan shoving a collapsible wheelchair through the bars of Kal's cage. Once it was through, he aimed his rifle at Kal. "Now get your fat ass in there before I shoot you."

"You're not planning to shoot." Kal slowly came into view as he walked around the chair and sat in it.

"True." Ryan held the gun steady. "I also don't want to haul something as heavy as you if I don't have to. Fasten the straps."

Kal fastened straps around his ankles and another set around his waist and torso before placing his arms on the armrests. Ryan lowered the rifle and unlocked the door.

"Remember, I can shut you down with the collar if you try and escape." He darted in to fasten the wrist restraints.

Kal hadn't moved. Tears filled Martha's eyes, and she bit down on her knuckle to keep from crying out. *I'm sorry.* She hoped he could hear her thoughts. *I'm so sorry.*

It was even worse when Ryan opened Patrick's cell. She couldn't see, but she heard his high-pitched scream, a desperate squeal like that of a dying rabbit. It echoed until it was abruptly cut off. Martha leaned forward and saw Patrick sprawled on the floor with Ryan standing over him.

"Damn loocy tried to bite me." Ryan's expression didn't look sane.

The doctor ignored him, clattering off to one side.

"There was no need for this kind of violence," Kal said quietly. "He was afraid and didn't understand what you wanted."

"Shut it!" Ryan roared. He lifted Patrick and dumped him into another wheelchair. Yanking the straps, he fastened the gangly teenager in place before wheeling him out of sight into the tunnels.

"He's a real charmer, that one," Annika called out.

"I don't understand why you insist on antagonizing him. It's entirely counterproductive." Dr. Coulon was nearby. *Is he close enough to see me crouching in the dark?*

"Nothing else to do around here," Annika replied.

Martha wished she had the powers that the others did, something that would let her whisk out of the dark like a masked avenger and stop all of it from happening. Instead, she could only stay hidden and hope that the doctor gave her an opportunity to creep back up the stairs.

Ryan returned and grabbed Kal's wheelchair. Kal called out cheerily, "It will be all right. Be strong until we meet again."

There was a long silence as the metallic rattle from the chair faded away.

Be the fierce kestrel. She couldn't fight them directly, but there had to be a way. *I need to think.* The grinding of rubber wheels on concrete announced a new arrival.

"Place him in the far cell. Make certain the collar is secure," Dr. Coulon directed.

Martha leaned forward again, cautiously trying to see more from her limited vantage point.

"These aren't the accommodations I reserved." Despite some slurring, the man's voice was immediately recognizable. *Andrew.*

Oh, shit. Andrew's right arm hung limply at his side, probably dislocated. Scrapes showed through rips in his clothing, and a heavy metal ring circled his throat, much thicker than the usual shock collar. Martha's already-battered heart threatened to break at the thought of what this news would do to Lou.

A few moments later, Ryan returned with the second new subject. The shock was less, but Martha was still horrified to see Lily slumped in a chair with a dark bruise on her cheek and a collar that matched her brother's.

"Be careful. I bartered a great deal for these subjects." Dr. Coulon moved into Martha's view again. He faced the cells. "Allow me to explain the rules. I am Dr. Coulon. Try to avoid boring me with the usual empty threats or attempts to bargain. You are here to further my research into *occulata hominem*. I will not tolerate any behavior that could interfere with that research. Cooperate and you can avoid punitive measures."

"But you can't avoid meatloaf night," Annika added. "It's totally cruel and unusual punishment."

Andrew ignored the banter. "I'm surprised. No attempt to lie and claim we won't be harmed if we play nicely?"

"Lying to you would be useless and counterproductive." The doctor turned away from the cells, and Martha held her breath, wondering if he would notice her. But he only picked up a worn leather notebook and began flipping through the pages. "My work will damage you, but it is in my interest to keep you alive as long as possible. Special Investigations believes my primary focus is to see whether or not you transform after death, but after careful thought, there are other areas I would like to explore."

"We won't cooperate." Lily's growl sounded like Lou's, only lighter. Martha suppressed a surge of guilt at her earlier wish for someone with powers to arrive. She hadn't meant anything like what was happening, and it didn't look as if Lily's powers had done her any good.

"You will." Dr. Coulon was matter-of-fact. "They tell me that you have a romantic attachment to the man captured alongside you. The preliminary blood tests conducted en route have revealed that you are pregnant."

No. The news hit Martha like a punch to the gut, and she knew it must be ten times worse for her friend. Lily's face went pale, and her lips were pressed together and shaking.

"The reproductive rates among *occulata hominem* have been something of a mystery. They rarely mate outside of their own subspecies, and the inheritance of gifts does not follow straightforward genetic predictions. To have a fetus to study in depth as it develops will be most useful." Dr. Coulon closed the notebook with a satisfied clap. "If you prove difficult, I will find other suitable subjects. Now, you will sit quietly while Mr. Blake releases you from the chair. If either of you causes trouble, you will regret it."

Ryan was thumbing the shock-collar remote. *There must be collars underneath the metal rings.* Martha held perfectly still. *Just do it. Don't fight right now.* They wouldn't hear her thoughts, but that didn't stop Martha from thinking them as hard as she could. Regardless of the reason, Lily and Andrew did cooperate. Andrew grunted in pain as his wrist restraint was removed.

Dr. Coulon walked toward Martha's hiding place and began to remove surgical tools from the cabinet. She closed her eyes, wondering what she would see and if her courage would be sufficient.

"Mr. McBride, it's been such a challenge trying to find you." Priya smiled graciously and bowed her head. "Thank you for accepting our invitation."

The man in the chair didn't speak, not that she expected him to with the gag shoved deep in his mouth. His muscles were rigid as he fought against the restraints, glaring at her. He'd been kept in isolation for the past twenty-four hours but showed no sign of mental or emotional distress. *He's as strong as Karan said he would be.* She still would prefer a transformative, but she could work with McBride.

"My brother is delighted. He would be here today, but he had other business to attend to. Besides, he knows that I can take care of these matters better than he can." She turned to one side and lifted the cover off a delicate china bowl. "I regret that our prior obligations left us unable to greet you when you arrived. Would you care for some soup?"

Her demeanor was throwing off his expectations. The clanking soundtrack of his struggles slowed, and Priya hid a smile. Like all military men, McBride had prepared himself for confrontation and torture. An aggressive man would still have been facing a snarling beast trying to break free. But a gracious and demure woman offering food triggered his deepest training to be polite to a hostess. It undermined his resolve to resist.

She reached over then undid the soaked cotton strips binding his mouth closed, removed the gag, and set it aside. "My mother used to make me vegetable soup when I was a girl. I wish you could taste it, but I'm afraid the recipe died with her. Still, I think you'll enjoy this chicken soup. I understand it's a traditional American comfort food."

She cradled the bowl in one hand and spooned up a small amount of the rich yellow liquid. McBride pulled his chin back. "My mother told me not to eat with kidnappers."

His defiant gambit was so transparent that she laughed aloud. "What a delightfully specific piece of parental advice."

He pressed his dry, flaking lips together.

"Are you afraid it's poisoned? That wouldn't be terribly logical, Mr. McBride. We've gone to a great deal of trouble to get you here, and it's in all of our interests to make sure you're in good health." She sipped at the spoonful of broth. "Perfectly safe, I assure you. There's no need to be frightened."

"Where's Lily?" he demanded.

He should have eaten first. *Ah well, I'm not his mother.* Priya placed the bowl back on its table, covering it with the lid to keep it warm. "She is under the care of our doctor."

"I want to see her." The restraints clanked in emphasis.

"I'm certain you do. You love her a great deal, don't you? I saw how you tried to free her. It was quite touching." It was a terrible weakness, but at least it offered a less messy option of persuasion. "But I'm afraid that she's being held on the other side of the continent for now."

A flicker of fear in his eyes told her she had cracked his emotional armor.

"You may not recall properly. You were given quite a cocktail of drugs, as I understand. You are now on the east coast. Only a few hours walk from New York, if you were unlucky enough to manage to escape."

"Unlucky?" He spat the syllables at her, trying to surprise her into revealing something.

"I doubt you could reach her before I—or one of my representatives, should you happen to kill me during your escape—

contacted her." Seeing her threat hit home sent goose bumps dancing along her arms. "Instead, I would think that you would prefer to protect her."

McBride swallowed hard, slumping as the fight drained out of him. "What do you want?"

Priya hid her smile by picking up the bowl of soup again. Men were so predictable. First they blustered then threatened and eventually collapsed when anyone had the audacity to counter their efforts. "You're going to help us make sure that the public understands what a danger the *lalassu* can be. Throw a few cars around, punch some people through walls. There's a whole range of possibilities, and I encourage you to be creative. Or simply recreate the latest action movie, because it doesn't matter how attractive people find violence in film. There will always be a difference when they're truly in danger."

"And why would I do that?" There was a little quaver in his voice.

Good. There is still fight in him, and presumably he is saving it for the right target. Priya stirred the broth. "Do you know how many people are angry at your wife, Mr. McBride?"

Silence. He probably assumed it was a typical threat, but she had something much more creative in mind.

"The video of her transforming into a bear was what revealed the *lalassu* to the world. Many of them blame her personally. But they aren't the only ones who would target her. Hate groups across the globe are using her face as the prime target for their rage." *And with only minimal prompting on my part.* "If you provide a suitably dramatic alternative, you could take her place as the poster child. They would target you instead of her."

He still wasn't saying anything.

It was a gamble, but one Priya was fairly certain of. She'd examined the reports from Bear Claw carefully. There had been numerous captives closer to him than the woman, but he'd chosen to attack her cage with his bare hands. And no matter his strength, crumpling steel would have hurt badly. The palms of his hands had been bruised when he'd arrived. He would do anything she asked if it would protect his wife.

"I do this, you'll let her go?" he asked.

"I will keep her away from the general population at Woodpine, out of reach of those who are angry at her." *Not out of the doctor's hands, but I will ensure he doesn't perform any experiments that would have permanent side effects.*

"How do I know you'll keep her safe after I've done what you want?"

His question gratified her more than she could let on. It was so frustrating not to be taken seriously, even if it did carry some advantages. "As long as you continue to cause public fear and chaos, she will be protected from the *lalassu* who blame her. I won't even hold it against you if you try to rescue her."

He watched her stonily.

"What I'm offering is the carrot, Mr. McBride. But there is a whip as well, if you prefer. Our doctor is quite eager to examine her and understand how her bloodline is able to perform their remarkable abilities. If you are unwilling to cooperate, I can see if her brother would be more amenable."

"It's not much of a choice," he said through clenched teeth.

"You aren't listening carefully. I'm not requiring you to attack innocents for the demonstration. I will be releasing you on one of the hate groups who would slaughter everyone you love in a heartbeat. Doing so helps to keep your wife safe. Isn't that worth some cooperation? But in the end, it's up to you."

His fists slowly loosened, and he let his fingers dangle free.

"I thought you were a logical man." She lifted the bowl again. "Soup?"

Chapter Twenty-Seven

"Please, just stay here." Hood braced himself in the doorway of the trailer, even though he must have known he couldn't stop Lou from leaving.

"Out of my way." Lou didn't want to hurt the other man, but his nose was clogged with the scent of death and his heart with memories of trailers carrying their lifeless loads from the helicopters into the camp. He'd recognized Malila first, with her distinctive reddish-brown fur. She used to bawl for him in the forest when she got lost, and he would collect her and bring her back to the Colony. There had been no sign of her cub—her first and last. Then he'd spotted Elxeli's dark fur and worn claws. No more drumming crashes would echo through the forest as the male pounded his paws against hollow trees for the sheer joy of it. Next were Jis's namesake white paws, which had gone limp. Then Ts'eli, who had earned his name with his croaking call.

Hood had dragged him away before Lou could identify more of his friends and charges. Perhaps he had anticipated that Lou would erupt in another rage, but the pain was too new and fresh. It didn't seem real. It couldn't be possible. If he ran to Bear Claw, surely he would find them all sunning themselves on the cliff caves in the Colony. They couldn't possibly be dead and carried away to the camp.

To return back to the trailer and discover Martha missing was another devastating blow.

"I can't let you go out there. Bernie's ghost says that Martha is all right for now, but she won't be if you go charging in." Hood was still talking.

Grizzlies were not social animals. They lived mostly solitary lives, except for their mates and cubs. Given time and space, Lou might have been able to convince himself that there was nothing to be done for Elxeli and the others. But when he'd discovered that Martha was gone, and Bernie relayed that she was trapped in the lab, it had stretched his control like overstrained leather. The slightest pressure could snap it.

"Harley is setting up a distraction that'll get the doctor and Ryan out of there." Hood had said it before, and Lou guessed the man was trying to buy time.

Mentioning the torturer and the scavenger was the wrong choice. Lou's nails began to grow longer, harder, and sharper. He longed for the simplicity of the fur, the calm of primal purpose.

"Look at yourself! You have to stay here. I will get her out, I promise." Sweat shone on Hood's bald head. "Martha would want you to stay and protect Bernie."

It was a new entreaty, and it slipped in between Lou and the fur like a flimsy plastic lid. It wasn't enough to block the most determined effort, but it was enough to create some breathing room. He hadn't had so much trouble controlling the shift since the awful days after his father's death.

"We don't know what's going on, and we need someone to protect Bernie." Hood repeated, his gaze shifting to the girl reading on the sofa, curled up as if oblivious to the struggle fewer than ten feet away.

Lou hesitated. Every instinct pushed him to rescue Martha. But Hood had a point. Lou was on edge, his nerves and emotions raw. He didn't know the human world or its customs, and he doubted he could pretend to be harmless, with rage boiling in his heart.

Hood sensed the confusion and pounced. "I swear on my daughter's life that I will bring Martha back safely."

Lou nodded, reluctant but convinced. "Go."

Hood didn't need to be told twice. Lou watched through the window as he hurried away, moving through the milling throng of staff without disturbing them.

"Ugh. I wish they'd let me stay with Eva." Bernie flipped the page of her book. "I bet she could have got me something to eat while we were stuck in the kitchen."

"You're hungry?" Lou had some supplies hidden away. He didn't dare dip into them too deeply in case they needed to leave, but he could spare something.

"No. Just bored." She tilted her head as they talked, as if he might vanish if viewed from another angle.

Lou made himself close the door and took up a post near the window. Between rumors and the helicopters, the camp resembled a disturbed insect nest—lots of activity but not many apparent results.

"She'll be okay, you know," Bernie called. "Henri has been checking on her and reporting back to me."

Lou frowned but didn't turn around. Even after a relatively short time, he'd gotten tired of the constant refrain of *Chuck says* coming from Bernie. *Why isn't the ghost taking the limelight now?*

"Henri's nice, like a gentleman prince from a fairy tale. He dresses like one, too, in a long coat and those puffy neck things. I don't think he's really that old, though. It's more like playing pretend." Bernie's attention was on her book, not her words.

Lou pretended not to pay attention. If he reminded her of his presence, she would snap her mouth closed and resist any attempt he might make to pry. If he couldn't rescue Martha himself, perhaps he could help her daughter by being a listening ear. Watching the child's reflection in the window, he settled into the relaxed state of mind that he used to conserve energy and waited for Bernie to speak again.

"He talks funny, but I like it, especially when Chuck's being mean and staying away." Bernie shrugged, turning the next page. "He does that sometimes. But he always comes back. I'm the only one he can talk to."

Andrew's warnings about the child ghost replayed in Lou's memory. *Overwhelmed with jealousy and anger.*

"He can be such a bully. He's acting mad because he thinks it'll make me do what he wants. Except I want to stay and find a way to help everyone. Once it's settled, then I can leave." Bernie suddenly looked up, and her face went red as she dropped the book.

"Leave?" Lou turned, pinning her in place with the same intent gaze that his grandfather had used on him.

"I don't have to tell you." Bernie folded her arms.

Lou didn't argue or lecture, but he kept watching her. It was the truth. She didn't have to tell him anything. He wasn't her family or shaman, and no matter what she chose, he would continue to protect her. But he heard the undercurrent of uncertainty in her voice and guessed that she needed to talk to someone even if she didn't want to. He could sympathize with that.

Bernie fidgeted, her fingers plucking at her clothes and the sofa. Lou waited patiently, putting his own worries on ice in an effort to flush out hers. Bernie was like a little pack mule. Yank on her halter, and she would dig in her heels, but pretend not to be interested while holding out a bit of carrot, and she would follow a person anywhere.

Bernie heaved a sigh and muttered. "Leanne and I were going to leave on the commuter plane." She waited, obviously expecting him to respond, which would then let her avoid the rest of the conversation.

But he'd learned his patience from the hardest teachers possible, his grandfather and the wild creatures of Bear Claw. A twelve-year-old girl wasn't a challenge.

"I was tired of running all the time and pretending to be like the other kids. Leanne said we could start a new life somewhere and she would teach me." Bernie's lowered gaze stayed fixed on her hands, which busily wore through her jeans. "After what happened with the collars, I wanted to stay and find a way to help. I mean, I'm like all of the people over there. I just haven't gotten caught yet."

His heart softened, but he kept his face stern. Her plan to run away was a childish decision, but she was still a child, so he wouldn't get angry about it. Her words showed the beginning of a noble character starting to break through the soil.

Her next words undermined his developing pride and reminded him of the danger. "Leanne and Chuck are both unhappy about it. Leanne's tired of being stuck in camp, and Chuck… I think he blames Mom for what happened to me back in Perdition."

Lou's frown deepened, and his arms tensed.

"I'm mad at her, too. I mean, she gave me up and let them take me away. I know that Mr. Dalhard had that weird touch-you-hypnosis thing, but she's my mom. She should have been able to resist. Or she shouldn't have called him in the first place." Bernie's hands stilled on her jeans, her fingertips tucked underneath her palms. "She shouldn't have wanted to give me up."

"You're right," Lou said gently.

Bernie looked up in surprise.

"Andrew told me what happened to you." Lou sat down cross-legged on the floor so that he wasn't looming over her. "And I've listened to your mother."

"What?" Bernie demanded skeptically, leaning back and slamming her arms across her chest to create a barrier. "Did she tell you how it's not her fault?"

"No." Lou snipped the girl's budding anger. "She knows it was her fault. She'll regret it every day for the rest of her life."

The wind was stolen from her sails, but Bernie wasn't finished. "Good."

"It was one decision." Lou kept his calm despite his increasing worry. Shouldn't Hood and Harley be back by now? "She gave you up, but she also gave herself up to give you a chance. And she gave herself up many, many times."

"I didn't ask her to." Bernie's arms loosened.

"She is a mother. Mothers are the fiercest fighters, but they don't always win. When I was a boy, my mother lost herself when my father was killed. Then she sacrificed herself to save Lily and Mark. Is she a good mother? Or a bad one? Which decision counts more?" He waited while Bernie thought about his words.

"I'm sorry about your mom," she whispered.

He nodded, accepting without pushing for more.

She leaned forward. "Mom said what people do is what matters. All the things they say or promise doesn't matter as much as what they do."

Wise words. "It's true."

"So I guess that what matters now is what I do." Bernie tapped her fingers on her knee. "I want to be someone who helps."

"You will," he promised as footsteps crunched outside. *Someone is coming. Several someones.*

He rose to his feet, moving to stand between Bernie and the door. If it was an attack, he would take them all down.

The door opened, and all he saw was Martha.

She rushed to Bernie, touching the child's face, shoulders, and arms as if to verify her daughter was safe before wrapping her in a rough hug. Only then did her eyes raise to Lou.

"Mom, I'm fine." Bernie pushed free.

Martha nodded. She took a hesitant step toward Lou then threw herself at him. Her arms wrapped so tightly around him that he couldn't draw a full breath. He cradled her, breathing in her scent to reassure himself that she was truly back and unharmed.

Hood and Harley were watching from the doorway. Harley coughed. "We'll go now. Try to keep from doing anything else dangerous until we've all had a good night's sleep."

"Wait." Martha lifted her head so she could face them. "Thank you."

"Thank us in the morning." Hood's eyes were dark with future worries. "The helicopters are disabled, which means someone is going to be screwed in the morning. And there's still panicking and fighting from the riot we provoked. No one is walking away from this one."

"I know. But thank you anyway," Martha said quietly. "Now we have a chance to get Kal and Patrick out of detention. And we need a plan to rescue the others."

"Tomorrow." Hood waved as the two men left to check on their own daughter.

"Are you okay, Lou?" Martha raised her eyes to his, still holding him as if he was her lifeline.

Now that you're back. He hoped she could feel the words.

"Did Hood and Harley tell you? They… they raided Bear Claw." Her eyes were fixed on him, searching for any sign of pain.

"I know." His throat was narrow from relief and sorrow.

"They did?" Bernie asked, creeping closer again. Martha pulled her into their embrace.

"Yes, baby. But we're going to get Lily and Andrew out."

Lou stiffened. *What?*

Martha pulled back, looking between him and Bernie. "I thought you knew."

He shook his head, his teeth clenched as he fought to keep his human form.

"He saw the dead bears from the Colony." Bernie tugged her mother away from him, her wide eyes fixed on his.

"But Chuck must have—"

"Chuck took off. Henri's been helping us, but he doesn't know who Lily and Andrew are. He didn't say anything." Bernie's chin firmed as she backed Martha farther away.

Lou had never been more grateful than he was in that moment. His bear roared just below the surface, wild and primal. He couldn't be sure he would be able to keep control.

"Listen to me, Lou. We'll get them out." Martha pulled Bernie's shoulders and tucked her daughter behind her.

He sank down onto his knees, his fist braced against the floor, pushed down by the weight of his failure as Ekurru's Guardian. He'd already been scraped raw by the sight of his friends and kin being hauled down the road like so much garbage. Anger, grief, and fear threatened to drown him in a flash flood of unfamiliar emotions. Memories sliced into his soul. *Lily, a gap-toothed girl and rambunctious cub, always running faster and climbing higher than the others. Andrew, pretending to be solemn and grown-up but crying in his bed at night after their father died.* His fist clenched as he wondered if Mark, Lily's twin, had been anywhere near Bear Claw. He should still have been safe at the university at Juneau, but he might have gone home to visit. *What about Grandfather? Or Setsuné?* His fingers dug into the floor. *Is there anyone left?*

He hadn't felt so helpless since the days he struggled to keep Kots'éen alive. Since then, he'd had focus and purpose as the provider and protector of his family—until Martha came to Bear Claw.

He roared as his body thickened, transforming to the fur. His collar and waistband choked him before breaking. Colors dimmed, and the stale air inside the trailer stung his muzzle. The floor creaked under his weight. But he already felt calmer. His animal instincts were offended by the violation of his territory, but it was his human side that felt outraged and violated. The bear would wait for an opportunity, not waste energy seeking one out.

Movement to the side caught his attention, and he swung his head toward it. Martha took another step in his direction, moving very slowly. Her clean-sunshine scent soothed both sides of his nature.

"Hi," she whispered, lowering herself carefully to one knee.

"Mom?" Bernie's worried question cut through the quiet spell.

Martha waved her back, keeping her own attention on Lou.

He snorted and shook his body, enjoying a satisfying ruffle of his fur.

"I know you're worried about Andrew and Lily, but I want you to listen to me. We'll find a way to get them out. From what they say, Mark and your grandfather are still safe." She kept her hands folded on her knee instead of reaching out to touch him. A wise choice from his fierce kestrel.

The fur brought clarity, separating him from the turmoil of his emotions. The targets of his rage were not in sight, and therefore the rage was banked against future opportunities. But enough of his human awareness remained to make him edgy and restless. He'd heard what Dr. Coulon did inside that pit of a lab. His brother and sister were in the grasp of a monster. He grumbled and keened in short bursts.

Martha didn't turn away from him. "You have to come back to me. Please."

His mate. Such limited words for such a wonderful thing. He stretched forward and nosed at her hands. She inhaled sharply but held her ground, demonstrating the bravery that had won both halves of his heart.

"Lou. Please," she whispered. "Come back to me."

She was meant to fly free in the skies. He couldn't be the one to cage her inside a life she would hate. But he could watch and remember the brief time where she perched beside him. He would not allow the filthy scavenger to clip her wings.

The shift to the skin drained his energy. He knelt on the floor among fresh tatters of yet another set of clothing. Martha let a long sigh of relief escape, plunking back to sit on the floor. Bernie scrambled to sit beside her, and Martha wrapped a protective arm around her.

Lou aimed his first words at Bernie. "I'm sorry."

"Do you do that every time you get upset?" the girl asked.

"Most times," he replied honestly. Once his emotions became too turbulent to control, his body would demand the relative clarity of the fur. It became inevitable.

"Would you have hurt us?" Bernie was the one who asked, but he saw Martha's lifted head and intent interest.

"No." He wouldn't vow against property damage, but he would

never hurt Martha or Bernie. They had become part of his family, as much as any of his siblings. "I am angry at what happened. Not at you."

"I'm glad one of us is certain about that." Martha's fingers tightened on her daughter's arm. "Bernie, get him a blanket, please."

Lou nodded ruefully as the girl scampered away. "Do we have a kettle?"

Martha tilted her head. "Are you thinking of trading it for a new outfit?"

He smiled, even though the joke was weak. "No. But I have a tea that I should drink. It will help me to sleep and keep me in the skin. Andrew—" He paused, fresh emotion ripping into him. "Andrew made it for me."

She didn't ask any more questions, just got to her feet and plugged in the small electric kettle. Bernie brought him the blanket, and he wrapped it around himself before searching out the packets of medicinal herbs. As the tea steeped, he took Martha's hand. "Thank you."

"For what?" She frowned as if confused.

For being you. For helping me. There were too many reasons, and the feeling was too large to trap inside words. "For everything."

She was quiet as he finished the tea. Sleepiness pulled at his mind as he trudged to their shared bedroom. He fell down onto the bed and dove into slumber, but as the blackness closed in, he heard Martha's whispered reply.

"You're welcome."

Anger

Chapter Twenty-Eight

Martha dared to stroke Lou's silky black hair as he slept. The anti-transformative tea had knocked him out completely. He'd slept through the night and the morning. Between the riot and the sabotaged helicopters, the whole camp was on lockdown. All staff and internees were to remain in their trailers and barracks. Only the guards had freedom of movement. At least it meant that Lou wasn't expected at the construction site, and Martha didn't have to go in to the medical office. As a bonus, given the stranded soldiers, Ryan and Dr. Coulon needed to exercise at least some caution. Most importantly, Annika should be safe for the moment, and Kal and Patrick couldn't be whisked off to some Dalhard Industries lab.

She still couldn't process all the events from the day before. It didn't seem like any of it could have happened. The kiss, the attack, Lou's outburst in the forest, the arrival of the Bear Claw survivors, and Lou's transformation in the trailer… None of it felt quite real.

"It was a hard day," she said softly. Given all that had happened, it seemed wrong to be grateful, but she couldn't help it. Her fingers trailed down his warm skin, noting the deep lines around his mouth. Even while he was sleeping, he seemed like he was on guard, standing between her and Bernie and anyone who wanted to hurt them. It had been a long time since she had someone she could count on for more than looking outraged. She stood up before she could give in to the impulse to kiss him.

A faint tap on the door broke her thoughts.

"How's everyone doing here?" Harley asked, holding out some applesauce and granola bars for breakfast. Behind him, the camp seemed completely deserted, with everyone sealed inside their own compartments.

She let him in and closed the door. "We made it through the night. Lou is still knocked out."

"Hood and I have been working on a plan to get Lily and Andrew out. Actually, to get all of us out." Harley grimaced, automatically checking over his shoulder although he couldn't possibly see anyone through the trailer wall.

"What kind of plan?" Bernie's question made them both jump in place. She stood in her doorway, still in her pajamas.

"I didn't realize you were up. Are you hungry?" Martha held out the plastic containers.

"I want to know what kind of plan." Bernie's mouth was set in a thin line, but she didn't seem as much angry as detached.

Is this defiance? Or should I treat her like an adult and include her in the planning? There was no map to guide Martha, and she had the sinking feeling that she'd missed a turning point in the mother-daughter relationship.

"It involves hijacking the commuter plane." Harley's shoulders twitched apologetically. "Just long enough to get us all out of here."

"You can't be serious." Martha searched his face for some sign that it was a bad joke. "There are armed guards… And do any of us even know how to fly it?"

"I've done some time on a simulator, and we're hoping that Lou or one of his siblings have experience on a bush plane." Harley's hurried words were not reassuring.

"And if they don't?" *Please let plan B be better.*

"Then we force the pilot to fly us."

It's not better. "No."

"Lou and Hood could scare the pilot a little. It's only a few hours, and then we'd be safe in Juneau, able to scatter into hiding." Harley lowered his voice. "I know it's not great, but things are getting worse. This is the only way to get what we know out there."

"What about Leanne?" Bernie asked.

Harley shook his head. "We can't take everyone with us. The more people we have, the more likely we are to be caught."

"I suppose we won't be looking for Kal and Patrick, either?" Once again, Martha felt trapped between impossible choices. On the one hand, she could keep her daughter and Lou and his family safe. On the other, she would be abandoning Kal and Patrick and all the others here. She knew which one she'd have to choose, but it would leave a scar.

Bernie started to shout. "We can't—"

Martha put her hand over Bernie's mouth. "Please. We don't want to be heard."

Harley checked the windows.

Bernie glared at her, and Martha took a deep breath, removing her hand. "Please give me and Harley a chance to talk about this. I don't want to abandon our friends."

Her daughter didn't say anything, but her expression shot accusing barbs to sink deeply into Martha's conscience. Bernie spun around and slammed the door behind her.

"I'm sorry," Harley said.

"It's not your fault. It's mine." Martha felt hollow. "She doesn't have any faith in my ability to do the right thing."

"If it makes you feel any better, Eva is being just as vocal about what a cowardly thing we're doing." Harley winced. "And I can't exactly argue with her."

"Is there any way we can… I don't even know what to ask. Overthrow the camp?" Martha sank down into the uneven chair at the small table. "Rescue everyone?"

"I wish there were. But we've examined it from every angle. As long as they have those shock collars, even a few guards can shut everything down. I'm good with tech, but I haven't been able to find a way around them, and I've been looking. Tamper with them, and they give a lethal shock."

It was not the news she wanted to hear.

"If we stay, I think we're going to disappear into those cells. We've maybe got a few days, if we can keep our heads down and not cause trouble." Harley joined her at the table. "Eva and Bernie are too young to realize that the good guys don't always win."

"I'm not sure I count as one of the good guys with Bernie right now." Martha tried to smile, but it slipped away too quickly.

"I don't think I've been one of the good guys since Eva first learned to talk." Harley's grin was equally fleeting.

"I'm completely out of my depth. I have enough trouble with regular parenting decisions, let alone this sort of major moral crisis." Martha ran her hand over her head, smoothing down the stray wisps of hair. "When Bernie was in therapy, everything was regulated. It was exhausting but predictable. And then we were in hiding, and it was all about keeping her safe. I feel guilty for thinking this, but if we succeed, then there's a chance she could have a life like the other kids."

"And maybe you can, too?" He covered her hand with his. "You're not selfish to want something for yourself as well as for Bernie."

Martha realized she was watching the door to the bedroom where Lou was still sleeping. "I'm not sure those things are compatible. Especially not with what just happened at Bear Claw."

"If you have a chance to be happy together, you can't let that stop you." Harley sighed. "Maybe it'll work, and maybe it won't. But not giving yourself the chance is something you'll always regret."

"With so much going on, it makes our feelings seem less important." The weight of responsibility tasted suspiciously like fear in her mouth.

"Take a piece of advice from someone whose relationship has always had to contend with external big-picture crises." Harley's gaze went inward, focused on the past. "Hood thought the same way you are right now. When we met, we were taking down a big human-trafficking ring, and he was so caught up in doing the job that he ignored all of my signals. If I hadn't taken matters into my own hands, he never would have realized that it's possible to be effective and happy. Don't let the big picture paint over your feelings for each other. There's always room for a dash of personalization."

"Thanks." She leaned back. "It's been a while since I talked to anyone about relationships."

"Glad to be of service. And it's nice to talk to someone who knows the truth about us. I really miss our friends back home." He sighed. "I know Hood is all freaked out about someone finding out that we're gay and attacking us, and I get that it's a real threat, but what gets to me most is not having our friends."

"I can understand that." She got up to walk Harley to the door.

He gave her a hug before leaving. "Promise me you won't give up on a happy ending."

She promised and closed the door behind him. *First, there's another relationship I need to work on.* Martha tapped softly on Bernie's door.

No answer. She hesitated, wanting to respect her daughter's privacy. But they needed to talk. Maybe there was too much to break through, but she had to try. Trying to give Bernie plenty of warning, Martha slowly twisted the knob and opened the door.

The room was empty.

"They're not looking. Go now."

Bernie followed Henri's instructions, slipping behind the guards and through the gate into the inner camp. It had been easier than she'd imagined to get away. She'd opened the window, crawled out, and dropped to the ground.

I'm not abandoning Leanne. She couldn't believe her mom was planning to walk away. After her talk with Lou, Bernie considered forgiving her mother, but her anger had grown fresh and hot once more.

There was no one in the camp. No children played. No adults hung around and talked. No people went back and forth to work details. Bernie crept to Leanne's door and cautiously knocked. Worried murmurs rose and fell inside, and she looked around anxiously to see if anyone had noticed her.

The door opened, and Dolly peered out, her short dark hair making a greasy cap for her round face. "Oh, it's you. Go away."

"I need to talk to Leanne." Bernie stood firm.

"And I need to not be tased again." Dolly scowled, her thick hands opening and closing.

"I brought food." Bernie held out her backpack, full of half-eaten foil packets leftover from the night before.

Dolly snatched the backpack and started poking through it. She left a narrow gap, barely wide enough for Bernie to slip inside the barracks. The other internees were crowding forward, filling up the broad aisle between the stalls, but Bernie made her way back to Leanne's bunk.

Her teacher was curled up on her cot, wrapped in blankets. "Did you save any for me?"

Bernie handed over two plastic cups of applesauce and a crumbled granola bar.

"So what brings you out? Surveying the damage?" Leanne gestured at the rest of the barracks. The internees were fighting over the food. Dolly punched one girl in the face and carried away three packets. Two sisters managed to rip one open, sending the chicken and potatoes to the ground in a wet splat. A couple had secured two packets and were sharing them with their three children.

"I wanted to talk to you." Bernie stared down at her hands. If she were bigger and more powerful, then she could fix all the problems. But she had to do what she could.

"So talk." Leanne opened the granola bar's wrapper and poured the broken bits into her hand.

"We're leaving," Bernie blurted out.

Leanne eyed her. "I thought you wanted to stay and save us all."

"I do. But it's my mom. She says we have to go now. The doctor has Lily and Andrew."

"And who are Lily and Andrew?" Leanne frowned.

It took a little while to explain, but eventually Bernie got all the information out. Leanne sat on her bed, tapping her skinny fingers.

"I guess it's always different once your own family is involved. So they're going to retreat and leave us all to rot," she hissed the words between her teeth.

"But you can come with us. You wanted to go." Bernie didn't understand why Leanne was angry instead of excited. "Chuck says it's all going to be perfect once we're out of here."

Leanne's angry mouth softened. "Is that what he says?"

Bernie frowned in confusion. "Of course."

Leanne glanced around. "Is he here?"

Bernie shook her head, confused. Leanne looked as if she was afraid, but Bernie didn't understand why she would be afraid of Chuck.

"There's something I've been wanting to tell you." Leanne gestured for Bernie to move closer. "It's about Chuck. Do you know why there aren't many old ghosts?"

"Gwen says it's because they lose themselves. Chuck has trouble remembering things sometimes, but I remind him." He didn't like realizing he'd forgotten things, and he sometimes got upset at Bernie for reminding him.

Leanne gripped Bernie's arms. "It's more than remembering facts and details. We aren't meant to exist without bodies, at least not here. Without a body, there's something broken, and a ghost becomes more dangerous. When we see a ghost like that, we have to send it into the light."

"What if they're not ready to move on?" It sounded mean. "What happens when they go into the light if they're not ready?"

"I don't know. No one knows what happens on the other side of the light. But it stops them from hurting people here. Do you understand? Sometimes there's no other choice."

That made sense to Bernie. "So how do you do it?"

"It's not easy. You know how you push ghosts away, using Chuck's energy mixed with yours?" Leanne asked.

Bernie nodded.

"To send a ghost into the light, you do the same, except you keep it from leaving. There's a kind of mental twist that tightens the energy around it. And then you'll see the light open and pull the spirit in." Leanne's grip loosened. "Do you understand?"

"Sort of. Chuck can help me." She'd keep an eye out for dangerous ghosts but was far more concerned about making sure that Leanne was with them when they left.

"Bernie, you need to be careful with Chuck—"

Henri suddenly appeared in front of them. "*Petite*, your mother is looking for you."

"I'll be back for you. I can bring my mom's clothes for you, just like we planned." Bernie stood up.

"She can't go by herself, Leanne. You need to go with her." Henri flickered for a moment. "The guards—"

"She'll be fine." Leanne scratched at her shock collar as if she wanted to rip it off.

Bernie wasn't as confident about that but didn't want to say so. The idea of going back outside and facing angry guards made her stomach churn.

"She got here by herself," Leanne continued. "You can help her to get home."

"Sure, I can." Bernie's voice cracked, and Leanne's sharp eyes snapped back to her.

Bernie tried to seem confident and mature instead of scared. But she wasn't sure what to do with her hands, so they ended up flailing a bit, first crossing over her chest and then trying to hide in her pockets.

Leanne huffed. "Come on. Let's get it done."

Chapter Twenty-Nine

Martha peered at the ground, wishing she had Lou's tracking skills. She'd hoped to see some sign of Bernie's passage, hopefully something that would let her find her daughter quickly. She was already past Hood and Harley's trailer and didn't want to backtrack.

It's not like there's any question where she would have gone. The squat barracks in the inner camp stood in isolated rows. Bernie must have snuck through the gates to see Leanne, which meant that Martha would have to go after her. Stiffening her spine, she marched over to the gates. A confident attitude would help her to bluff her way through.

"Ma'am, you need to return to your trailer," the young man at the gate called, putting down a steaming tin mug.

She didn't slow her steps at all. "I have to go inside the inner camp."

He moved to stand in front of her. "You can't. We're under emergency protocol. No one is allowed in or out of the inner camp."

She eyed the guard. He didn't seem comfortable in his uniform jacket. His cheeks and chin were still rounded with baby fat. It gave her an idea to try. Softening her voice, she widened her eyes. "Please, I need your help."

The young man swallowed and looked around.

Martha kept her distance, not wanting to spook him. "My daughter isn't in our trailer. I think she snuck out to see her friends in the inner camp. Please, I need to check."

"I haven't seen anyone, ma'am. I wouldn't have let her through." His chin lifted in pride.

I doubt he's even reached twenty years old yet. Martha summoned up her best maternal evil eye, the one that could make grown men feel like small boys caught sneaking cookies before supper or standing over the shards of something they'd been warned not to touch. From the way he shifted and tried to avoid meeting her eyes, she'd found the correct expression. "What is your name?"

"Paul Graysmith, ma'am."

"Paul, have you been at this post for the entire morning?" Martha kept her voice cool to maintain a sense of authority.

He nodded, freezing when Martha tilted her head.

"You didn't take any breaks?" She pointed to the tin mug, still steaming on top of the gate post. "Not even to get coffee?"

"It was really quick. I was only gone for a minute." He bit his lip, seeming to realize his error.

"She could have gotten through while you were away." Martha stepped toward the gate. "Let me see if she's there."

He started to chew on his lip, obviously unsure what to do.

"Please, just let me go in. No one has to know," she said quietly. "I need to make sure that she's safe." She waited, certain that Lou's outburst yesterday must have made the guards nervous about watching over the *lalassu*.

"All right. But hurry up, please, so we don't both get in trouble." He proved that not all of the guards at the camp were callous predators, and Martha sincerely hoped he wouldn't be punished for it.

"And what do we have here?" Ryan boomed, dashing that particular hope.

"Sir, we have a missing child—" Graysmith began.

"I'll take care of this." The anticipatory cruelty in Ryan's eyes set a spark of fury smoldering at the base of Martha's spine. "Back to your post, Paul."

"Well, sir, maybe I should help her." The boy's shoulders pulled back, and he stepped between Martha and Ryan.

His attempt at gallantry was sweet, but Martha could see it was ultimately doomed.

"Maybe you should mind your own business," Ryan snarled. "Ken! Travis!"

Two more guards came running. To distract herself from her fear, Martha wondered how many guards there actually were. There seemed to be a lot of them for the total number of staff and internees.

"Ken, take Paul back to his trailer so that he can spend some time thinking about his career path," Ryan ordered. "Travis, guard the gate, and don't let anyone through."

He grabbed Martha's arm and pulled her a short distance away.

"Let me go." She pulled free. "I'm going to get my daughter."

"Lost her again, have you? Sounds like you're not a very good mother." His smirk widened. He was enjoying her defiance, which only made her angrier.

Martha peered over Ryan's shoulder at the other guard, Travis, half-hoping that he would interfere. But he turned away, pointedly ignoring the two of them. *I guess he's seen what happens to people who defy Ryan. I'm on my own.*

"Maybe I should escort you to the medical building. Maybe you didn't hear, but one of your precious loocies managed to smash up part of the forest." His gaze went up and down her body, and it didn't take a genius to figure out what he planned to do in the relative privacy of the medical building.

Think! She couldn't let him take her someplace he felt he had control. But the fact that he was trying to get her away from the open area meant that he didn't feel entirely immune to others' opinions.

Ryan leaned in close. "I like it when you pretend like there's a way to get away. It lets me look forward to breaking you."

She recoiled in disgust at his words and closeness, turning away. She spotted the three men in military fatigues walking along the road to the landing field, probably soldiers trying to fix the helicopters that Hood and Harley had sabotaged. Her mind snapped to attention. They worked for Dalhard Industries, so she couldn't rely on them to be decent people who would stop Ryan to protect her.

"Women like you pretend that you're better than guys like me," Ryan muttered, leaning in even closer. "You pretend you don't spread your legs like all the others."

The lattice fence pressed into her back, even through the insulation of her coat. The soldiers were coming closer, and she needed to figure out a way to drive Ryan back. A fierce fighter would have slapped the sick smile off of his face. His evident enjoyment of her fear told her he wasn't about to give up easily.

He stepped back, lifting his rifle. He pointed the barrel right at her as he grabbed her hand. "Come on, Doc. I think I need a real thorough examination."

She wasn't a fierce fighter. She couldn't force him to leave.

"Do you need a reminder of our conversation yesterday?" He checked over his shoulder. Travis was still studiously ignoring them. Martha could see the soldiers taking note of the situation. None of them showed any signs of alarm.

Ryan yanked her hand toward his crotch.

I'm not a fighter. I'm a nurse.

"Feel that?" he whispered.

Martha looked him directly in the eye and squeezed hard. Twice. "Yes. I do."

Ryan dropped her hand, gasping in pain. His jaw tightened, and his face flushed in anger.

She pulled her hand back slowly, avoiding the appearance of panic. Pitching her voice to carry, she began to speak in a clinical tone. "I assume you wanted me to check for parasites? Luckily, there are no irregular growths."

The soldiers started hitting each other and laughing. Ryan turned, glaring at them.

Martha continued. "You're right to be concerned, since penile parasites can cause severe complications, including rashes, open sores, and prolonged periods of impotence."

She was making every word of it up, but the uncertainty and disgust on Ryan's face was worth whatever karmic price she'd have to pay for the lie.

"Puts a new meaning into having ants in your pants, huh!" one of the soldiers shouted, elbowing the others.

The outcome of her gamble was still uncertain. Ryan was furious at her clinical mockery, trembling on the edge of control. If she showed any sign of fear, he would unleash his rage on her. She needed to tip him back into the realization that further action would make him seem even more foolish.

"Generally, I prefer to do such examinations in private so as not to violate doctor-patient confidentiality." She kept her voice calm. "However, since you were worried enough to insist on an immediate exam, I can put your fears to rest. There are no signs of worms, ticks, or other parasites."

It was too much for Travis. He let out a bark of laughter.

"You bitch," Ryan hissed.

Martha stepped away from the fence, moving so that he couldn't pin her again.

"Can't say I blame you!" a new voice shouted. "I wouldn't wait for an exam from her, either."

Ryan's face twisted into a smirk as he turned to face the soldiers. Martha kept her head high and slowly moved toward the gate. From the way Travis was sniggering, the encounter would make its way through the camp at record speed.

"Mom?" Bernie's voice had never been so welcome. She was standing right by the gate, and Martha took her hand.

Thank you. Martha kept her eyes fixed on Ryan, aware that he would pounce on any show of weakness. He was a bully, and while she might have temporarily won a round, the game wasn't over. It was only a matter of time before he came after her again, and he'd want to pay her back for his humiliation.

Walking away with her head high and her daughter in tow, she listened for signs of pursuit. But despite her wariness, she still couldn't help but enjoy a sense of satisfaction at having fought back, if only in a small way.

"Parasites." Leanne chuckled to herself. She wouldn't have guessed that the soccer mom had it in her. However, the amusement quickly faded. The woman and her merry band of heroes were going to get a lot of people killed with their knee-jerk panic. More importantly, they were going to fuck up Leanne's escape.

Their plan to sneak everyone onto the commuter plane was ridiculous. And when they got caught, they would trigger massive reprisals.

"He's gone off," Henri reported. "The guard isn't looking. You can go."

She didn't waste any time, retracing her steps back to the barracks. Dolly let her in, and a few minutes later, Leanne curled back up in her frigid bed, seething about the inequity of the universe.

"You're backing out of our deal." The thin, childish voice chilled her more than the sunshine could warm.

"I'm not. Your girl's mother is changing the plan," Leanne muttered.

"Change it back," Chuck said.

"Cheer up. The way their luck is running, your girl will get herself shot."

An icy incorporeal fist plunged into her chest, and Leanne gasped.

"If she's killed violently, she'll cross into the light," his voice whispered in her ear.

Leanne jerked away. "I should blast you into the light."

"Hey, Looney, keep it down! It's bad enough in here without listening to you ramble," Dolly shouted.

"Leave her alone," Henri joined in.

Chuck shouted, "Piss off, frog eater—"

"Enough!" Leanne got to her feet. The entire barracks fell quiet, watching her as if she'd shifted from good-story crazy to dangerous crazy.

"All right, Looney, we'll keep it down." The Asian girl came closer, trying to be soothing. She was usually the barracks' peacekeeper, but Leanne could never remember her name.

"Leave me alone." Leanne walked to the front door.

"We have to stay inside." The girl shifted to block her way. "Remember?"

"I'm crazy, not an idiot. And if I have to stay in here for one more second, I'm going to prove how crazy I am." Leanne stared at the girl without blinking. "Out of my way."

The girl backed down. Leanne fixed her stare on each of the other occupants before opening the door.

"Leanne, wait!" Henri's shouted warning came too late.

Ryan was waiting on the other side. "Just the woman I was looking for."

He didn't wait for her to reply before forcing his way inside. "You had our nurse's little brat in here, didn't you?"

Leanne didn't answer. None of the others said anything, either. But she knew it couldn't last.

"First one to answer gets rations. You all must be getting hungry by now." Ryan nudged a piece of discarded foil packaging with his toe. "Or maybe you've already eaten."

"The girl brought it," Dolly said.

"Good for you. I'm a man of my word. Travis, take the lady to the kitchen," Ryan called out. "In fact, take all of them. And then take them to detention."

A few of them cried out but stopped as soon as Ryan touched his belt. None of them wanted to suffer through the burn of the shock collars again.

Leanne stood silently while the others filed out. The frightened expression on the children's faces tugged at her heart, but she held still. Ryan's reputation for sadism was well established. It was why they'd all breathed a sigh of relief when the camp forced him to take a two-week vacation after nearly murdering two internees.

Once they were alone, Ryan began the questioning. "Why does the girl come to see you?"

Playing crazy wouldn't get her out of his grasp. "She likes my stories. She feels sorry for me."

"Bullshit. There's no way that some suburbanite kid braves a lockdown for stories. So what is it?"

She wondered if Chuck and Henri were still here. A little ghostly interference would be welcome.

"You haven't been cooperating. Haven't joined a work shift. Hell, half my guards are scared to death of you." Ryan started to pace back and forth. "Why is that?"

"I'm colorful." Leanne tugged her blanket tighter around her arms.

"Be careful." Henri's low whisper brought a dangerous surge of relief. She needed to keep her wits sharp.

"If that's all, I'll send you to detention with the others. Let the doc figure out what's so special about you." Ryan studied her closely and smiled. "You don't like that."

"Of course not." She swallowed. "What do you want?"

"Leanne, don't," Henri pleaded.

"I want to know what the bitch is doing here. Is she sneaking you extra rations? Is she a reporter? What?" Ryan's face was inches from hers.

"We'll figure something out. You don't have to do this." Henri's desperate plea didn't change the odds. It was an easy calculation of hatred versus survival. Defying the guards to avoid a work detail was one thing, but doing it with a man barely hanging on to his sanity was suicide. Those who challenged Ryan had disappeared before, and Leanne had no intention of becoming one of them.

"She's one of us," she said.

Ryan started at her, confused.

"The whole family is." Leanne doubted that Martha had any actual gifts, but if it came to a choice of who was going to suffer in the doctor's custody, it wasn't going to be her.

"She's a loocy?" He wiped his hand on his shirt and grimaced as if he wanted to vomit.

"They're planning to escape, along with the prisoners who arrived on the helicopter." She couldn't let him know that she knew about the secret lab. He would kill her for certain.

"When?"

"On the commuter plane." If there was any kind of justice, Ryan would be too busy with his revenge to pay attention to the flight. And if all attention was elsewhere, then Leanne would find a chance to escape. She needed to get away from Bernie and away from Chuck's attention as soon as possible. With luck, the unstable ghost would forget about his threats. A twinge of guilt tried to creep up from her conscience, but she shoved it away. Chuck wanted someone else to do his dirty work, so Bernie should be safer without another medium around for him to bully.

Ryan's eyes weren't sane despite her efforts to cooperate. "Tell me everything," he said.

Chapter Thirty

Martha dropped Bernie with Hood and Harley. They would keep a close eye on her while Martha brought Lou over, assuming he was awake. After everything that had happened, she didn't think it would be prudent for their group to split up.

She eased open the door to the trailer, wondering what would be waiting. She was thankful when the place seemed to be grizzly free. Lou was stretched out on his bed with his feet dangling over the edge and one muscular arm thrown up over his head. His long hair was silky smooth despite what must have been a night of tossing and turning. His tight T-shirt hugged his broad chest, outlining each firm curve, but Martha found herself wishing he still slept naked.

As she watched him, the confusion in her mind stilled. They were in a horrible situation. He'd seen his family and friends killed and knew his home had been attacked. She and her family were under immediate threat by people who were taking lessons from the Nazis. They were trying to overthrow a prejudiced conspiracy, and they could end up being killed for their attempts. Faced with all of that, worries about caring too much for Lou or how they could build a life together seemed much smaller. *There's no point in trying to keep my heart safe for a future that may or may not ever happen.*

Take a chance on a happily ever after—or at least a happily right now. She called his name, not sure how he would react to being physically jostled awake.

His eyes opened immediately, and he sat up, showing no sign of drowsiness. "Are you all right?"

"I'm fine." She looked down at her hands. "A little nervous, though."

His gaze sharpened, but he waited, trusting her to tell him what was wrong without prompting.

"I've kind of made a decision." *Could I sound any more like an awkward teenager? Do you like me? Check yes or no?* Maybe she should take a page out of Lou's book and forget the words that seemed so embarrassing and inappropriate.

She took the three steps to the bed then bent down and kissed him. Just a brief touch of their lips sent her heartbeat into orbit. She opened her eyes and bit her lip, not sure how he was going to react.

He smiled at her, and her heart didn't only skip a beat, but it began to dance, leaving her light-headed.

"There are so many reasons why we should be careful or be afraid, and right now I don't care about any of them," she said as she sat down beside him on the bed. "I want to be with you, even if today is all we have. Do you…?"

He wrapped his hand around hers, lifting her fingers to his lips and pressing a slow and sensuous kiss into her palm. "Are you sure?"

Her other hand tightened in the bedclothes, and she pressed her thighs together against the surge of warmth between them. She nodded.

He smiled slowly, his strong thumb stroking the back of her hand. "You are brave and beautiful. I admire you more than I can say. I want to help you to be happy."

The effort behind his words touched her as much as the words themselves. She smoothed his hair away from his face. "Can we take this moment just for us and not worry about what the future holds?"

"I want that, too. But first, I must tell you something." He took a deep breath. "You are my mate."

Like Ron and Lily? It seemed impossible. They hardly knew each other. But whenever she thought about the future, he was there. She could no longer imagine her life without him.

His lips brushed along her wrist and made her wish she'd worn short sleeves.

"I won't trap you. I want you to fly free," he said, unbuttoning the cuff of her blouse and sliding the loosened sleeve up her forearm, baring the skin.

"I trust you," she said breathlessly.

It seemed that whispered consent was what he'd been waiting for. He lifted his head, his eyes dark and mysterious with desire. Her mouth dried, and a spasm quivered deep in her belly. For whatever reason, the gorgeous, sexy man beside her wanted her as much as she wanted him. And she wanted him so badly that her body ached for his touch.

He bent over her wrist again, and Martha had a fevered flashback to the vampire romances of her youth. He tasted her as his nibbled kisses moved up the sensitive skin, mixed with quick probes from his tongue. Her heart raced, spreading a warm flush all over, blending with tingles of anticipation.

She shifted, moving to straddle his lap. Knowing his cock was so close to her core's budding slickness kicked her body's reaction to the next level. She wouldn't have protested if he'd stripped off her clothes and plunged into her then and there. But she also couldn't wait to get her hands and mouth all over him.

He cradled her hips in his hands as she settled, his big hands anchoring her. He was watching her, studying her with a seriousness that she'd never seen from a potential lover. It was as if nothing, not even his own ego, was more important than getting it right, and it didn't seem necessary to clutter the moment with more words and worries about what might happen next or what their relationship would be. For the time being, they wanted and cared about each other. She trusted him, and he trusted her.

She slid her arms around his neck and slowly undid the leather thong holding his hair back. The silky strands flowed free, cascading over her hands in a stimulating caress. She cupped his face between her hands, enjoying the vulnerability of his masculine beauty. There was such strength, but it was all laid bare before her, open to her touch and no one else's. It was a side of her strong grizzly that no other saw.

She leaned in, brushing aside the hair from his shoulder so that she could place a kiss on the sensitive place just below his ear, where his neck and jaw joined. The tendons immediately tensed, and she thrilled at knowing it was because of her touch. She kissed the same place again, this time swiping it with the tip of her tongue. Her reward was a full-body shudder running through him and his hands sliding down to cup her buttocks.

She kissed all along his granite jaw, returning greedily to his mouth. As soon as their lips touched, the kiss took on a life of its own, swelling and moving without their conscious control. Everything else faded away, subsumed into the interplay of lips and tongues that fanned the blaze ever higher. Dizzily, she heard the rip of cloth and realized she'd torn open his T-shirt in order to get her hands on his chest. *His ridiculously muscled chest.* The memory brought giggles bubbling to her lips.

He broke free, searching her face. *He's making sure I'm okay.* Such tender concern dissolved her lingering self-restraint. It was absolute proof that she was safe with him and could allow herself to surrender to her desires. She eyed the uneven rip running from hem to just below the collar, spreading it open with her fingers.

He smiled in feral approval of her tactics before reclaiming her mouth for his own.

As his tongue thrust into her, she gripped his shirt collar in both hands and yanked in opposite directions, with little to no effect.

"Damn it," she said breathlessly between kisses. He smiled against her lips, and his hands came up to cover hers, wrapping around her fingers as he stole another blood-igniting kiss. With a wrench that seemed effortless, he tore apart the collar and hastily discarded the remnants of the horrid barrier.

She ran her fingers along his chest like a blind woman reading survival instructions in braille. The crisp hair dragged on her fingertips as she stroked his broad pectorals, moving down over his taut stomach. His low and throaty growl was almost a purr as she undid his jeans.

His hands crawled up her chest, undoing the first button of her shirt. She broke free of his intoxicating kiss, a last-ditch surge of protective uncertainty threatening to spoil the mood.

"Trust me," he whispered, leaning his forehead against hers.

She nodded then gasped as he gently tilted her back onto the bed, holding her as if she were as precious and delicate as a glass sculpture. For once, being treated with care didn't seem like a criticism of her abilities—it was because he cherished her. He leaned over her, surrounding her with his strength as he stared intently down into her eyes.

"I dreamed of this," he reminded her.

"Me too," she whispered. Then she said the words that snapped her remaining lifeline. "I want you."

He bent over her, his mouth trailing kisses along her neck. She buried her hands in his hair, guiding him along the trail to her pleasure. He slowly parted her blouse, unhurriedly savoring her flesh. Her nether reaches clenched and tightened, eager to receive the same attention, but his patience was greater than hers. Unclasping her bra with surprisingly nimble fingers, he stripped it and her blouse off then tossed them to the side. Then he lowered his mouth to her breast, drawing her nipple deep inside his mouth and flicking it with his tongue.

She tensed, a truncated cry escaping her stiffened lips. His tongue continued to tease and roll, alternating with hard suction. Her hips thrust up, her slick folds desperate for his touch. She struggled to open her pants, needing to free herself from their imprisonment.

Without ceasing his attentions to her breast, he captured her wrists and guided them away. She could have howled in protest, but he transferred his mouth to her untouched breast, and what came out was more a groan of broken encouragement. He pinned her wrists to either side, the grip light enough to allow her to escape if she desired—except that would have meant him stopping what he was doing, and she thought she might explode from pent-up sexual frustration if he did.

His gentle attention was nothing like what she'd fantasized about, but if it was the sort of skill that a lifetime of primal living provided, she would insist that every male over sixteen be sent to the Arctic. Delicious tension rolled across her, and she trembled in anticipatory shivers as he worked her sensitive nipples. He left her skin sweat slick, her vulva primed and aching, and her appetite roused for more. She wasn't even close to being satisfied.

She became aware of cool air circulating across her bare thighs and dimly realized he'd somehow finished undressing her while she'd been distracted. *My turn.* She clasped his head, forcing him to lift it. Her whole body felt as if electrical currents were writhing just under her skin. She wanted to feel his weight on her, his thighs pressed between her legs, and his arms around her. She wanted his presence to anchor her experience in reality, not in another fantasy where she stroked herself to satisfaction and awoke to empty arms.

Attacking his mouth, she clung to him, pressing as close as humanly possible. His muscles trembled under her fingers as he tried to hang on to control. She wanted him to lose control, or rather, to be the one who could make him lose it. She wanted his raw, uninhibited passion and desire.

She wrapped her legs around his waist, grinding her hips against his as she plundered his mouth. He had braced himself on his elbows, and she could feel how tight his biceps were, the veins coming to the surface like a restraining harness. The sight brought on a deep feminine satisfaction. She felt intently powerful and desirable, a wanton goddess demanding proper worship.

And goddesses did not wait. Squirming around to take his earlobe between her teeth, she growled her command. "Inside me. Now."

He went still, his eyes meeting hers. For a long second, a distant twinge of fear made her worry that she'd gone too far. Then his civilized veneer cracked, and she saw the wild man underneath. As a final act of patience, he tested her folds with a finger before recapturing her hands and securing them over her head.

The tip of his heavy erection probed at her opening. She panted, trying to take him inside, but he held back for a long, agonizing moment.

Then he thrust into her in a single hard push. She was so wet and eager that he slid his full length into her inner canal without a hint of resistance. Leaning her head back, she moaned. It had been so long that she'd forgotten how satisfying it felt to be filled.

He pulled back, leaving her to tremble in emptiness before filling her again. She locked her ankles behind his back, arching her back and hips to let him go deeper. His hands tightened around her wrists, and he sped up, thrusting harder into her.

There were no words left in her mind, only ecstasy as a powerful orgasm built, plunging her into shuddering waves of gasping delight. He was still pounding into her body, driving her higher and deeper until everything else vanished into a prolonged series of fiery climaxes.

Finally, his cock spasmed inside of her, triggering yet another orgasmic cascade. He collapsed onto her, his weight anchoring her before she could dissolve entirely. Their sweaty skin clung together, and she was half crushed into the bed, but it didn't matter. The trivial discomfort meant that her reality had shifted into one in which a wonderful, smoking-hot man wanted her and had just made love to her.

Chapter Thirty-One

"I find it difficult to believe that he has agreed." Karan hovered over the monitor displaying Ron McBride's containment unit. The live feed showed Ron pacing back and forth in the tiny basement cell. Priya had spent a great deal of time and money to convert the former farmhouse into one of Special Investigation's holding facilities. There were no neighbors for miles and no need for an extensive staff who might have been tempted to go public.

"He's idealistic but not a fool." Priya stretched out on the low leather sofa, sipping a glass of merlot. "He'll be ready for the rally."

"Leaving him loose is a mistake." Karan repeated himself.

Priya hid her grimace behind the wine glass. She'd explained it a dozen times in the politest terms. Marks from restraints would undermine the story they wished people to tell. It might be unlikely that anyone would think to examine their patsy too closely, but she saw no need to risk inconsistency. *Look at how people still obsess over the details of the assassination of JFK.* She had no desire to be overthrown ten years in the future by a mob determined to find retroactive justice.

Karan was still obsessing. "The Humanists' rally is in less than two days. You should keep him sedated until then."

"Sit down, and have some wine," Priya sat up to pour her brother a fresh glass. "You know, it reminds me of the bottle we stole from that trader. What was his name again?"

"Kadri." Karan smiled, and Priya smiled back, grateful he'd turned away from the blasted screen. He joined her, claiming the chair that matched her sofa. "He was the most appalling liar."

"Every year, he'd tell us ridiculous stories." Priya deepened her voice to mimic the long-dead peddler. "I fought the dragon for twenty days and twenty nights, and only after I plunged my sword into its chest did I discover this marvelous collection of necklaces and bracelets."

"All of which looked suspiciously similar to the ones he had shown us the year before." Karan chuckled.

"Exactly." *This is why I reached out to him again after all these decades.* She had wealth, power, and influence long before hacking Karan's computer to let him know she was still alive. But there wasn't anyone else who could remember the boastful Kadri or the songs their mother sang or any of a thousand other details from her childhood. No matter how much her brother annoyed her, he filled a hole in her life. "I have my people planting evidence on social media. Hundreds of genuine pro-*lalassu* protesters are planning to show up at the Humanists' rally. The atmosphere should be delightfully tense."

"What about the police?" Karan swirled the blood-dark wine in his glass.

"They're planning an extra presence to prevent tempers from flaring into violence, but I have a few carefully planned distractions arranged to ensure they don't arrive too quickly." Special Investigations would be available as a backup, and there would be three snipers ready to take McBride out of the picture once he'd created sufficient havoc. As much as she would have liked to have him available for future demonstrations, he was too dangerous and unpredictable to leave loose on the game board. Priya continued, "The man downstairs needs to become an embodiment of rage. He will spend the next forty hours wondering what is happening to those he loves. He is learning that he is helpless to save them in the way he most craves. We will provide him with an opportunity to release the anger on those who have threatened what he cares for. The emotion will make his performance much more believable."

"He is dangerous." Karan set down his glass without drinking from it. "He has already escaped from us more than once."

"And never once on his own initiative." Priya kept her voice low and sweet despite her building frustration. "The first time, you set him up to betray the little girl and her friends. The next, he was taken by the *lalassu*. For the third, he was in the hands of our agents when one of those shape-shifting bears took out the entire team. And most recently, it was the police detective who arranged for McBride to serve as a witness."

"I assume there is a point behind this litany of disappointments."

"McBride is a soldier. He sees himself as a protector and a hero. We aren't asking him to go against his instincts, except in working with us." Priya had studied the man's file extensively. "He needs the time to think on our offer and realize that a deal with the devil is his best choice."

"You are too confident in your predictions." Karan shook his head.

Priya's smile hardened. *How dare he dismiss my work. His own efforts haven't yielded much success.*

"We need backups in place in case he pulls another surprise out of his hat." Karan seemed to belatedly realize he'd made his sister angry. "I'm certain your insights are correct, but the last two years have taught me that those around the Harris family have a particular talent for disrupting even the most diligent plan."

"What would you propose?" They were not family as they looked at one another. It was purely business.

"For your social media campaign, have you created accounts in McBride's name?"

Karan's question caught Priya by surprise. "Of course we have. We've been using them to engage online with members of the Humanists and several other hate groups." *Does he really think so little of me?*

"I assumed as much, but I never act on assumptions. I believe we need to have something more, something that will require your delicate touch with online records and digital trails."

Flattery could only soothe so many stings to her pride. Priya nodded coolly.

"Can you create evidence of radicalization over the last two to three years?" Karan asked. "Posts with groups that advocate violence? The ideology is irrelevant. When the FBI, Homeland, and Special Investigations begin looking into McBride, I want them to discover a man who has been searching for a target for his violent impulses."

"That would dilute our political message." She shook her head. "We don't want this to be dismissed as the actions of a madman."

"I also want you to create medical and police records. Ones that show McBride being forcibly treated for drug and alcohol use. Numerous arrests for intoxication, petty theft, and the like."

Priya considered her brother's request. McBride's true records already showed issues with addiction. The more severe it was, the less sympathy the public would have for him. "You want him to appear as a monster."

"I want him to be irredeemable." Karan's usual serene mask dropped, revealing a sadistic, eager gleam. "No matter how deeply anyone digs, all I want them to find is more and more evidence of a man who should have been locked up years ago."

He wanted vengeance. It wasn't about plans for the future but about paying for the past. He left Priya with no recourse. "No."

Her brother went very still. "No?"

"No." She was gentle but firm. "I won't allow a personal vendetta to divert resources away from the task at hand."

"You forget yourself. You need me." Karan drew back, glaring at her icily.

Priya began to laugh, which only made him angrier. His behavior was so ridiculous, so over the top, and so melodramatic that she couldn't help herself. "Perhaps you'd like to have him target the President in a needlessly complicated scheme as well?"

He opened his mouth, but she cut him off before he could launch into a tirade.

"In order to tilt public opinion and create the sort of chaos we need, we need to keep the message simple and on target. People cannot be allowed to dismiss McBride's actions as a sociopath's outburst, they must see his violence as a natural outcome of his status as a *lalassu*," Priya lectured. "You've watched how the public react to acts of terror. Support for control measures increases only to be slowly eroded by the inevitable bureaucratic inefficiencies and stories of sympathetic individuals. The initial fear we created by revealing the *lalassu* is nearly gone. The public have had too much time to consider and think rather than reacting emotionally." She paused, waiting to see if he would accept her logic or continue to fight.

Karan did not attempt to speak, but the ticking muscle in his jaw told her that he was far from convinced.

"You are correct, though." She poured herself a fresh glass of wine, watching her brother through her lashes to measure his reaction. The tiny flutter of his flexing jaw muscle subsided, and his hands flattened on his thighs, which meant she could proceed. "The Harris family and those around them have a talent for disruption."

"And what is your suggestion?" His voice was barely above a snarl.

"Quite simple. We guarantee a sufficiently frightening demonstration, regardless of their interference. McBride's history can work for us. He could quite plausibly have planted an IED or two or more—something poorly designed and unstable, to create plenty of casualties on all sides." Mass injuries would work more effectively than a few deaths. "Our experts can explain how his enhanced strength somehow damaged his devices. It doesn't even need to be plausible to increase the blame."

"If he survives, he could undo everything."

Priya inclined her head, graciously accepting her brother's concern and ignoring his tone. "He cannot outrun a sniper's bullet. And if the manner of death does not bring you satisfaction, consider that his death will be painful and public, coming as a result of actions he finds morally reprehensible and in the full knowledge that we have his most important people in our custody. He has lost everything that means anything to him, and he failed to stop us."

Karan's lips quirked. "I suppose I will have to be satisfied with it."

She sipped her wine to hide that she gritted her teeth.

"And you have taught me a valuable lesson tonight, sister dearest."

She forced herself to smile pleasantly at him. "And what lesson would that be?"

"Not to underestimate you, with your smiles and flattery. I knew you had a talent for manipulation, but tonight has shown me how truly skilled you are." He rose to his feet, buttoning his jacket. "I will return home for the rest of the evening. Do stay and enjoy a celebratory glass of wine.

You've certainly earned it."

Irritation soured the sweetness of the grapes on her tongue.

"You need not worry about my actions. You have convinced me that the most satisfying course of action will be to proceed as you suggested. But in the future, I will pay much closer attention when we cross swords and intentions."

"The new staff members arrive today." Dr. Coulon chose not to waste time with greetings or small talk when Martha arrived for work after three days of lockdown. He didn't even look up from his notes.

It had been incredibly stressful with all of them crammed into Hood and Harley's trailer. With four adults and two teenagers, there hadn't been any opportunity to further explore the feelings between her and Lou aside from that one glorious afternoon. Lou had ended up spending most of his time out patrolling the woods in bear form, while Martha dealt with Bernie's increasingly volatile emotions. Neither Chuck nor Henri had been to see her, and Bernie was feeling understandably abandoned. It had frustrated and worried Martha as well. She'd tried several times to sneak into the secret lab to check on Andrew, Lily, and Annika, but Dr. Coulon was always either there or in his office. He must have left to sleep at some point, but she couldn't figure out when. *Just when a ghost would have been useful, there isn't one to be found.*

"They will need to be tested to determine if any of them are *occulata hominem*," he said.

Martha nodded politely even though he couldn't see her. There had been a lot of debate as to whether or not Martha should return to her job. Eventually, she and Harley had prevailed, insisting that it was best to proceed as if everything were normal. With the helicopters disabled, Kal and Patrick would be transferred on the commuter plane, which they all hoped would allow for a rescue.

"This lockdown has put me behind on my own work. You will perform the testing."

I can't. Martha pressed her lips together to keep from blurting out the words. She couldn't be the one responsible for painting a target on someone with a few swipes of a cotton swab, not to mention that they'd hoped to get Lily, Andrew, and Annika out while the doctor did the testing. "I'm not familiar with—"

"You'll find the directions with the supplies."

"Yes, sir." *Why did I expect the mad scientist to be helpful?* Martha escaped to the front room, desperately trying to think of a new plan. Hood and Lou were waiting nearby. Harley, Bernie, and Eva were waiting at the trailer with the essentials packed, ready to flee. Bernie was upset about leaving the bulk of their things behind, but they could only take what they could carry.

First things first, the horrid test. It took her twenty minutes of searching through the cupboards to find the stack of sealed cheek swabs and vials of chemical solution. A battered typewritten instruction sheet was folded on top of them.

As she read it, Martha's jaw clenched in anger. She'd seen the test in Bear Claw when Michael had brought it, but at the time she'd been more concerned about making sure that she and Bernie got false-negative results than in understanding how the actual test worked. It used a similar technique to a home pregnancy test, except that it tested for a protein rather than a hormone. If the protein was present, the chemical solution would change color from clear to cloudy. Someone had decided that the protein was linked to the genetic variation between *lalassu* and the general population.

Except it wasn't. Martha wasn't a geneticist, but anyone with even a cursory medical knowledge could see the inherent flaws in relying on such a simplistic method for a new field of research. It wasn't just that the test failed to catch *lalassu* who didn't produce the protein, but the notes at the bottom of the test shared that its creators had been well aware that it also produced a significant number of false positives. Up to thirty percent of the positive results were for people who showed no evidence of powers, even under "rigorous testing," a term that made her skin crawl.

It was information that needed to be made public. She slipped the folded paper into her pocket. *None of these bastards are going to get away with this.*

Next, she dumped the vials of chemical solution down the drain. No one would have their lives ruined by this the again if she could help it. *I can claim there's a problem and insist that Dr. Coulon come to the Hub. Then Lou and Hood can get everyone out.*

She grabbed a bottle of drinking water from the counter. As she began to pour, the medical office door opened, and one of the stranded helicopter pilots walked in.

"What are you doing?" he asked suspiciously.

"It's not important. Did you need help?" She put on a bright, slightly ditzy smile. "I'm sure you must be looking forward to getting back to civilization."

He stepped back, frowning. "He was right. You're sabotaging the test. You're one of them."

The door opened again, and Ryan stepped in, rifle ready and aimed at her. "What did I tell you? How else can you explain what happened that day? She used her powers on me."

A sinking feeling in Martha's stomach told her that bluffing would be futile, but she still gave it a try. "What are you talking about?"

"You're one of the loocies." There was no lust for power in Ryan's expression, only disgust. "You tried to seduce me, but I saw through you."

"You're going to have to come with us, ma'am. I don't know what you tried to do to Mr. Blake, but you can't get away with doing it to both of us." The soldier pulled a thin gray strip out of his pocket—one of the shock collars.

"I don't know what you're talking about. I was tested. You were there." Martha heard the quaver in her voice and knew she wouldn't be able to bluff her way out of it.

"You're one of the freaks who can fool the test. But don't worry. I sent men to round up your daughter and your husband, so you'll have plenty of company while you're in detention." Ryan laughed, a thin, brittle sound that held very little sanity. "Do you know what he's going to do to you? He'll cut you into bits, trying to find out how you work. And then he'll start cutting up your little girl—"

Fury overcame caution. Martha threw herself at him, fingers stiffened into claws. It must have surprised him because she managed to hit him, leaving long red scratches across his face.

The rifle came up and hit her in the chest, knocking the breath out of her. She dropped to the ground. It felt painful and hollow, as if her ribs had been caved in. But her medical training gave the real answer. He'd hit her solar plexus.

She tried to kick him, but the soldier grabbed her and pinned her arms to her side. Ryan grabbed her by the hair, hauling her head up. Martha's eyes watered with pain.

"I'm going to enjoy watching him experiment on you," he hissed.

The door banged open again, and an ear-splitting roar filled the room.

Martha's knees banged painfully on the floor as she abruptly fell. Blinking, she raised her head. Hood had tackled the soldier, and they were grappling, bent over the counter. She turned toward where Ryan had been, but Lou's broad back blocked her view.

She scrambled to her feet, not sure how to help but ready to do whatever she needed to. Lou's shirt was stretched nearly to the breaking point as he slowly lifted Ryan with one massive hand wrapped around the bully's throat.

Ryan clawed at Lou's hand, trying to break free. His face was red, and his eyes were bugging out. Clinically, Martha realized he was going to pass out at any moment.

"What is going on here?" Dr. Coulon demanded irritably from his office door.

CHAPTER THIRTY-TWO

With Hood holding the soldier and Lou focused on Ryan, it was up to Martha to stop the doctor. Ryan's rifle lay on the floor, and without giving herself time to think, she snatched it up. "Stay there!"

Hood, the soldier, and Dr. Coulon all stared at her. Ryan started to gag, and his heels banged against the wall. Hood used the distraction to smash the soldier's head into the counter. While the other man was dazed, Hood let go and took the rifle from Martha, aiming it at the glaring soldier and the frowning doctor.

More than happy to let him play the role of armed guardian, Martha turned her attention to Lou. His mouth was distorted with heavy fangs, and long, narrow claws sprouted from his fingers. Ryan's face began to turn purple, and Martha realized there were only seconds left. As much as she hated Ryan, she didn't want him dead. "Don't kill him."

Lou didn't immediately respond, but the tooth-rattling subsonic growl stopped.

Martha put her hand on his shoulder. "Please. He deserves to stand trial for what he's done."

"He hurt you." The low, rough voice didn't sound human, but Martha understood.

"I know," she said softly. "But you don't need to hurt him."

Lou let go, and Ryan dropped to the ground, gasping for breath.

"You're both dead," Ryan snarled, holding his throat.

No good deed goes unpunished. Martha stroked Lou's broad back. He was still breathing heavily through a mouthful of fangs, but the claws had retracted. Under her touch, the sharp teeth slowly receded.

"Fascinating," Dr. Coulon said. He ignored both Hood and the gun trained on him. Instead, he seemed much more interested in observing the changes.

With Lou calmed down, Martha grabbed some long strips of tough cloth from the cupboard. They were meant for bandages and slings, but they would do for restraints. "Can you hold him?"

Lou's eyes lit up with pleasure. He picked the limp Ryan up with one hand, letting the other man's feet dangle above the floor. Quickly, Martha tied Ryan's hands behind his back, not bothering to be careful about his circulation.

"The doctor next," she said. Lou dropped Ryan on the ground and walked with her to Dr. Coulon.

"Is the transformation voluntary? Or is it triggered emotionally?" The doctor's eyes shone with excitement, and he put his hands behind him without any prompting.

Martha tied him up without answering. The soldier required both of them, but his hands were bound without incident, giving them a few minutes of breathing room.

"Are you all right?" she asked Lou.

"It's hard to keep control when someone threatens you," he said. "I don't want you to be afraid."

"I'm not afraid of you," she whispered. "I'm your fierce kestrel, remember. You can trust me."

"I'm going to be sick," Ryan interjected. Martha shot him an angry glare before returning her attention to Lou.

"He tried to hurt you." Lou's voice deepened as he glowered at Ryan.

"And he failed. Let's go get the others, and then we never have to see him again." Martha tucked her hand into his, turning to face Ryan. "Someone else can take care of the garbage."

"All right," Hood said. "Time to get moving. Martha, you go first. Lou and I will follow with these guys. And in case anyone has any bright ideas, after a few months in this place, I am more than happy to shoot any of you. And if any of you even think about harming her, then I'm not going to stop Lou from ripping you into pieces."

Even with only blunt human teeth, Lou's savage smile carried threat.

"You can't possibly think this is going to work." Dr. Coulon sounded puzzled. "This is pure sentimentality."

Hood bent down and yanked the remote trigger for the collars out of Ryan's pocket. "Let's go. On your feet."

Ryan opened his mouth, probably to complain or threaten, but he never got a chance. Lou hauled him upright, keeping his hand wrapped around the other man's neck.

His throat would be incredibly swollen and bruised from being choked. Remembering her own bruises, Martha enjoyed unprofessional satisfaction in his discomfort. Trusting Hood to manage the captives, she went ahead to unlock the secret door.

"I'm impressed by your resourcefulness, Martha. You would have made an excellent permanent assistant." The doctor went quietly.

"What the hell is this place?" the soldier asked as they descended the narrow stairs. His eyes widened in alarm as they passed the plastic curtain and he saw the bloodstained examination chair and the occupied cells on the far wall.

Andrew sat up. "What are you doing here?"

"We're going to get you out." Martha found the keys behind the file cabinet and unlocked his door before moving on to the next.

Annika glared at the doctor as she stepped out of her cell. "Captivity is a good look on him. Death would be better."

"Put them in the cells," Martha ordered. Lily wasn't moving. She hadn't reacted to their presence at all. Concern contracted her lungs, locking down her breath. "Lily, are you all right?"

"She's been tortured for days by a psychopath. She's outstanding." Andrew's peevish reply stabbed into Martha's guilt.

Slamming the cell door on Ryan, Lou growled, moving to stand between his twin and Martha.

"You can't be serious." Andrew stared at his brother as if he'd never seen him before. "Her?"

"Hey, if we're escaping, can we get on with it?" Annika interrupted.

"Maybe save the heartfelt family reunion for somewhere that's more *Dr. Phil* than *Jailhouse Rock*?"

The doctor was the only one still loose. He shook his head. "I am sorry that you've decided on this path. Finding a replacement will be difficult."

Andrew began questioning Lou in a trippingly liquid language.

Martha opened Lily's cell and hurried inside, where the other woman lay curled up on the cot, her tan skin dulled by a film of tacky sweat and a sour-yellow undertone. Her pulse was thready and irregular, and she was breathing in shallow, panting sips.

"What did you give her?" Martha demanded.

"He's been draining blood from her ever since she arrived," Andrew said.

If Martha had held the rifle in that moment, she could have shot the doctor for his cruel indifference. "It could be hypovolemic shock from blood loss. She needs a transfusion immediately. Help me get her out of here."

Andrew pushed her aside, examining his sister himself. Lou immediately pulled his brother back.

With a start, Martha realized Andrew's pupils were dilated. "He gave you something. What was it?"

"I don't know," he replied, blinking hard and shaking his head. "It's like being drunk and sleep-deprived at the same time."

They both waited to see if the doctor would volunteer the information, but he stayed quiet as Lou picked up Lily. Hood put Dr. Coulon in the cell and locked the door.

Hopefully, whatever it is will subside on its own. Martha wouldn't waste any time waiting for his cooperation. She turned to Andrew. "Do you know her blood type?"

"Yes. We're all the same type. But you can't use my blood, not with whatever he pumped into it." Andrew clung grimly to the edge of the chair to keep his balance.

"All right. Lou, roll up your sleeves. Annika, see if you can find something to keep her covered. She needs to be kept warm." Martha rushed to the tool chest, yanking open drawers until she found what she needed. Turning, she found Lou standing next to Lily, his shirt discarded to one side.

"I don't think he's big on clothes." Annika smirked in approval. She'd moved over and was supporting Andrew.

"What the hell is going on here?" the soldier demanded again.

"Dr. Coulon has been systematically experimenting on the internees," Martha snapped.

"We needed to discover their abilities." The doctor shrugged.

"Except that at least a third of the people in your camp aren't *lalassu*. They just had the misfortune to be tagged by your ridiculously defective test." Martha took a deep breath. She needed to concentrate on Lily. "Andrew, do you have any last-minute words of advice? Is this different for skin-walkers?"

He shook his head. "We don't usually worry about this kind of thing. With a big wound, we can transform and replenish a lot of the blood that we've used."

"All right. So if we stabilize her enough to get her outside and she can shift, we'll be in good shape." Martha hoped she was right since there was no more time for talking.

"Very interesting. Could you give me my notebook so that I can take notes?"

They ignored the doctor's request.

"Is she right? Are there people trapped with the loocies?" the soldier asked.

"The *lalassu* are people, too." Hood's growl wasn't as impressive as Lou's, but it still echoed in the underground lab. "No one deserves what the people here have been through."

Martha ignored them. Lou reached over to squeeze her hand, offering his strength as a rock for her to use as a foundation. Martha swabbed his arm and inserted a needle attached to an IV hose. When the crimson stream replaced the air inside, she inserted the other needle into Lily's arm.

There was no immediate reaction, for which she was grateful. She needed to judge how much blood to transfuse, both for Lou's safety and Lily's.

Thank you. She mouthed the words to Lou and was rewarded with a hint of a smile tweaking the corners of his mouth.

"I clearly missed way too much down here." Andrew swayed on his feet despite Annika's supporting arm. "I thought you didn't trust her. You thought she'd break and put everyone in jeopardy."

"Spare me the daytime drama. I hate you all," Ryan moaned.

"Can we tranquilize him?" Annika glared at him.

"Did you really think that?" Martha asked Lou quietly. She couldn't exactly blame him if he had, but it still hurt. She liked being his fierce kestrel and knowing that she had his respect.

"Yes," he said, just as quietly.

"Oh." She should have known better than to expect him to lie to spare her feelings. *Okay, time to put on the big-girl panties and take a moment.* She had been broken, ground down, and ready to snap at the slightest pressure. But Lou had not treated her as a fragile burden. He protected her, cared for her, and was proud of who she had become.

Lou was watching her warily with real fear in his eyes. There were no protective barriers between them, and he was probably feeling vulnerable. Martha swallowed her hurt. He'd called her his mate. He wanted her to fly free. He didn't see her as damaged, something to be discarded or replaced.

"Well, that was before," she said firmly. "And this is now."

He smiled at her.

"So from now on, I expect you to trust me the same way I trust you. Even if you're not there, I'm still your fierce kestrel." Her own smile was shaky, but underneath, she knew they had something solid.

"That's sweet. I'm glad you turned out to be stronger than we thought." Whatever he'd been given, it was making Andrew chattier than Martha could have imagined. "I was afraid that you'd spill everything you knew if you got captured."

"And I thought drunk dialing was awkward," Annika muttered. "This is way worse. Is he going to break into song or start moaning about lost loves or tell us how much he loves us?"

"We'll just have to smile, nod, and avoid eye contact if he does." Martha shook off the insult behind his words. If he still said them once he was sober, then they would have a problem. She checked Lily's pulse and was relieved to feel it evening out along with her breathing.

"At least yours is keeping his mouth shut."

"I am not drunk, and I resent the implication. I'm entirely the victim here." Andrew straightened up. "Lou has always been the upstanding one who embraced his role as a Guardian. Until we needed him, that is."

"Take him upstairs," Martha snapped. She could already see the invisible weight of blame settling on Lou's shoulders. The plastic curtain rustled as Annika obeyed her instructions. Martha focused on her mate. "What happened at Bear Claw is not your fault."

"It was a difficult assault," Dr. Coulon mused. "Another transformative might have turned the tide."

"Shut up!" Martha shouted before turning back to Lou. "It was not your fault."

The pain in his eyes stole her breath. "I should have been there."

"No. They shouldn't have attacked. They shouldn't have killed your family. This is their fault, not yours." She took a deep breath and checked Lily's pulse again. "I think she's stable enough to move."

She doubted that her impassioned plea had changed much. Feelings didn't obey words and logic. As she pulled the needle out of Lou's arm, she resolved to do whatever it took to root out the horrible guilt. She would take a page out of Lou's book of communication and show him that he was not to blame. She pressed a cotton ball over the pinprick of blood. He covered her hand with his, cradling her cool fingers against his warm muscles.

"Are you planning on killing us anytime soon? Because if I have to listen to this any longer, I'll blow my own brains out," Ryan groaned.

"Don't tempt us," Hood snarled.

"Lou? What are you doing here?" Lily asked weakly as Lou picked her up. Martha and Hood followed them up the stairs. Andrew and Annika were waiting, the former slumped in the doctor's chair. Martha helped Annika to pick him up and support him as they left the medical building.

The camp was still deserted, but Martha's heart pounded hard enough to leap free of her chest at any moment. Any second, she expected to hear shouts demanding that they stop and surrender, but they made it from the medical building to the Hub without incident.

Harley, Eva, and Bernie were waiting inside the empty cafeteria with clothes for Andrew, Annika, and Lily. Hood and Harley embraced, drawing Eva in with them. Martha went to hug Bernie, but her daughter evaded her, sticking close to Eva.

"What kept you? The kitchen staff is going to be here soon. I was ordered to be here in less than an hour to begin getting ready for the new arrivals," Eva warned.

"There were complications. Do you have the film?" Martha asked.

"Right here." Harley patted an orange-and-brown backpack beside him.

"What about the others?" Hood nodded at the two other identical backpacks.

"Emergency supplies. In case things go wrong."

If they could get to the airfield before anyone realized what they'd done, they might have a chance. "Can you help Lily? I want to check on Andrew."

Lou put Lily in a chair. She was a little more alert but still very weak. A few tables over, Andrew was slumped over again in his own chair, with Annika steadying him to keep him from falling off.

"Did I mention that I hated the wilderness even before this all started?" Annika grumbled. "Why couldn't they have built their prison in a five-star hotel with attached spa service?"

Martha coaxed Andrew to raise his head. His skin was flushed, and his eyes struggled to focus. Whatever the doctor had given him was worse than she'd thought, but without knowing what it was, she couldn't risk giving him anything to overcome it.

"He was always there for me. When Mom checked out, he was there. When Grandfather made me leave school to become a shaman, he was there," Andrew muttered. "But when men attacked us, he wasn't."

Martha tilted his head back so he could meet her eyes. "He loves you, and what you're saying is hurting him."

"You're the one who will hurt him by making him choose." Andrew pulled free. "He's tied to you forever. I don't want to pick up the pieces when you break his heart."

The mating bond. She remembered Lily telling her how empty she had been during those long months when they waited to see if Ron would return after testifying against Dalhard. She didn't think the couple had spent a night apart since then. *Is that why Lily is so much worse off than Andrew? Because she's separated from her mate?*

She realized she was concentrating on Lily and Ron to avoid having to think about the implications for her and Lou. Suddenly, his comments about her flying free sounded less like a compliment and more like a goodbye. *We can deal with it when we're safely out of here. For now, I'm not going to make any decisions based on the ramblings of a drugged man.*

Annika tossed her former rags in the trash bin. "This is definitely the most therapeutic rescue I've ever taken part in. What's next, group share?"

"Hopefully, that can wait until we're safely away from here." Martha summoned up a smile for the joke.

"We should get moving before the new arrivals get here," Hood said. "We need to be in place when the plane lands."

Martha and Annika supported Andrew. Lou carried Lily, despite her protests that she could walk. Bernie stayed near Eva and her fathers. *Only a few more hours, and then we'll finally be safe.*

Chapter Thirty-Three

"The coast is clear," Henri said dejectedly.

Leanne hurried between the trailers, crouching in her new hiding place. Henri still wasn't happy with her, but at least he'd stopped moaning about what she should do. He thought that she should have defied Ryan, and then she and Henri could confront Chuck. Then she and Bernie would be able to pair up for an exorcism like television heroes. He didn't understand how dangerous it could be or how low the chance of success was. Keeping him on a short leash so that he couldn't warn Bernie had been difficult for both of them. She'd eventually ended up threatening him with his own exorcism if he kept bringing it up.

Two men walked past her, talking in low voices.

"I heard they found a new loocy, one that can shatter steel."

"Don't be silly. It was probably a lightning strike. Maybe it triggered one of the mines."

"We haven't had any thunderstorms, and they never installed the mines. Detention is full. They'd only do that if they were trying to find some new power."

They passed out of earshot. The whole camp was tense after the lockdown. Leanne scratched at her collar.

"Clear," Henri told her. He was still angry, but he'd forgive her once they were back home. They'd been partners too long to hold grudges.

She reached Bernie's trailer. It was locked, but the mechanism was old enough to pop open with a firm twist. *Cheap construction. Should have gone with a better contractor.* Leanne snuck inside. The cheap carpet reeked of cigarettes, making her long for a smoke even though she'd quit over a decade earlier. But the novelty of having solid walls around her was almost enough to make up for it. They had proper furniture, unrestricted food, and warmth. *They live in comfort while we starve and freeze.*

"I'm not going to be their whipping girl anymore," she said. It had taken every scrap of her cunning to stop Ryan from sending her to detention with the others. She'd spent the last three days huddling in a cold barracks, waiting for the right moment and listening to Henri complain about her ethical choices.

She checked the first bedroom and found the dresser was full of children's clothes. Martha's clothes were in the second one, the one with two twin beds. "Trouble in marital paradise, I see."

"Please let me warn them. It won't take long," Henri pleaded.

"They've caused enough trouble." Leanne picked out a set of clean clothing and began stripping out of her filthy rags. "And notice they've managed to walk away from most of it."

"It's not right, Leanne."

All of her fear and anger boiled over. "Would you rather I let him kill me because I didn't answer his questions? He still would have gone after them, but I would be dead."

"You didn't have to tell him everything. You could have lied, made up something plausible instead of telling him all about their escape plan."

Maybe. Or maybe it wouldn't have been enough. Leanne had taken the less-risky bet, and she didn't need a dead historical cosplayer to keep nagging her about it. She walked into the small bathroom and turned on the shower. The lukewarm water felt heavenly as she scrubbed the accumulated grime out of her skin, banishing Looney forever.

She wasn't a monster. She didn't like the fact that she'd betrayed Bernie. It was a decision that she knew would never rest easily on her conscience. But smart people did what was necessary to protect themselves. "I can't rely on anyone else to save me."

Henri wasn't convinced. "They're different. If we all worked together—"

"No"—Leanne stared at herself in the mirror—"they aren't

different. They might have good intentions, but so far they've made a complete mess of everything. Before they came, the guards were cruel, but they weren't crazy. There hadn't been a mass tasing. We need to get out of here."

He didn't say anything in return. She could still sense his presence hovering nearby.

"What do you think?" She fingered the collar around her neck. "Is my hair enough to cover it?"

"What about Bernie?" Henri asked. "Chuck is still trying to kill her. You can't leave her to deal with him on her own."

"How does me staying help her? Even if she believes me, she's the one who has to exorcise him. And if she doesn't, then he'll be after me." She rubbed at her chest, remembering the icy fist plunging into her heart. "Do you want to find out his limits the hard way?"

"No."

"Once we're on the plane, you can warn Bernie about Chuck. Then she'll know." It wasn't much of a reassurance, but it was what she could do. She leaned closer to her reflection. She definitely needed a scarf or something to cover the collar. "It's all we can do."

"He's not going to do the test?" Mrs. Fitz repeated Martha's words in disbelief.

"He's delaying," Martha clarified. "He'll do the test tomorrow, but for now he's focused on examining the people in detention, and he needs my help if he's going to get it all done for tomorrow."

"And what does he expect me to do in the meantime?" Mrs. Fitz sniffed.

"He asked that you do the usual orientation. In fact"—Martha leaned closer—"he said that your instinct was the most reliable test that he had."

Mrs. Fitz's hand fluttered to her chest. "He said that?"

Martha nodded. "Absolutely. He said he knew he could rely on you to handle things in his absence."

"Well, of course." Mrs. Fitz straightened. "He knows I've always had a keen eye for any impostors who try to sneak past our system. Very well, tell him I will take care of it."

Martha left, suppressing a smile as Mrs. Fitz began to bustle around the office with a renewed sense of self-importance. *Maybe I am cut out for this secret-agent stuff after all.* The others were waiting at the front of the Hub along with the other staff who were preparing to leave on rotation.

The truck pulled up as Martha stepped out from the doors. Lou helped her up into the back, his fingers squeezing her hand briefly. It was hard to keep a triumphant grin off of her face. There were still plenty of things that could go wrong. Someone could notice that Lily was still half-unconscious, remember that Lou and Martha would be unlikely to be rotating out, or realize they didn't recognize Andrew or Lily.

Bernie was slumped into the corner, sulking like a veteran teenager at being forced to leave. Eva sat next to her, pretending to read a magazine. Hood and Harley were on the opposite bench, making sure Andrew stayed quiet. And Annika deserved the Oscar for the best performance of boredom that Martha had ever seen.

The woman next to Annika seemed familiar, but it was difficult to place her. Long brown hair was caught up in a bun, showing traces of dampness. She didn't match the appearance of the construction crews or guards. *Kitchens?* Her narrow, bony fingers alternately clutched a black carry-on bag or fidgeted with a flowery scarf wrapped around her neck.

Oh my God. Martha quickly turned her gaze toward the floor as she realized why the woman looked so familiar. The scarf was Martha's, as were the tan sweater and black pants. The modest makeup did a good job at disguising her, but there was no doubt that the woman was Leanne.

Martha couldn't draw attention to her without risking herself and the others. And she wouldn't do it in any case. If she could have snuck the entire camp onto the commuter plane, she would have. *Please let Kal and Patrick be there, too.*

They arrived at the airfield in a flurry of activity. The newly arrived staff waited in a cluster, and soldiers were moving around the three helicopters at the edge of the field. Presumably, the replacement parts had arrived on the plane. Martha still wasn't sure what Hood and Harley had done originally, but she was grateful it had worked. Even more promising, there were armed guards standing in front of a small shed nearby. There were likely prisoners inside, and those prisoners were probably Kal and Patrick.

Martha hopped down from the truck and went to stand near Bernie. Keeping her voice low, she said, "Keep your face still and look at the woman next to Annika."

Bernie's forehead wrinkled in disbelief and confusion but she did as asked. Martha could tell the instant she recognized Leanne from the way her eyes went wide.

"Don't say anything," Martha cautioned. "Look back at the ground or at the trees."

Bernie stared off at the trees, but her hand crept into Martha's.

I might not be forgiven, but at least I could show her that we're not abandoning her friend. From the way Leanne stood stiffly off to one side, she had recognized them as well. Martha trusted the other woman's common sense was strong enough to play along.

A tug on her hand drew her attention back to Bernie. "Mom, it's Chuck. He came back."

"That's good." *Not entirely good, but if it made Bernie happy, I won't complain.*

"He must not be mad anymore." Bernie frowned. "Henri's upset. He's shouting at Leanne."

That wasn't reassuring news. Martha was about to ask why when a chill ripple passed through her, like a cold breeze on damp skin but one that went right through her insides.

"Oh no," Bernie whispered.

"What's happening?" Martha asked. Everyone was shifting uneasily, glaring suspiciously at one another.

"Don't," Bernie said, reaching out.

One end of the scarf wrapped around Leanne's neck began to move.

It tugged loose as if being pulled on a string. She grabbed at it, but it slipped free, unwinding to fall at her feet and revealing the shock collar.

"Loocy!" one of the armed guards shouted.

Leanne ran, racing toward the forest.

"He did it. He did it to her," Bernie repeated numbly, releasing Martha's hand. She started walking to where the scarf lay on the ground.

Two sharp cracks popped in the air, followed by a thud.

Leanne lay motionless in the field. The armed guard lowered his rifle.

And then chaos erupted.

The other staff started to shout and scream in fear, running in all directions.

"Bernie!" Martha shouted, trying to reach her daughter's side. A man blundered into her, knocking her down. For the second time that day, she found herself on the ground and breathless.

Annika shoved Andrew away from her and took off running. Lou shouted for Martha, but she couldn't quite get to her feet. Dazed, she watched as Eva grabbed Bernie's hand and pulled her away from the bedlam. Hood and Harley took their daughter and Martha's, protecting them.

Soldiers were arriving, brandishing handguns and shouting orders. Andrew was on the ground, laughing bitterly. Lily knelt with her hands wrapped around her lowered head.

Another sharp crack. From the rifle aimed at Annika.

She stumbled but didn't slow for more than a step or two. The guard cursed and fired again, but she disappeared into the trees.

"Don't move, or I'll shoot." The barked order made Martha realized she'd missed her chance to escape unnoticed. A soldier a few feet away pointed his gun directly at her.

Three soldiers surrounded Lou, but from the way his shoulders tensed, he was ready to fight his way out, either as a human or a bear. *He can't.* There was no way he could survive direct hits from such a short distance. If he attacked, they would all open fire and keep firing until he dropped.

I can't let him lose control. If she was in danger, he would do whatever he had to in order to protect her. Martha couldn't let that happen. She lifted her hands slowly into the air, signaling surrender. Hood and Harley had vanished. Andrew and Lily were in no shape to run. *I won't get anyone killed today.* Her eyes found Leanne's body. *Anyone else.*

"Stay down!"

Martha obeyed but kept her gaze on Lou. *Please, don't let them hurt you.* Surrendering was frightening, but it was better than certain death.

Slowly, Lou lowered himself to his knees with his hands raised. Martha breathed a sigh of relief that doubled when she realized that Hood and Harley had taken the backpack with the film and the other evidence they'd collected.

Bernie is safe. Hood and Harley will get her away from here. Martha watched, hoping for an opportunity, as the guards spread out. Maybe they could blend in with the other staff and find a new opportunity to escape.

A second truck arrived at the scene. When Dr. Coulon and Ryan stepped out, it killed the last of Martha's faint hopes.

The doctor spoke briefly with the guards, pointing at Martha, Lily, Andrew, and Lou.

"Get everyone on the truck. We'll process them down at the Hub!" Ryan shouted.

The crowd of potential targets thinned, leaving Martha feeling very exposed. The doctor came toward her, sauntering as if unconcerned.

"It was a rather daring attempt. As I said before, I am impressed with your skills," Dr. Coulon said.

The truck drove away, leaving the four captives alone with a dozen soldiers and a handful of guards, along with the doctor and Ryan.

"Escape attempt." Ryan spat into the grass. "Shoot them."

Martha winced, waiting for a bullet to smash into her body.

"Hold." Dr. Coulon sounded bored, but no weapon fired. "Take them back to my lab."

None of them wants to end up on his bad side.

"You can dissect them later." Ryan leaned down to grab the dropped rifle.

"Stand down, Mr. Blake." There was steel in the doctor's quiet statement.

Ryan scowled, clearly unhappy at being reminded that he wasn't the ultimate authority. "Fine. On your feet."

Lou slowly got to his feet then helped Lily to stand. Martha did the same with Andrew.

"Start moving," Ryan ordered. When they hesitated, he raised his rifle. "Go on, give me an excuse to shoot you all."

"I would prefer you aren't damaged, but I'm willing to compromise if needed." Dr. Coulon turned to walk back to the truck. "Come along."

"We'll need another metal collar for the chief," Ryan said. Then he pulled a thin gray strip out of his pocket. "But I've got your necklace right here, baby."

Martha held still as he fastened the collar around her throat, snugging it tight. *Don't let him see that you're afraid.* It was the only victory she could still achieve.

Her world dissolved in tingling fire that lashed through her body.

As her vision cleared, she realized she'd dropped to her knees and that Andrew was in the same posture beside her.

"Try anything, and I drop her again, Chief." Ryan glared at Lou, who was being held back by four men. From the fury on Lou's face and the tense effort on the others', it took all four of them to hold him back.

"I'm okay," Martha gasped. "Please, Lou, I'm okay."

Lou rocked back on his feet, angry but no longer fighting to break free. He stood still as they fastened another shock collar around his neck. They were all captives.

Chapter Thirty-Four

Bernie's wrist ached where Harley had grabbed it. They had outrun the guards and their guns, and they were stuck in the stupid forest, and Hood and Harley were arguing over what to do next. She still couldn't believe that Chuck had revealed Leanne's collar. It hadn't been an accident. He'd blasted Henri away then yanked the scarf off. And he'd looked right at Bernie while he did it.

"What part of our history together makes you think I'm someone who knows how to live off the land?" Harley sounded like he wanted to shout.

"We need to keep moving." Hood kept looking around with every puff of wind that rattled a branch.

"So we can get lost and die of exposure?" Harley shook his head. "We should stick close to the camp."

"We should try to rescue them," Eva suggested.

Great, now all three of them are arguing. Bernie was tired of listening to the so-called grown-ups fight.

"Bernie, psst." Chuck poked his head out from behind a tree.

She shook her head. She wouldn't talk to him, not after he'd gotten Leanne killed.

"C'mon. Don't be mad at me." He leaned forward. "You need to get away from them before the guards hear them."

"I'm not going anywhere with you," she whispered. Hood, Harley, and Eva were getting loud.

"I know you're mad, and I'm sorry that I did it without talking to you. I had to act quickly. Leanne betrayed you." Chuck sat down beside her. "She told Ryan that your mom knew about the secret cells and that you were planning to escape."

"She wouldn't do that," Bernie said defiantly. "Besides, where were you for the last three days?"

"She held me back, just like we held back the other ghosts."

Something about his explanation didn't seem right. The bond between them hadn't felt as if it were stretched or blocked, which it would have if Leanne had banished him. But then again, Leanne had been worried about Chuck and talking about exorcism. It was all too complicated, and there was no one that she could turn to for help.

"I can prove to you that you can trust me. The woman from the cells is nearby, but if you don't get to her soon, then the guards will find her." Chuck pointed into the trees. "She's through there."

Bernie got to her feet. "Okay, show me."

She followed Chuck through the trees, her steps dragging. What Chuck said didn't make sense, but he'd always looked out for her before.

"She's up here." He jabbed his finger toward the upper branches. Peering up, Bernie could see a slim figure in white among the needles.

"Can you get down?" Bernie called out.

"Be quiet. The guards are close," Chuck warned.

Bernie repeated it.

"Shit. Hold on," the woman replied. Pine needles rained down as she dropped through the branches, landing near Bernie. She stood up, wincing. "That seemed like a much better idea before I actually tried it. Now, who the hell are you?"

"I'm Bernie. Martha is my mom. And you're Annika."

"And you're not easily intimidated. Good on you, kid. Are you all alone out here?" Annika looked around.

"There's Chuck, but you can't see him. He's my ghost." Bernie folded her arms. If the woman wanted to call her crazy, then they might as well get it out of the way.

"The guards are coming," Chuck warned.

"Ghost. Yeah, sure. Why not?" Annika shook her head.

"We have to go. Guards will be here soon. Hood, Harley, and Eva are over there." Bernie pointed. "Try to be quiet."

Annika followed her as Bernie led the way back to the others.

"See, I told you that you could trust me." Chuck walked beside her.

She wanted to believe him. It was reassuring to believe that he had her back, that he would protect her, like always. But she couldn't ignore what he'd done.

As they emerged from the trees, Eva noticed them first. "Bernie! Where did you go? We were so worried."

"I found Annika. She was stuck in a tree." Bernie glanced over at Chuck. "Are the guards still coming?"

"I wasn't stuck. I just hadn't thought through my exit strategy." Annika ran her hand through her short dark hair, leaving it sticking up at odd angles. "What about you? Do you have a plan to get out?"

Chuck flickered. "The guards are going the other way."

"We had a plan. Be on the damn plane when it left." Hood frowned. "Didn't you get shot?"

Annika turned around to show the hole in the back of her thin cotton shirt. "Impenetrable skin."

"Impressive," Hood said.

"Not really. It's literally only the skin. As in, sticks and stones will break my bones but paper will never cut me. So it hurts like hell where they shot me, but it didn't kill me." Annika exhaled in pain. "I didn't even know I was a loocy until I came here, and now I have the lamest superpower ever."

As they talked, Bernie turned to Chuck. "Can you check on Mom, Lou, and the others?"

"They got captured. Now she can know what its like to be stuck in a lab and experimented on." Chuck grew darker, flickering in place.

His anger frightened her. She was just starting to accept what her mother had done. She didn't want her to be hurt by the doctor.

"Is she actually talking to a ghost?" Annika asked. The others nodded.

Right, because I look like I'm crazy. Leanne had been right. Even other *lalassu* couldn't accept a medium. A big tear dropped from Bernie's cheek.

Her mom was in the secret lab and was probably going to die. Her friend was dead, and there was no sign of her spirit, which meant Leanne went directly to the light instead of stopping to say goodbye. Chuck might be going crazy, and she couldn't trust him anymore. And they were making fun of her. It was all too much.

"I'll show her who's real." Chuck seemed to suck all of the light into himself, becoming pure shadow.

"Go away," Bernie said sullenly.

The darkness faded. He seemed surprised. "You can't mean that."

"Just go away." She pushed at him with her mind. She didn't want to see him or have to fight with him. She only wanted for him to leave her to be miserable in peace and quiet.

"Fine." He scowled before vanishing. She could still sense him lurking nearby but didn't care. Another tear dripped off her cheek.

"Can I sit down?" Eva asked.

Bernie shrugged, hunching into a ball of misery, knees tucked to her chest.

Eva sat down beside her and wrapped her arm around her. She didn't ask any questions, for which Bernie was profoundly grateful. They sat there while Hood and Harley argued with Annika some more about whether or not they should stay close to camp.

Martha supported Lily as they walked through the underground tunnels to the lab. Behind her, the steady beat of Lou's footsteps and the irregular pace of Andrew's stumbling ones gave her some comfort that she wasn't alone. Ryan marched behind them all, ready to shoot any of them if they faltered.

Dr. Coulon glanced back. "When Mr. Blake told me that you were one of the *occulata hominem*, I dismissed it at first. I assumed you might be searching for a family member, but I didn't expect you to steal my lab subjects."

Martha said nothing, keeping her lips firmly pressed together. There was a bright light ahead of them. *I guess that explains where all the power from the generators was going.* As they drew closer, her flippancy changed to horror and nausea.

Bright lights illuminated a large, open surgery, complete with a metal examining table. The giant lights made it impossible to ignore what was on the table, the head of a bear with red-brown fur, its skull split open to examine the brain within. *Oh my God. I think that's Malila.* Martha swallowed hard, wishing she could shield Lou from the sight. Automatically, she looked back over her shoulder at him.

He might as well have been a robot, walking past it as if it were just one more stretch of hallway strung with heavy electrical cables.

Andrew said something in his native tongue, the anguish and pain needing no translation. Ryan slammed his rifle into Andrew's knee. He immediately began to collapse, but Lou held him up. Andrew launched into a snarling litany.

"I expected the serum would loosen your tongue, but I didn't expect you to lose all sense of decorum. This is a place of science. You should act like it," Dr. Coulon scolded.

Martha began to laugh in bursts of hysterical giggles. *Is he really complaining about us showing a lack of propriety about medical torture?* Her outburst earned a slap across the face.

"Shut it, loocy." Ryan shoved his gun in her face. "Get moving."

Martha swallowed the remaining giggles, slowly getting back to her feet with her hands raised nonthreateningly. Ryan seemed disappointed with her compliance but satisfied with the evidence of her fear. It was more power than any hasty groping could have offered, and he was clearly savoring it.

All too soon, they reached the lab and its empty cells. Dr. Coulon frowned, and Martha quickly guessed the cause. There were four prisoners and three cells.

"How did you get out, by the way?" Andrew demanded as Ryan shoved him into a cell.

"Door just popped open." Ryan grinned. "But don't worry, I'll double-check yours."

A flash of irritation crossed the doctor's face, but he said nothing. *I don't think they got out by themselves. Maybe someone came to check on them.* It wasn't promising for the four of them pulling the same trick.

"Put me in the same cell as Lily. She needs medical attention, and I'm still a nurse." Martha straightened. The blood transfusion had helped, but Lily was still swaying on her feet. Even as Martha watched, she started to collapse. Lou caught her before she could hit the floor.

Dr. Coulon stared at them for a long moment before nodding. "Both of you in the middle cell."

Holding tightly to her dignity, Martha walked inside. Lou followed her and put Lily down on the bed.

"I'll take care of her," Martha said in a low voice.

There was no reaction from him, only stony silence as he turned and walked away.

Dr. Coulon picked up a syringe and plunged it into Lou's bare arm. He grunted, his face twisting in pain as he dropped to his knees.

"No!" Martha shouted, charging forward. The cell doors closed, sealing off any hope of a last-minute escape. She rattled the bars. "If you hurt him—"

"It's a tranquilizer. Calm down." The doctor lifted an eyebrow, the overhead lights turning his glasses into blank circles. Ryan grabbed Lou's arms and dragged him into the cell to her left.

"You didn't have to do that. He was cooperating." She glared at him.

A solid thunk from the other cell made her wince. It sounded like his head hitting the hard concrete floor. *Nonononono. I'm sorry. Please be okay. I should have fought.* The thoughts kept chasing themselves around her mind like whirling discs on a carnival ride. She felt nauseated and as if she were going nowhere.

Lily moaned, and Martha crawled back to the cot. The clang of a closing cell door rang out. To hide her building fear, Martha knelt beside Lily, checking the other woman's pulse and temperature. Footsteps began to move out of the lab, but she refused to look up. Lily's vitals were much steadier than before, so hopefully it was healing sleep and not a hypovolemic coma. *Please let Bernie be safe. Please let Lou be okay.* She kept her eyes down, not wanting to see Dr. Coulon preparing for a new round of torture.

The silence stretched, and Martha found herself straining to hear some warning click of an instrument on a metal tray. Eventually, she stole a glance, only to discover they were completely alone. Dr. Coulon had evidently left with Ryan.

Andrew snored in the cell to her right. But there was no sound from the cell on her left. Holding on to the bars, she stared at the stained restraint chair and the rows of gleaming tools laid out on the small surgical table.

"Lou? Are you all right?" she called out softly.

No answer. No sound of movement. The cell could be empty as far as she knew.

"Henri? Are you here?"

She waited a long moment and then tried again. "Chuck?"

No sign of the ghosts, not that she'd necessarily know if they were there. Martha rubbed at her arms, the cold already seeping into her skin. She was completely and utterly alone, unable to help her daughter, her lover, or herself. *I should never have gone to Bear Claw. Then Lou and the Colony would still be safe.* Except then she wouldn't have known him, which made the loneliness clench around her like a soggy blanket. Her pessimistic side berated her as selfish for implying that good sex could potentially balance out mass slaughter. But her wiser side prevailed. The slaughter would have happened regardless, and the universe was not such an evil place as to demand such a monstrous bargain. *Besides, it's more than sex.* He'd believed in her, the first one to do that since Derek left. He'd trusted her. *And look where that got us all.*

"I'm so sorry. I didn't know what else to do." Martha clamped her lips closed over her babbling effort to exonerate herself. She could only imagine how irritating her words would be to Lou under the circumstances if he was awake. "I wish I could change it."

Still nothing.

"I know we can still find a way to fix this," Martha heard herself say. She was flabbergasted at the apparent optimism of her subconscious.

I should have learned some useful skills, like picking a lock. Instead, I tried to make things seem like our old life for Bernie. The thought of her daughter made her hands shake and her stomach spasm in protest. *Hood and Harley will keep her safe and get her out of here.*

All three siblings were unconscious and relying on Martha. She took a deep breath, but her mind kept whispering of potential tragedy. Dr. Coulon could have made a mistake with the dosage. *What if... what if something happens, and the last thing I did was disappoint him?* He'd been so silent as he walked away, giving no hint of his emotions or even a twitch to remind her that he had faith in her. There'd been no sign that she had ever been anything other than a responsibility to him. Martha tried not to read too much into it, but the uncertainty sapped her strength. She sat down beside the cot, leaning against the cold cinderblock wall. Tucking her hands under her arms, she wondered if she would be at risk for hypothermia before much longer. The adrenaline that had been carrying her abruptly petered out, leaving her exhausted.

Chapter Thirty-Five

Lou could hear Martha and Lily's soft breathing echoing off the hard walls when he awoke. He lay very still despite his awkward position on the floor with one arm twisted underneath him. The sting of antiseptic in his nose told him that he wasn't alone.

The doctor had been clever, dosing him with a tranquilizer. It had stolen hours that he could have used to escape. With privacy, he could have tried to pop the hinges on the cell door or break the lock. Even in his human form, he was much stronger than a human would expect.

If he'd thought he could kill the guards and soldiers before one of them got off a lucky shot at Martha or his siblings, he would have done it. But he hadn't dared risk their lives.

"You must be getting uncomfortable in there by now." Dr. Coulon spoke as if they were in the middle of a friendly conversation. "You might as well move, since I know you are awake."

Lou rolled over without saying a word, staring at the doctor who treated his people like science projects.

"I see the family resemblance with your siblings. Tell me, do you share physical properties in your animal form as well?" The doctor picked up a leather notebook and pen.

No other guards were present. Of course, that didn't mean much with the collar around his neck. Curiously, there was no heavy metal ring like the ones around his siblings' throats. He should be able to shift to the fur if needed.

"Not talkative, hmm? A shame. You and your siblings were quite informative before. I gained a great deal of information." He flipped back a few pages in the notebook. "I've been writing down as much as I can remember, though I would like to know more. Your brother mentioned that the transformation can allow you to heal some injuries. Would that only apply to minor lacerations and abrasions, or could you heal something as dramatic as an amputation? Do severe injuries echo between the two forms?"

Lou stayed silent and motionless, hoping to tempt the doctor into coming close enough to grab.

"You caused quite a stir over the last few days. At first, we thought we had missed a major ability among the internees. When Mr. Ryan told me it was actually one of the staff, it was quite surprising." He sounded excited but detached, as if it were all a fascinating puzzle. "While you were unconscious, I ran the genetic tests myself, and none of you register the *occulata hominem* protein. I would assume that you were a completely separate species if it weren't for your sister."

Lou noticed that the doctor used the plural when discussing a failure but liked to claim credit for himself.

"I'm quite eager to see the DNA results for her and the child. It should open up some fascinating lines of study. Though I must admit, I am growing tired of these primitive conditions. A modern lab with modern equipment would allow me to be much faster with the tests. I left the bulk of my subjects in Juneau, as there simply isn't room here."

A low growl built in Lou's throat. This man talked of Lou's kin as if they were mere lab rats.

"I had hoped you might be willing to share information, but it seems that you're not as useful as your siblings. You'll be on your way shortly to my patrons." Dr. Coulon closed the notebook.

Lou waited for Dr. Coulon to continue, but the doctor failed to follow the pattern of fictional villains, leaving his captive audience in the dark about his plans. Instead, he walked out of the lab.

"If you have a chance to escape, take it," Andrew said quietly.

Lou grunted. He wouldn't abandon Martha or his family.

"Don't make me have your death on my conscience. There's enough already." His twin sounded much more clear than he had before. "I tried to fight when they came, to do what you would have. It's not as easy as it looks."

"Never was." Lou touched the wall between them. "We don't have much time. Take care of Martha and Lily."

Andrew stayed quiet for a long moment. "Don't give up. Don't go out in a heroic blaze of glory. And don't you dare act like this is goodbye."

Footsteps approached. As much as Lou wanted to tell his twin that he had no intention of surrendering, he couldn't. Not when the doctor returned to the lab with a loaded syringe.

"Extend your arm out between the bars," he said.

"What's going on?" Martha's sleepy voice interjected.

"Ah, Mrs. McKinnon, so pleased to see you're awake. Do tell your husband to cooperate."

"No," Martha replied quickly. A swell of pride straightened Lou's back.

"Why must you persist in forcing me to resort to base threats?" Dr. Coulon seemed genuinely surprised and disappointed in their lack of cooperation. "Extend your arm through the bars, or I will activate your wife's shock collar."

The needle of the syringe glinted in the overhead light. Slowly, Lou walked forward and put his arm through the bars.

"No, don't! I'll be okay. Don't do it," Martha pleaded.

He held his arm steady, watching the doctor, planning ways to strike if the opportunity presented. "Fly free."

"Lou, you can't do this," she begged. "You can't let him make you do something because he threatens to hurt me. I won't be a leash on you."

I am Guardian. It was his purpose to place himself in danger so that others would not be hurt. He would not go down without a fight. When the doctor came close enough, Lou would grab him and slam him into the bars for his threats.

The doctor seemed to guess his plan, approaching from the side. Lou tried to twist his arm to grab but the needle jabbed deeply into his muscles, injecting an icy stream into his veins.

"I dislike melodrama." Dr. Coulon stepped out of range. Martha was shouting as oblivion smothered Lou's senses. Her shriek of pain was the last thing he heard before blackness swallowed him.

The plane roaring overhead woke Bernie from a fitful sleep. She stared at the dark-blue sky as she realized that their best chance at escape went with it. Eva and the adults were still asleep, wrapped in the extra clothes from their bags. Hood had won the argument about not having a fire after dark. It would have been too easy to see.

"Hey, *petite*." Henri's soft greeting didn't surprise her.

"Hi. I'm sorry about Leanne. You must be mad at me and Chuck." Bernie folded and re-folded a corner of her jacket.

"Never at you, Mademoiselle Bernadette. None of this is your fault." Henri's pale hand passed through her cheek. His touch was gently cool like her mother's hand when Bernie had a fever.

"Is Leanne still here?" Bernie made herself ask. "I wanted to say sorry to her, too."

"No. She went into the light. The last thing I felt from her was surprise and joy." Henri smiled. "It was very comforting."

"Oh. I guess you'll be going on, too." *Leaving me alone. Again.*

"I considered it. I've been afraid of the light for a long time, but after sensing that, I don't think I will be again. But I couldn't abandon you with a half-mad ghost." He settled beside her, softly glowing in the predawn darkness. "I've been keeping watch to make certain that no one discovered you. And I've been checking on your mother and friends."

"Is she hurt?" Bernie's nightmares had been filled with images of Chuck attacking her mother the way he'd attacked Leanne.

"The doctor has not been gentle, but no permanent harm was done. He put Lou on the plane just now, headed for the east coast. The other two with your mother have not been hurt."

"Have…" She needed to ask but hated the possible answers. "Have you seen Chuck?"

"*Non.*" His mouth narrowed. "He cannot be saved, *petite.*"

He didn't sound angry, which somehow hurt even more. Bernie squeezed herself tighter into a ball. She'd made too many mistakes. *I'll never be a hero like Michael or Dani.* She wanted her mom so badly that it burned in her throat and behind her eyes. "He was my friend."

"Maybe he was once, but he's not right in the head now. He thinks that if you die, you and he will be together forever. He wanted Leanne to kill you."

Bernie stared at Henri in shock. "You're wrong."

"I wish I were," he said softly. "You need to know something. What he's trying to do isn't right, and it's not your fault. None of this is because of you."

Bernie hid her eyes and whimpered deep in her throat. "Yes, it is."

"Absolutely not. Chuck is unstable, and it has affected his mind and his judgment. None of that is about you," he said. "These people are here to help you. They care about you."

She didn't deserve help. "I'm s-s-sorry. I m-messed everything up."

"This is what life is about. Making bad choices and then learning to fix the mistakes. The only truly unforgivable mistake is to refuse to try when the opportunity presents itself." Henri tilted his head, watching Annika's sleeping form. "Such as this one. She seems like a delightful young woman. Perhaps I should serenade her in the moonlight?"

"She can't hear you," Bernie said.

"Ever the pragmatist. Leanne was more inclined to see the romantic…" Henri trailed off, and his grin slowly faded.

"Do you wish she'd stayed?" Bernie wondered how long Chuck had wanted her to become a ghost. Had it been right from the beginning?

He shook his head. "I'm glad she's at peace, even if I'm not eager to join her. Have I told you how I died?"

"No." Bernie uncurled, sitting up straighter.

"I was very young when I died, still in college. I took a corner too quickly on my motorbike and skidded, snapping my neck instantly. It took me a while to realize I was dead, and I couldn't accept it. There were so many things I still wanted to do and experience."

Bernie rubbed at her arms, trying to smooth down the pebbly goose bumps.

"You know, I can understand your Chuck. I spent a lot of time doing silly things like sneaking into forbidden places. But it quickly lost any meaning. No one could see or hear me. No one would ever see or hear me again, not from the living world. And you've talked to ghosts, *petite*, so you know they're not the best conversationalists. I needed a friend."

"So you found Leanne." *Just like Chuck found me.*

"She found me, playing around with a Ouija board when she was your age. Once she realized she could hear me directly, she was quite intrigued by the possibilities of what we could accomplish together. It was good to be part of a team and even better to have someone who could listen to me. Before we met, I felt as if I was fading away, disappearing along with people's memories, but Leanne made me feel real again."

They were silent for a while, watching the sky shift from deep blue to a dark lavender.

"If your friend Chuck has truly been around as long as he says." Henri paused. "I can only imagine how lonely he must be. I only died twenty-three years ago, and sometimes I feel as if it's been closer to a hundred. But here's the important part: even if he is lonely, that doesn't give him the right to try and take away your life. If he were a real friend, he would want what is best for you instead of what's best for him."

"I know." Bernie sighed. "I keep thinking about when I was little. He used to get mad when I played with the other kids. Then he'd tell me that it was because they were planning to hurt me. And he'd try to get me to hurt them back. I thought he was trying to protect me."

"And now?" Henri asked.

I'm sorry, Mrs. Anderson, but we can't keep Bernie in the program. She's simply too aggressive. One of the adults at her first therapy program had said that after she punched another child in the face repeatedly. Chuck told her that the other child had been about to bite her. Bernie's stomach soured as she wondered if Chuck had been lying. After the incident, her mother took her to a new doctor, one who gave her the pills that made her head feel funny. "I don't know. He was right about the scary lab and Mr. Dalhard."

"But he's not right about your mom and about the rest of us," Henri reminded her.

"Do you think he'll be back?" Bernie wasn't sure if she wanted him to return.

"Yes. I can still feel him." Henri looked off into the trees. "I don't know why he's keeping his distance. Maybe there's still some human part of him that feels bad about what he's done. Or maybe he's planning something even worse than what he's already done."

"I don't know what to do," Bernie said quietly.

"Yes, you do. And I wish you didn't have to, but you're the only one who can make sure he can't hurt anyone else."

That's what heroes do. They stop people from getting hurt. Maybe there was still time to be a hero.

"You're gonna listen to this frog eater, Bernie?" Chuck appeared in front of her. He was building up to a blast again.

Reaching out mentally, Bernie hooked into Henri. When Chuck's energy wave hit, she held Henri in place. He flickered a few times under the brunt of the attack. Needles shook loose from the trees as the branches lashed back and forth. Eva sat up, her teeth chattering and hands shaking. Hood sprang to his feet, searching for a menace he could sense but not see. Harley crouched, covering his eyes from the wind-driven debris. Annika scrambled backward, putting her back against a tree.

"You're picking him over me?" Chuck's hurt stung deeply, but Bernie held fast, keeping Henri anchored to her. Birds squawked as they took to the sky in alarm.

"He's helping me. You aren't," she shouted.

Chuck's attack harshened, sinking into her mind like cat claws.

Bernie shrieked, clutching her head. "I thought you were my friend!"

"So did I," he growled, looming like an impenetrable shadow.

"You have to stop him, *petite*!" Henri shouted, flickering faster. Cuts appeared on Eva, Hood, and Harley's skin as they were scratched by needles and grit in the flailing wind.

Bernie struggled to her feet, glaring at Chuck. "Stop it!"

He was fighting her, but Bernie dug in, ignoring the pain and concentrating on one thing. *Make. Him. Stop.*

A rumbling boom crashed down on them like a thunderclap. It sent a rippling rush through the trees, and then it was all over. There was only the soft patter of debris dropping to the ground.

"What the hell was that?" Annika demanded.

Bernie searched for Chuck, casting out her mind. She could still sense him, so he hadn't been exorcised. A thin thread of hurt and betrayal sifted through their connection, and her heart ached for him. But she could also feel Henri. His warm pride was like the sun beaming down on her.

"Well done, *petite.*"

CHAPTER THIRTY-SIX

"He is certain?" If the contact at Juneau had erred with something so critical, Priya would ensure he did not survive another hour. But she couldn't suppress the thrill of excitement. *And to think I nearly didn't take the call.* Using her cell phone in the safe house could have alerted someone to its location, but the news could change everything.

"I spoke with Dr. Coulon myself. The new captive is a transformative. He has been tranquilized and is en route to you now. The doctor asked me to pass on his pleasure at being able to provide what you had originally asked for."

Priya noted the details of the flight with delight before terminating the call. Finally, she possessed all of the pieces she needed for her original plan. McBride would terrify with his strength and destruction, but he wouldn't spark the same revulsion as someone who was both a minority and essentially inhuman. There were still vast reserves of racism that the new transformative would tap into, and she could ensure that anger stayed aimed at the *lalassu* instead of superficial variances in skin color. *Nothing unites bigotry like a new target for hatred.*

She checked the video feed from McBride's cell. He had been digging at the walls again, scraping his fingertips raw.

"Such useless defiance." She began to prepare his evening meal. "There's still a piece of you that thinks you can win, isn't there?"

If it had been her in that cell, she would have been lulling her captors into a false sense of security, not continually reminding them of her potential lack of cooperation. Defiance allowed a prisoner to rattle the cage, but it wasn't sustainable. He should have been ready to cooperate with her, but he still resisted.

With the new transformative on the way, she could terminate him. He was no longer essential to her plans. She stirred thick chicken stew into the rice, watching as the liquid dissolved. Adding a drop or two of poison would have taken care of things efficiently. *Still, it would be wasteful.*

And yet, she wondered what she could do with two demonstrations. There were multiple rallies planned for the next day, but two *lalassu* attacks would distract from one another in the media. It could even end up provoking someone's suspicions. And two working together could potentially overcome the safety barriers that she had already put in place.

What if they weren't working together? The idea provoked some pleasing possibilities. *Could I turn them against one another in an inhuman fight to the death?*

She transferred the chicken, vegetable, and rice mixture to a cardboard bowl on a stiffened cardboard tray, none of which could be turned into a weapon against her or himself. Satisfied, she carried it down the stairs to McBride's cell.

The door to his enclosure was two-inch steel with two small openings. The first was a window to look inside, and the second was a narrow slot for the meal tray. Priya would have liked to be in the same room to better observe his expressions and posture, but she had no wish to place herself in harm's way.

"You must be hungry, Corporal McBride," she called out softly.

His face filled the window. "Let me out of here."

"In due time." She motioned for him to back away from the door, and he reluctantly complied. "Or are you offering to trade your wife's freedom for yours? Has the course of true love run its path?"

As she unlocked the tray slot, she watched McBride out of the corner of her eye. Anger and fear alternated, with his clenched fists and widened eyes choreographed by the pulsing throb of the veins in his neck and forehead.

He grabbed the tray from her roughly, eyeing the mixture in his bowl with suspicion.

"Oh dear, I thought we were past the paranoia of poisoning. Do you want me to taste it first?" A hint of mockery ran under her demure pose, and from his narrowing of his eyes, he'd caught it.

"A fork would be nice," he replied.

Priya nearly clapped in delight. He'd decided to play her game after all, responding to her as a hostess instead of his captor, which meant it was time to change the rules again. "I wish we could trust you with one, but you haven't been building our confidence."

"Since you're planning to use me as a disposable political prop, I don't see a lot of trust falls in our future."

"Trust falls are such an interesting exercise. Essentially meaningless except as a demonstration of commitment to an arbitrary group." Priya shrugged, keeping her eyelids lowered so that she could watch him without seeming to. "Trust is only truly demonstrated with the unexpected. Your trust in us warms my heart far more than any number of blindfolded collapses."

"I don't trust you as far as I can throw you." He moved closer to glare at her through the window.

Priya smiled delicately. "I imagine that would be quite a distance, given your abilities, but I'll accept that you meant it as a colloquial statement of distrust. which is a pity. I suppose your recent efforts are a result of you rethinking your choice to cooperate."

"The first duty of a captive is to escape," he said. It was a soldier's doctrine.

"Even at the risk of harm to your wife and child?" she asked softly.

McBride froze in place, and Priya suppressed laughter. The doctor's report could not have come at a better time. Her captive looked completely lost with his gaping mouth.

"Congratulations, by the way." She turned away from him, twisting to speak in profile over her shoulder. "Perhaps I'll arrange for you to have a cupcake or something so that you can celebrate."

"Lily is pregnant?" he asked hoarsely before shaking his head. "No. It's a lie. A trick."

"Not at all," Priya said smoothly. "Perhaps I'll have the doctor do an ultrasound so he can send you a picture."

"Keep him away from her!" McBride slammed against the door.

Priya barely even flinched in her startlement. "My, I hope you kept better control over your temper at home. That is hardly the way to speak to the woman who holds your beloved's life in her hands. Especially when she doesn't need you any longer."

His jaw gritted so hard that she wouldn't have been surprised to see blood leaking at the corners from a literal bite to his tongue. "You've given up on your demonstration."

"Not at all. But I have someone new in mind for it. You were always my second choice, and as you've decided not to cooperate…" She shrugged and began to walk up the stairs.

"No, please! I'll do whatever you want!" he shouted.

Priya slowed. "Why should I believe you?"

"Because whoever you have won't be as scary as me." His hands poked through the meal slot. "I spent time hiding in some of the roughest places you can imagine and doing things that still keep me up at night sometimes. And because you're right. You do hold Lily's and my child's life in your hands. So I'll do whatever you want."

It wasn't the pregnancy that had tipped him over, it was the realization that he was disposable. Priya made a mental note for future captives. Although his wife's life had always been on the line, he must have believed that they would somehow triumph. It took the immediate threat to gain his cooperation.

She moved closer, studying him openly. "You must truly believe that you are in love with her. It is the only conceivable reason why you would value her life over your own. I've never felt that, you see, and so I've never quite understood it."

"Then I feel sorry for you." He spit out the words like so much soggy paper.

"Do you? I am over six hundred years old. I heard Beethoven play and watched Picasso paint. I have lived experiences that you can only imagine." She let her voice become breathy and low. "I understand beauty and lust, greed, and art. But I've never been tempted to delude myself into placing another person above myself."

"What about your brother?" He threw out the accusation, obviously expecting it to bite deeply.

"Are you hoping to divide us? Or to make me believe that he and I don't share an agenda?" she asked innocently, as if inquiring about a character in a film. "I suppose I shouldn't tease you, not after all the work I've put into you. It's rather simple. My brother and I are allies and partners. It does not mean that I value his input more than my own. We're working toward the same goal. You are willing to die for a woman you've known for less than two years and a child you only learned about five minutes ago. And believe me, with all of the work we've done on you, we know that you are giving up a significant allotment of years. Yet I don't see any signs of hesitation."

"If you'd felt it, you wouldn't." McBride's statement reeked of superiority, and she smiled at his conviction.

How stable are those foundations? "I imagine that those who destroy their lives for drugs would say the same. It's an all-consuming high." She laughed quietly. "And we both know how far you'll go for your next fix."

The cardboard tray he'd been holding suddenly crumpled in his grasp, sending an explosion of rice across the tiny cell.

"Is this your next addiction? Sacrifice yourself to prove that you are more than a junkie who escaped through pure chance?" Her words sank home like shining daggers plunging into unprotected flanks. "Or will you selfishly allow your woman and your unborn child to die in more meaningless attempts to escape your fate?"

"You have my word. I'll do what needs to be done, no matter what it is. As long as they're safe, that's all that matters." He shoved the ruined food back through the slot.

"You'll have a chance to prove yourself, though I'm afraid the stakes are now higher than before." She met his eyes through the thick window. "I'll give you a chance to defeat your competition and prove that you are the one we should rely on. But I'm afraid this will be a winner-takes-all gladiatorial match now."

His shoulders dropped as her words sank in.

"Either your opponent dies, or your wife and child die." She paused for effect. "And he will have received the same instructions about you. Kill you, or what he cares for will find a grave."

The defiance drained out of him completely, leaving only panic. "I'll do it. I'll kill him. As long as she's safe."

"Very well. I can allow one more chance." She met his eyes. "But never forget this, Corporal: the moment where you made the wrong choice. I won't be so forgiving next time."

"Martha?" Lily called weakly, waking her from a light doze. In the artificial light of the lab, it was impossible to tell how much time had passed, but Martha's arms and legs were cold and stiff, making it hard to move.

"I'm here." She only had to shift a few inches to be beside the cot again. "How are you feeling?"

"Tired. Foggy. Cold." Lily answered. "Is the baby okay?"

"I haven't seen any signs of a miscarriage, which is good." There was no need to terrify her friend with all the possibilities, especially when they couldn't do anything about it.

"Good." Lily's eyes closed briefly. "I guess I finally got to see an expert."

"Next time, maybe we can go with another referral." It was a terrible joke that fell flat in delivery, but it still made Lily's smile appear for a brief time.

"Did anyone… who else is here?"

Bernie got away. Hood and Harley have her. She couldn't say it out loud. If they didn't know, then Martha wouldn't be the one to tell them. "Andrew is in the cell beside us. Dr. Coulon gave him something that made him loopy for a while, but he's sleeping now. Annika got away."

"What about Lou?" Lily struggled to sit up, but Martha held her shoulders.

"You need to lie still, okay? The doctor took Lou away." She'd screamed her throat raw until the collar had knocked her out. She kept thinking of the brightly lit autopsy suite down the hall and wondering if the metal table had a new occupant.

Lily closed her eyes, and tears leaked out from behind her thick lashes.

"It's my fault. The doctor threatened to hurt me. But even before that, if I hadn't surrendered… he would have fought." Martha didn't think she'd ever be able to forgive herself for that decision. "I was scared he would be shot, so I put my hands up—"

"We're not immune to bullets." Lily winced. "I got shot once, and it hurt like hell. And the last thing Lou would ever want is to see you get shot. Especially now that you're mated."

Martha's jaw dropped. "How on earth did you know about that?"

"I saw how he looked at you. I've never seen him look at someone like that. Lou's not big on words, but I've learned to read between the lines." Lily's delight only made Martha feel worse.

"Andrew said I would break his heart." The painful words dropped from Martha's lips like glass spikes, each aimed directly at her soul.

"Andrew's full of shit." Lily's declaration held the ring of truth of an aggrieved younger sister.

The two women started to laugh, a sound full of equal parts irony and pain.

"We'll find a way." Lily squeezed Martha's hand.

She believes that. Martha couldn't. She didn't have the certainty of youthful optimism any longer. Once again, her hopes for a better future had been snatched away. But she couldn't do the same to Lily's hope. "You should rest. When you wake up, we'll figure out what to do next."

"We need to find Ron," Lily added, her free hand moving protectively to her belly.

"Maybe he got away."

Lily shook her head. "I remember them taking him. He tried to get me out of a cage. But I don't know where they took him." Tears began to puddle on her lashes again.

"It'll be okay," Martha lied. As the hours passed, they held each other, trying to ward off one another's heartbreak.

Action

CHAPTER THIRTY-SEVEN

"No tests."

"You think you have the power to enforce such a decision?" Dr. Coulon's brief laugh jabbed like a wasp's sting.

Martha held firmly to her refusal to cooperate. Lily was not in shape for whatever test the doctor had planned. Holding tightly to her patient's hand, Martha stared the doctor down. "You've already put her life in jeopardy once. She needs time to recover."

Inside, she was quailing, but she channeled Lou's granite-faced determination for the exterior. It didn't matter whether or not she could physically prevent the doctor from carrying out his horrible experiments. Lou wasn't there to protect his sister, so Martha needed to stand up. She had a duty to her patient and her friend.

"Martha, don't." Lily struggled to get up, but Martha squeezed her hand, hoping the other woman would understand the signal to stay still.

The doctor stared at her, obviously weighing his decision. If he wanted to forcibly move her, he would have to bring in one of the guards, which would mean a delay in proceeding with his work, his all-consuming priority. He would do it if he wanted Lily's next procedure badly enough. And if he wanted it that badly, it was worth resisting with every breath in Martha's body.

"I can concede your argument. The subject may rest." The doctor still stared at her as if imagining her skin peeled back under a dissection knife. "But that means I move on to my next planned experiment. You,

Mrs. McKinnon.”

“Me?” It would have been an excellent point to rattle off a witty catchphrase like a heroine in a movie. Except those heroines had the advantage of never truly being in danger, while she was acutely aware of the menace behind Dr. Coulon’s relatively calm demeanor.

“I would like to discover your abilities.” He pulled out his notebook.

“I don’t have any abilities.” Martha doubted he would take her word for it. But the longer she could keep him distracted, the more Lily would recover and the better chances they would all have for escape. “I’m not a *lalassu*.”

“A number of internees have tried that ploy, but I have discovered there are ways to discover the truth. Pain, sensory extremes, and electrical stimulation have all been effective in revealing an *occulata hominem*’s powers.” He made a note in the book. “We’ll begin with electrical stimulation.”

Lily’s fingers clenched on Martha’s hand. Martha’s throat was dry as sour bile rose.

“Or you could allow me to perform my experiments on my current subject.” Dr. Coulon’s smug smile gave Martha the courage she needed to untangle her hand from Lily’s and step to the front of the cell.

“Whenever you’re ready, Doctor.” She kept her head high.

He unlocked the door and gestured for her to step out. As she did, she saw Andrew watching her from his cell, his fingers locked around the bars.

The clang of the door closing reminded her there was no retreat. She eyed the monstrous examination chair. She couldn’t make herself walk toward it and quietly lie down, allowing him to strap her into the restraints. *Better me than Lily. Or Bernie.* She tried to push herself, but her feet were rooted to the floor.

Sudden pain lanced through her body, radiating from the collar she’d forgotten. Martha dropped to her knees, her hands coming up to claw at the narrow band. Her fingers were too rigid and clumsy to search for a clasp. The electrical current must have locked her vocal cords, because she couldn’t scream. Her mouth was rigid and distended as if she were trying to swallow prey whole, but not a sound came out of it. Her vision began to blur as the agony continued to build, swamping every nerve.

Then it abruptly stopped.

"You son of a bitch!" Lily cursed weakly.

On her hands and knees, Martha could only pant in place as her ability to think slowly returned. She reached up to touch the nylon strip with its bulge for a battery and a transmitter, running her fingers along it.

"No sign of supernatural abilities at the lowest setting." The doctor held up the shock collar remote. "The technology comes from Dalhard Industries. Nanowire fabric allows for direct contact with the nerve endings in the skin, and the ends can be directly sealed, making it impossible to remove without an authorization unit. Even attempting to cut it will produce an enormous shock, sufficient to cause a heart attack in some cases. We will proceed to level two."

The second jolt was even worse than the first. The pain was like a burn, scraping everything raw before bathing it in fire. Tears leaked out of Martha's eyes as she shook on the floor. She couldn't remember a time before the pain or a future after it. The only thing that existed was the anguish shredding her skin.

When it stopped, she was numb. Her unmarked skin didn't make any sense to her dazed brain. Sweat dripped onto the concrete floor, leaving a constellation of dark circles around her. Lily was halfway off the bed, whispering apologies.

"It was developed for interrogations, but the mental effect was too great. Subjects couldn't remember their secrets, much less the questions they'd been asked. Luckily they kept some prototypes, and it does serve as admirable crowd control." Dr. Coulon eyed the two women.

"It's… okay," Martha gasped. She crawled forward and hauled herself upright, turning to face the doctor. Her hands were shaking, and her knees felt as if they might collapse at any second, but she was standing.

"No sign of supernatural abilities at level two." The doctor wrote a brief note. "You could shorten this process significantly by cooperating. Tell me what powers you have."

"N-n-none." Martha braced herself for the next shock, but it didn't come.

"Then tell me about the other *occulata hominem* in this camp. Who else made it past our tests? What secrets are your contacts in the camp hiding?" He paused, pen poised.

It was the moment that Lou's family had feared, when she would spill their secrets to spare herself pain. *I will be the fierce kestrel.* She took a deep breath. "Your tests are inherently flawed, but you already knew that." She took a deep breath. "Your methods are barbaric, and history will condemn you in the same breath as Mengele. You won't be remembered as a genius but as a bigoted butcher."

Her attack on his legacy struck home, and he triggered a fresh wave of agony. Martha slammed into the chair, and her vision failed. When the pain subsided, she caught Andrew watching her with sympathy and regret. *I'm not doing this because of what he said. I'm doing this because I will not be the one who betrays Lou and his family.*

"Last chance, Mrs. McKinnon." The doctor's poise showed strain. His clenched jaw and the rigid tendons in his neck telegraphed his anger.

If she refused him again, he would take out his frustrations on her. She wasn't just going to be subjected to a sociopathic doctor's experiments but to those of a vicious sadist avenging his pricked ego. She looked him in the eye and spoke the words to seal her fate. "I have nothing else to say to you."

"If it weren't for the collars, we would outnumber the guards," Harley suggested.

Bernie sighed. It was morning, and they still didn't have any idea about what to do next.

"They don't give up, do they?" Henri asked.

"And if we could give everyone grenade launchers, we'd be better armed," Hood snapped. Lack of food, shelter, and sleep had stressed everyone's temper.

Harley recoiled with hurt in his eyes. Eva's chin quivered as if she was trying to suppress tears.

There must be something we can do. Bernie didn't think they would last much longer. From the way she was twitching, Annika was ready to crawl up another tree.

"Perhaps I can help?" a new voice asked.

"Who are you?" Henri demanded.

Bernie frowned as the tall thin man with the black caterpillar mustache walked through a tree. "Mr. Marshall?"

The others all turned around to face her. Hood ran a hand over his skull, and Harley exhaled sharply.

"Who is she talking to?" Annika asked.

"Ghosts," Eva whispered.

"It is really off-putting when she does that." Annika wrapped her arms tightly around her ribs. "It's worse than listening to half a cell-phone conversation."

"Shh!" Bernie waved at them to be quiet. "Mr. Marshall, what are you doing here?"

He seemed lost, looking at the trees as if unsure where he was. "I felt something. It was like a storm, but it pulled me in."

"The fight between you and Chuck," Henri explained. "Any ghost within a two-mile radius would have felt it."

"Does that mean more ghosts are coming?" Bernie asked.

"They might." Henri shrugged. "If Chuck doesn't blast them away. So what did you mean that you could help us?"

"You were talking about the shock collars. I spent a lot of time studying them, both before and after I died." Mr. Marshall seemed much more coherent than he had at the schoolhouse.

"Bernie, who are you talking to?" Hood came closer, moving slowly and looking around as if he expected to run into someone.

She explained about Mr. Marshall and what he'd told her.

"Wait, I think I know who he is." Annika hunched her shoulders, tucking her hands deeper under her arms. "I watched a guy try to cut his collar off once when we first got here. He was some hotshot electrical engineer, and he thought he could get around it. Stole a set of bolt cutters and got someone to promise to cut it as fast as they could. The guy cut it off, but Mr. Genius was already dead. The collar stopped his heart."

"That was me," Mr. Marshall confirmed.

"If we can get rid of the collars, then we'd have a chance at a real uprising." Harley absently plucked needles off a nearby pine tree.

"No offense to the dead guy, but is he sure he knows what he's doing this time?" Annika asked. "Last time, he thought he had the answer, and it didn't go so well. We're not going to get a lot of recruits if we kill the first few off."

The ghost smiled sadly. "I've taken a lot of time to study the collars since I died, and I've followed the guards to get a closer look at the transmitters. I know much more than I did before. The key will be to disable the collar first with an electric shock. It will disable the tampering safeguards for a few seconds, allowing the fabric to be cut."

After Bernie relayed the message, Harley nodded. "That might work. But where would we get an electrical charge? There are generators among the staff trailers and in the administrative building but none in the camp itself."

"We can use ghost energy. Like this." Mr. Marshall walked over to Annika and put his hands around her throat.

"What the hell?" Annika jerked away, her hands batting ineffectually through the ghost.

He dropped his hands. "Tell her to hold still."

Bernie shared what Mr. Marshall was doing.

"Hell no. I am not volunteering. I've had enough of being a guinea pig." Annika huffed and refolded her arms.

"It's not a great test if we can't cut off the collar." Harley walked toward Annika, peering at her neck. "We need to find a knife or cutters."

"You guys don't have a knife? What kind of rescue op is this?" Annika held still while Harley took a closer look at the collar.

"If you have complaints, we'd be happy to escort you back to the doctor," Hood said dryly.

"It's better than a soap opera, isn't it?" Henri plopped down next to Bernie. "How are you holding up, *petite*?"

"Tired. Cold. I want it all to be over," Bernie told him.

"Thanks to you, it's closer to being over than ever before." Henri smiled. "Without you, Mr. Marshall wouldn't be able to tell them what they need to know to make sure that this camp doesn't hurt anyone else. Your mother is going to be very proud when she gets out."

"You think so? That she's going to get out?" She was too tired to hope that things would go their way for once.

"Even if we can get the collars off, how do we get back into camp?" Annika demanded.

"One problem at a time." Hood shook his head.

Harley straightened. "You never listen."

Henri grinned. "With such a perfect partnership, how could we fail?"

Chapter Thirty-Eight

Lou couldn't tell for certain whether he'd actually struggled back to consciousness or if he was dreaming, but the sour stink of old urine and rotting garbage didn't seem like something he would dream. He gagged and coughed, trying to clear his nose and mouth of the stench.

"Hey, he's waking up." The voice sounded afraid, pitching higher at the end.

Lou forced his eyes open, blinking against the rough grit. Metal walls surrounded him on all sides except one. A grid of bars stood between him and a young man standing on the other side of the metal box, who spoke into a phone and clutched a pronged metal stick as if his life depended on it.

Not a dream. Lou rolled his shoulders and shifted his neck, but he couldn't feel any sign of one of Woodpine's shock collars. The mental fog of multiple druggings was rapidly being replaced by the clarity and focus of anger. It would be easy to shift to the fur to exact revenge. He needed to keep himself in check until he could find out what happened to Martha and his siblings.

A small door at the end of the box opened, and a tall man with golden-tan skin and dark hair entered. "Hello, Mr. Charging Bull. We have not had the pleasure of meeting officially. My name is Karan Samil, and I am the CEO of Dalhard Industries."

Lou didn't reply. He doubted the man was truly interested in exchanging meaningless pleasantries, and the sooner Lou could find out what this Karan wanted, the faster he could snap the bastard's neck and get out of here.

The young man in the uniform made a hasty exit, leaving the metal stick with Karan. The other man toyed with it, running his fingers along its black surface.

"This van is currently parked at the edge of a park," Karan said, gesturing at the metal walls. "Inside the park, people have gathered to demand the government start dealing with the menace posed by the *lalassu*. They want sweeps to discover *lalassu* who are pretending to be human, deportations to more camps like Woodpine, and possibly even executions. It is all driven by fear, of course, but that makes it all the more desperate."

He seemed to think the threat of his words was obvious, but Lou was far more interested in Martha and his kin. There was no reason to waste his time with fools wanting to gather together in a park to try and drown out their own fears with angry shouting. He held back a growl, flexing his fingers to keep them from curling into fists. The urge to rip apart the bars and attack Karan was surprisingly difficult to suppress.

"There are also those who think the government is being unfair in confining anyone for the crime of being born different. They are demanding the camps be shut down and *lalassu* identify themselves so that everyone can learn how terribly normal they are. It is the American dream at its finest: scream debate through chants and slogans and prey on fears and uncertainty, all with neither side listening to the other. It is a war of words, and victory comes with annihilation of your opponents, not understanding." Karan smiled and bared his teeth like a predator. "But I doubt any of it matters much to you up in your forest enclave."

Lou was starting to think that Karan had taken him for the sole purpose of having an audience. Like Dr. Coulon, the man seemed to desperately need to explain himself rather than letting his actions stand on their own.

"You are going to show them that they have everything to fear from the *lalassu* in their midst." Karan tapped the stick on his open palm.

Snorting in disbelief, Lou shook his head.

His refusal didn't seem to bother Karan. "This is likely the moment where you expect me to threaten your brother, sister, or perhaps your fictional wife, all of whom I have in my control. However, I do not share my sister's faith in such measures. I prefer something more direct."

Lou kept a tight throttle on his bear. Karan wouldn't be taunting him if he didn't want him to shift to the fur. And if that was what Karan wanted, Lou needed to avoid it.

"You are having trouble keeping your temper. Do not bother to deny it." His captor smiled. "I injected you with a drug my company developed for combat. It increases rage while decreasing the ability to feel pain. Unfortunately, a significant number of subjects became completely psychotic."

His arms shook with the effort to hold himself back. *I will not give in.*

"You still believe you can win against me. How very sad." Karan sounded disappointed and resigned. "Very well. Allow me to be clear. As we speak, your brother in law, Corporal Ron McBride, is in another van similar to this one on the other side of the park. In a few minutes, you will both be released, and you will do your best to kill one another."

No. Lou's muscles rolled and shifted, fighting to transform.

"If either of you attempts to escape, then everyone you love will die." Karan jabbed the pronged end of the metal stick into Lou's side, and electricity jolted through his body, stinging like thousands of bees on the inside of his skin. It shattered his ability to control his form.

He writhed on the floor, and his body tried to shift rapidly as the muscles contracted and spasmed beyond Lou's control. His hands scratched at the floor with long sharp claws sprouting from his fingers. His jaw broke and reformed as a muzzle then collapsed back into blunt human teeth. It was agonizing and nothing like a usual transformation. He roared with the pain, the sound ending in a grizzly's angered bellow.

He slammed serving-platter-sized paws onto the ground as the bear seized control from his dazed human mind. Sniffing the air, he realized that Karan had left at some point. But the two large doors at the end of the van were ajar, letting in a sliver of daylight.

Equally blinded by rage and the urge to escape and find his tormentor, Lou shouldered open the doors and leapt to the ground. Immediately, he began to hear high-pitched shrieks of alarm. At the edges of his blurred sight, movement began to speed up, and the shouts of panic got louder.

This isn't right. Lou forced himself to think like a human instead of react like an animal. He made himself shift back to the skin.

"He's one of them!" a woman shouted.

A half-eaten sandwich came flying out of the crowd and pelted Lou with a glop of tuna salad. A teenage boy stood on the fringes of the group, clutching his paper cup of soda, ready to let it fly if the tuna wasn't a sufficient deterrent.

Lou glared at him, and the boy went pale, his Adam's apple bobbing. Wiping away the clinging mess, Lou sized up the area and saw a few anemic trees in round circles of grass amid an expanse of concrete. Massive buildings hemmed him in on all sides, locking the sun and sky in a gleaming vault of glass and steel. Traffic crawled past the outer edges, clouding the air with acrid smoke and greasy grit, and more people than he could easily count were crammed into the artificial gap in the infrastructure.

Whatever drug they had given him still clouded his mind, poking at his anger and refusing to let it settle. There were too many people, too many smells, too many bright lights and loud sounds, and too much for his mind to accept. His instincts were screaming at him to rage and run, find his way back to Woodpine and protect his family. The idea that Martha was in the hands of the doctor, vulnerable to the callous orders of men like Karan, it made him want to howl to the sky. His kin had been slaughtered in his absence from Bear Claw. He wondered if history would repeat itself and he would be unable to protect Martha and Bernie.

"What is he doing?" Karan demanded, glaring at the monitors in the surveillance van. It had all begun so promisingly, but the shape-shifter simply stood there, naked and aloof. Priya shifted between six different feeds, preparing them to broadcast to the world media. And instead of a compelling drama, all he had was footage of a man wiping tuna off his chest.

"It seems your drug was not as effective as you'd hoped." Priya sounded smug, as if she was preparing for a puerile I-told-you-so.

"Why is no one attacking?" Some of the crowd were pulling out their phones to take appreciative pictures.

"Patience, brother. They only need to remember that they were afraid." There was a click. "Corporal McBride, your brother-in-law doesn't appear to care about whether or not your wife and child survive. Because of him, Lily will die unless you get out there right now and take him out."

"No… I can't." The faint protest was scratchy with interfering noise.

"Then I will call Dr. Coulon now." His sister's tone brought renewed pride to Karan. She sounded genuinely regretful, a masterful performance. He had never been able to adequately fake emotional reactions, relying on a neutral mask of benign pleasantry to avoid detection.

"No! Wait!" McBride's voice was tight with panic.

"Your wife has five minutes left to live. If you would like it to be longer, kill the skin-walker." An atypical harsh note injected bite into Priya's orders. "Tick tock, Corporal. The clock has already begun."

Karan spotted the disturbance on the monitors as McBride left the second van. People abruptly went from milling around to scattering for the edges of the park. The former soldier leapt high above the crowd, clearing heads by five or six feet and landing in the middle of the small park. "He certainly took your instructions to heart."

"Snipers, be prepared to take out the target on my signal." Priya muted the radio and chuckled quietly. "It's all about finding the proper motivation. Now your skin-walker will have to fight for his life. No matter how much he wants to thwart us, he will want to live more."

Like everyone else, Lou was startled when Ron suddenly appeared in the air and landed hard enough to send a cloud of dust rising from the concrete. People were running between them, trying to find escape routes to safer vantage points at the edges of the park. The surprise broke the thin bonds on his self-control. He snarled, preparing to launch into an attack.

Ron slowly stood up from his crouch. He was dressed in combat fatigue pants and a faded gray cotton undershirt. As he straightened, his expression undercut Lou's rage, giving him room to think again. Ron's haggard and drawn face didn't seem to indicate rage. Instead, his set jaw and narrow mouth were more determined than angry. But his eyes were what struck Lou hardest. There was no hope left in them. It was the gaze of a man who was already lost in pain and torture and who only hoped to spit in the eye of death before it swallowed him whole.

"I'm sorry." Ron walked forward, his fists raised. "They have Lily."

Lou nodded, not bothering to protest or argue with his sister's mate. "I know."

"They want me to kill you." Ron choked on the words. "Or they'll kill her."

You can't let him make you do something because he threatens to hurt me. I won't be a leash on you.

Martha's words filtered out the anger flooding his mind. He had no doubt that Karan and the doctor were ruthless enough to carry out the horrors they'd promised. They were the real enemies, the manipulators pulling strings.

Ron charged him. Lou bent forward at the waist and met Ron's tackle with a shoulder to his brother-in-law's chest. The impact slammed through them both, reverberating like a vibrating drum skin. Lou grappled with Ron, locking his arms around the other man and trying to take him to the ground.

Ron's strength was impressive but meaningless if he didn't have the leverage to wield it. His fist pounded down on the armoring slab of muscle on Lou's back. Lou grunted with the blunt pain of each blow, but he wasn't feeling snapped ribs or shots to vulnerable organs. Lou twisted, planting his feet firmly before lifting Ron off of his. Ron hung off Lou's shoulder, feet dangling and leaving him momentarily at a loss.

"Go down. Pretend to be hurt," Ron whispered.

That wouldn't satisfy the manipulators. No matter what they did, Martha and Lily would be in enemy hands, along with everyone else. And the best case would be that Ron and Lou would have crippled one another, reducing their ability to defeat the real enemy.

Slamming his brother-in-law to the ground, Lou winced at the click of Ron's jaws bouncing off each other. *I'm sorry.* He rolled onto the other man, trying to pin him down with his own weight.

Ron got a foot wedged between them, planted on Lou's hips. He kicked, thrusting Lou up and over the immediate battlefield.

The kick itself whooshed the air out of Lou's lungs. A tree trunk cracked into his back as he slammed into it. The blow sent him gasping, unable to draw a breath as he dropped to the ground and sprawled awkwardly on the concrete. It was hard enough that Lou half expected to discover his legs locked in some kind of paralysis.

"Don't make me do this!" Ron begged. "Stay down!"

Ron was on him before Lou had a chance to evaluate any injuries. Between the drug and the adrenaline flooding his system, he wouldn't feel the pain until much later. Ron's hands scrabbled at Lou's neck, trying to get a death grip.

Lou grabbed Ron's wrists and tried to bend them away. But the other man was too strong and too desperate. They needed to find a way out of this rigged death match.

He needed to trust his fierce kestrel to find a way to protect herself and Lily, to escape from their enemies. He needed to believe in them instead of their captors. If Karan had told the truth, then Lou would lose no matter what he did. Either his beloved or his sister would die. So Lou refused to accept their lies as realities. He shifted to the fur.

Unable to keep a grip, Ron was thrown off as Lou's mass increased. Lou rolled over and planted himself on all four feet. Dimly, he was aware of shrieks and screams, but his attention stayed focused on Ron, who didn't look any saner than before.

Rearing up to an impressive twelve feet, Lou roared and came crashing down onto the pavement. The ground shook with the impact. Hopefully, the display would also send the innocent gawkers fleeing for safety.

Ron charged at him again, and Lou swiped him with a paw, careful to keep his six-inch claws extended out of damage range. His brother-in-law's enhancements would prevent or heal blunt trauma but not a slice.

The blow sent Ron tumbling end over end, smashing through a park bench. He popped up onto his feet, ready for the next round. His fists were clenched, and his cheeks were drenched in tears. Lou braced himself.

Ron took two steps forward and then stumbled, flailing to keep his balance. Something bright blue caught Lou's attention from behind the other man.

Ron got to his knees and tried to launch himself like a runner. But he sprawled face down on the ground with outstretched arms and twitching fingers.

"What is happening?" Karan shouted from the van.

"Snipers, fire!" Priya ordered. But there was no response from her teams on the perimeter.

No. Karan refused to believe that once again his enemies had managed to snatch victory from what should have been certain defeat.

"We need to get out of here." Priya dropped her headset and crawled into the front seat.

"No! Call the doctor and tell him to kill the hostages!" Karan grabbed at her arm.

"The snipers have been taken out." She tried to wrench herself free. "We need to trigger the explosions before they have a chance to leave. Unless you want to be caught in it, we need to leave right now."

He wanted them dead and destroyed almost more than he wanted to live.

"If we can activate the bombs, they will die. Believe in me, brother," Priya insisted, but Karan could only stare at the screens, his hands squeezing his sister's flesh. *My enemies must die.*

Lou cautiously shifted to the skin, wanting human eyes to verify what his bear ones had seen. A tufted metal cylinder stuck out of Ron's back, and the fibrous, fluffy end was an intense bright blue.

Four people, two men and two women, were running toward him, dodging through the last of the evacuating crowd. Lou recognized Michael, and he guessed the dark-haired woman alongside him was his mate, Dani. The other man carried a long rifle and a shiny police badge. The fourth woman had sandy-blond hair caught in a ponytail and delicate features, but she moved as fearlessly as Dani.

"Sorry," Michael announced breathlessly. "We came as quickly as we could, but we had to stop the snipers on the roof. Are you all right?"

Lou nodded once. The blond woman knelt to check Ron's pulse.

"Damn, that is a lot of naked man right there." Dani's smile quirked toward a deep dimple in her cheek.

Michael didn't seem upset by his mate's comment, only rolling his eyes and shaking his head with a smile as he knelt beside the blond woman. Although he wore his leather gloves, he didn't touch Ron or the woman.

"I'm Lieutenant Joe Cabrera," the man with the gun introduced himself. "You want a jacket or something?"

"No. Is Ron all right?" Lou asked.

"He's alive. I had to guess about the dose of ketamine." The blond woman stood, keeping her gaze fixed firmly on his face. "I'm Cali, by the way. And trust me, as much as Dani is enjoying the view, we need to get you covered up and out of here. Special Investigations will be on the way."

Joe trotted a few feet away and picked up a checkered blanket lying beside a pair of abandoned backpacks.

"All right, if the public nudity part is over, then we might as well go." Dani crouched down and lifted Ron as if he were no more than a doll. Given that the unconscious man was several inches taller than she was and easily double her weight, the feat impressed Lou.

"That's my girl," Michael commented fondly as Joe handed Lou the blanket to wrap around himself.

Whatever reply Lou might have made was lost in the thunderous roar of an explosion.

Chapter Thirty-Nine

"Martha? Come on, you need to wake up and have some water." Lily's voice pulled Martha out of a pleasant dream and back into aching reality. She opened her eyes and winced at the brightness of the lights.

"Try to sit up," Lily coaxed.

Arms slipped underneath Martha's shoulders, lifting her into a seated position. Her whole body ached as if in the grip of a powerful flu, but she supposed that, under the circumstances, she should be grateful it wasn't worse. Panic gripped her, and she turned toward the lab. No doctor.

"He left a while ago," Lily said through flattened lips. "I convinced him to let us stay together."

"Did he hurt you?" Martha asked. The other woman looked much better than she had before, alert and without the papery tone to her skin.

"No, he concentrated on you today," Andrew spoke from the other cell. "I wanted to say that I'm sorry."

"I couldn't let him experiment on Lily again." Martha accepted the plastic container of water.

"Not about that, although I am sorry you had to go through it. I'm apologizing for what I said to you before, about hurting my brother." Andrew paused, leaving Martha to wonder if she was supposed to say something in return. Accepting the apology seemed trite under the circumstances, but she didn't want to alienate him further. After a deep breath, Andrew continued, "Lou was the one who had the hardest time when our father died. They'd been hunting partners since before I can remember. He stepped up and became a parent when our mother couldn't. It wasn't easy for him, and he wasn't very nurturing… In fact, he could be grouchy as hell."

"Tell me about it," Lily said, adding a younger sister's vote of solidarity.

Martha wished she could see Andrew as he kept talking. "But he cared, and he did it all. The money he got for furs and leathers went to us. If there wasn't enough food, he claimed to have eaten in the bush."

"He's a good man. I know that," Martha said quietly. "It's one of the reasons I love him." *Wait, love?* She hadn't meant to say that. She didn't remember the doctor injecting her with anything, but there were several foggy points in her memory. *Why did I have to say it now? This isn't how declarations of love are supposed to work.* She wasn't supposed to be trapped in a cell while the man she loved had been sent far away by a psychopathic doctor.

"When he said he would come with you, I thought he was sacrificing himself again." Andrew's voice broke. "I wanted him to do something else, something that would make him happy instead of taking care of everyone else."

"Andrew, you don't owe me any explanations. He's your brother. I understand that." Martha reached out to Lily to let her know that she was included in the broader sentiment.

"I have to say this. When I first saw the two of you together here, I realized you were mated. I'd never seen Lou so focused on any one person. But I thought you would abandon him, and I hated the idea of him suffering again. Because it's more than a biological drive for him. He loves you, too. I know him better than anyone else, and I can see it in how he trusts you." Andrew's words caused Martha's breath to catch in her throat and tears to gather on her lower lashes. He continued. "He could have shifted and taken on the guards. He could have fought against the doctor. But he didn't want to risk hurting you."

"Just like you didn't want him to get hurt," Lily said.

"When you begged him not to let you be a leash, I knew you cared about him more than yourself. He deserves that. You do, too," Andrew finished.

Their support meant a lot to Martha. It would mean more if they weren't trapped in cells about to be killed—*no, that's not how this is going to end.* Her worst fears had come true, and it hadn't broken her. "Enough depressing talk."

Lily looked up at her in surprise.

"We're still alive, and we still have a chance. Annika and the others are still out there." Martha stood up. "We're going to find a way out of here."

"I'm open to suggestions." It was refreshing to hear Andrew's dry sarcasm instead of sincere apologies. It put Martha in more familiar territory instead of on the brink of disaster.

"If we can get out of the cells, then there aren't many other physical barriers." She tugged at her collar, reminded that there were blockages other than locked doors.

"Excellent plan. A little vague in the middle, but we can work on it."

"Andrew, stop being yourself." Lily stood up next to Martha. "I could pretend to be sick again, and then we both rush him when he opens the door."

"He can drop me with that remote." Martha told herself it wasn't cowardice to want to avoid ever feeling that pain again.

"We can both pretend to be sick. Then he won't be prepared for it." Lily's optimistic enthusiasm firmed into determination. "I'm not going to die in here. And I'm not going to let them use me as a hostage for Ron."

Martha nodded agreement. Not dying or being a hostage wasn't much of a goal, but it was better than nothing. And if it meant that she would have a chance to see Bernie and Lou again, she would seize it with both hands and never let go.

"Are you ready?" Hood asked, keeping his voice low as he eased the knife under the young woman's collar. He and Bernie had snuck into the camp several hours before and set themselves up in Leanne's old barracks. After all the arguing, it had been much easier than any of them could have expected. With Henri and Mr. Marshall as undetectable scouts, they'd been able to walk right in.

"I'm ready." The young woman lifted her chin and closed her eyes.

Bernie held up her hand as Henri stuck his hands through the woman's throat and held them there, intersecting the shock collar. Henri grimaced but kept his hands steady. *"Bien."*

Bernie dropped her hand, and Hood sliced through the collar. The woman stepped back, her hand at her throat, blinking rapidly. For a moment, she stared at the thin strip of fabric in disbelief before viciously kicking it off to the side. Then she hurried away, and the next internee, an older man, took her place.

Out of the corner of her eye, Bernie watched the woman embrace a man holding a baby. He'd had his collar removed a few minutes before. They were smiling together like a happy family.

"Bernie?" Hood gently recaptured her attention.

"Sorry. Mr. Marshall?" Bernie pointed at the skinny, gray-haired man waiting to have his collar removed. When the ghost had suggested that the spiritual energies of the dead could be used to short-circuit the collar defenses, she doubted that he had anticipated spending the next few hours sticking his hands into people.

But it was working, even though both Hood and Harley had been skeptical. Word spread through the camp like wildfire. Eva and Harley were quietly going through and bringing the internees to the barracks then escorting them back in groups.

The old man's collar joined the others on the floor. He straightened as if freed from a much bigger weight than a half ounce of nylon. Bernie felt taller herself, proud to be doing a hero's work.

"That is the most peculiar sensation," Mr. Marshall mused, looking at his hands.

"Uncomfortable, you mean," Henri griped.

It wasn't any more pleasant for the living. Bernie noticed they kept rubbing their throats, and a few complained about an icy sensation.

"Why don't we take a break? If Henri is up to it, maybe he can check on Martha and the others," Hood suggested quietly.

"I'll be back in a minute, Bernie." Henri vanished.

A tapping at the door announced Harley's arrival with a new batch of internees. As soon as he came in, Harley made a beeline to Hood. "How are you holding up?"

"All right." Hood glanced around before taking Harley's hand. "How about you?"

"I keep waiting for someone to betray us," Harley sighed. "I expected there would be someone who wants extra privileges or who has been promised that they can leave if they cooperate with the guards. But everyone has been on our side and ready for a revolution as soon as they find out we really can get rid of the collars. Now I find myself more worried that someone is going to start the uprising before we can free everyone."

"I'm more worried about what we're going to do after the revolution. We're still stuck in the middle of nowhere, and we can't fit everyone on that tiny commuter plane when it comes back," Hood grumbled. "Where's Eva?"

Henri reappeared as Harley replied, "She's talking about going after the people in detention."

"Shit," Hood cursed.

"She'll be okay. I told her to wait until we free the rest of the camp, then we could get the rest out with their help. She's expecting the call soon."

"Don't know where she gets her optimism." Hood chuckled, still obviously proud of his daughter.

"Is my mom okay?" Bernie asked.

"Scared but okay. The doctor is working on the dead bears," Henri reported.

She was afraid to ask the next question, but it came out anyway. "Did you see Chuck?"

Henri shook his head. Bernie turned to watch Hood getting ready to head out and collect the next group. They had a deactivated collar to attach around his neck with a hair clip. It was enough to fool the guards at first glance. Once a group came to the barracks and their collars were removed, they were escorted back to hide and wait for the signal. When the signal went out, those who could fight would come out to take on the guards and take over the camp. Some were eager to vent their frustration on the people who had kept them imprisoned. Some just wanted to go home. But all of them were ready for change, and she was part of making that change happen.

A chill crept up the back of her neck. Henri and Mr. Marshall abruptly vanished. Bernie slowly turned until she could see Chuck standing behind her.

"Hi, Bernie," he said quietly.

None of the living were aware of what was happening. Hood took his group out while Harley organized the new arrivals. She looked at her toes.

"It was a lot easier before, when they thought you were crazy."

Bernie glared at him.

"I meant we didn't have so many people trying to tell us what to do. We didn't have so many people paying attention to us." Chuck pretended to lean against the barracks. If he hadn't been concentrating, he would have gone right through the wall.

She wasn't in a mood for nostalgia. "I like this better."

"Come on. Didn't you like it when it was the two of us against the world?" Chuck grew darker, and the temperature of the room began to drop. "I took care of you."

"Bernie?" Harley asked.

"It's Chuck. He's here." The roof creaked. The internees clustered together, reaching for each other's hands. Bernie glared at Chuck. "Stop it."

"Come with me, and I'll leave them alone." He held out his hand.

"No," she shouted. Her anger felt like a palpable presence, like a wall at her back. "Because of you, people looked at me like I was crazy, and I got put on drugs that kept my brain foggy, and then I thought I was crazy because I heard and saw someone who wasn't really there."

"That was your mom's fault," Chuck insisted. The walls of the barracks began to creak and bend.

If it kept up, someone was going to get hurt. She hurried to the door, knowing Chuck would follow her.

"Bernie! Wait!" Harley called out.

"I know what you've done to get me in trouble," Bernie shot back at Chuck. "You wanted me dead."

"If you cared about me, you would want to be with me." Chuck got even darker, turning into a solid black outline with glowing eyes. "But you wanted to be a hero. And this is what happens to heroes. They get to hide in the cold and dark because there are always more bad guys than heroes."

The posts holding the walls up began to shake, sending dust steadily sifting down. Bernie jumped outside as the internees scrambled for the door. Harley tried to force his way to her but couldn't push through Chuck's dark presence. Bernie waved at him to stay back. She didn't want anyone else to get hurt.

"You're all going to get caught"—Chuck wasn't finished with his tirade—"just like your mom. I made sure of it."

She turned to face him. "What are you talking about?"

"I opened the doors so the doctor could get out. I knew he'd catch her before she could leave." His smile was too twisted to belong on his face.

Henri had been right. He wasn't her friend anymore, and he couldn't be saved. A whirlwind buzzed around her, except nothing was moving. It was only in her head, which made it hard to think and concentrate. She fell to her knees. "Go away! Leave me alone!"

"Can you make him stop?" Harley shouted. He was hanging on to one of the posts.

Bernie shook her head.

"Then we have to get out of here before the guards come." He pulled himself closer to her, holding out his hand. "Come on."

"Back off!" Chuck roared, swiping long black claws at Harley.

"No!" Bernie screamed and reached out to block the strike even though she knew Chuck would pass right through her flesh.

Except this time, he didn't. The claws bounced as if they'd hit a solid wall.

She could feel the wall in her mind, as if it were a part of her. Chuck snarled, turning on her.

A second wall sprang into being between them, meeting the first to form a corner.

"That's it, Bernie." Henri suddenly appeared beside her. "Close him in."

She made two more walls, blocking Chuck's exit. She was panting, and her eyes were sore as if she'd been crying, but the mental walls held firm.

Chuck paled, returning to how he'd been when she'd first seen him. A skinny boy in gray overalls and a pale shirt with a cap on his head said, "Bernie, don't do this."

Harley's hands clamped on her shoulders, but she shook him off.

"Now tighten the walls. Close him in," Henri prompted.

She held out her hands and began to close the gap between them. The walls contracted around Chuck.

"I don't want to go into the light without you." Chuck held out his hand. "We're friends. Friends should stick together."

"No, friends should want each other to be happy." Bernie stood up, wobbling for a moment before catching her balance. "I want you to be happy. Go to the light."

"You have no idea what's in there. Everyone talks about it as if it's so wonderful, but no one knows for sure because no one comes back from it." Chuck looked up at her. "Come with me, then we'll find out together."

She shook her head.

"I thought we were family. Family isn't supposed to hurt each other." He pushed back against the walls, but Bernie kept them strong.

"Then why are you trying to hurt her? You need to go into the light," Henri said.

Chuck's face crumpled in fear. "I'm sorry, Bernie. I didn't mean it!"

"This is what he needs," Henri said quietly.

I wish I didn't have to. She kept pushing the walls inward, making the space inside smaller and smaller.

"I don't want to die!" Chuck pleaded, already squished into a box too small to stand in. "You're killing me."

Rough hands grabbed at her again, threatening her control. She flailed, trying to break free. "Leave me alone. I have to finish this."

"Bernie, please!" Chuck reached out to her.

She wanted to believe that she could go on being friends with him, that he'd learned from his mistakes, and that he'd never try to hurt her again. But she couldn't. "I'm sorry, too, Chuck. I wish you could be my family again."

"His family will be waiting for him." Henri's quiet words made Bernie start to cry.

"I'm his family, too." Her hands started to tremble.

"I know, *petite*."

The area inside the walls was growing warmer, but not a scorching heat that could burn. It was more like the gentle warmth of a blanket or an embrace.

"I'm scared," Chuck whimpered.

There was something on the other side that couldn't quite be put into words, but it wasn't threatening. The closest description that she could think of was that it was like knowing a warm glass of milk and cookies was waiting for her after a long walk home in the rain. "I don't think you have to be."

A shimmering flicker appeared beside Chuck, and he seemed to relax. As it grew, he began to smile. "I think I see my mom... and my brother."

Bernie could sense him growing lighter and somehow younger, as if the long years alone on Earth were being stripped away from him. He felt happy, and she sighed in relief. She'd hated the idea of forcing him into something that scared him so badly, even if it was necessary.

He looked up at her with all of the craziness and the hurt gone from his eyes. "I'm sorry. Really sorry this time for all the things I did to you. Leanne was right. I got lost and did some horrible stuff."

Bernie had no idea what to say. She couldn't tell him that what he'd done was okay. But she didn't want to say goodbye and still be mad at him. "You were my only friend for a long time."

His smile was a little sad, as if he understood what she couldn't say. "I'm glad I'm not anymore. Will you take care of her, Henri? Be her friend?"

"I promise," Henri said.

"Then I think I can go. I hope you win your revolution. Good luck, Bernie. I'll miss you." Chuck faded into the growing brilliance.

The walls disappeared from Bernie's mind, and she sat down hard.

"Are you okay?" Harley knelt in front of her.

As she touched her face, she realized that she had been crying. "I… I think so. I'm not sure what to do next."

Harley pulled her close for a hug. "None of us are when we lose a friend."

CHAPTER FORTY

"We should be at the airport," Ron grumbled from the back seat of the car. Lou would have preferred to be airborne as well, rather than stuffed into the front seat of the low-slung sports car.

"If you want Special Investigations and Dalhard Industries to know that you're not dead, then be my guest," Dani replied, her knuckles standing like white beads against the stark black of the steering wheel. She took the next turn at such a high speed that Lou grabbed at the plastic bar inside the door to steady himself. In the rearview mirror, Michael was pale and hanging on to his own door.

Lou would have thought that a woman who served as a conduit to the divine would be more cautious. When the first rumbles of the explosion began, Dani had grabbed them and shoved them into the doorway of a local shop. They had pulled a few other people with them, but there hadn't been time to clear everyone out of the way. The front of the shop had been smashed in by debris, but they had managed to escape through the back. The Goddess's direct intervention through Dani was the only reason they had managed to survive, so Lou was inclined to trust Dani's instincts for the time being.

"Once we've had a chance to check in, we can ask Gwen if there's news." Michael seemed determined to be cheerful.

"Gwen is your sister, the medium, right?" Ron asked. Lou remembered hearing the name from Bernie's lessons and Andrew suggesting that she might be someone that Bernie could talk to, using ghosts as a kind of messenger system across the continent. But he also remembered the warnings about her stability and mental health, how she often got confused, mixing up events from the past, present, and future. Having Bernie follow in Gwen's footsteps was one of Martha's greatest fears.

"We've got a rush on getting you the false papers you'll need to get back to Woodpine." Dani sped into another turn with the tires squealing on the road.

Ron opened his mouth to say something but suddenly clapped his hand over it, his shoulders heaving as he scrabbled for a fresh plastic bag. It was the third time he'd vomited since waking up from the tranquilizer dart. Lou had little sympathy or tolerance. If he'd been willing to trust Lou instead of their captors, the others wouldn't have needed to chemically subdue him. Lou took a deep breath, hoping his irritation would pass along with whatever drugs lingered in his own system. His worry about Martha, Bernie, and his family unsettled his normal patience.

"Fucking ketamine." Done vomiting for the time being, Ron scrubbed at his closed eyes with his palm.

"Don't worry," Michael said. "Dani's family has been using this house as a safe house for a long time, and Joe has promised to do what he can to make sure the investigation doesn't get this far."

Lou didn't care about investigations or *lalassu* politics. He needed to know that the people he cared about were safe.

They turned onto a narrow country road, and Dani finally slowed to a less hackle-raising speed. They arrived at a small farmhouse surrounded by ancient trees. The walls were cheerfully painted a pale green and the wraparound porch stained deep brown. An addition made of heavy stone, without visible windows or doors, stretched out to one side. The whole thing struck Lou as off. The roof wasn't steeply pitched enough to deal with heavy loads of snow, and the walls didn't seem solid enough to insulate against winter's cold.

As they got out of the car, Ron grabbed Lou's arm. "They said she had five minutes to live."

Unsure if the other man meant the statement as an accusation or an apology, Lou said nothing.

"I can't lose her." The lines around Ron's eyes made him appear just as haggard as he had when he'd first shown up in Bear Claw, running from his past and his addictions.

Neither can I. Lou shook off the other man's grip and walked up the porch steps. He wasn't going to let his brother-in-law waste any more time. If Gwen could use her medium gifts to talk to the dead and find out what had happened, then that was what they needed to concentrate on. A strange hollowness cramped his stomach, worse than spring starvation. If Martha was dead, he didn't know if he could go on. He would take care of Bernie for her, but like his own mother, his heart would already be in the spirit world with his mate.

"Welcome to Freak Central." The door was opened by a young man with curly dark hair who bore a remarkable resemblance to Dani.

"This is Vincent, Dani's brother," Michael said. Lou remembered the young man from the year he spent in Ekurru after being brainwashed by Dalhard.

"And a total pain in the ass. I've been considering going pro, but I can't pass the medical exam." Vincent grinned. "Good timing. Eric should be back soon with your papers."

Eric was the older brother, and Vincent was the younger. His irreverence reminded Lou of his own younger siblings. He hoped Mark was still safe at school. *Martha will keep Lily safe.* Lou's hands tightened into fists.

"How is she doing?" Dani asked.

"Still crazy." Vincent shrugged. "But more in a whimsical way than a straitjacket way for now. You should see her before that changes."

They left the light and airy kitchen for a narrow and dark hallway that was barred with a heavy wooden door. Lou waited impatiently, though not as visibly fidgety as Ron, while Vincent hauled the massive plank of rough-varnished wood open.

Behind the door, dim candlelight flickered. Lou's eyes adjusted quickly to the low light levels, but a bang and a muffled curse behind him suggested that Ron's did not. Dani pushed past them to join a young woman sitting cross-legged on the floor. Her thin limbs and pasty skin reminded Lou of a picture he'd seen of a cave spider, a creature born to darkness and unable to bear the light.

"I don't want to talk to Chuck." Gwen looked up at her brother with wide, frightened eyes. "He's going dark, dark, dark, and it's too far for me to follow. I'll lose my way in the forest and be eaten by the wolf."

"Hey, no one wants to eat Gwen cutlets. But we need to know if Martha, Lily, and Andrew are okay. Can you do that?" Vincent knelt in front of his sister.

Gwen jerked away from both her siblings and crawled across the floor. "I told you about the fight. Gods battle in the streets, film at eleven. Can't tell the stories without everyone seeing, peering, and visualizing. It's all in the image… a picture is worth a thousand words, but which words? What words can hold the picture, pinning it down for history and leaving a hundred bleeding holes… Holes in the dike, with a child's fingers to plug them all, but the waves come washing it all away, clear like the flood…"

"This is who we've been relying on to pass messages?" Ron growled. "What about my wife?"

"Hey, back off," Vincent replied with quiet menace. Dani stood up, her arms tense with anger that was mirrored on her face.

Ron had the grace to look embarrassed. "Sorry."

Lou watched Gwen as she rambled away with her eyes darting around the room and her fingers twitching. She was held behind walls of stone for her own safety. There was no electricity that a ghost could use to enter, and the specially constructed wards only let a few trusted spirits even come close. It was what Martha feared for Bernie, a lifetime of madness and captivity.

Slowly, he knelt on the floor, not wanting to intimidate the young medium with his size. Gwen met his steady gaze with her own haunted one.

"All hail the King of the Forest. Not a lion but a bear, shaped to hide as a man." She giggled. Then she scowled at Vincent. "I'm still not talking to Chuck. Not ever again. The old ones become demons as they forget their place and names. They become hungry and cruel, and then they are truly damned for all eternity because there's nowhere else they can go."

Bernie had said something similar about old ghosts. Lou waited until

Gwen's roving gaze fell on him. "Because they can no longer remember their ancestors."

Gwen beamed with the giant grin of a girl who got ice cream and a balloon in one afternoon at the fair. "Exactly. I knew you would understand, Growling Bear."

The hairs on the back of Lou's neck crawled. Growling bear was the literal translation of his bear name, Notaku. His grandfather had given him the name, dreaming it in one of his shaman dreams. Lou rarely used it, and he doubted that anyone would have shared it with the girl. She was even more powerful than his previously generous estimate.

Dani and Vincent both seemed ill at ease with their sister. They clearly cared for her deeply but were uncomfortable with her strangeness and unpredictability. After a lifetime with both his grandfather and his twin, Lou wasn't intimidated by spiritual power or its unconventional expression. "Gwen, you are a seer. You can see what is hidden."

Her grin vanished. "Nothing is hidden for me. I see it all. It's too much."

"Please," he whispered.

Gwen stared at him, her huge brown eyes like midnight pools. Like the hawk, she saw past the surface and into the distance. He didn't care if she saw his secrets, scraping to the core of his soul. She pulled her fingers out of her sister's grasp and reached up to trace along his cheek from his eye to the corner of his mouth. "Take me outside."

"Gwen, you can't—" Vincent began, with what seemed like real worry overcoming his irreverent attitude.

"I have to. There's too much confusion in here." Gwen grimaced, rubbing her head. "And I wasn't kidding. I can't talk to Chuck. He's on the edge of losing everything. Down, down, down into the rabbit hole, and then it will be off with their heads."

"If we take you outside, the ghosts will overwhelm you. They'll be drawn to the house, and you'll never get any peace." Vincent glared at Lou. "She's not doing this."

"There's a way. Bernie told me. I can push them back for a little while." Gwen slowly got to her feet. "And I don't need you to make my decisions. I'm not a doll, kept in the dark to play with. You can't sing the songs, play the games, and then tidy me away until next time. I can do this before the dead swarm like bees on honey."

"Maybe we should forget this if it's going to hurt her." Michael stepped between them and the door.

Dani shook her head. "If Mom was here—"

"Then she would already know what was going to happen, which would actually be kind of comforting because then we'd already know if it was a mistake." Gwen put her hand on Lou's shoulder. "Do it quickly. There's no time to waste. More and more voices will start to shout, and then it will be like listening to a poem being recited during a football match."

She was worn, fragile from the constant battering of fate, and swaying on her feet. But like his kestrel, there was a strong core underneath. His hand steadied her. "Are you sure?"

"Yes. I can do this." Gwen straightened, clinging tightly to Lou's arm. She glared at Vincent, who had his mouth open to protest. "Don't. I'm not broken, and I'm not a child. I know what I'm doing."

"Okay, but when Dani kills me, I'm coming back to haunt you, and I'm going to sing nothing but polka music." Vincent smiled at his sister before turning a serious expression back to the others. "Once you cross the salt barrier, she's going to begin to hear the voices. Try to get her outside. It's easier to deal with ghosts outdoors than it is in the house. Once we have the information, or if she gets overwhelmed, bring her back inside as quickly as possible."

Lou nodded. Vincent opened the heavy door, revealing the thick line of salt crystals outlining the barrier between Gwen's refuge and the rest of the world. Gwen went even paler, but she took the first step. Lou supported her, lightly resting one arm around her back with his hand on her elbow and the other cradling her other hand. From that position, he could catch her if she fell or gather her up if he needed to carry her.

They crossed the dark hall into the kitchen, where the last of the afternoon's light flooded the room. Gwen squinted and twisted her head but crossed the linoleum in her bare feet. Dani sprinted ahead to open the porch door, and Lou guided Gwen across the porch, down the steps, and onto the grass. She stared down at the mixture of brittle light brown and soft green.

"Does it always smell like that?" She inhaled deeply then lifted her head to look at the leaves shifting in the wind. She shivered in her thin shirt and leggings.

"Are you cold?" Lou asked.

"No," Gwen said sadly. "They're coming."

Lou could imagine voices in the rattling of leaves in the evening wind, but he knew he was deaf to the voices Gwen would hear. She closed her eyes, leaning into him as she breathed hard.

"I need someone to go to the Woodpine evaluation camp and see what's happening." Gwen opened her eyes and stared at an empty place a few feet away. "I won't talk to anyone until that happens."

She was shaking like a newly hatched bird. Lou wondered if he would find himself in the same position with Bernie one day. It brought new immediacy to Martha's determination to do better for her child than Gwen's parents had managed for her. His mouth tightened. He would do whatever was necessary in order to make sure Bernie did not end up fighting her battle alone.

Gwen's attention snapped to another spot on the lawn. "Who are you?"

There was no answer that anyone else could hear, but it didn't stop Lou and Ron from holding their breaths as if to listen.

"They brought Henri. He's been helping Bernie," Gwen reported through bloodless lips. "He says Chuck has moved on."

Ron opened his mouth as if to demand answers, but Lou's glare convinced him to shut it again.

"Andrew, Martha, and Lily are not hurt." Gwen's words earned a shout of thanks from Ron, but Lou didn't voice the relief thawing his own snow-choked fear—not when he could see the lines in Gwen's face deepening with effort.

Behind Gwen, Dani's hands crept up to her head, and she started to sway on her feet. Michael immediately ran to her side, murmuring too quietly for Lou to catch what he said.

"Incoming calls have right-of-way," Gwen muttered, her thin fingers clutching at Lou's arm. "Henri thinks he can get them out of the cells, but there's a bigger problem. Do you hear the people sing? Angry men and women rising up with blood in their hearts. Riots and cornered animals biting back."

Somehow, the internees had revolted. Angry mobs didn't always pick their targets carefully. He had to get back and get his family out. All of them.

"I think I need to go back now." Gwen gasped, her eyes wide with pain and fear.

Lou picked Gwen up and carried her back to her room. Vincent helped his sister to settle into her nest of quilts and blankets. Then he nearly shoved Lou out of the room and closed the door behind them.

Dani slouched over the kitchen counter, cradling her head as if she had one of Andrew's headaches from his early shaman training. "We have to get you back to Woodpine now."

"The Goddess sent a direct message." Michael supported his lover, letting her rest against him. "We're almost out of time, but Dani and I won't be able to go with you."

Lou studied the pair, both showing signs of exhaustion and pain. Whatever happened in those few moments outside, it had taken an extreme toll.

"Why can't you?" Ron asked.

Dani straightened, fear clouding her gaze. "Because we have to go to a place called Founder's Pass."

Chapter Forty-One

"We can't raise his suspicions. We have to act scared." Lying on the cot, Martha didn't think it would take much in the way of acting skills. Dr. Coulon had frightened her before, but after the round of torture, he terrified her.

Lily shook her head, pacing the tiny cell. "If we act too meek, he'll be suspicious."

They'd been arguing for what felt like hours, though Andrew had already lapsed into silence. Martha exhaled in exasperation, her breath condensing in a white cloud. She sat up. "What the…"

"It's freezing in here." Lily rubbed at her arms. "When did that happen?"

White frost condensed on the metal bars. Martha and Lily backed away from the door but quickly hit the rear wall.

"It's a ghost," Andrew said grimly from the other cell. "I can sense him."

"Chuck?" Martha called out tentatively. She wasn't sure if she should be relieved or scared if it was him.

"No," Andrew replied. "This isn't him. It's someone else."

The lock clicked.

Martha didn't hesitate. She grabbed the latch, hissing at the sting of the cooled metal, flung open the door, and stumbled through. Lily followed a heartbeat behind.

"Thank you," Martha said to the apparently empty air. The frost began to fade from the bars, suggesting the ghost was no longer in the room.

"A little help?" Andrew's cell door remained securely latched. Luckily, the keys were still behind the cabinet.

Footsteps echoed on the stairs between the medical building and the lab. Martha grabbed the keys and twisted open the lock before Dr. Coulon pushed back the plastic curtain. He frowned as he realized his test subjects were loose.

Lily shouted and launched herself at the doctor. He dodged, and she fell to the ground. The doctor began to reach into his pocket and Martha realized that if he got his hands on the collar remote, this fight would be over.

She dropped the keys and ran the few steps necessary. She grabbed his wrists, locking her hands around them. Dr. Coulon's eyes flashed as he tried to yank free, but Martha hung on with the strength of suppressing hundreds of tantrums.

Lily kicked at him from the floor, her feet tangling in his legs. He fell, dragging Martha down with him. Something small and plastic tumbled out of his lab coat, skittering across the concrete floor. She awkwardly jabbed at it with her foot, trying to send it far out of reach without letting go of the doctor's wrists. Her flailing kick missed.

Dr. Coulon ripped his hands loose and shoved her back into Lily. Martha landed hard on her shoulder and hip, the wind knocked out of her. *Get up!* Her body refused to obey her frantic demands, reminding her that middle-aged women did not spring to their feet like action heroes. Any second, she expected to feel the pain ripping through her body.

"Martha! Over here!" Lily shouted.

Crawling to her hands and knees, Martha got moving. She saw Lily sitting on top of the doctor's chest. He flailed and shouted at her, trying to buck her off.

"Got it!" Andrew held up the remote.

The doctor managed to twist out from under Lily's weight. Before he could get to his feet, Martha flung herself on top of him, knocking the breath out of him. He shouted as he tried to lift her off, but Martha went limp, making herself dead weight. But it wouldn't last long. His rage-filled eyes promised retribution as he struggled.

"Sedative!" she shouted, holding on grimly. Glass clattered as Andrew pawed through the vials of medication.

Dr. Coulon jerked underneath her, but Martha kept her weight limp, holding him down like a lead-lined blanket. A second jerk was less powerful, and she hoped it meant the sedative was taking effect. She didn't dare move.

"Martha, he's out." Andrew's voice penetrated her dazed determination. Strong hands, similar to Lou's but not quite the same, lifted her. Dr. Coulon was sprawled on the floor, his glasses askew and his eyes closed.

Andrew helped her to balance on her feet with a hint of a smile on his face. "I don't think they'll ever make a movie out of that particular action sequence, but it was effective."

Martha scanned the room. "No one else is coming?"

"No sign of anyone so far." Lily seemed unaffected by the rough escape, prowling about the lab and poking into the cupboards and shelves.

Martha should have been reassured. After all, the place had obviously been constructed to make sure no one could hear screams and struggles. The sinking feeling in her gut would not allow her to relax. She looked down at the unconscious doctor. "What should we do with him? He already got out of the cells once."

"We'll have to hope it doesn't happen again." Andrew grabbed Dr. Coulon's shoulders and dragged him into a cell.

After he was locked inside, they hurried up the steps to the medical building. As soon as Martha pushed open the bookcase, it became clear that all was not as it should have been in the camp. Irregular popping punctuated angry shouts. *Gunfire.*

The three of them slipped out of the medical building. The Hub and the outer camp were abandoned. No guards stood by the gates to the inner camp. Bodies lay sprawled in the churned mud, some in uniform but most in the mix of rags and layers that the internees wore. Martha swallowed hard against building sadness. *I'm sorry. This isn't how it should have been.*

People were shouting angrily in the distance. As much as she wanted to believe that Hood and Harley would have gotten Bernie away from the fighting, her instincts told her that her daughter would be right in the middle of it.

"You should stay in here," she said to Lily.

"Hell no." Lily started to push past, but Martha caught her arm.

"You're pregnant. If a stray bullet catches you, it doesn't matter how badass you are. You can't shift into a bear with that ring around your neck. You and Andrew should stay here." Inspiration struck. "In fact, you two should go to the Hub."

Lily opened her mouth as if to argue then reconsidered. Martha remembered how her own pregnancy had crept into her awareness, a kind of *I can do this—oh no, wait, I can't because I'm pregnant.* Lily's hand crept to cover her abdomen. "We have a better chance of escaping if we stay together."

Two Hispanic men crept around the barracks, one of them holding a small child. The other had his hand pressed against a dark wet spot on his shoulder.

The pair looked terrified, and Martha's heart went out to them. "This isn't about escaping anymore. We need to stop this."

"You can't be serious—" Whatever else Andrew planned to say failed to materialize when he turned to Martha.

I'm tired of dealing with anger. I'm tired of taking the easy path and not saying anything. "Most of the people working here aren't evil or even aware of Dr. Coulon and his secret lab." She took a deep breath. "We're the ones who started this uprising. And now people are dying on both sides. We owe it to them to stop this if we can."

"And how do you propose we do that? Ask the mob nicely? Or maybe you want to start with the not-so-evil guys with the guns?" Andrew's sarcasm was thick enough to serve as winter insulation.

"They're scared, cold, and hungry. They've been hurt. That's where we'll start." Martha signaled to the two men to come to them. "Andrew, get medical supplies, and then you and Lily take them to the Hub. It should still be deserted with everything going on. Open up the kitchen and start treating the injured. I'll come to you once I've found Bernie and the others.”

The two men and the child were close enough to listen, and she didn’t want them to hear her and Andrew bickering. She summoned up the comforting smile she’d used during long nights in the ER. “What are your names?”

“I’m Nicolás, and this is my brother, Sebastián,” the one holding the child said, his voice thick with tears. “They killed my wife…”

“I’m sorry.” Martha could feel her own eyes starting to glisten. “This is Andrew and his sister, Lily. They’ll take you somewhere safe and warm and take care of your injuries.”

The two men were skeptical at first, arguing briefly in Spanish. Then Nicolás shook his head. “She’s the one who’s been treating injuries in the camp. It’s not like we have a better offer.”

Sebastián nodded, earning Martha’s gratitude. She didn’t want to waste any more time arguing, not when Bernie was out there. *Hold on, baby. I’ll be there for you soon.*

“They still have not recovered the bodies.” Karan poured himself a generous portion of peat-brown whiskey. The office in the safe house was amply stocked, but he was making a severe dent in their supply.

“Patience, brother.” Priya’s attention was on her computer screens as she checked various social media accounts and news websites. “Clearing such a large amount of rubble takes time.”

The explosion had caused two buildings to collapse in the square. At five and six stories, respectively, they made for a lot of concrete and rebar to clear away. The city was projecting weeks before the area could reopen, and estimated casualty counts were in the hundreds. Police were scouring the rubble and had already shared their suspicion that the bomb had been a homemade device similar to the one used in the Oklahoma bombings.

Priya could have given them exact details, but it wouldn't have served her purpose. Eventually, they would piece together enough fragments to decide that it bore significant similarities to explosives that McBride would have seen in the Middle East during his tours of service—ones whose plans were readily available online and whose materials could be traced back to online purchases she had planted in a false computer history for McBride. It could take months for all of the evidence to be uncovered. Throughout it all, she would manipulate the media with carefully worded discoveries. By the time she was done, the people would be demanding mass testing, mass incarceration, and even executions.

That, in turn, would provoke retaliations from the *lalassu*. Hotheads on both sides would escalate. Paranoia and distrust would divide the communities, and they would be looking for someone to lead them out of the chaos. She and her brother would be perfectly positioned.

"We should not have used the transformative." Karan began to pace around the office. "It was a reckless disruption of the plan."

Turning from her computers, Priya regarded her brother coolly. "It was a calculated risk."

"How calculated could it have been?" Karan fumed. "Dr. Coulon only contacted you the day before the rally."

"Are you dissatisfied with the result?" A knife strapped to Priya's ankle was reassuringly close. A gun rested in a tear-away pouch under the desk. Her brother's behavior was shifting from understandable to alarming.

"They knew each other. That is why they refused to kill one another, even with your threats." Karan sounded exactly like their father had when he'd been in a temper.

"It was never necessary to the plan to have them kill one another," Priya reminded him. The footage of the two of them fighting was rapidly going viral. The superhuman leaps and punches and the transformation from human to animal and back fascinated and terrified. "We got what we needed, and they are both dead now, along with Danielle Harris and Detective Cabrera."

"I want to see their bodies," Karan insisted.

Such melodrama. Priya weighed the cost of adding additional resources to the recovery effort. She could claim humanitarian intentions, claiming to want to search for survivors in the rubble. It could be a minor public relations coup for Special Investigations.

A crawling tag on one of her screens caught her eye: *Unknown Savior Pulls Woman and Child to Safety During Riot.* Subconscious alarms sounded in her head, and she quickly found links to a video.

A gray-streaked woman filled the screen. "It was amazing. He picked me and Natasha up and carried us inside like we weighed nothing. The woman shouted that we needed to get to the back. She was so calm that I assumed she must be a policewoman or an ambulance driver or something. They took everyone through the back, and it was just in time. The whole front of the store was smashed in. We had to crawl out of the back door into an alley. They saved our lives. I only wish I knew who they were."

"A miracle. If our viewers have any information—" A click ended the cheerful anchor's plea for assistance.

Priya sat silently in her chair. *What are the odds that the people in the story are our targets?*

Glass and liquid crashed into the wall as Karan threw his whiskey. "I told you they had a talent for disruption."

"How could they possibly have known?" Priya stared at the screen, trying to calculate the odds. They could have subdued the snipers. It was unlikely but not impossible. There were any number of ways that they could have discovered the snipers' presence. It would take a coordinated effort to remove the agents without anyone being able to signal about the attack. She recalled the tranquilizer darts they had used to subdue the soldier. *They were prepared.* A mole in Special Investigations was the most plausible explanation, someone who could have tipped them off about yesterday's demonstration.

But they could not have known about the planted explosives. Priya had constructed and placed them herself, not trusting anyone else. Karan had been the only other living soul to know about them, and he wouldn't have undermined their goals.

"They specialize in achieving the impossible." His tense shoulders distorted the clean lines of his suit.

At last, Priya could sympathize with her brother's obsessive focus on the Harris siblings and their collaborators.

"Their psychics are more powerful than we could have anticipated." Karan's shoulders slumped. "They've destroyed everything we've worked for."

"No. They haven't," Priya said slowly. "Even if McBride and Charging Bull survived, there is no place where they can hide. People are already demanding swift reprisals from the government to ensure that this never happens again. Chatter is increasing among the intelligence communities. The landslide has begun, and it no longer matters where a few pebbles have bounced."

Karan snorted. "You have not seen what these particular pebbles can do. They escaped your snipers and explosives. They rescued the patsies we intended to blame. If one of them goes public—"

"They will appear insane and paranoid. Government-sponsored kidnappings? There is no proof." She could still spin events to their advantage and use the media to protect herself and her brother. As she examined her computer, she found a heated editorial beginning to circulate. A few keystrokes arranged for it to be shared with several biased journalists who would ensure it received wide distribution.

"Are you certain? The transformative was one of several caught trying to escape. He has a connection to the prisoners from Bear Claw. We cannot be sure what they managed to obtain." Karan smoothed down his rumpled suit jacket. "We have to contact the doctor at Woodpine."

A prudent suggestion. Priya contacted the support personnel at their lab in Juneau and directed them to get in touch with the camp. A few moments later, there was an alarming reply.

"We can't raise anyone at Woodpine, Ms. Jeevan."

"When was the last communication?" Priya asked.

"Two hours ago."

Matters were unraveling rapidly. They could not afford such a loss of control. "I want a strike team on its way in fifteen minutes."

"Yes, ma'am." The connection ended.

Priya leaned back. It had been over eighteen hours since the explosion. If their captives left immediately afterward for Woodpine, they could already be at the camp. It could be part of a coordinated mass-rescue effort.

"This is a disaster," Karan snarled.

"Panicking will not help," Priya snapped back. "We need a plan."

"Your plans are what got us into this mess in the first place. Too many convolutions, chances for the Harrises to disrupt them." He dismissed her year of effort with a wave of his hand.

Priya held tightly to her temper. Fighting with her brother was counterproductive. But she would remember his dismissal and the ease with which he blamed her. It was not a lesson that she would easily forget.

"No optimistic words about how our goals are still in reach? The plan still intact?" His mockery only firmed her resolve.

Fingering her golden bangles, she stood. *Never again a slave.* Karan seemed oblivious to her anger. She smiled and said quietly, "Fortune favors the brave, dear brother."

"And what do you propose the brave do?"

"Clear the playing board. Wipe away all of the opposing players."

Chapter Forty-Two

It didn't take much work to get the Hub open and ready for the internees. Martha got the heaters running and the kitchen powered up while Andrew searched for food and Lily tended to their first rescues, Nicolás and his brother Sebastián. She hoped that the combination of warmth and food would help tempt people away and reduce the potential for violence. "All right. I'll find Bernie and the others—"

Andrew grabbed her arm. "Don't get sentimental about the guards. You might not think they're all evil, but I'm sure that plenty of them are sick and twisted jerks who enjoyed having targets to take their rage out on."

"I'm not naïve. I know they're not innocent." Martha took a deep breath. "There must be a way to separate the bad guys from those who deserve a second chance."

"How?" he demanded.

"I don't know." She met his gaze. "This camp is done. There's no way for it to recover. The guards are on the run, the staff is terrified, and the internees are desperate. If we can get people calmed down and taken care of, then we can start working on getting everyone evacuated to someplace safe. But we can't do that if we're dodging bullets or angry mobs."

It wasn't enough to convince Andrew. "You don't think the *lalassu* are entitled to some revenge for what they've been through?"

"They deserve justice. They deserve to get their lives back." The passionate words spilled out of Martha in a way she'd never expected. "Killing won't get them that. Revenge won't get them that. They're entitled to be angry. I'm angry, too. Everyone should be angry about what happened here. But I want the people responsible to pay for it, and aside from the doctor, they're not physically here. I want every person in this camp who has suffered to be able to stand up and tell the world what happened here."

A look of respect replaced his angry expression. "Be careful. Lou will never forgive me or himself if something happens to you."

"And I'll never forgive myself if something happens to Bernie while you and I are arguing." Martha stepped back.

"Go. Lily and I will take care of things here." Andrew turned back to the kitchen, and Martha left the Hub, plunging deeper into the chaos.

Moving slowly to avoid getting caught in crossfire, she stopped to check the bodies lying in the mud and to look for people hiding from the violence. Most of the prone figures were beyond her help, but there were a few she arranged to be carried back to the Hub. Those hiding seemed to be grateful to have someplace to go. Luckily, no one seemed to question her motives, although a few recognized her as staff rather than an internee. It seemed she'd made an impression by treating their injuries and infections.

As she got closer to the shouting, she realized the gunfire had tapered off. There were also a lot more people around, all of them focused inward to the center of the crowd. She spotted Hood's dark bald head standing above the others and fought her way to him.

"Martha?" His jaw dropped when he saw her. "When— How?"

"We got out. Is Bernie okay?" She gripped his arm to keep from getting pulled away.

"She's with Harley and Eva," he shouted above the crowd noise. "We were trying to get rid of the collars, but there was an incident with Chuck."

Martha formed an *o* with her mouth.

Hood hurried to reassure her. "Bernie's okay. She got rid of him, and she said she would send Henri to help you guys get out. I'm glad to see it worked." He gestured at the angry mob. "We were going to mount a rescue, but things got out of hand. Before we knew it, we had a full-blown riot."

A fresh burst of gunfire caused them both to duck automatically.

"The internees have trapped a bunch of guards in one of the barracks. The guards have been trying to keep them back with their guns," Hood said.

Martha's plan for a peaceful resolution took a step back. "They're firing into the crowd?"

"No. It's mostly over their heads."

Maybe there was still a chance. She told Hood about her plan to get the internees over to the Hub.

"It's possible. If we take out the guards, take their weapons, and try to keep bloodshed to a minimum, it could work." Hood grimaced. "I've seen this sort of thing before. People want payback, and they'll turn on each other when they don't feel satisfied… Oh, shit."

The crowd began to chant. "Burn! Burn! Burn!"

"We better get up there." Hood started pushing his way through to the inner circle, Martha following in his wake. As they got closer, there was a strong scent of gasoline and smoke. Coughing, Martha realized the crowd was surrounding one of the barracks, crowding the broken-down door. At the opposite end of the building, three men were working on something near the ground. Broken bits of furniture and irregular planks were heaped together with thin trickles of smoke creeping out of the gaps.

"It's not catching. The wood is too damp." One of the men threw a plank to the side in frustration. He was a big fellow with a long, scraggly gray-brown beard and ponytail. From his tattoos, Martha guessed he'd probably been a member of a motorcycle club before coming to Woodpine.

"Add more gas. Then it'll burn." The second man was skinny and pale, with sharp cheekbones and sunken, wild eyes. His fervent gaze stayed fixed on the barracks with a zealot's intensity.

"I'm not blowing myself up to smoke them out," the third man grumbled, scratching at his patchy brown beard and greasy hair.

"Wait," Martha shouted. "Let me talk to them."

That got the crowd's attention. All of their eyes turned to her, and the fierce hostility hit her like a blow to the chest.

She held her ground. "We've taken over the Hub. There's food and blankets there. Anyone who wants to can go there and get warm and fed while we figure out the next steps to getting all of you home."

Some people at the fringes of the crowd began to turn and walk toward the hulking administrative building. Those who remained were eager for blood.

Martha tried again. "Let me talk to them and get them to surrender to you."

She searched the crowd but didn't see any faces she recognized. She'd hoped to see one of the internees that she'd helped, but the tense faces with narrowed eyes and mouths all began to blur together in their collective anger.

"She's one of them!" a woman's voice shouted.

The people near Martha reached out to grab her, but Hood suddenly stood between her and them. His arm darted out, and then the closest one was kneeling on the ground, his wrist caught in Hood's grasp. He'd twisted the hand hard enough that the wrist must be close to breaking.

"No, she isn't." Hood's voice boomed across the camp, cutting through the furious muttering. "We came here to gather evidence about what happened to you. Martha found evidence against the doctor and his experiments on you. She found documents that prove their test is flawed. She snuck food to those who were trapped in the doctor's secret lab, despite the fact that Ryan Blake threatened her life when he found out."

The hostility level lowered but didn't disappear entirely. A young woman stepped forward, and Martha recognized her as the one with a burned arm from her first day.

"She stood up to the guards for me," she said.

"She's still one of them."

Martha didn't see who spoke, but from the crowd's reaction, she hadn't entirely won them over.

"Let her go," the zealot from the fire called out. "If they shoot her the way they did the others, it's no loss to us."

The surface of the crowd bobbed as people nodded, some of them looking downright gleeful in anticipation of her demise.

Sure, trust the crazy guy. At least it was a chance. Martha approached the barracks slowly. "Hello?"

"Back off, or we'll shoot!" It sounded like a young man, panicking and on a hair trigger.

"Please, don't." Martha raised her hands over her head. "I'm unarmed, and I only want to talk. Can I come to the door?"

She couldn't make out the low conversation that followed her request, but she didn't have to wait long for an answer. The same voice called out, "Okay."

First hurdle down. Ten steps took her to the broken door. "Is anyone hurt?"

"They ripped open Frank's leg. He's bleeding pretty bad."

Martha put a foot inside the barracks, but Hood caught her arm. "Negotiations first, medical attention second. Or you're going to become another hostage."

Reluctantly, she placed her foot back on the ground. "We can't treat Frank until we know it's safe. If you toss out your weapons, we can escort you to someplace secure. The camp has been taken over and is going to be disbanded." She wasn't sure if it was the right word, but it was more important to keep talking.

"We can't let the loocies escape!" an older voice interjected. It was tight, as if the owner was in pain. Martha wondered if it belonged to the wounded Frank.

"The *lalassu* never should have been here in the first place," she said firmly. "Being born different doesn't make someone an automatic criminal. But no matter how you feel about it, are you ready to die to keep this camp running?"

Silence.

"I have evidence of what's been happening here." She wasn't sure if they still had the film she'd collected, but the doctor's records were all intact and waiting in the secret lab. "Medical experimentation, torture, people kidnapped based on a faulty chemical test. But even if you don't believe me about that, then trust what you've seen for yourself. Inadequate shelters and food, mass-inflicted punishments, and no chance at appeal or to prove that a person isn't a threat. They've been judged guilty without any chance at ever proving they were innocent. That can't be okay with you when you take the time to think about it."

More silence. She held her breath. *They must realize how wrong this camp is.*

"Sounds like they ain't interested in surrender." The biker man crossed his tattooed forearms.

Martha turned around to face the shadowed interior again. "Please. Come out, and you won't be hurt."

A man walked forward into the light, his hands raised to his shoulders. His pinky finger was missing on his right hand. Martha recognized him from her first day. She helped him out of the barracks, and he stood facing the mob with a stoic expression on his face.

"I just wanted a job." His voice projected clearly over the murmuring crowd. "This was the first paycheck I've had in a long time."

"I lost my job when you people arrested me." An older woman shoved her way to the front, her chin jutting out and her eyes wild with anger. "I was a nurse, and I never even knew I had any powers. But you took me away and dumped me up here."

"The people who made that decision aren't here," Martha said gently. "The men in that building can give testimony and make sure they pay for their choice. And if you're a nurse, I could use your help. I can't take care of everyone all by myself. Please, will you help?"

"I won't tend any of them." The woman spat on the ground. "But I'll help the people from the camp."

"Thank you." More movement inside caught Martha's eye. Two men walked into the light, carrying a third between them. As they came closer, she saw the blood-soaked pant leg and realized it was the injured Frank.

"Will you really help him?" the one on her left asked. With a start of surprise, Martha recognized him as Paul Graysmith, the young guard from the camp gates. He still looked barely old enough to be out of high school but much more worn and afraid.

"Put him down on the floor so I can dress his leg." Belatedly, she remembered Hood's warning. "How many more are in there?"

"It's only us. Mr. Blake took a bunch of the guards and took off." Paul lowered the injured man.

Which means Ryan is still out there. Martha's mouth dried. She doubted he would surrender as easily as these men had. Numbly, she examined the leg wound. It was deep, but not spurting. If she stitched it and wrapped it well, it would be fine. She issued the necessary instructions. By the time he was ready, most of the crowd had dispersed, presumably for the Hub. The drama of the moment was long over, but there were still some men and women standing nearby with hate-filled eyes.

Martha couldn't blame them for their anger—it was justified—and as she helped to carry Frank to the medical building, she couldn't help feeling that she deserved to be the target. She'd slept comfortably while they froze. She'd eaten while they starved. *Maybe I didn't do all that I could have, but I'm doing what I can now.* It wasn't perfect, but it would have to do. She hoped things would go better once everyone got some sleep and food. Straightening, she moved as fast as she dared without making Frank's injuries worse, eager to see her daughter.

Hood and Harley brought Bernie to the medical building as Martha finished stitching up Frank's leg. No sign of injury marred her beautiful daughter, and Martha breathed a silent prayer of relief.

Bernie ran to Martha and threw her arms around her. Martha held her tightly, ignoring her unwashed hands. "I'm so glad you're safe."

"We'll take Frank to the Hub and put him with the other staff," Hood offered. He and Harley lifted the injured man and carried him out the door, leaving Martha and Bernie alone.

"Harley made me and Eva hide while he and Annika went into detention to get everyone out." Bernie sounded disappointed. "Henri kept an eye on all of you for me."

"Thank you for sending Henri to help us." Martha pulled back so that she could see Bernie's face. "Hood told me what happened with Chuck. I'm sorry."

"I was, too. But then I could feel what he felt when he started to go into the light. It was like it washed all the bad stuff away. He was like my friend again."

"I'm glad, honey." Martha smoothed away Bernie's hair then realized she'd left red smears on her daughter's cheek. She found a cloth and wiped at the marks before scrubbing her fingers clean.

"We didn't even know that ghosts could pick locks until Chuck said he'd done it so the doctor would get out." Bernie glanced at the office door. "He's still down there, isn't he?"

"Yes." They'd checked on him before she started to work on Frank's leg. He was still unconscious from the sedative.

"He hurt you really badly." Bernie's lip started to tremble.

Martha held her closely. "He did, but I'm okay. And he's not going to hurt anyone else ever again." She hesitated, wanting to know but unsure if it would be too much for her daughter. "Did Henri check on Lou?"

"He and Ron are okay. There was a big fight that scared a lot of people, but they didn't get hurt. Not even when the building blew up." Bernie pulled free from the embrace. "Can we go get something to eat?"

"Of course," Martha said automatically, not sharing her daughter's calm acceptance of such things. *A building blew up? A big fight?*

"Lou isn't as grouchy as I thought he was. He's actually a pretty good listener," Bernie commented as they walked to the Hub. "I miss him."

"Me too," Martha said softly. *Please be safe, and come back to us soon.*

Chapter Forty-Three

If Lou never took another plane again, it would be too soon. He gritted his teeth as the wheels bounced on the airfield. He'd spent ten hours of flying with a ninety-minute stop to refuel, and every minute had been spent worrying about Martha, Bernie, Andrew, and Lily. If Dr. Coulon or Ryan hurt any of them—the package of trail mix crackled as he crushed it in his fist.

"We're still not getting any signals from the camp. But it's not on fire, so that's a good sign." Vincent's sense of humor hadn't improved from what Lou remembered. If Dani hadn't insisted on her brother accompanying them, Lou would have refused to let Vincent get within five hundred miles of Bear Claw again. From the expression on Ron's face, he was of a similar opinion.

No guards rushed out to meet their tiny plane as it slowed. The helicopters were gone, and presumably the soldiers were with them, which was a relief. The plane finally stopped, and Lou jumped out of his seat to open the small jet's door and lower the stairs.

"Thank you for flying Air *Lalassu*. Make sure your tray tables and seatbacks are in the upright and locked position. Because it's the last chance you'll have to be in control of anything ever again." Vincent unbuckled his seat belt and leaned back.

"Shut up," Ron growled.

Lou couldn't get the door to release. He gripped it in both hands, ready to tear it out of the frame.

"Hey!" Vincent leapt up and tried to shoulder Lou aside. "If you break the plane, that's bad. Remember?"

"Open it." Lou stepped back, his shoulders and neck aching from the effort of staying in the skin.

Still muttering, Vincent twisted the mechanism, and the door unfolded from the plane. Lou ignored the short stairs and jumped to the ground. Ron followed him, only a second or two behind.

"That's the Hub?" Ron pointed at the administrative building, clearly visible in the distance. Lou nodded, and the two men began to run, ignoring Vincent's protests.

Where are the guards? No one challenged them as Lou's strides ate up the distance between the airfield and the Hub. A few people shouted at him as he passed the rows of staff trailers, but his focus stayed fixed on the doors separating him from the people he cared about. While Ron and Vincent took over the Hub, he would go through the tunnels and get Martha, Lily, and Andrew out. And if anyone got in his way… *No mercy.*

He burst through the front doors and skidded to a halt. The long cafeteria was full of people who blocked the view like trees in a forest. *Where had they all come from?*

"Chief? Where have you been?" Tom stepped forward, his hand still wrapped in a bandage.

"Kicking ass in full view of television cameras, from what I hear." Andrew emerged from the milling throng. "Glad to see you won."

Lou clasped his brother's shoulder as human words failed him. *Where is Martha? And Bernie and Lily?*

"You would not believe what's been going on here, Chief. Did you know they were keeping people locked up in some weird basement?" Tom shook his head. "It was crazy. Now the guards are all locked up, and they say we're all going to get to go home."

Lou repressed the urge to swat the boy out of his way and go searching for his family.

"Martha is all right. She's the one who organized all this. I'm not often wrong about people, but I'm glad I was in this case," Andrew said softly. "Bernie is fine, too. She finally banished Chuck but picked up a new ghost, Henri. This one seems more stable."

And she did it without Andrew's help. Lou doubted anyone else would have picked up the professional sting in his twin's words. But all Lou felt was pride. Bernie was another fierce kestrel, just like her mother.

The doors behind him banged open as Ron and Vincent charged in.

"Lily and the baby are all right, too. She's not listening to me about getting some rest but doing well nonetheless." Andrew raised his voice. "We finally got the blasted metal collars off a few hours ago. Lily has been helping Martha up in the front office."

People were clogging the short hall between the front office and the cafeteria. Some were lying down and bundled in blankets, while others were eating out of an assortment of plastic bowls and cups. Lou pushed past them all with Ron right at his heels. As they rounded the corner, he searched the crowd's faces for Martha or Bernie. But he kept finding stranger after stranger.

"…through enough." Martha's adamant declaration pierced the noisy chatter, giving him something to track. Lou stepped around a pair of teenage girls and finally spotted what he was looking for.

She was talking with Hood. Her blond hair was in what had probably been a sensible braid but was frayed and puffy like a shedding bison. Her eyes were dark and shadowed as if she hadn't slept since they'd last seen one another. She wore a mismatched oversized sweatshirt and jeans that were too short for her, revealing several inches of pale ankle. Her hands were making slashing motions across her waist as she argued with Hood.

Lou had never seen anything so beautiful in his entire life. For a split second, his human and bear halves were both floating in sated relief. His mate was safe.

"Ron!" Lily's shout broke the brief moment of contentment.

Martha broke off her argument to scan the room. Her eyes met his, and it was like the first glimpse of sunlight after the long arctic winter. The brilliance was too much for dark-dazzled eyes to bear.

She walked away from Hood as if she couldn't quite believe what she was seeing. Her eyes swept over him as if searching for injuries.

Lou couldn't wait any longer. He rushed forward and swept her up in his arms. Finally, he could breathe her scent, feel her warmth, and know in the most primal way that she was unharmed.

"You're back. You're really back," she whispered against his chest, her fingers curling into his shirt to latch on.

He tilted her head up to capture her mouth in a fierce kiss. As their lips met, the hubbub around them disappeared from his awareness. The only thing he cared about was the woman in his arms, the soft press of her body against his, and the fire blazing below his belt, demanding that he demonstrate how much he'd missed her.

From the way she responded, she'd been just as worried about him as he had been about her. Her hands crept up his neck and twined into his hair as she deepened their kiss, adding red-hot coals to an already raging fire.

"Mom? Lou?" Bernie's question was the only thing that could have broken through. "Public place."

Martha pulled back but kept her forehead pressed against Lou's. Their breath intermingled in hot puffs of air. "I wasn't sure we'd both live long enough for me to tell you this, but I love you."

"I love you, too," he whispered, leaning in to steal a quick kiss.

"Oh, don't start minding the audience now. They're certainly not." Vincent jerked his head toward Ron and Lily, who were still intertwined.

Lou ignored him, his attention focused on Bernie. She was turning away, with lowered eyes and her hands curling around her stomach. He called her name.

As she lifted her head, she made an effort to smile, but he saw the uncertainty and fear lurking behind the supportive mask. She'd already been abandoned by one parent, and it was perfectly human to wonder if he would end up supplanting her in her mother's affection. "I can give you guys some privacy. It's no big deal. I should probably talk to Henri anyway and find out what's going on."

Lou knelt in front of her, still holding Martha's hand. "You might not be my daughter in blood, but I would like you to be mine in spirit."

"Are you serious?" Bernie looked at each of them in turn. From Martha's firm squeeze on his fingers, he guessed that she approved of his offer.

"It is up to you," he said. "And you don't need to decide now. I will be in both of your lives from now on."

"Yes, you will." Martha's eyes were shining as she smiled.

For an answer, Bernie threw herself at him, wrapping her arms around his neck for a rare and generous hug. He held her tightly, promising to keep them both safe.

"This is sweet and all, but we've got other stuff that needs to be taken care of," Vincent interrupted.

Lou shot him an irritated look as he rose to his feet.

"He's right." Martha straightened, her expression sobering. "We've rounded up most of the guards and staff. The worst offenders have been put in the cells below with Dr. Coulon. Those we aren't certain of have been confined to their trailers. Mrs. Fitz had some choice words to say about it, but we convinced her it was in her best interest to stay put."

"I've had Henri searching, but we can't find Ryan anywhere," Bernie added.

"He's got at least three armed men with him. They ransacked the warehouse badly enough that we can't be sure what they've taken," Martha said. "We've been keeping the internees in the Hub so that he can't ambush anyone. We've been trying to get rid of whatever is blocking satellite signals. The lab at Juneau has been trying to reach us through the shortwave radio."

Vincent grimaced. "It's a safe bet that they've realized they're not in charge anymore. They'll be sending in a team to fix that."

A ripple of fear went through those watching and listening.

"Last bombshell," Vincent said, "there's no way we can evacuate everyone before they get here."

There were signs of panic in the faces around them. Wide darting eyes, rapid movements, and shuffling feet suggested that people were starting to think about escaping.

"Now listen to me, people. You all know the game has changed over the last year." Vincent sounded uncharacteristically serious. "It's time we added some rules of our own. They know we're out here, but they don't know everything that we can do."

He turned in a circle, looking at everyone. Then his mouth spread in an infectiously confident grin. "I'd say it's time we showed them."

"He's right." Martha's voice carried easily over the worried mutterings. "We've worked together so far, and we're not going to abandon each other now. So let's start preparing. If you have abilities, this is the time to share them. Then we can figure out how to stop anyone who comes here wanting to put a collar around our throats again."

Scattered applause began to build. Lou surveyed the crowd. Some people still seemed afraid, but most of them were determined. They'd broken free and had no intention of being captives ever again. Even the former staff were on board. Tom was nodding and clapping along with the internees.

"I'll start taking notes. I've got a good idea of what different bloodlines might be out there," Vincent offered.

"I'll go talk to Hood and Harley and coordinate." Andrew lowered his voice. "Martha, you've been going for nearly twenty-four hours now. You need to rest."

"There's still so much to do." She bit her lip, looking up at Lou.

He noticed the dark shadows under her eyes.

"We're going to need you later. You're one of the few people who both sides of this camp trust. For now, take your family, and get some rest for a few hours." Andrew glanced over to where Ron and Lily were sitting together. "I'm going to insist on the same for her."

"What about Hood and Harley? And Eva? They've been working as long as I have." Martha frowned.

"They took a break about six hours ago. So did I, if you remember. You're the only one who hasn't." Andrew gestured toward the door with his chin. "Go. Use one of the trailers so that no one bothers you."

"Come on, Mom. I'm wiped." Bernie leaned against her mother with a yawn.

Martha reluctantly agreed, and the three of them left the Hub. The camp was quiet, almost peaceful.

"We buried Malila and the others," Martha said softly as they walked. "Andrew did a ritual to ease their spirits into the next world."

The news soothed Lou's aching conscience. There were still the cubs imprisoned in the Juneau facility to rescue, but at least his kin were no longer being carved up for science.

"What happens next?" Bernie asked.

"We'll have to find somewhere to live," Martha said. "We're still going to be fugitives."

Bear Claw wasn't safe any longer. As much as Lou wanted to return to his home, his family would need a fresh sanctuary. His ancestors had migrated from Northern California before, and they would migrate again. They would find somewhere to bring Mark, Grandfather, Setsuné, and whoever else was left.

"Hood and Harley still have all the evidence we collected." Martha opened the door to their trailer.

"Wait!" Bernie shouted, grabbing at her mother's arm. Lou instantly went on the alert.

Martha stepped back, checking with her daughter.

"There's someone inside." Bernie backed away, pulling her mother with her. Lou stepped between them and the trailer door as it pushed open from the inside.

Ryan stepped out, holding something in his hand. "Little bitch spoiled my surprise. And after I waited so long, too."

Lou pushed Martha and Bernie back, preparing to tackle the man.

"Ah! Don't take another step, or we'll all die." Ryan held up the object in his hand. It was a small plastic square with long wires leading back into the trailer. "This is the trigger for a bomb that I've rigged under this trailer. I let go of this button, and it goes boom."

As much as he wanted to rip the man limb from limb, Lou couldn't risk Bernie and Martha's lives. It was one thing to trust Martha to protect herself, but bombs didn't respect fierceness. "I'm the one you want. Let the others go."

"No, I'm pretty pissed off at all of you." Ryan's fist tightened on the detonator as he eyed Bernie, who stood half hidden behind Martha. "How'd you know I was inside?"

"Henri told me," Bernie said. "He's a ghost."

"You're a better liar than your mom. How'd you really know?" Ryan shook his head. "It doesn't matter. Get inside."

Lou wasn't about to obey the instructions of a madman with a bomb, much less trust Martha and Bernie's lives to him. *Could it be a bluff?* The construction crews hadn't used blasting caps or dynamite.

"We're not going anywhere with you. That thing probably isn't even real." Martha held her ground.

"Pain in the ass to the end. You ruined everything," Ryan hissed, stepping forward. "It's real enough. We planned to set up mines outside the fence, but it didn't work out. Everything was still sitting in the warehouse. I wanted to make sure that none of you got away."

He might be right. Lou could have overpowered him if he'd had a gun. He wondered whether the bomb was powerful enough to hurt Martha and Bernie if Lou threw himself on top of Ryan.

Bernie was muttering to herself under her breath.

"Please, let my daughter go," Martha pleaded. "She doesn't have anything to do with this."

"So she can go running to get help? How stupid do you think I am?" Ryan's eyes darkened.

Lou would try jumping on him and hope that it would give Martha and Bernie time to run.

"It's going to be okay," Bernie said suddenly. "We can go inside."

Lou frowned, and Martha shook her head.

"Trust me." Bernie stepped out from her mother's grasp. "Please. I don't want anyone to get hurt."

"Smart kid. Get moving." Sweat glistened on Ryan's face and neck.

"No. I refuse to cooperate to make it easier for you to kill us." Martha straightened. "You're a coward and a bully, and you might want to hurt us, but I doubt you're actually willing to kill yourself to do it."

There was no sanity in Ryan's eyes. His thumb lifted off the button. "Wrong."

Lou covered Bernie and Martha with as much of his body as he could, shifting to the fur to increase his size in a desperate attempt to shield them. He growled as he waited for the explosion.

Bernie reached up and petted his muzzle. "It's okay."

He lifted his head at an agonized yell from Ryan. The man stood beside the trailer, jabbing the button on his trigger over and over again.

"Henri pulled the wires. He's getting pretty good at moving stuff," Bernie shared.

Martha blinked in surprise then smiled. "Thank you, Henri."

Lou straightened his legs and growled at Ryan. The human screamed and tried to run.

It was easy for Lou to catch up in a few loping strides. He knocked the scavenger down with one platter-sized paw. Ryan tumbled to the ground, and Lou made sure he stayed there, despite the man's writhing and shouting. He growled, making sure his captive got a good look at his sharp fangs.

Bernie shouted back, "No one messes with my family."

CHAPTER FORTY-FOUR

As Martha crouched beside Bernie in the scant brush surrounding the airfield, she wished she'd been able to take the nap that Andrew had suggested. Instead, she'd spent an hour installing Ryan in the cell next to the doctor then supervised the removal of all the explosive devices from the trailer and then gotten caught up in a debate about how to handle the incoming Special Investigations team. By the time she'd gotten everyone to agree to at least try nonlethal means, there wasn't enough time for her to relax and get any real rest.

I hope this works. Their plan was more of a rough guideline than a detailed masterpiece. Hood and Harley were manning posts around the perimeter of the airfield, each of them with a team of *lalassu*. Andrew and Lou had both shifted to the fur. Andrew waited near the road, prepared to cut off any exit. Lou lay nearby, his paws stretched out beside his long snout. Annika, the most vocal advocate for shooting them all and worrying about the details later, had sulked when denied one of the guards' rifles but brightened when given the job of securing any captives. They discovered a box of new shock collars in the warehouse, and Annika's thumb was ready for the trigger.

Ron had lost the argument with Lily about her staying safely away from the field of combat. The pair were a short distance away, but Martha couldn't see any sign of them through the brush. On her other side, she could see Vincent, leaning against a tree trunk with a bright-orange hard hat over his eyes. He looked far more relaxed than he should for someone leading a ragtag force against a well-trained special-ops invasion.

"Henri says the helicopters have been spotted," Bernie said in a low voice, thrilled to be included. Allowing her to use Henri and Mr. Marshall to coordinate the different groups was safe enough, and Martha trusted that either she or Lou would be able to whisk her away if the need arose.

Bernie had also coordinated communication with Gwen and the rest of the Harris family. Virginia hadn't been pleased to learn about her daughter's field trip outside of the ghost wards, but she still used her impressive organizational talents to coordinate an evacuation for the camp. If they could prevent the Special Investigations team from recapturing the internees, they could have everyone safely away within twenty-four hours.

A rapid thwat-thwat-thwat announced the imminent arrival of the helicopters. Vincent was supposed to be coordinating the attack, but he wasn't moving. Martha wondered if she should take over. *No one could possibly sleep through this.* It must be one of his perpetual jokes.

The helicopters appeared over the trees, coming in fast to land. Martha used balled-up mittens as makeshift ear protectors, and Bernie did the same. Lou nudged her with his nose and moved away to get into position. Martha offered up a final general prayer for luck and a more specific one for her family: *Please be safe.*

As the first helicopter's landing skids touched the dry and withered grass, a soldier wearing full combat armor and scanning the horizon with his rifle peered out of the open door. The other two helicopters landed a short distance away, their blades kicking up a wall of wind-blown grit amid a deafening roar from the motors.

The roar abruptly went silent.

The rotors on the top of the helicopter still turned but were slowing like an unplugged fan. Inside the nearest one, the pilot frantically pushed buttons with no effect. White frost painted the nose of each helicopter, evidence of the ghosts disrupting the engines' electrical signals. Martha exhaled softly. *Phase one is done.*

A half dozen soldiers hopped out of each helicopter with their weapons raised. They stayed in a tight formation as they abandoned the useless machines.

Leaves rustled beside Martha as Vincent stood up and walked onto the airfield with his hands held high over his head. "Ladies and gentlemen."

Guns swung around, and triggers clicked, but nothing fired.

Another sigh of relief passed Martha's lips. *Phase two is successful.* Four of the internees had the ability to psychically suppress small fires. Anything bigger than a candle would be beyond them, but the tiny sparks to launch a bullet were well within their abilities. They could only do it for a short time, but Vincent's actions allowed them to time their efforts.

From his grin, he loved the attention. "I'm afraid that we've had a change in management, and you are no longer welcome here. However, we know it's been a long flight, so we're more than happy to put you up in the same accommodations that you planned to use for us."

"You don't want to do this," one of the soldiers called. "I'm sure we can talk this out."

It was Martha's cue. She stood up and followed Vincent onto the airfield, keeping her hands visible. It was a peculiar feeling to not be able to trust men and women wearing the uniform that was supposed to be a symbol of protection and security. But she had become one of the people forced outside of the ranks of those protected, and those she cared about had been defined as an enemy by a quirk of genetics.

"There isn't much to talk about. This camp is an atrocity based on a lie." She explained the faulty test, the shock collars, and the experiments in a few terse, charged sentences.

From their reactions, it was news to about half the soldiers—but not to the other half.

"I can understand that you're frustrated, but armed revolt isn't the best way to accomplish your goals. You need to be reasonable."

"Reasonable? Is it reasonable to imprison people who haven't committed any crimes? They've been reasonable enough, and now they're leaving." Martha glanced over at Vincent.

"As fun as sharing these facts has been, it's time for you all to throw down your weapons and surrender," he instructed.

"We can't do that—"

Vincent lowered his hands. "Don't make the mistake of assuming that it's a choice."

Phase three. A family of telekinetics who had been arrested for manipulating the gambling tables in Vegas responded to Vincent's signal. The guns clattered down onto the ground.

Before any of the soldiers could retrieve the weapons lying at their feet, the fighters who were waiting in reserve stepped forward. Lou, Lily, and Andrew were magnificent in their bear forms. Hood, Harley, and Ron were quietly impressive, standing ready to attack. Dozens of other internees backed them up, some of them with eyes literally blazing with power. Martha wasn't sure what the variously colored glows meant, but it certainly gave a clear message of intimidation.

It was the moment of truth. The psychics who suppressed fire were tapped out. The telekinetics wouldn't be able to drag the heavy guns out of range. If any of the soldiers decided to fight, they could grab the weapons, and the *lalassu* wouldn't be able to stop them. The internees would have numbers on their side, but many of them would get hurt or killed before the soldiers were subdued.

"We're giving you an opportunity to surrender so that no one gets hurt." Martha couldn't see the soldiers' eyes behind their face shields, but she stared at each of them in turn. "Please take it."

For a long, tense minute, she thought they were going to fight. But then they began raising their hands in surrender. Led by Annika, a group of volunteers came out and kicked away the weapons, stripped off the combat gear, and bound the soldiers' hands.

Vincent's rounded shoulders suggested he was disappointed in the surrender. Maybe he'd been hoping for a more gladiatorial response. Martha could only feel relief. *We're going to get out of here.* She and Lou and Bernie would find a place for their family.

"Should have known better than to expect a fair fight from you loocies," one of the soldiers muttered as Annika stripped off his combat armor.

She snorted. "Guns versus starving people. Sounds totally fair to me."

Vincent sauntered over and picked up one of the discarded

handguns. Catching the complainer's attention, he snapped the gun in half with his bare hands.

The soldier flinched.

"You know," Vincent began conversationally, "I'd hoped to find some Sirens in camp, then we could turn you all into our willing supporters. I guess they could use their talents to avoid capture. Most of the powerful *lalassu* could. What you have here are the ones who aren't so powerful. They have minor gifts, like snuffing out candles or knocking over a beer can. But the funny thing is, working together, those minor gifts took out your entire squad in less than five minutes."

From the angry glare, Martha didn't think the soldier appreciated Vincent's point.

"Don't worry. We'll be out of your hair soon enough. Once we're gone, we'll make sure someone comes to pick you up." Vincent's smile took on a hard edge. "When you do, pass on a message for us. We aren't playing by your rules anymore. You didn't want us among you? Fine. We're more than happy to never deal with your stupid prejudices again because we're not going to be living under your control anymore."

Martha's spine stiffened with pride. She moved to stand beside Lou, burying her hand in his ruff. No more passively accepting what the world had to offer her and hoping for the best.

Vincent's pause was only for dramatic effect. "Oh, and if you're stupid enough to think that you can come after us again, I suggest you rethink it. We're done hiding. So if you attack, we will come back at you with all of our abilities, and it won't just be the minors. You don't stand a chance against us."

"Well, that was exhausting, *petite*." Henri threw himself down in front of Bernie with his arm flung over his eyes as she packed her things from the trailer. "More days like this one will be the death of me."

She giggled. "You're already dead."

"Then I'll probably be fine." He sat up and poked a finger through the box. "But it was tiring. I don't think I've ever tried to do so much physical interaction before. I don't know how poltergeists do it."

"Thank you for getting my mom out of the lab." Bernie glanced at where her mother and Lou were curled up together on the bed, both sound asleep. It still didn't seem real that they were going to be a family. Most kids would probably have been upset at the idea of a stepdad, and Bernie still wasn't sure how it would all work out, but she hoped Lou would keep the worried, empty look out of her mother's eyes.

"Picking a lock was definitely easier than seizing a helicopter engine." Henri shrugged. "When do you leave?"

Is he planning to go into the light now that everything is over? Bernie folded a shirt and carefully put it into the box. "We'll be on the last flight out with Lily and Ron. Mom wanted to make sure that everyone was okay."

"What about the evidence you collected?" Henri asked.

"Hood, Harley, and Eva took it with them when they left with the first groups. They'll make copies and make sure it gets out to the public." Bernie picked up another shirt, avoiding Henri's gaze. "Thanks for sticking around after Leanne went. I guess this is goodbye."

He drifted up a few inches in surprise. "Are you kicking me out? Exorcising me from your life?"

"I thought you'd want to move on and be with Leanne or something," Bernie muttered, resisting the urge to kick the boxes. *I can so be mature.* "You said you weren't afraid of the light anymore."

"It doesn't mean I'm in a hurry to jump into the existence-ending brilliance. Besides, you could use me." He tilted his head to one side. "Don't you want to find out more about this Founder's Pass place they're sending you to?"

"Bernie, who are you talking to?" Martha asked sleepily from the doorway.

"Henri. He's offering to tell us about Founder's Pass." Bernie leaned back to see if Lou was still asleep. He was sitting up in bed but wasn't making an effort to join them, instead giving them the space they needed without intruding.

"Are you worried about going there?" Martha sat down on the sofa, patting the seat beside her.

"I don't know. It'll be weird, not hiding who I am and having other *lalassu* around." She leaned against her mother the way she used to when she was little and scared by the voices in the dark.

Martha held her with one arm wrapped around her shoulders. "From what I understand, it'll be a retreat of sorts. *Lalassu* will have the choice to come and live there if they want to live openly and without having to be afraid of what the government or anyone else will do to them."

"It used to be an old mining town, but no one has lived there for years," Henri shared. "There are rows and rows of houses with no one living in them."

Bernie told her mother what Henri said. "It sounds kind of creepy," she added.

"It does," Martha crinkled her nose and smiled. "But after a year of living in that cabin, I bet we can make it into something great."

"At least I'll have my own room." Bernie glanced again at Lou. "And you can help us to fix it up."

"Count on it," he rumbled in his gravelly voice. It was nice to listen to when he wasn't being all growly. It made Bernie feel safe—like he was watching out for her.

But there was something she needed to ask. "Do you think this is all over? The government will admit they're wrong, and people will realize they didn't need to be afraid of us?"

Martha slowly shook her head. "I wish it were, but people are going to be even more afraid now. Look at how scared they were when they saw the video of Lily transforming. When they watch the video of Ron and Lou fighting, it's going to be scary for a lot of people."

"But we're not running and hiding anymore, like the odd fellow with the curly hair said," Henri added.

Bernie smiled. "You mean Vincent?"

"Between you and me, I think he practiced his speech in advance, don't you?" Henri winked.

"What about Vincent?" Martha frowned, having missed the ghostly part of the conversation.

"He said we're not going to hide, and we shouldn't have to. People will just have to get used to us," Bernie finished emphatically.

"That they will, sweetheart. We've got a much bigger family now." Martha kissed Bernie's forehead. "Family takes care of one another."

Lou rumbled. "And protects each other."

"Exactly."

Epilogue

Martha shifted the full bag of groceries to her other hip as she left the newly opened store. The selection still wasn't great, but it was improving. She spotted patches of yellow and orange in the trees, reminding her that summer was coming to an end and school would be starting soon. She turned toward the nearby playground, where kids swarmed over the swings and climbing equipment. "Bernie, time to go."

Her daughter's lanky form separated from the other children and dashed to meet her, her eyes shining with excitement. "Livy says the new family has kittens that they're giving away. Can we go see after supper?"

"Sure. We can definitely drop by." They began walking down the cracked roadway. It had been six months since the mass escape from Woodpine, and new *lalassu* families were still arriving at Founder's Pass on a regular basis. Not everyone had wanted to live in a former mining town somewhere between Utah and Colorado. A few internees had returned to their homes and their families. But most of them had set to work, updating the abandoned houses that had been sitting vacant since the nineteen sixties. The town was becoming a home in exile for those who didn't want to be vulnerable to the world's changing fears and a destination for those rescued from other secret labs. They still hadn't found Kal and Patrick, but the search continued.

The footage of Ron and Lou fighting had become an international reference: the Jackson Square Attack. It was being referred to as a new 9/11. Over a hundred people died in the explosion, and three times that were injured. There were calls for stricter controls over the *lalassu* and their abilities, and a bill to require mass testing was once again on the front page of the newspapers.

Yet those same newspapers were being very quiet about the fact that the *lalassu* had effectively taken over a piece of United States soil and were no longer recognizing government authority. Sometimes they were mentioned alongside survivalist cults, a fact that offended Martha to no end, but it was as if the government wanted the public to forget about them.

If it keeps them away… The fearmongering made her angry, but she recognized that it also kept potential exploiters away. Like the patrols of those with combat-oriented powers, it had become a part of their lives. Bernie went to school with dozens of other children, and learning to use their abilities was a regular part of the curriculum.

Lou volunteered regularly for the patrols, sometimes spending up to a week circling the perimeter of Founder's Pass. He still found it hard to adjust to so many people being around on a daily basis. Martha had become the head of the medical clinic, dealing with everything from Lily's pregnancy to general checkups to stitching and plastering the aftermath of accidents. It might not be the life she'd pictured, but it held far more happiness than what she'd hoped for over the past ten years.

Bernie chattered the entire walk home, full of ideas about kitten names. *Maybe I shouldn't have said we'd go.* It didn't seem fair to make a decision about a pet without talking to Lou first, but he wouldn't be back for another week. He and Andrew had gone back to Bear Claw to see if they could find any other survivors. They'd tried to find the cubs from the lab in Juneau, but the building had been deserted when they arrived. Doc had stayed in Bear Claw to protect what was left of the Colony, but the other families at Ekurru had joined them as soon as Founder's Pass opened.

Lily was hoping the biologist would join them, but Martha had her doubts. Doc's heart was in the wild. If he couldn't stay at Bear Claw, he would probably search for some other remote location, maybe join one of the Russian skin-walker clans. In the dark, pessimistic corner of her mind, Martha wondered if Lou would have liked to do the same.

Once they reached their small bungalow, Martha put away the groceries. There was a brief interruption as she sent Bernie back to the front door to deal with the sneakers that had been aimed in the general direction of the mat but hadn't quite managed to land on target. With that incredibly unfair and onerous requirement complete, Bernie's door banged shut.

Spying her daughter's backpack on the floor, Martha picked it up. *A little reminder that kittens come after homework might help tone down the attitude.* Her mind half-preoccupied with what to make for dinner, Martha went to knock on Bernie's door. That's when she noticed the empty laundry basket.

Frowning, she went closer to make sure. Lou had woven the basket from narrow willow branches, and it wasn't particularly big—certainly not big enough to appear empty when it should have several days of clothing in it. But it was unmistakably empty, with not a scrap of fabric to be seen inside. For a moment, her breath hitched in her throat as old fears rose up.

She closed her eyes and took a deep breath. There was no reason to assume anything dire. Maybe Lily had sent Ron to pick up their things for a joint load at the common laundromat. She knew how much Martha hated the dark cramped building that always seemed to smell of mildew. *She's being nice, and I'm being paranoid.*

Even as she thought the words, the front door opened. *Did I forget to lock the front door after we came inside?* Not everyone in their newfound community was trustworthy. Martha had already dealt twice with addicts who assumed that, since she was the head of the clinic, she could provide the drugs they craved. She snatched up the heavy walking stick from her bedroom, ready to defend herself and her child.

"Martha?" a low, gravelly voice called. "Bernie?"

It can't be. Martha couldn't believe it until Lou came into view at the head of the narrow hallway, a large bundle in his arms. His slow smile reminded her exactly how long it had been since he left.

As she hurled herself into his arms, a small part of her brain calculated whether or not she could arrange for Bernie to go stay with Lily and Ron for the night. His toe-curling kiss was nearly enough to bring her to orgasm on its own and suggested that Lou might be okay with such a plan.

"Hey, Lou, did Mom tell you about the kittens?" Bernie shouted from her room. She'd stopped coming out to greet Lou immediately. As she put it, she had no desire to watch "old people making out."

"Kittens?" he rumbled, breaking free of their kiss to raise one eyebrow.

"Apparently, there are kittens who need a good home. But what are you doing back so early?" She couldn't stop herself from caressing his broad chest. *And I'd be stupid to try.*

"We found Setsuné." His lips brushed against her temple.

It was wonderful news. They'd worried that Lou's great-grandmother might have been one of the skin-walkers killed during the attack.

"She had Malila's cub kept safely hidden in the forest. Andrew is bringing them back here to live in the caves I found to the east." He gave her one last kiss before breaking free to pick up the bundle he'd dropped on the floor when she'd rushed to welcome him home.

Martha blinked as she realized what it was. Laundry, freshly washed and folded and wrapped in a sheet. He'd come home early and taken care of the laundry without being asked, just because it needed to be done, and that way, she didn't have to do it. It was one of the sweetest ways that he had found to tell her that he cared about her, all without saying a single word.

"I love you, too," she whispered, putting aside the laundry to show him how much it meant to her.

"Hey, I was thinking—oh." Bernie stopped herself mid-bound. "I'll come back later."

"What is it?" There was no hint of frustration or impatience in Lou's voice, and Martha loved him all the more for it. He treated Bernie exactly as a father should, never giving her any cause to doubt his affection for her but also holding her to a standard of behavior.

Bernie bit her lip before answering. "Well, I kind of asked Henri to go have a look at the kittens, and he said that two families have already been to the new family's house."

"And you're worried that if we wait until after supper, there won't be any kittens left," Martha guessed.

"Then, we go." Lou bent down and picked Martha up in his arms.

She grabbed at his neck to steady herself.

"You were on your feet all day at the clinic." He shifted her around so that she was sitting up and facing forward with her arm balanced across his shoulders. *Only my Lou could carry me around on one arm as if it was no big deal.* It was delightful, but she wasn't sure why he'd done it until he bent down to pick up Bernie with his other arm.

Her daughter squealed, laughing in excitement as he carried them both across the main room, crouching to get them all through the front door. Then, with one held securely on each side, he started to walk.

As much as Martha enjoyed the care and attention, she wasn't entirely sure she approved of the plan. Lou began to walk down the street, leaving their house behind—with their shoes still inside. "Are you really planning on carrying us the whole way like our own personal He-Man?"

He smiled at the laughter peeking through her words.

"We can walk, you know." She felt a moral obligation to protest but no real desire to leave his arms.

"Oh come on, Mom. This is awesome." Bernie grinned from ear to ear. "Livy said they're on Third Street."

Lou hefted them into a slightly better balance, his long strides devouring the ground at a rapid pace. Since he'd helped with the new construction, he probably knew better than Bernie where new arrivals were settling.

Martha's lips brushed his cheek as she whispered, "Thank you."

Her tongue darted out in a lightning caress, and his arm shivered in an answering tremor. She would definitely suggest that Bernie could pay a visit to Lily and Ron later. "I'm glad you came home early."

"You are my mate and my love. And we are a family." He turned his head to bestow a quick smile to each of them. "There is only one path forward."

Her mind immediately went to all the lovely physical ways he demonstrated his love, and a rush of flames swept over her cheeks and belly.

"Marry me."

She went still. "What?"

Bernie's eyes were shining with non-kitten-related excitement.

"Marry me. You are mine for the rest of my life, and I'm yours for the rest of mine. We're together for now and whatever the future brings." He smiled.

There was only one answer that a sensible woman could give when faced with such a proposal. She nodded and gave him a long and lingering kiss. After years of feeling broken by life, she was finally whole again. She was fierce and ready to soar.

Thank you for reading.
If you enjoyed this book and have a moment,
please leave a review.
It's one of the best ways you can thank an author.

If you're not ready for the fun to end,
check out my website www.jclewis.ca
for a chapter by chapter author commentary.
I share inspirations for my characters and scenes,
some of the more interesting bits from my research,
and all sorts of other tidbits.

Look for the mirror and step on through…

You can also sign up for my newsletter to find out about new
releases, contests and my appearances.
Sign up at www.jclewis.ca.

The story continues in book five: *Division*

Read on for a sneak peek…

What separates the truly persecuted from the posers?

The *lalassu* have taken over the abandoned mining town of Founder's Pass and effectively sundered themselves from the rest of society. In return, the rest of the world is becoming even more afraid and reactionary. Assaults and accusations are flying and suspicion reigns supreme.

But it's not all smooth sailing inside the boundaries of Founder's Pass, either. Factions are ripping the community apart. Those who have been part of the *lalassu* secret society for generations are used to living an itinerant life, not being cooped up in one tiny town. They're not happy and they're looking for someone to blame. Those who have been recently identified as *lalassu* are struggling to cope with the twin burdens of isolation and learning to use their abilities. Tensions are high and waiting for any spark to explode.

Annika Hirdwall used to be a casting agent in Los Angeles, finding the right people to be Tall Man # 2 or Woman With Stroller. It might not have been the most exciting career but it certainly beat being held in a sub-Arctic evaluation camp under the control of a psychopathic researcher. She'd much rather go back to sorting through headshots than training to be a superhero.

Vincent Harris has always been allergic to responsibility. He'd much rather see himself as the wise-cracking sidekick than the hero in the spotlight. But more and more, he's becoming the one that the people in Founder's Pass turn to when they have something to complain about. And they have a lot to complain about, taking up time that he could be using to find out more about one intriguing new addition with dark eyes and a damaged soul.

Coming soon …

For updates on when *Division* will be available, join my newsletter. Or you can check out my blog every Monday for updates on my writing progress. You can find them both at www.jclewis.ca.

Thank Yous

The first thank you goes to my two boys, who have learned to ignore me typing and muttering to myself, and who are very proud of me (even though they haven't read the books and I've ignored my younger son's advice to include time travel and dinosaurs). They are my ultimate fans and I'm super-proud of both of them.

Second thank you to my extended family. The shout-and-share family network is awesome. They continue to share and recommend my work, even those who aren't romance readers. They are my original and irreplaceable street time.

More thank yous to my best friends: Christina, Erin, and Sarah. They keep reading and cheering, pick me up when I need it, and kick my butt when I need that. Girl posses are great and everyone should have them.

Thank you to 'Nathan Burgoine and Nathan Frechette, who both patiently explained micro-aggressions and how they can accumulate into pain.

Thank you to the ladies of ORWA, particularly Eve Langlais, Twilah St. Cyr, Lucy Farago, and Christine Enta. They've been patient, supportive, and helped me through life's challenges.

Thank you to Kristen, whose wonderful support inspired the tag line for this book. No one should ever try to mess with a mom who has a mission. I was able to get this book out because she held me up when other aspects of my life tried to drag me down. She is a real life superheroine standing up to monolithic villains.

Thank you to Red Adept Editing, particularly Sara, Kate and Amanda. They are patient and precise, polishing every chapter into a gem.

Thank you to Streetlight Graphics for yet another amazing cover.

Thank you to Nada and Lauren who keep on supporting my work and giving great reviews.

The last thank you, as always, goes to my readers. Book by book, the numbers are growing. Thank you for your emails and your reviews. They mean the world to me. I can't say it enough: Thank you! Thank you! Thank you!

About the Author

Jennifer Carole Lewis is a full-time mom, a full-time administrator and a full-time writer, which means she is very much interested in speaking to anyone who comes up with any form of functional time-travel devices or practical cloning methods. Meanwhile, she spends her most of her time alternating between organizing and typing.

She is a devoted comic book geek and Marvel movie enthusiast. She spends far too much of her precious free time watching TV, especially police procedural dramas. Her enthusiasm outstrips her talent in karaoke, cross-stitch and jigsaw puzzles. She is a voracious reader of a wide variety of fiction and non-fiction and always enjoys seeking out new suggestions.

For more information about *Judgment* or other books of the *lalassu*, including my Under The Covers author commentary for chapter by chapter bonus and background information, you can go to www.jclewis.ca. You can also find Jennifer on Facebook and Goodreads as Jennifer Carole Lewis. You can also follow her on Twitter at @jclewisupdate or email her at jclewis@pastthemirror.com.

© Ryan Parent Photography